FEVER CITY

Tim Baker

FEVER CITY

Europa
editions

Europa Editions
214 West 29th Street
New York, N.Y. 10001
www.europaeditions.com
info@europaeditions.com

This book is a work of fiction. Any references to historical events,
real people, or real locales are used fictitiously.

Library of Congress Cataloging in Publication Data is available
ISBN 978-1-60945-287-2

Baker, Tim
Fever City

Book design by Emanuele Ragnisco
www.mekkanografici.com
Cover photo: Studio portrait photo of Veronica Lake
taken for promotional use. Date: circa 1952

Prepress by Grafica Punto Print – Rome

Printed in the USA

Nothing is as it appears in a world
where nothing is certain.
—LUCRETIUS, *On The Nature Of Things*

CONTENTS

FEVER CITY

BOOK ONE
Fever City

CHAPTER 1
New Mexico 1964

The sun rises fast in the desert. There is no warning, no subtle intimation. It is a brutal transition; the end of night. The beginning of suffering.

Hastings stands outside, sipping the too-hot coffee, trying to feel the turn of the planet as it bows to its star. His dog comes to his side, its head lifted in awareness, one forepaw raised. Hastings scans the landscape. Everything seems motionless at first but then he sees it: the cloud of dust defining itself as it fans away from an approaching convoy.

Three black cars.

Coming fast.

For him.

Three cars. That means at least six men. Maybe as many as twelve if they were smarter than the last ones. He sends his dog running into the countryside, watching until Bella disappears amongst the sage grass. He has already saved one of them. They always sacrifice the animals first, spilling the easy blood. No gas chamber for the household pet. But it shows they mean business.

The cars are approaching.

He must act fast.

There is a buzzing inside his head, familiar and comforting. The first time he heard it was when he went hunting with his stepfather. An internal drill, coring its way through his skull. Not going in, not going out. Just present. Being there. Like the gush and swell of blood he could feel in his arteries as he sighted on the deer and exhaled silently, taking the first pressure; totally still, as close to death as the deer itself.

He had missed on purpose.

It just didn't make sense, taking that animal down. For meat? There was an icebox full back in the house. There was only one reason to kill it: to remove a thing of beauty from the world forever.

He can still feel the sharp sting of his stepfather's hand across his ear; how it burned in the cold morning air. His first ever lesson in philosophy—moral decisions are never painless.

Hastings removes the submachine gun from its vault behind the bookcase. He knew what had to be done that morning with the deer. And he knows what he has to do now.

The cars buck over the ground, corrugated from two weeks of flood and fifty of drought. The house appears, large windows glinting in the dawn light like the eyes of an animal caught in the glare of headlights: unmoving; intuitively awaiting disaster.

Two doors slam with the resonance of a 12-gauge, footsteps brisk not with determination, but worse—with business. He can tell by the casual, efficient glances they give the terrain as they cross to the house: these men are professionals. They have done this many times before.

The others wait in the cars, undispersed; careless. For this brief moment, they're still within target. In seconds they will all exit; will light cigarettes and piss and spit into the red earth; adjust flies and belts and revolvers; check their ammo; worry their shaving rash as they head round the back, hoping to find a woman or two they could strip and torment; something to distract them from the monotony of murder.

In this swift, fatal interlude, the choice is his: hit the cars first and remove them from the picture, or start with the two men arriving at his front door.

He adjusts his earplugs. The cars are parked head to tail; the hubris of overwhelming superiority. He steps through the window of the laundry into the morning sunlight just as the driver gets out of the lead car, his cigarette falling from his mouth when he sees Hastings.

Metal disintegrates in pockmarks of agony, the cars rocking wildly, sinking fast on newly dead tires, windows going red then exploding.

Heightened, searing silence.

Nobody moves.

The husks of bullet casings click as he steps back inside. He checks the cameras. Nothing for a long moment. Then he sees them, shadows of fear moving in their black-and-white world. Taking up ambush positions. To hell with that. He grabs a rifle, opens all four gas cylinders, rips out the generator's fuel valve and exits through the cellars.

The house is in full, exposed view, the sun in their eyes. He runs everything through his mind. Passports and drivers' licenses. Cash and car keys. Weapons and ammo. He has them all. The phone numbers he has in his head. He looks at the cars through the rifle's telescopic sight. Nothing moves except for the wicked wave of flies above pools of blood. If they were halfway experienced, the two inside would have noticed the surveillance cameras by now. That would make them sick with apprehension.

He aims at the window box outside the kitchen, where Luchino's C3 is still stored, and fires, his face to the ground with the explosion, blue energy rolling across him, the hush and sucking evaporation of gas; and then the ticker tape of debris.

He runs across the ground, weapon at the hip, flashing back to the beaches, the wet sand, the palm trees; the sting of a bullet in somebody's chest. They taught him well. He was young back then; methodical. It's like the Jesuits. It stays with you. Kill shots through all three cars. Re-kill shots. No one survived the first attack.

Then he waits, sitting on his haunches, until the flames in the house subside enough to allow him to enter. Two shots rise up to the sky; echoless in the vast New Mexican desert, already gone just like the smoke. He looks at his watch. Eight o'clock. They would have rung in by now. The people who had sent them would know that they had missed. He takes a glowing piece of furniture—the bookcase maybe—and lights his cigarette with it.

Hastings gets into his '63 Thunderbird, the black mirror-gloss camouflaged by red desert dust. He slams the door and drives away, not looking back. He'll head towards the dry riverbed and collect Bella. And then he'll disappear.

Again.

T he call comes long before dawn, Cate picking up the phone and handing it to me without even answering. The bedroom is lit by the full moon, the shadow of the blind cord hanging like a noose above our bed.

The receiver is cold in my hand.

Everything is about to change.

Schiller tells me what's happened in his telegraphic style. Old Man Bannister. Called the Police Chief himself. The Bannister kid is missing. Looks bad. They want to talk. To you. The soft burr of wires and electricity showers into my ear. Then there is a savage click. Someone has been listening in. I swing out of bed.

Earlier in our marriage, Cate would have protested; she would have tried to pull me back into her warm embrace. And if I had insisted on going, she would have kissed me good-bye; made me promise to be careful. Now she turns her back, pulls the covers up. Before my shoes are laced, she will be drowsy again. By the time my car key enters the ignition, she will be asleep. The crickets pulse all around me, stewing on the problem: a two-year courtship plus a five-year marriage equals nothing. And now a stranger's missing child thrown into the mix. The child we can never have. The 'stranger' is one of the richest men in the country. And the child the subject of speculation even before he was born.

The headlights probe the night for weaknesses, tunnelling a way through the darkness towards Holmby Hills. Pampered lawns proudly display placards and campaign slogans. Up here it's a Nixon landslide but my gut tells me Kennedy can still pull this one off. I switch on the radio. *Cathy's Clown*. I change stations. There's a number from Trane's new album. *Spiral*. More my style.

The estate is northwest of Greystone Park, at 696 Laverne Terrace, just outside the jurisdiction of Beverly Hills. The gates are wide open, an ambulance and three patrol cars sitting outside. I sound my horn as I enter, passing under the wrought-iron arch above the gates, with the name of the estate written in fancy scrollwork—*High Sierra*.

The slick smack of macadam is replaced by the worry of gravel, the car skidding on the turns going up, like me on unfamiliar ground. The trees retract as lawn takes over, a vista opening up: all of LA jewelled in streetlight. A butler is walking towards me before I even stop the car, gesturing towards the house with mute disdain. Every light is on, terror and hope thriving side by side. There's someone over by a grove, digging. I call out to him as I go up the stairs. 'Find anything?' He shakes his head and goes back to his work. Schiller's waiting in the doorway. Even his huge frame is dwarfed by the size of the entrance.

Schiller guides me into the living room. 'Old Man Bannister's upstairs with his wife.'

'Which one?'

Schiller stares hard at me. 'Don't start.'

'I have to know who I'm dealing with.'

'Betty Bannister.'

I knew her from the papers. I couldn't remember if she was number three or four. 'She's the mother, right?'

'Jesus, Alston, they're just married.'

'There's your motive. She kidnaps the kid 'cause it's not hers.'

'Who said anything about kidnapping? This is still a missing

persons case until I say otherwise, got it?' Schiller looks
around, dropping his voice. 'The walls have ears in a house like
this.' Houses like this were not meant to be lived in.

'How long have they been searching?'

'Six hours before they called the Chief.'

'The kid would have shown up by now.'

'You don't know this place. Believe me, Alston, the longer
you nose around this joint—'

'The more complicated it gets?'

He's staring at a decanter full of whiskey. 'The more dirt
you'll find. Isn't that why they always call in a private dick? To
shovel through the shit?'

'So, who was the last person to see the kid?'

'The nanny, Greta Simmons . . .'

'Let's go and have a friendly chat with her.'

'Can't. She's gone.'

'There's your suspect. She's already skipped town.'

'It's her night off, and will you can it with that suspect stuff.'

'So what happened?'

'Greta put the kid to bed. Then she went out for the night.
Twenty minutes later, when the other nanny checked—'

'The *other* nanny?'

'It's Rex Bannister, for Christ's sake. When the other nanny
checked, the kid was missing.'

'So send a car to collect Greta Simmons.'

'She's a live-in nanny. Christ knows where she is. Probably
out somewhere trying to get laid . . .' His voice trails off, but this
time he's looking past me, out to the reception area. I turn. Betty
Bannister is gliding towards us, a floor-length silk robe wrapped
carelessly around a black negligée, her hand extended as
though I were the mayor. 'You must be Mr. Alston,' she says,
her voice warm and strong as morning coffee.

'How do you do?'

'Mr. Schiller—Captain Schiller, told me so much about you.'

Schiller's eyes protest.

'Won't you come this way, Mr. Alston?'

I turn to Schiller, who nods darkly and goes back inside the library, heading towards that decanter. As far as he's concerned, it's intermission and the bar has opened. Mrs. Bannister indicates the staircase.

'Not a very agreeable man, Mr. Schiller . . . '

The first testing question. It must always be rebutted. 'Not a very agreeable profession, being a cop.'

'Yet perhaps nobler than private investigator?'

At the beginning of every case there is this moment, when the client can't quite believe it's come to this—they actually need a private investigator. It is a moment when the enormity of their situation hits them; a moment of revolt. Of panic. Of denial. A moment when they turn against the very person they expect to help them, questioning how a man can make a living snooping through dirty laundry—maybe even theirs. This is when the fee is suddenly doubled, or the case declined. This is the only moment of power. Once you decide to take the case, you are locked into the gravitational pull of the client, and gravity always pulls down.

'I didn't ask you to drag me away from my wife in the middle of the night.' I turn and start going down the stairs. Her hand takes mine; soft, warm, surprisingly strong. Determined. 'I hope I can make it up to you one day.' I look up at her, at the way her gown has opened, providing shadowed glimpses. She mounts the stairs, speaking over her shoulder. 'This way, please. My husband is anxious to speak with you.'

'Tell me about Greta Simmons'

'There's nothing to tell. I had as little to do with the boy as possible.'

Had. 'And was that your decision, or Mr. Bannister's?'

Without answering, she opens a large door with a crystal handle. Old Man Bannister is by the windows, sitting in a wheelchair. He gestures dismissively at a doctor, who snaps a medical bag shut and strides out of the room with the dignified anger of an insulted ambassador. I turn back to Mrs. Bannister. She smiles before she puts out her hand. 'Good evening, Mr. Alston. Please don't hesitate to call should you require any- thing.' I feel the loss as soon as she withdraws her hand. 'I am entirely at your disposal . . . ' This time she doesn't try to hide the teasing inflection in her voice.

I cross the room. The Old Man gestures for me to sit down; clears his throat. *'Evil is rampant.'*

I wait, but there's nothing more. 'Mr. Bannister, if you could please just start at—'

'Did you not hear me?' He leans forward, red-faced.

'Evil is rampant?' He nods. 'What exactly does that mean, Mr. Bannister?'

'Mathew 24:12: *Evil and sin shall be rampant, and the love of many shall grow cold.'*

I had expected many things from Old Man Bannister but not Bible verse.

'If you understand that, you understand everything.'

'Everything about what, Mr. Bannister?'

'This household. Her. What my life has become.'

'What has your life become, Mr. Bannister?'

His face fills with slow, bitter exasperation. 'Mr. . . . '

'Alston. Nick Alston.'

'Mr. Alston, if there's anything in the world I am certain of, it is that I love that boy above all else and consider him not just my son, but my only heir.' He clears his throat, shifting his weight in his chair. The emotion genuine. 'Unfortunately, several months ago my lawyer started receiving representations from a man claiming to know the identity of the boy's true father.'

'I see . . . '

'This . . . person stated that he would commence court proceedings to remove Ronnie from my legal custody unless a significant sum of money was deposited into an account in Mexico.'

'And did you pay this money?'

'I am old, Mr. Alston, but I am no fool. To acquiesce to a demand such as that would only be to invite every felon in the state of California to feast at the same trough of iniquity.'

'Have you ever been subjected to blackmail attempts before this incident?'

'What happened before is of no concern to you.'

'I beg to differ, Mr. Bannister.'

Old Man Bannister pushes himself fast towards me, his arms shaking from the effort. He sits upright and rigid: an uneasy man soon to die. 'I will not tolerate contradiction.'

I whistle. 'I can see you're still a tough old bird despite all the doctors and nurses.'

He gives a harsh, dry laugh. 'And I can see you're not one to mince his words.'

'So, allow me this. What do you tolerate less: contradiction or kidnapping?' Old Man Bannister sags back against his wheelchair, worn out. 'Cigarette?' He looks at the offered packet, torn between easy temptation and righteous denial. He shakes his head. 'Tell me, when were you first blackmailed?'

The Old Man stares at me, his head inclined to the side, as though a tainted fluid were slowly draining from his ear. It's too much for him. He gestures for a cigarette, his fingernails rasping against my hand as I follow it with a lit match. What does it matter, this greedy old man is already on borrowed time. 'Tell me, Mr. Atlas . . . '

'Alston . . . '

'Mr. Alston . . . Tell me, have you read Balzac?'

I blow out the match, shake my head.

His eyes gleam with the malice of superiority. '*Behind every great fortune there is a crime*. Balzac was wrong. Behind every great fortune there are *many* crimes. Oh, don't look too shocked, Alston.'

'I'm not the shocking kind.'

He laughs, his wheeze ghosted by smoke. I gesture towards a decanter, and he nods. I pour us both generous shots. 'These were not my crimes, per se; they were crimes thrust upon me, extorted payments to corrupt and lazy officials to facilitate access to instruments of business I had every right to enjoy in the first place. These were the very first instances of blackmail. I was the victim, Alston, but I was guilty too. I consorted with these evil men. I also profited from these crimes; they permitted an unjust advantage over my competitors.' Old Man Bannister sighs as he sips his whiskey. 'One day, a newspaper reporter came to interview me, in this very room. It was not an invalid's sickroom back then, but a place of study and reflection. The reporter had done his research. He was blunt. Avaricious. He demanded payment for his knowledge. I determined to silence this reporter. Not with cash but with fists, Alston, brutal, compelling fists. They knocked the reporter's teeth out, one punch at a time. You may remember it; Goodwin James?'

Everyone who was old enough remembered Goodwin James. His working over was legendary. Only real pros could have inflicted that much damage without killing a man. His photo did the rounds—a good-looking, arrogant young man with a chip on his shoulder the size of his IQ transformed into a monster. I stare at Old Man Bannister, a slither of terror now overtaking me. He stubs his cigarette out against the wheel of his chair. 'You can therefore imagine my reaction when this man stepped forward, claiming to know the identity of Ronnie's father and demanding payment for his silence.'

Where can we find his body? is what I want to ask, but instead I play it safe. 'And who was this man?'

'*Was*, Mr. Alston? Is. I haven't had him killed. Not yet, at least. This man, Mr. Alston, is called Johnny Roselli.'

I gag on the whiskey.

'I see you know of whom I speak.'

Choose your words carefully. 'Mr. Bannister, have you ever considered just paying Roselli and letting sleeping dogs lie.'

'Sleeping dogs never just lie; they always awake, savage and ravenous. You are not here to give me advice, you are here to find my son, and when you do, you are here to deal with Roselli.'

'That's a tall order, Mr. Bannister.'

'That's why I chose you.'

'To tell you the truth, Mr. Bannister . . . '

'I am not interested in the truth. Or even justice. I just want peace.'

'I'll do my best . . . '

'You're not a Boy Scout, Alston. I want more than best.'

CHAPTER 3
Dallas 2014

L uck is not a state of mind, it is a physical condition; it is a climate, an ecosystem where fortune and providence are born; where blessings and accidents lurk in the foliage, assisting one passerby—ensnaring another.

In this jungle of chance, fate and circumstance are two sides of the same coin, not opposing entities. Fate is when you try to make sense of luck, circumstance when you no longer have the strength to do so. Death at twenty. Death at eighty. That's the real difference between fate and circumstance.

There are all types of luck: good, bad; equivocal. Dumb luck. Most often, there is unregistered, unacknowledged luck: happenstance.

But when luck is married to conspiracy, it always becomes unlucky.

Adam Granston is well over eighty yet his voice is quick and solid, and his movements belie the crumpled face, the tobacco yellow teeth, the watering eyes. He threads the audiotape with the care of an old tailor. 'The signals are clear and followed with military precision. The first horn is to let them know Oswald is coming. The second orders them to kill him.'

I nod with a betraying intensity. What the hell was I doing in an old lawyer's over-air-conditioned Dallas apartment fifty-one years after an assassination? Some leads have a way of sounding interesting when you hear them on a phone. But when you're sitting drinking weak coffee and listening to the panting of an ancient beagle in the corner, you begin to have serious doubts.

I lean forward as the hiss of memory and time unspools; a once-familiar sound, a pause for contemplation that has almost been removed from our consciousness. Then comes a general, blurred commotion, voices indistinct but excited, and the slap of movement through a crowd. A radio announcer's voice cuts in, oily in its professional confidence; sinister in the context of what you know is about to happen. The glib announcer is talking about T-shirts. He's performing his professional patter. This could be a football match or a parade.

But it's going to be a murder.

The old Texan raises a finger, his eyes liquid behind the inquiry of their magnified lenses. A klaxon is sounded, and immediately afterwards the announcer says that Oswald is coming. Voices rush and whisper all around the car park, jealous ghosts seeking the medium's attention. I lean in closer, still staring at Granston, who raises a second finger. The horn sounds again, and instantaneously the shot is fired, so clear that I can hear the whistle of the bullet as it turns through the rifling of the .38 Colt Cobra's barrel, husks a passage through the air, billows through the charade of the clothing's defence and thuds into the fatality of flesh. I can see my own face reflected in the man's glasses as he nods.

The announcer seems as stunned as I am. 'Oswald has been shot,' he says, his voice stripped of all confidence. This is no longer a carnival sideshow. This is history. The announcer has passed through the assurances of his microphone and has become part of his own audience: he has been caught living in wonder, and in awe. 'Oswald has been shot,' he repeats, the disbelief sucking his voice of timbre. 'Holy mackerel . . .'

This was in 1963. When disbelief was registered with phrases like *holy mackerel*. That was back in the old days, when the constraints of the airwaves regulated the private home. Today it is the other way round, when reality television begins in the public home and shatters the constraints of the airwaves.

The announcer's voice accelerates; wavers—nearly flutters and dies. Just like the victim, already being transported away in an ambulance. A phantom voice, charred with liquor and inside dope, slurs into the mike. 'Jack Ruby is the name.' The announcer repeats this information, his voice rising in disbelief. How can such knowledge be transmitted so quickly? The stranger's voice sounds pleased with the effect it's had. It continues with the punch line. 'He runs the Carousel Club.'

This is too much for the radio announcer. He can barely repeat this last item of news. I imagine him keeling over, cowboy boots clattering into silence. Holy mackerel indeed.

This moment of murder, when justice was denied and the truth killed as surely as the skinny kid with the bruised face was captured live on television and radio. Beep. Beep. Bang. The Morse code of the new Cool Media. The birth of a different kind of experience: Real Time. At that very moment, we were all sucked into the vortex: the witnessing instant of history, right now as it happens. It would be only one small step to the moon landing, one giant leap to the Berlin Wall.

I look up at the old man, who's tapping his temple. 'See? What the hell did I tell you: it was a conspiracy. They all knew about it in advance. They were all in on it.'

'And who exactly are *they*?'

His laugh is the unforgiving chuckle of an embarrassed father watching a worthless son fail yet again in public. 'They are not us.'

But who is he; this old man with the angry spittle on his lips? 'Us?'

'Patsies. Oswald said it himself, in the station before they shot him. We were all patsies.'

'How were you a patsy, Mr. Granston?'

His laugh is more a shriek, a rasping intake of breath sucked through a web of mucus. He looks up at me, his eyes whittled with blood vessels. 'Because I was the man on the car horn.'

The hum of air-conditioning needles the uncomfortable silence. He had me going there for a second, too. It was like my time in Ciudad Juárez, when people would read about the killings in the papers then pretend that they had witnessed everything. Granston was typical of most people: he wanted in on history. It didn't matter if he were only a footnote. Not for a crime this big. 'So you'd like me to write that you were part of the conspiracy?'

He bumps the table getting up, the undrunk coffee bridging the lip of the cup. The dog takes a shot at raising its head but doesn't quite make it. 'We're done here.' He sounds like a frustrated felon dismissing his incompetent lawyer. The door is already open. I take a step back to the table, but he blocks my way. In the corner is a sound almost like a growl. 'I knew your father when he was working on the Bannister Case.' Another pathetic lie to get my attention. He sucks in breath; half succeeds. Coughs up indignation and mottled phlegm. 'A travesty of justice.'

'Knowing's not the truth.'

'The truth, Mr. Alston . . . ? I thought you were just after a story?' He smiles, his teeth a row of decaying tombstones, yellowed by winter frost. 'Look all you want, you'll never find the truth. Not here, in Dallas. Mind your step.'

I turn to go, the sun spitting blindness, and I miss the curb, nearly turning my ankle. There is that same, mirthless laugh behind me. Indecent in its divide from joy.

The car is an assault on survival, the air torpid and pressing, like the blast from the crematory door. I turn the air-conditioner up high and think of the child left in the back of the station wagon by his father. The psychologists called it quotidian amnesia; that cycle of mindless routine that most families succumb to. Turn off the alarm, turn on the coffee. Toothbrush, car keys. Drop the kids off . . . The detail the father missed in his exhaustion with the everyday. His wife was sick. She normally took the boy to school on Thursdays. The kid fell asleep in the backseat, the way he always did. That was how they got him to sleep in his first year: they just put him in the car and drove. The dead boy was my welcome to Dallas. On radio talk shows strangers demanded the death penalty for a father on suicide watch. Events are big when the victim is small.

I drive off, squinting into the setting sun.

CHAPTER 4
New Mexico 1964

Hastings was heading south to Ciudad Juárez. He would disappear in the barrios of the hard town and when he knew he had lost them, he'd start travelling west through Mexico before heading up the coast to Los Angeles. They were expecting a frontal attack, explosive and loud. They were expecting Samson in the temple. But they'd wake in silence and feel the cold bite of the *navaja sevillana* scouring their throats. No time for panic, not even for pain; just the quick sting of realization: it's over.

He was allowing six months for the trip. He didn't want to return until well after the elections. Otherwise they might think he was going after LBJ too. Bella sat in the passenger seat next to him, her head half out the window, breathing in the strange fragrances of chase.

He had received the call almost a year before from Ragano, a mobbed-up lawyer for Carlos Marcello and Santo Trafficante. They had condoned a hit and Sam 'Momo' Giancana would control it. There was the first problem. Giancana, like all vain but unintelligent men, surrounded himself with stupid lieutenants; men like Johnny Roselli. The money was two hundred thousand down; three hundred thousand after. Ragano levelled with Hastings up front. This hit would be no picnic. High security. High probability of capture. Capture meant death—no one could ever be allowed to testify.

There was no mention of the target. Hastings figured

Castro or some other foreign bigwig. Or maybe someone domestic, causing problems for the syndicate, Jimmy Hoffa or Howard Hughes or maybe even J. Edgar Hoover. Someone big enough to be scary.

Roselli set the meeting at the old Monogram Pictures Ranch. Hastings got there two hours early, checked for sniper and ambush positions, and then hid three weapons in separate locations. Bella sat in the slim shade of a stand of eucalyptus that filled the hot air with the scent of medication. Roselli arrived late with two cars full of goons. A display of power that only made him look weak. The two of them went for a stroll along a horse track, the hoods watching them with binoculars, Bella padding silently at their side, her bouts of sudden, frozen attention making Roselli nervous. 'What the fuck is that?'

'Nothing.'

'He's seen something.'

'It's a she. And she's just scenting.'

Roselli looked around, his pale face sweating in the sunshine. 'Do you believe what they say, that dogs can sense ghosts?'

There was no point in sharing the truth with a man like Roselli. 'I don't believe in ghosts.'

Roselli stared at him for a long moment, sweat trailing like tears down his cheeks. 'A man like you don't believe in nothing.'

Hastings whistled and Bella trotted up to him. He raised his chin and the dog sat. 'I believe in well-trained dogs.'

'I seen a ghost once. Willie Bioff. That fink!'

'So why did he come back to haunt you?'

'I didn't say he was haunting me. I just said I saw him, right after he died. Reflected in the swimming pool. Practically shat in my trunks. There was this fucking dog barking. No one could shut it up.'

'Bella doesn't bark.'

'All dogs bark.'

Hastings looked back at the parked cars. 'I suppose we're far enough away to talk?'

'Sure,' Roselli said, wiping his face with a monogrammed handkerchief. 'So here's the deal. You, Chuckie Nicoletti and a Frenchman. The best.'

The best. Charles 'Chuckie' Nicoletti had killed his own father when he was 12 years old. Not even a teenager and an Oedipal hit to his belt. He was Chicago—that meant Giancana was watching carefully. Hastings figured the Frenchman was Albert Luchino, a Corsican killer and drug runner for the French Connection. Rumour had it he was the lead gunman in the Trujillo hit. Fearless. Flashy. Highly dangerous to work with. And Hastings. War hero. Purple Heart. Honest man betrayed. Husband; widower. Lover. Loner. Loser.

'Three shooters, one patsy.'

'Who's the patsy?'

'How the fuck do I know?'

'Do the other shooters know about me?'

'I don't know about you—are you in?'

Dumb question. There was only one answer now. If Hastings said no, Roselli would nod and talk about some amusing bullshit or his bad hip on the way back to the cars. And then they would kill him, dismember him, and cover him in lime. 'I'd appreciate it if you don't use my name.'

'Fucking A. That's why I just said Frenchie and Chicago.' Except he'd used Nicoletti's name. It was impossible to tell if Roselli was just dumb, or if it was an act designed to misdirect and control. 'I'll call you fucking Elvis, okay?'

'Call me anything you want, except my name.' Hastings saw the glitter of a telescopic lens from the cars. The goons were scoping them for fun. He hoped the safety was on. 'How?'

'Two scenarios. The first is a bedroom whack, the broad included.'

'Where?'

'How the fuck do I know? Somewhere with a bed and a broad.'

'Security?'

'Heavy. Very. Always.'

'The second?'

'Sniper attack in public. Moving target, limited opportunity.'

'Who chooses the scenario?'

'A fucking telephone. What do you need?'

'I'll take care of it myself.'

'We can get you anything you need.'

'I'll take care of it myself . . . ' He was thinking of a Springfield Model 1903-A4 with custom mercury rounds for the sniper shot; suppressed .22 to the temple for the bedroom invasion. He didn't want any materiel from Roselli, which would be traceable, probably back to CIA.

'When?'

Roselli grimaced. 'As soon as possible. You'll all be on alert as of Saturday.' He slapped Hastings on the back. Bella froze, staring hard, her teeth exposed. Hastings signalled it was all right. Roselli laughed falsely. 'Half a million. Think about it. You can retire on this job.'

Of course he could retire. In style. But he would have to make do with a cool two hundred grand; they were never planning on handing over the second payment. They'd clip him first. They'd clip the others; they'd clip their own families and their children and anyone who stood in the way for that kind of money. The target had already become incidental. What was really at play was nine hundred thousand dollars, with the possibility of tracing much of the other six hundred grand. All Roselli had to do was move in fast and capture, torture and murder the top three hit men in the world.

'So who's the target?'

'JFK.'

'Jesus Christ!'

' . . . What are you, a Democrat?'

Hastings liked JFK as well as anyone could like a politician. He was young; he was bright. He was dangerously extravagant. Hastings knew all about Kennedy's father—the Rum Row days before he became ambassador. Before he sided with Hitler, he had sided with Frank Costello. Joe Kennedy wasn't drawn to Nazis, but what they had to offer: prosperous appeasement on the back of a warring Europe. His folks had emigrated from Ireland to escape poverty and brutality. What point was there in placing America in the heart of all that centuries-old hate? Joe Kennedy had voted for self-interest and was vilified, but that was all forgotten when Joe Jr. was blown from the sky; when PT-109 sank in the Pacific. Then Joe Kennedy became the father of heroes and decided to back JFK all the way. Hastings didn't care about Joe Sr.'s history, just like he didn't care that JFK couldn't keep his hands off women.

Not admirable but audacious. JFK was the first American president who looked his country in the eye and said: I have a hard-on for power and it makes me want to fuck. Men got off on that. It made them feel good about their own dicks. Women got off on it too.

But then Johnny Roselli came along and hung a bull's-eye on JFK's hat. It occurred to Hastings: was this all because of Nick Alston . . . ?

'The President. You're serious?'

'Fucking A.'

'But why . . . ?'

'Fucked if I know, Momo wants it done, is all.'

Except Giancana didn't have that kind of money. Neither did Marcello and Trafficante. One and a half million was Cold War level cash. Cold War level target. Cold War level hatred. They had to be mobbed up with CIA or Big Oil on this one. And they wanted Kennedy dead. They were so out of control, they might even be able to pull it off. Danger simmered in the heat haze. Hastings was trapped. He maintained the patter, trying to think through a survival strategy. 'Bedroom or sniper job, the getaway will be tough.'

'You've got five hundred thousand reasons to figure something out. Are you in?'

He was dead, no matter what he said. 'Stand-by from Saturday? I can do it.'

Roselli stuck out his hand, sealing the deal with a sweaty palm. 'We'll be in touch.'

Hastings watched Roselli stomping back up towards the cars. He could hear the swivel and stutter of Roselli's mind as he sweated through the sun, counting all the cash. CIA doesn't ask for receipts.

Hastings collected his stashed weapons, formulating his plan. He would kill the other hit men before they ever had a chance to kill the President.

Then he'd snatch their dough.

And start running.

CHAPTER 5
Los Angeles 1960

The mansion's cellars are vast, vaulted crypts of damp and gloom, the stone walls protected by the turrets of wine racks, hills of coal and the easy clutter of the always frugal super-rich. Coils of fencing and electrical wire, half-full tubs of dried paint, ancient rugs crawling with mildew. I shine the torch on a set of steel doors, then turn to the butler. 'What's that?'

'The shelter, sir.'

He doesn't mean to call me sir but he can't help it. Any question fired at him would always elicit the same automatic response. Yes, sir. No, sir. Three bags full, sir. I try the doors. They're locked. 'Do you have the key?'

'No, sir.'

'I see. What's your name?'

'Morris, sir.'

'Morris, can you get one?'

'Get what, sir?'

'A key . . . '

There is an uncomfortable pause. This scenario was never discussed in Good Butler School back in London. 'The shelter is off-limits to all but Mr. Bannister, sir.'

'And Mrs. Bannister?'

'One would assume so.'

Sir. 'Though you don't know?'

'That is correct, sir.'

The strike of my match makes him start. I light my cigarette, then watch the flame sizzle on a cobweb. 'How about Ronnie?'

'Naturally sir, members of the immediate family . . . '

'I mean, did he know about the shelter?'

'I cannot say, sir.'

'Make an educated guess, Morris.'

'Possibly, sir.'

'He came down here?'

'In the cellars? Rarely.'

'Did he play on his own?'

'There are two nurses and two nannies.'

'How about other kids?'

Morris shakes his head.

Lonely kids. Only child. I knew all about it. Solitary hide-and-seek, always half-expecting your secret friend to pop out. I have a hunch. 'Go get the keys, will you?'

'But, sir . . . '

'Jesus, man, look at that door. That's an honest-to-god bomb shelter. What if the kid's locked himself inside? What if the air filter's off and he's suffocating while you're standing there not getting the keys?'

Morris stares hard, not seeing me but the movie I've just projected. He jumps to the end credits: Fired Butler played by Morris. The echo of his footsteps fades as he hurries away.

Silence. A faint whiff of sewage. And the fast, light patter of something falling softly in the distance. I step into a narrow passageway supported by the shadows of high brick porticoes that arch into the gloom. My shoulders brush either side of the walls as I enter further into the dark passage, the calcified walls flaking, ceding the obscure, olfactory mysteries of decay, mildew and the spectral neglect of entombment. There is the same cloying dampness you find in the bottom of the cargo hold of an ancient freighter; the feeling that an ocean is press-ing all around, penetrating by minute degrees the rust-stained hull. Something drifts down from the ceiling, scattering lightly all about me. The match smacks the darkness away, loose soil raining all around me, like the warning of an imminent cave-in. I look up to the ceiling, but it's out of reach of my light. I scan the ground ahead. There is a stone column, like a well or a massive foundation pillar rising up in front of me, blocking the way. Something foreign yet familiar lies half hidden in the loose soil. As I reach for it, the match goes out. I feel along the moist earth in the dimness. A shoe. The excitement at its discovery is pierced by its high heel. So not the kid's but maybe it belonged to the nanny. I shove it in my jacket pocket and work my way around the stone column, burning my fingers with matches as I check the ground and the sides of the walls. No signs of any other items of clothing. No footprints. No doorways or further passageways. Nothing. Not even an opening small enough for a cat, let alone a kidnapper with a child.

I head back the way I came and hit a dead end. Panic settles like a fog. I freeze, taking short breaths, the trickle of soil hissing softly against my shoulders. Is this what it's like: the tomb; the final, narrow resting place. The shower of soil from above . . . ?

I put my back against the wall and stick to perimeters until I come back to the column. It was the lavish sweep of the curve that confused me, amongst all the straight, nocturnal lines. I ease my way back out into the spatial luxury of the main cellars. Behind me there's a secret scuttle. Too light for a man with a knife. Too assured for a lost kid. A rat. Or a giant spider, like in *The Incredible Shrinking Man*.

I shiver and go over to the shelter, brushing the soil from my shoulders and hair. I tap on the door. The kid's not in there; if he is, he's already dead.

I nose around the rest of the cellars. There is a door at the end of one of the larger passageways. It opens. I hit the lights.

It is a large, circular chamber with a giant gold and purple pentagram painted on the ceiling. The way it's been painted, there could almost be eyes staring down from its centre. In the middle of the room is a round stone altar. Something hangs from it. Four restraints at compass quadrants. One side of the wall is lined with monks' habits with cowls. A pipe organ squats at one end of the chamber. I bet that's good for a laugh. Opposite is a huge brick fireplace. Nice and cosy, only I don't think it's ever been used for roasting marshmallows. There's a heavy red velour curtain concealing an entrance into a large changing room. More costumes, some in leather. A black satin cape. Golden sandals. Some wizard outfits. Riding crops, leather handcuffs. There's even a light-lined theatrical makeup mirror for showtime. I can imagine what happens when this curtain goes up. I come out, almost walking straight into Mrs. Bannister. She looks over my shoulder, staring straight into the changing room. 'Some show . . . '

'I wouldn't know. All that was way before my time.' Her eyes glitter with amusement. 'What . . . ?'

'It's not like this place is snowed under by dust.'

'We have a staff of nineteen.'

'Quite a little army.' I glance back at the circular marble table in the centre. 'Now that's a conversation piece, if ever I saw one.'

'It's from the middle ages.'

'It doesn't look six hundred years old.'

'I mean Mr. Bannister's middle ages. That agitated time of life when men get up to strange things.' She looks at me, her green eyes challenging. 'Tell me, how old are you, Mr. Alston?'

'Still young enough to imagine what that table must have looked like when it was laid . . . '

'Altar, Mr. Alston . . . '

She jingles something in front of my eyes and smiles. Her mouth is large with a slight overbite that heightens her high cheekbones. 'For the shelter.'

I take them with a nod of thanks, opening the door for her. 'I can hardly wait to see what's inside.'

'Relax, Mr. Alston, it's a model of humble utility.' She closes the door and then there is the tumble of bolts.

'It wasn't locked before.'

'It is now.'

'Tell me, Mrs. Bannister, what do you think has happened to Ronnie?'

'I haven't the faintest idea. That's why I suggested they call you.'

'You?'

She nods. 'You helped out a friend of mine. Judy Turner.' She drops the name with false modesty. Only very close friends used Lana's real name. 'She spoke highly of you.' She takes the torch from my hand. 'What did you do for her?'

'Client confidentiality.'

'Stompanato had it coming to him.'

'We've all got it coming to us. The trick is to make sure we're ready when it does.'

'Really, Mr. Alston? I thought the trick was to hide.' She moves the torch. We're standing in front of the shelter. I have trouble finding the keyhole. She guides my hand towards it. 'Just slip it in and turn. That's normally all it takes.'

'I'll try to remember for next time . . . ' I shine the torch into the interior. So this is it: at the end of the world, this'll be the last place standing. Steel and concrete walls on the outside. Supermarket on the inside. Canned food, bottled water. First-aid kits. Gramophone and records. Radios, torches, an old wall-mounted telephone, and books, books, books. What the hell else would there be to do but read? And maybe pray. There's a toilet hooked up to some kind of septic system. Shaving equipment. Rifles on the wall. A man could live six months easy inside here. Although you certainly wouldn't want to bump into him coming out. 'Cosy, isn't it. A real home away from home.'

'Don't make fun, Mr. Alston. Every family in America dreams of having one.'

'Dreams . . . ?' I take the torch and get down on my hands and knees, looking under beds. 'Don't you mean nightmares?'

She sits down on the bed opposite me, her robe opening, revealing the graceful lines of her legs. 'Find anything?' I get to my feet, dusting off my knees. She shakes her head at the cigarette I offer. There's the snap and flare of a match. 'The thing you need to understand about my husband, Mr. Alston, is that he is a very thorough man. When he decides on something, he follows through, right to the end.'

I mask my eyes behind smoke. 'Except when it comes to marriages?'

'I'm sure you feel better, now that you got that off your chest.'

'All I meant was . . . '

Mrs. Bannister stands, cinching her gown tight with a silk belt. 'What you meant to do was to humiliate me, but I think you've achieved only the contrary. Now instead of standing there ogling me, don't you think you should be doing your job?' She tugs the cigarette from my mouth, but the paper sticks to my lip, tearing it. I let out a curse, my finger coming away wet. First blood to her.

She drops my cigarette to the ground, grinds it under her gold sandal, then dabs at my lip with a silk handkerchief. 'I hope you don't think it was intentional.'

I smile at her, tasting blood. 'I don't think you're capable of performing any act that isn't.'

The smile that's been hovering across her lips ever since we met is gone. She moves closer to me. Her eyes widen, searching my face for a truth. 'I'll take that as a compliment.' She brushes past me, so close that her hair passes across my lips. My bleeding lips. I hear her stumble and shine the flashlight for her, but it goes right through her gown, illuminating a perfect silhouette; a naked shadow puppet. 'Mind your step, Mrs. Bannister.'

She turns, standing proud in her spotlight. 'And yours as well, Mr. Alston. I would so hate to see you fall.'

CHAPTER 6
Dallas 2014

There is the dislocation of sudden darkness, the doors swinging shut like a spring trap behind me, the sour stench of beer rising up from damp carpet. 'Hello, pilgrim.'

I turn around, shaking the proffered hand, a sweat-shining face spilling out of the shadows. 'Lewis Alston . . . '

'Hell, I know who you are. I recognized you from your Twitter photo.' He leans in close, scenting the air with a sweet, boozy haze. 'Personally, I stay away from all that internet bull-shit. Just look at PRISM. What a circus. The less the NSA knows about my whereabouts, the better.'

For all, by the look of things. 'Mr. Jeetton, I presume?'

'At your service. Speaking of which?' He holds up an empty glass of ice. 'Bourbon and Coke's my pleasure.'

One of these. Every journalist has lived through one of these. The man with the dope and the rope—the rope in this case free booze; as much as he can drink while talking fast enough to keep you interested.

'Now I can tell you're an intelligent man with a powerful focus, I mean it. The average person coming in here, first thing they do is glance up at the television. All of them; eyes drifting to the TV. Doesn't matter what's on; could be football, girls, cars . . . Goddamn talking heads. But they've got to look, not because it's interesting but because it's there, dominating the space. Irresistible. Like candy or pussy in a box. But you, you're different. You live in your own space. You understand that, you'll understand what I'm about to tell you.' He slams his glass down. There is the rattle of freshly bereaved ice. 'Don't mind if I do . . .'

'If you do what?' Just for the pleasure of stringing him along.

He frowns. 'Have another drink, of course.'

Of course. 'Mr. Jeetton . . .'

'Call me Tex.'

Original. 'You're not driving, are you, Tex?'

'You fill up this here glass and I'll let you drive me home.'

Tempting invitation but I think I'll pass. There is the riot of new ice against glass and the inexplicable mix of dry burn and sick sweet. I take out my phone and start recording. I'll give him five minutes, or two drinks. Whichever comes first. He catches me looking at the time.

'Nice watch. Zodiac Sea Wolf. Collector's item.'

Already weighing my worth. 'A gift from my father. Now Mr. Jee—Tex. You said you had some information, something about E. Howard Hunt?'

'Hunt was in the CIA as you well know.'

Sometimes realizing the difference between a lead and a waste of time comes down to something as small as a definite article, or lack thereof. No one who knew anything about CIA called it *the* CIA. It was the first gatepost. He had just stumbled.

'He was in on the JFK hit. And probably on Bobby's too.'

'Tex, do you know how many people are supposed to have been in on the hit?' I did. I had spent months researching every conceivable conspiracy theory for my book on the assassinations of the Kennedy Brothers. 'E. Howard Hunt was an unsuccessful novelist, CIA operative and burglar. What makes you think he was a successful presidential assassin?'

'The same thing that made him unsuccessful in everything else. Complete lack of imagination. He never anticipated the consequences of anything he ever did, including JFK.'

'So how exactly did Hunt fit in?'

'The way every patsy does: He was pushed. Marginalized. There was no other place for him to go but with the conspirators. They were the only ones who would still have him after Bay of Pigs.'

'What was his role in Dallas?'

'He was the benchwarmer. The man who picked up the phone and put the suitcases on the plane. Always doing, never thinking. And then it blew up in his face.' Tex leans forward, the stench of soda-masked booze saturating the air. 'He was expecting a reward. But when he started to see what was happening to the witnesses . . . ' The famous 'murdered witnesses' to the JFK Assassination, most of whom had actually died of natural causes. Jeetton shrugs with a gesture of helpless magnanimity. 'He realized he was lucky to be spared.' Some luck. When a president needed a leak fixed, Hunt was told to take his plumbing tools to the Watergate Building. Unlike Nixon, no one spared Hunt his prison time.

Tex pulls out a crumpled piece of glossy newsprint, unfolding it carefully. There is a photo of three men being marched across a Dallas street by two escorting police officers. I recognize them instantly. The notorious Three Tramps, detained shortly after JFK's assassination. Tex's nicotine-stained fingers caress the photo. 'The small one here is Hunt. This one up front was a Frenchman. And this one, in the middle? That's Philip Hastings.'

Ice from the machine rattles the silence. 'The Philip Hastings from the Bannister case?'

That's one conspiracy theory I've never heard before. Tex nudges his glass towards me. That has to be a three-drink revelation. 'One and the same.' He taps the photo of the small Tramp. 'Of course you know E. Howard Hunt was Deep Throat.'

'Deep Throat was Mark Felt.' Felt was furious because he thought he was next in line to become FBI chief, and when he didn't get the promotion, he started blabbing. Behind most whistle-blowers, there's usually a backstory of paranoia, wounded pride and vengeance. 'Everybody knows that.'

Jeetton stares at me, his eyes hooded with alcohol and exasperation. 'You liberal reporters come down here sniffing round for information . . . ' Here we go. ' . . . And when you actually get it, you turn your noses up because it's not what you want to hear.' He looks into his glass, drains what dregs might still be lurking there amongst the caramel-coloured melting ice, the heat of his resentment flushing the too-small space between us. Normally he should be saying these things on a phone to a shock jock in a radio studio, not a stranger in a bar.

'It's not because I don't want to hear it; it's because I know it's wrong.'

'Because the *Washington Post* or the *New York Times* told you it's wrong?' He slams his glass down hard on the bar counter, making the stale peanuts jump in their miserable saucer. That's it. He's lost his free drinks after two rounds: a new record for Mr. Tex Jeetton. 'You and your goddamn Political Correctness.'

The tell-tale sign of the irredeemable bigot: the vicious sneer in the voice, like a death-choke, whenever they utter those two, detested words. Politically Correct. It deprives them of the easy racial epithets they'd been freely using all their lives; that shorthand all extremists employed to create their simpleminded world of segregation and apartheid; of anti-Semitism, sexism and homophobia. Of concentration camps and plantations. Then someone came along and said: you can't say those words anymore.

'Tex, I can see I made a big mistake . . . '

Fear and anger tremble across his drink-scarred face. 'So blinded by mirrors, you don't see what's staring you right in the face.'

He says it as though it were verse from Conspiracy Theology: the religion of the post-Atomic Age. In the beginning, the

Roswell Saucer crashed. And on the Seventh Day we get the Gemstone Files because, hell, there's just no time to rest when shape-shifting lizards are sitting in Buckingham Palace. When empty skyscrapers are being destroyed with controlled demolitions. Duck and cover, everybody, and don't forget to look under the bed when you're down on the floor—you might find a fake lunar rock.

Why do so many people believe in Conspiracy? Is it simply easier to think you are being manipulated than to accept that the forty-five years you just put in working at a job you hated to pay off an overpriced mortgage were all wasted, with nothing left to show for your suffering serfdom other than a loveless marriage, ungrateful children, and some loose change?

Or is it because we have all forsaken God but not our innate need to believe in the unknowable? In the Big Secret hidden behind the curtain. Something awe-inspiring; brighter than the Wizard.

In this sad world, E. Howard Hunt is the iceberg apparent, the tiny fraction of the massive, submerged enigma; Atlantis, the hidden continent of conspiracy. 'And what is staring me in the face, Tex?'

'That Hunt knew about the Bannister kid.' I hold on to the bar. His smile is a leer of triumph, the facial equivalent of a kick in the balls. 'You smart-aleck, liberal greenhorn. Snooping around these parts with your nose in the air, and all the time you ain't got a clue what's buried under the very earth you're stomping on. Well, I'll tell you what's buried there, tangled up amongst the skeletons and the oil. It's the Truth, son, just as plain and ugly as a wart on a toad's ass. So you can wipe that stupid look off your face and buy me another drink, jackass.'

CHAPTER 7
Los Angeles 1963

Roselli had been quick with the down payment. The money had arrived the day after the meet at the Monogram Ranch. Roselli was trembling at the proximity of such wealth; so many possibilities. Forty Eldorado Biarritz Caddies lined in a row. An eighteen-hole golf course in Key Biscayne. Ten thousand call girls. Except that if Roselli wanted a car, he'd steal it; if he wanted land, he'd kill for it; and if he wanted a girl, he'd rape one. He had absolutely no need for money, which only made him want it all the more.

Roselli's eyes entertained betrayal as he whispered instructions to the three bagmen who carried in the loot, concealed inside hefty duffel sacks. There was a moment when Hastings watched Roselli in the reflection of the drinks cabinet, his hand dropping to an ice bucket, where he had camouflaged an S&W .38 nickel-plated revolver. A five-shooter. One for each gangster and one left over, just in case. Hastings could hear the flat, damp roll of Roselli's brain struggling with a believable story for Momo. Scotch tumbled into heavy crystal. Hastings scooped a fistful of ice, dropped it in a glass, the handle of the piece exposed, Roselli's greed retreating behind the logic of fear. He wouldn't have to reach for more ice, he wouldn't have to kill Roselli. Yet.

Hastings waited until after they had left, watching the cars retreating down the street. He knew there was a tail out there somewhere. Roselli wasn't that stupid. One sack on his back, one in each arm. Down the cellar. Through the plate in the wall. Along the storm water canal. Up by what passes for a river in LA. He had a '57 Plymouth inside a rented garage looking on to the canal. The car started up first time. Hastings headed south towards Long Beach.

He stashed the dough in his safe house in Chula Vista. A Chubb customized anti-blowpipe key and combination double lock hidden inside an underground tank. Chula Vista was his lifeboat in case the good ship SS America hit a reef. Ten minutes' chase distance to Tijuana. Disappearable. He wanted all options open. Especially flight. He made it back to LA after midnight. Fourteen hours for a 300-mile round trip, half of that making sure no one was tailing him. That there was no surveillance. That's what being sure does: slows movement down to a molasses creep. Gives you time to see the faces behind the windows, the wires under the car; the glint of gunmetal through the branches of a tree.

Hastings entered back through the cellar, closing the secret door soundlessly behind him; listening. He waited an hour down there, until he was sure, then came up, checking all the doors and windows for signs of entry. Nothing. He unbolted the front door, so that it was just on its latch, and spread canvas on the floor in front of it. Then he waited in the shadows scoping the street, the jacaranda trees outside trembling with betrayal. Just after three a car pulled up on the far corner. Two men got out, walking hunched away from the streetlights, casing windows for witnesses. There weren't any. This was a respectable neighbourhood. There was the rasp of the latch being lifted, then they were inside; violent faces masked by darkness. One of them tripped on the canvas and cursed. Maybe he knew at that very moment what was about to happen. Four suppressed shots. The hammer of two falling bodies. Then silence. Hastings sat there, alert, straining for an indication of departure, a spirit shifting away.

Outside, the street was empty except for a draining moon and the weaving flutter of bats.

He set to work with towels and tape, staunching the bleeding as he ID'd the goons. Dallas. Joe Civello's boys. Chicago owned the Midwest, Texas, the West Coast. This was Roselli's way of trying to recuperate the money via one of the back doors. Roselli would have arranged a cut in exchange for the tip. A nice piece of safe pie with enough deniability to probably get away with it.

Hastings wrapped them in separate bundles, and hauled them through the house and into the garage one at a time. Getting them into the back of his Mercury Colony Park was hard work. They were both big men, heavy with guilt.

He drove south down small, modest roads unused to crime, and dropped them into the sea off Bluff Cove. Their bodies hit the water with a light, unlucky slap. He watched the current take them out into the night. He checked the back of the car for evidence, and then headed back north. He would have to lose the car. But before that, he needed to call Roselli, just to let him know he was safe and sound.

S chiller is outside, swaying gently as he whistles to himself. A dozen patrolmen are spread out, going through the gardens.

'Any word on that nanny?'

'Nothing yet. We checked her room though. Nothing to suggest she was planning on skipping town.'

If she were planning on skipping town, she wouldn't exactly leave a sign on the door handle. 'You find anything out here?'

Schiller looks up at the rising sun then turns and squints at me, shaking his head. 'No footprints, tread marks, broken windows, forced entry . . . Nothing to suggest a snatch.' Schiller toes a flower out of the dew-wet soil. 'How about you?'

'There's no way the kid's inside. I even checked the bomb shelter.' There is a shout from one of the patrolmen, standing at the edge of the grove. 'Captain. Over here.'

We both start running, all the other cops sprinting too, a converging ring of blue targeting the grove. Some of the patrolmen, inexplicably, have already drawn their service revolvers. Perhaps they had sensed the evil; the violence that was about to ensnare them, the city—the entire country.

The Bannister case was about to go wide.

The officer who found it turns, pushes his way out of the ring and retches onto the manicured lawn. Schiller shoves his way through the wall of uniforms, me riding his wake. He stops so suddenly that I run into him. His curse whip-cracks across the morning.

I peer over his shoulder into the humming shade. Two female hands have started to flower from the soil, the slender fingers reaching up towards the light, the fine sheen of nail polish chipped from digging, the red tips curled like petals withering in the sun. The golden gleam of a wedding ring is barely visible; the promise of buried treasure. Something swells between the hands, the morning breeze lifting it like threads of gossamer: long fine black hair. I crouch down and gently brush the soil away from the forehead, the pursed lips grimed and cracked by dirt, the eyelashes heavy with the endless sleep of the tomb. Her face is tilted upwards, as though caught in the act of contemplative prayer. 'Does anyone know her?' I look up at the circle of stunned faces haloing this grave, still as death. No one moves. Then a cop crosses himself.

'You.' Schiller grabs him by the arm. 'Go find someone.'

'Who?'

'A gardener, someone in the house—anyone who can tell us who she is.'

I continue to free her face from the soil. Schiller kneels reverentially next to me. 'She was alive,' I whisper. 'When they buried her here, she was still alive . . . '

'How are you so sure?'

'Look at the soil under the nails, now look at the patterns on her palms. She did that to herself, struggling to get out. See how the soil's been driven under the skin? And look here . . . ' I gently purse her lips open. Schiller moves closer. 'You're kneeling on her throat.' He apologizes, moving back—a perfect gentleman. 'See how it's packed in the front corners of her mouth? She was trying not to swallow the soil . . . '

There's a noise behind us and the officer leads Mrs. Bannister through the wall of police. I watch her as she stares down at the corpse. Something huge ripples across her face. An enormous emotion that she grabbed by the scruff of the neck and hauled back, just before it had time to escape her. Admiration overwhelms me.

'You know her?'

'Elaine . . . '

Red. That's what's been bothering me about Mrs. Bannister standing there above me; she's still wearing her silk robe, but she's wearing a different coloured negligée underneath. I could swear it was black before. Why did she change?

'She work here?'

The question drives Mrs. Bannister's eyes away from the grave.

'She's Elaine Bannister. Ronnie's mother . . . '

I turn back to the half-revealed face staring up at us. Something has caught my attention. Schiller goes to speak, but I silence him with a finger to my lips. Everyone goes quiet, the cops all stepping back, as though expecting a geyser to erupt at any moment, showering them with scalding debris. I put my ear to the soil. It's uncanny, but for a second I could have sworn I heard a child crying.

Schiller's on edge. 'What is it?'

'Something's happening but I don't know what . . . ' I glance up at Mrs. Bannister. This time she can't control it, the emotion leaching her face of colour, her mouth gaping open in disbelief.

I turn back fast to the body of Elaine, and then I see it too: a tear slowly pushing a trench through the grime on her cheek.

Roselli didn't call until the last Saturday of October, setting a meet at 3 P.M. at the Hollywood Roosevelt. Roselli looked pale and nervous against the blue agitation of the swimming pool. Every time someone dived in, punching a hole in the water with a loud wallop, he looked up. In the distance a dog was barking. Ghosts lurked just outside his peripheral vision.

Hastings sat in the interrogating sunlight, feeling revolt at his profession; at the way his life turned out. An unknown father. A dead mother. A brutal stepfather. A tour in the Pacific. A homecoming marriage to a childhood sweetheart; an impossibly cruel story . . . that turned out to be possible. A tragic death that he should have been able to stop. Revenge and flight. Hands soaked in the blood of the innocent and the guilty. Nothing, except regret and self-hate. And a decade of menial work, trying to deny the calling that had chosen him in the Pacific: murderer.

During the war, Susan had been everything. She was the reason he suffered and fought to survive all those times when it would have been easier simply to give in to the call of death. She was his polestar, his way out of the torment of mosquitoes, mud and suppurating tropical ulcers, of dysentery and fear and the constant stench of decomposing human flesh. He came to understand that the point of the war was not to win or to lose but simply to teach each soldier the meaning of suffering; to remove them from their assumptions about humanity and kindness; to strip them of the sense of their own identity.

To change their world forever.

Only then would they allow themselves to be sacrificed, to gladly follow the whistle into enemy fire and the near certainty of oblivion. On this death journey of young men, all taboos were broken. Enemy soldiers were raped, tortured, murdered and mutilated. Civilians were gang-raped and beaten to death. Officers were shot in the back. Wounded were left behind.

Nothing exposed the tenuous membrane of civilization like war. Back home newspaper editorialists wrote about the good fight; politicians made speeches in Congress about brave soldiers dying for their loved ones. Grandfathers lamented the lack of gumption in the younger generation. But on the beaches of Normandy and the Pacific, words no longer existed. Conversation was dead in the face of the only law that counted. Kill or be killed. Survive. But how could you survive after all of that? The 'you' before the war was as dead as the bloated corpses washing up in the shallows. The 'you' after the war was just another dangerous stranger, to be avoided; above all never to be encountered alone and unarmed.

Hastings wept when the rain sent mildew blooming across Susan's photo, leaching the colour from her face, depositing a sick black stain there, a primitive totem; the Mark of Fate. It invaded his heart; took over its chambers one at a time. Insidious. Relentless. Shutting out the oxygen and the light. Hastings became the killer he was always meant to be. He even began to believe it was normal; this jungle suffering. But instead of killing, he should have been by her side, fighting to save her in the one place he thought she was safe: their hometown. After the war she broke his heart. He took his revenge, the only way he knew how. Then he ran and he hid. And he fell for a woman who was the opposite of Susan. He even thought he might be safe. But then came the Bannister case . . . One lousy break after another, driving him back towards the only job he ever did well. It was almost enough to make him believe in God. It sure as hell made him believe in the devil . . .

Hastings and Roselli sat in silence in the sunshine. Every day was the same in LA, the city's shadows slowly stalked, isolated, and killed under the tyrannous solar stare. Hastings believed in nocturnal amnesty. He had to hold out until the night, when the shadows rioted again, swarming in dark triumph. When the nicotine-yellow sky gave way to the jazz-blue heaven of despair. When he could sleep a few moments, imagining Susan still beside him. Pretending he hadn't done what he'd done after she'd left him.

He turned to Roselli. 'So what's it going to be?'

Hastings saw the pulse of a lie working its way up Roselli's neck. The impulse was enormous to end it right there, to slash Roselli's neck and watch his body pulsing red whorls of rotten life into the swimming pool, the clients screaming and backing away, a bellboy choking back sobs as he called the police and tried to describe the scene over the phone, the dog still worrying the horizon with its bark. 'Ambush. Sniper shot, like that Sinatra movie.'

'Where?'

'Soldier Field. Chicago. The Army-Air Force football game.'

'When?'

'November 2nd . . . ' His eyes narrowed. 'You said you were ready.'

'I am.'

'Well, fucking A, no problems then. Alderisio will be along for the ride.'

Felix 'Milwaukee Phil' Alderisio was Nicoletti's cousin and the best cat burglar in the country. He was also a sick and brutal killer. A Chicago setup on home turf featuring kissing cousin sadists. He and Luchino would do the job and get clipped coming out by Nicoletti and Alderisio. The mad cousins would score a bonus and Roselli a commission on the six hundred grand and whatever advance money he could recover. Everyone would be happy, except Hastings and Luchino.

Hastings finished his drink, masking his eyes behind glass and ice. If he told Luchino, the Corsican might flip and take out Nicoletti and Alderisio, and maybe Hastings for good measure. If Hastings pulled out, Roselli would make him an example to remember. Roselli had created the perfect trap without really meaning to.

'Your plan . . . '

'What's wrong with it?'

'For starters, Chicago . . . ' Hitting the President in Momo Giancana's home town was crazy. It'd be his own death warrant. Whoever had chosen Chicago must have done so because they wanted to take out two institutions for the price of one: the Presidency and the Outfit. The mob knew Momo could never withstand the heat. Momo was a talker. Momo was a turner. They'd move in fast and take him out before he could open his mouth and scream, 'State's Evidence.' Roselli too. They'd dice him up and feed him to the sharks. And then they'd turn on each other. It wasn't just Chicago that was at play, it was all the Midwest, it was Kansas City and St. Louis; it was Detroit. It was Texas and the Mexican border. All that shit coming up from South America. It was LA and the whole West Coast. Most of all, it was Vegas. It'd end up a civil war: New York against Trafficante and Marcello, with Meyer Lansky sitting on the fence as usual, a carrion bird, waiting to suck the bones of the dead. Alliances would shift, betrayals would squirm through the bullet holes. The whole Five Families would be up for grabs. Then the conspirators would move in, clean up and take over. It was too big to fight. They were all dead, JFK included, unless he figured something out fast.

'What the fuck is wrong with Chicago?'

The idiots didn't have a clue. That's why they were criminals.

Criminals were always lazy men who were also very, very stupid. 'Forget it . . . '

Roselli's eyes gave up trying to read his and drifted back to the swimming pool. 'You should see that Sinatra flick.' Hastings looked around. There were plenty of other middle-aged men staring at the pool, their eyes on the slim young women in bathing suits. But Roselli was gazing at the blue square; the door to the other world. The domain of ghosts.

Far away towards the hills, the dog kept barking.

J esus Christ, she's alive!' There is a roar of revolted disbelief. Hands dig and claw their way through the earth, freeing the unconscious woman from her sepulchre of newly-turned garden loam. She has been buried almost upright, tucked inside some kind of lead casing or pipe. She is naked except for a black negligée and a high-strapped golden sandal on her left foot. I take the forgotten shoe out of my jacket pocket. Right foot. Perfect match. I press my ear to her chest. If there's a heartbeat, I can't hear it. Medics arrive from the ambulance outside the gate, handling her in brutal yet effective fashion, opening up airways with hoses and suction. There is an audible gasp of breath, and then mud gutters from her mouth. I turn away, catching sight of Mrs. Bannister disappearing into the house. I run after her, leaving a trail of footprints from the miraculous earth.

She's on the other side of a huge hallway, her face in her hands. She stands upright, mastering her expression and her voice as she watches me crossing to her.

'She lives here?'

'Don't be absurd.'

'Why's that absurd?'

'The divorce was bitter. She lost custody of Ronnie.'

'So where does she live?'

'Now? I don't know.'

'When was the last time you saw her?'

'At the wedding.'

'Yours?'

'Hers. I was a bridesmaid.'

Mrs. Bannister was becoming more interesting by the second. 'You were friends?'

'More than that.'

Did she mean lovers? 'Could you be a little more precise, Mrs. Bannister?'

'Elaine is my sister, Mr. Alston.' Jesus, I hadn't seen that one coming. She smiles at my surprise. 'You didn't know? It was quite the scandal.'

'I bet it was . . . So what happened?'

'Rex . . . Mr. Bannister made a pass at me. He tried to seduce me. And he would have succeeded too if Elaine hadn't walked in on us.'

'I see . . . '

'I don't believe you do. Nobody understood what happened. Nobody believed. I was innocent. I was still a . . . ' She looks away with such embarrassed modesty I could almost believe her. Oh, this one is good, she's awful good. 'Let's just say I was easy prey for a powerful man of the world like Mr. Bannister. He swept me up in a passion I had never known before. I simply couldn't resist its power; even if I had wanted to.'

'I suppose your sister didn't see it that way.'

'She should have! That's how she became the fourth Mrs. Bannister. But she would have none of my innocence. For her it was simple: in a state of inebriation, her new, rich and immensely powerful husband had been bewitched by a provocative and jealous sister. A forgivable transgression . . . For him.'

'Even at her wedding?'

'A final fling before the marriage got under way. Except . . . '

'Except Mr. Bannister didn't want it to be so final?'

'Your perspicacity is commendable.'

'You didn't look too shook up back there when you first saw your sister.'

'I've always tried to keep my emotions private.'

'Except at weddings?'

'You have no right to make such a comment.'

'How about this for a comment: you were shown your own sister lying buried alive in your garden and you hardly blinked.'

'Our relationship was complicated.'

'Crosswords are complicated, Mrs. Bannister. This was your sister.'

'Half-sister.'

'Which half?'

'The mother . . . '

'And the father?'

'Mr. Alston, I need to rest. I've had a dreadful shock.'

'Who was your sister's father?' She looks at my hand on her arm, her eyes welling with tears, then turns away. Jesus, it suddenly hits me. My heartbeat accelerates with the perverse obviousness of the answer. 'Screwing his own daughter, is that it?'

'How could you think such a thing?'

'Then who was Elaine's father?'

'It's a secret.'

'Secrets are for sharing.'

'I can't, not this . . . '

'Tell me.'

' . . . Joseph Kennedy.' She starts to sob.

'The banker? The ambassador? That Joe Kennedy?'

'I don't want to talk about it anymore.'

'Does she ever see him?'

Her eyes widen with fear. 'She mustn't ever know. Not after . . . ' She struggles to regain control.

'After what?' She shakes her head. 'You've got to tell me, Mrs. Bannister. This may have a bearing on Ronnie's—'

'I don't give a damn about Ronnie! I don't give a damn about Elaine. I only care about Rex. Now find the boy and lift this burden from my husband before it kills him. That's what you're paid to do, Mr. Alston. Your job. Now do it.'

She storms away, her heels clicking fast across the oak floors. I look around the great hall with its trappings of wealth and privilege; its promise of the continuity of power. Crests, shields and arms, paintings and portraits; the severed heads of innocent animals. In other countries, in other civilizations—in Europe and Persia and China—these tokens of intimidation and supremacy took centuries to build; countless generations to maintain; innumerable wars to destroy. But in America they just appear overnight: spilling out of the back of a stolen truck; passed under a table in an envelope; whispered over a tapped wire. Delivered at the end of an untraceable gun. They arrive on the wings of crime but flower in the name of commerce and corporation. The swift, lonely power of Today. Parents are buried. Children yet unborn. There's just you. No yesterday. No tomorrow. The fuse of Now is burning bright. The slick instant of this very moment is all that counts. It's the Bannister Way.

Schiller raps on one of the windows. I step out into the dazzle of sunshine. 'Was the kid buried in there with her?'

He shakes his big head. 'We've dug it all back. That pipe she was jammed in gives on to an old well. Deep. There's no sign of the kid, at least not with our torches.'

'You better get a hold of a speleologist club.'

'A spelling what club?'

'Cave experts. Or Army Pioneers, anyone who can climb. You need to send men down with ropes, fast. I found what could have been a well down in the basement. What if the kid is stuck down there?' I run my hand through my hair, soil coming away. 'I just don't understand it . . . '

'Understand what?'

'There was no opening in the bottom of the well . . . and the top's covered with soil. How the hell did she get in?'

'Know what I think? They thought she was dead and buried her there.'

'You're wrong.'

'Give me one reason.'

'Why bury her in a place where they know she's going to be found?' Unless they wanted her found . . . 'Besides, I found her shoe down there in the cellars, near the well . . . '

'What shoe?'

'The right one, the one missing from her foot.' He shakes his head. He didn't even notice. That's the difference between a PI and a cop. One gets paid to think and one gets paid, period . . . 'Where'd they take her?'

'Linda Vista . . . '

'Linda Vista? Why not Mount Sinai? Or Cedars of Lebanon? They're both closer.'

'The Old Man's pumped a fortune into Linda Vista.'

'A philanthropist no less . . . '

'Knock it off, Alston. Even Howard Hughes stays there, and you know what he's like.'

Even in questions of life and death, social contacts mattered for people like the Old Man. 'Any word on her condition?'

'Too early to say. She looked pretty bad when they hauled her away.'

'So would you if you'd been buried alive. You know what's funny . . . ?'

'There ain't nothing funny about this.'

'Hold your horses and listen. Just when I got here last night, I saw someone digging over where they found her.'

'Why the hell didn't you say something?'

'I did. I asked him if he'd found anything.'

I walk over to the steps, staring at the grove, getting the angle and distance as approximate as I can. I try to summon the silhouette of the man against the glimmer of LA streetlight; listening to the sea conch of my memory. The rasp of a shovel digging; not the pad of it filling. 'I'm sure of one thing; he was preparing the hole when I saw him.'

Schiller stares at me.

'Meaning she would have been put in there after I arrived. But there's another thing. Look at that terrain. If she were already lying there, I would have seen her.'

'Not if she were behind the mound of earth.'

'But there was no mound of earth—not then. He must have just started.'

'The nerve of the guy.'

Nerve had nothing to do with this. It wasn't just cool calculation. It was certainty. They knew they could pull this one off. Either they were preparing a grave for Elaine Bannister . . . Or else they were preparing her escape route. And then got interrupted. 'Who else came through the gates apart from me?'

'No one.'

'How about the doctor who was here?' Schiller's eyebrows arch in acknowledgement. 'Any other no ones?'

'Well, the Old Man's attorney was with him.'

'You know him?'

'Name's Adam Granston. A Texan. Not your usual kind of lawyer. Rough around the edges. A heavy drinker. His clients are mainly oilmen.'

Oilmen. Crumpled suits and soiled cowboy boots. Red, sun-hurt faces hunched in half circles, whispering to each other about money, making nasty cracks about their wives. 'Anyone else?'

'LAPD. That's it. The ambulance was always outside . . . '

'They were there all night.'

'So . . . ?'

'Did they come inside to use the john?'

'You don't think a medic from an ambulance . . . '

'You're right, I don't think. But someone could have come in pretending to be a medic. Like the guy digging pretending to be part of the search.'

'He didn't pretend, you mistook . . . '

'He went along with it. That's pretence, okay. Now think, was there anyone else?'

This time Schiller actually stops and thinks. I can see him taking roll call inside that enormous head of his. 'That's it, except for . . . ' His voice trails away.

'For who?'

'Mrs. Bannister. She went out to look for the nanny after the Old Man finally went to sleep.'

'How long was she gone?'

'Forty-five minutes, maybe an hour.'

The red negligée. She'd met someone, slept with him, got changed and came back. She figured no one would notice with her silk robe. She hadn't figured on my prying eyes. 'Let's say she got back at five. Let's say she brought her sister with her in the back of the car. Let's say Elaine was drugged. They carried her to the grove, slid her into a goddamn pipe, and then buried her. By the time that's done, it's almost six. She comes to as soon as they finish. The soil's not packed so tight that she can't move, and the pipe's protecting her from its weight. And there's air coming up from the well. She struggles, nearly clawing her way out before she passes out. But she's still breathing—just—and then she's discovered not more than an hour later.'

'Right in the nick of time.'

'For her. But not for the people who put her there.' If they put her there. 'Let's take a look at Mrs. Bannister's car . . . '

Schiller leads the way to the garage, both of us passing under the hollowing bronze gaze of all those windows, blinded by the morning sun. What if someone inside had seen what had happened? They would have come forward by now, unless . . .

That's the thing about blackmail; it's like adultery. Once it starts inside a household, it's almost impossible to stop.

The garage is bigger than the church that Cate and I were

married in. Mythic names flash by in rows of blue and red and white. Bugatti. Rolls-Royce. Lagonda. Pierce-Arrow. Maybach Zeppelin. Hispano-Suiza . . .

At the end is a pink Cadillac convertible. Mrs. Bannister obviously shared the aesthetic values of the country. 'It's large enough, all right. Let's try the trunk.'

Schiller reaches under the wheel and pops it. I run my hands around the edges. It's clean.

I go round the side, staring into the backseat. Nothing. Then I spot it, half-wedged between the upholstery. I look away, waiting for Schiller to see it too.

'Nothing . . . ' he says. I lean in and snatch the cigarette lighter without him noticing, risking a quick glance. Gunmetal with engraved initials: EB. Elaine Bannister . . . I drop it in my coat pocket, then shiver with the implications.

'It's the air-conditioning.' We both look up at the mechanic, dressed in blue overalls. How long has he been here? 'Everyone shivers inside here. It's too cold, but what can you do? Humidity's bad for the leather.' I nod, steering Schiller out. Did the grease monkey see me? Tampering with evidence. Why did I do it? Because I thought Mrs. Bannister was innocent and that someone had planted her sister's lighter there? Or because I wanted to have something on her? The way she sat down on the bed, her gown opening between her legs . . .

This is why it's called a private investigation. Because we need to keep the discoveries, especially the ones we make about ourselves, confidential—hidden deep inside.

A cop comes running. 'They're on the phone.'

'Who?' As if Schiller doesn't know.

'The kidnappers.'

We race across the gravel, Schiller nearly tumbling, left behind as I overtake the officer and run up the steps, my shoes full of stones. Morris stands in the hallway, panic on his face. He points upstairs.

I take the steps three at a time.

Bannister's door is open. He holds an ivory-handled telephone in his hand. Mrs. Bannister stands behind him, her hands on his shoulders. A young policeman wearing earphones over his red hair listens in, his tape unspooling. I glance at him. He shrugs. 'What's your name?' He mouths back Sam. 'Sam, can you get a trace?' He grimaces, unsure, then his face goes slack with concentration, listening. His pencil hovers, waiting to find its mark.

'I want to speak to my son . . . ' For the first time, Old Man Bannister really sounds his age. 'I want him returned, unharmed.' I can hear the tone from the caller coming over the phone from across the room: Arrogant. Almost bored, as though reading from a text.

The kidnappers own this scenario. They hold the only card worth having: the kid. I lean in to Sam's headphones, listening. 'We will call with specific instructions.' A heavy lisp. Maybe a deliberate disguise. 'Do not involve the police . . . '

There's the bounce of echo as Mr. Bannister speaks, like a voice reverberating in a well. ' . . . But how do I know he's alright unless I speak to him first? I demand to speak to my son.' A pause and then the ungodly moan of disconnection.

The telephone next to Sam rings, making us all start. He picks up just as Schiller comes in, wiping sweat from his cheeks with a handkerchief. Sam looks at him. 'Captain. They got a trace.'

'Where?'

There is the scratch of a pencil obliterating itself against paper. Sam's hand falters, not completing the address. He looks up at Schiller, fear in his eyes.

'Well?' Schiller barks.

I glance at the half-completed address and swear. I turn to Schiller. 'From here . . . Jesus Christ, the call came from here.'

CHAPTER 11
Dallas 2014

Photos tell stories but their narratives are mainly fiction. *Death in Action* was just a stunt; *Les amants de l'hôtel de ville* were student models who had never met before, feigning their passionate kiss. Who made Trotsky vanish from the stage with Lenin? And what the hell happened to the Gang of Four? Take any actor's photo: his or her skin is airbrushed to seamless perfection—whether they like it or not. Oprah becomes Ann-Margret; Kate Winslet, Kate Moss.

Photos are stories that help us buy what we're supposed to; see what we have to. Understand all that we need to. Whether it's right or not. The proof is in the proofs. Truth becomes interpretation; interpretation manipulation.

To see a world in a grain of pixels.

Sam 'Momo' Giancana's photos are no different. They stare out at me from press book after press book in the air-conditioned office. His oversized head, weighed down by heavily-magnified glasses, seems to balance precariously on a small, stooped frame, giving him a deceptively benign appearance, especially when he's sporting a porkpie hat and shades. He could be just another favourite uncle on his way to the race-course or the retirement club for a couple of hands of pinochle.

But the photos are fiction.

Giancana was a brutal, disgusting man, capable of acts of both great and petty evil. His pride and ambition hid grievances that bordered upon paranoia and were fed by a need for generalized vengeance. His speech had a foul, keening sense of the sewer combined with a self-grandiosity that was almost lyrical in its absurdity.

He began his career as a hoodlum for the Forty-Two Gang, before becoming a wheelman for the Chicago Outfit, which was reinventing itself after Scarface Al Capone's arrest. Then Momo took a major step upwards by orchestrating the takeover of the South Side numbers racket through a series of annihilating racist attacks. He unleashed extreme sadists like 'Mad Sam' DeStefano and 'Milwaukee' Phil Alderisio onto the streets of Second City, USA, knowing that their rampages of unimaginable barbarity strengthened his authority—they were all 42-men and they were taking over the Outfit. Giancana was beaten up several times in one-on-ones in Vegas. A physical coward, afterwards he'd order his henchmen to exact revenge. Facial and genital trauma followed by unmarked graves in the Nevada desert.

Momo got messed up when he started fucking a pretty brunette in her twenties, sharing her with Sinatra and JFK. Judy Campbell had a big smile and a frank, open face, although her firm jaw should have warned them she was trouble with a capital T. Judy was an unlucky talisman. Her curse rubbed off on all who touched her. Sinatra lost his casino license. JFK lost his life. And Momo lost his war with Joey 'Doves' Aiuppa, who took over Chicago without a fight.

Momo got old. Momo got scared.

Momo ran away to Mexico, spending his last years in luxury running gambling rackets.

When he was finally nabbed, he squealed.

Under house arrest in Oak Park, not far from Hemingway's old joint, he was betrayed by the very institution he had owned for so long—Chicago law enforcement—his police guards mysteriously withdrawn just before an assassin pumped seven bullets into his head right when he was due to testify before the US

Senate Select Committee to Study Governmental Operations with Respect to Intelligence Activities. The killer took one of the sausages Momo was cooking—the mob never turns down a free meal—and left him lying there in the greasy smear of burning oil, bullet holes rimming his lips.

The question is a slap in the face: how could this worm of a man be responsible for the death of a president of the United States?

'Fascinating, isn't it?'

I look up at Miriam Marshall: real estate agent, conspiracy advocate, and surprisingly cheery survivor of alien abduction. 'Creepy is more the word I'd use.'

Mrs. Marshall nods understandingly. She has been through so much creepiness herself: interstellar travel, outer space organ transfer, internal brain tattooing. 'As you can see, Mr. Giancana organized it all.'

The finger has been pointed at Momo ever since the Magic Bullet started to pirouette. Momo had access to Vegas dough. Big Oil dough. Howard Hughes dough. CIA dough. And US Attorney General Bobby Kennedy was after him and his mobbed-up pals. What better way to get rid of Bobby than get rid of Jack?

'And why did Giancana organize it all?'

'Because he knew the truth about President Kennedy . . . '

'I don't think even JFK knew the truth about himself.'

'Mr. Giancana knew, because he was one himself . . . '

Oh-ho. One of what? Take your pick. Freemason; Catholic; Mafioso; Elder of Zion; Illuminati; Communist; Knight of the Golden Circle. Alien. Abductee. 'And what was Sam Giancana, Mrs. Marshall?'

'A homosexual of course . . . They know. They can tell others of their kind.'

Of their kind. 'And that would make Judith Campbell . . . ?'

She nods sadly. 'A transvestite. Just like Mrs. Kennedy.'

Jackie O indeed. 'I suppose she had the last laugh on Onassis then . . . ?'

She shakes her head. 'He was one too.'

'And how do you explain Maria Callas?'

'A castrati . . . '

Castrato. 'I see you've given this a lot of thought.'

'It's my life's work . . . '

'You have sources?'

'Gore Vidal, for one. He was a fellow abductee on the spaceship.'

Of course he was. 'Well, thank you, Mrs. Marshall.' I get up. Three days in Dallas and I haven't spoken to a single sane person so far. At least Mrs. Marshall isn't coercing me into buying endless rounds of bourbon and Coke. I actually enjoyed her coffee—the first decent cup I've had since arriving in the city. Her espresso machine sits dramatically in the centre of the room like a gleaming holy tabernacle.

She looks at me gathering my things together. 'But you're not leaving already?'

'Afraid so.'

'That's so disappointing, I prepared a PowerPoint presentation and all.'

'I'm terribly sorry.'

'I even had a section on the Bannister case.'

'Excuse me?'

'You know about the case, of course?' I think I nod. 'Mr. Giancana was involved.'

'How exactly was Sam Giancana involved?'

'It's in the PowerPoint presentation, right after the Adelsberg Suicides.'

I glance over at the door. Escape is only five strides away. If I stay, I will be subjected to an insane conspiracy theory based upon the prejudices of a deluded crackpot who believes in the existence of gaydar and little green men. But I may also be able to get a lead on one of the most persistent and enigmatic rumours surrounding the Bannister case. Before Elvis, there was the Bannister kid. Did he die or was he saved? Is he still alive today? Did he ever really exist?

What the hell, at least it's air-conditioned in here and I could do with another cup of coffee to wake me. I turn on the voice recorder of my iPhone. 'Can we perhaps start with the Bannister case?'

Roselli set the meet in Chicago for Halloween. Nobody laughed. Hastings left Bella at a boarding kennel in the canyon. She whined and scratched at the wire cage as he drove away, her face cleaved with anxiety.

Premonitions.

People used to have them before the marble temples and the men in robes, the newspapers and the radios, the pay slips and the railroad stations. People used to heed the warnings. They wouldn't get on the boat, they wouldn't cross the bridge at night. They'd turn when the whispers urged them to; they'd watch the flight of birds and harvest a day early. But in these modern times, premonitions were discarded like dinner scraps—left only to household pets.

Unless it was a hunch on the second race at Hollywood Park, no one listened to the internal voice anymore. But Hastings did, thanks to Bella. Hastings had lied to Roselli at the Monogram Pictures Ranch. Bella didn't bark but she did see ghosts. In July '62, just a week before the Brentwood break-in, Hastings had come back one night from a job—a fence who had stuck ten grand's worth of paste in with the merchandise he was passing on to DeSimone's people—and was going through the back door in the kitchen when Bella slowly lifted her head, trembling in fear.

Hastings thought she must have been poisoned, Bella was shaking so much. She had refused eye contact, her gaze frozen at a point always just behind him. Hastings did a slow circle around the kitchen, Bella's head rotating, following the invisible secret sharer who was tailing him.

Hastings went out the way he came in, strode all the way down the driveway, then made a loud noise with the keys as he came in through the front door, Bella waiting for him, her wagging tail hammering hard against the wall. She jumped up on him, unable to contain her joy, but when he tried to get her to follow him into the kitchen, she had refused.

He went in alone, stepping into a contained wave of cold air rising up all around, as if the kitchen had been built upon a layer of snow. It took him a minute before he noticed them: the smudge marks of wet footprints that had nearly dried. Men's shoes. He crouched down, and ran a handkerchief across the drying stains of red. The faintest trace of blood.

He turned to where Bella sat in the doorway, pleading with her eyes for him to cross the threshold back to the world without apparitions. The world where the dead did not return. He peered at her, moving closer. There was something wrong. Her breath was smoking in the cold. Her whiskers were coated in a thin white casing of frost about her muzzle. The cold ice tingled his fingers.

He gathered up a single suitcase and left forever. For all he knew the cold and the footprints were still lurking in that house. Many times he had tried to recall the footprints. Were they his? Or did they belong to the fence? He'd been waiting for the fence for two hours, sitting low in the front of a stolen car in the shadows he had made when he'd taken care of the streetlights. The fence didn't seem to realize he was already merging into darkness as he got out of his car, Hastings walking quickly across the soft, betraying lawn, his pistol fully extended, timing the shot with the slam of the door, the fence going backwards into the car and then forwards onto the lawn. Hastings caught a glimpse of the eyes right after the shot: not so much a regard as a physical affirmation of the passing of life. The swift

flutter upwards as they cast off their light and prepared themselves for the big stare into the Long Oblivion. Then he was
crossing the road, disappearing into the altered summer night,
looped with the shadows of assassination; with the loss of a
stolen life.

No witnesses.

Except for Bella.

Was the presence he and Bella had both felt that night
merely the last vestiges of the fence; a physiological registration
of extinction like that final look in his eyes? Or was it a manifestation of something else—life after death, the pursuit of
judgment; the suffusion of a restless, aggrieved life force?
Perhaps a shattered energy had contaminated him when he
fired the kill shot. The splatter of psychic evidence linking him
to the crime forever.

Or maybe it was simpler than that. Maybe it wasn't a ghost
that was haunting them in the kitchen; maybe it was just Hastings
and his past. A past that was catching up with him in Chicago.

'Well, look what that mangy, poor excuse of a cat dragged
in!' Roselli slapped Hastings on the back like he was arriving
at a Jaycee meeting in Waterloo, Iowa, everyone excited by the
quality of the wives who were being swapped that night.

Hastings peered through the curtains. Jack-o'-lanterns
flickered with orange malice from the windows of otherwise
normal households. Kids circulated with bedsheets and
broomsticks. Old people were taunted, cats tormented, children terrified. The Feast of Fear stalked the city, feeding on
superstition and confectionary. 'Close that fucking blind,
Jesus, the Feds could be watching.'

Indeed the Feds could be watching. Hastings could almost
hear the stutter of the shutters of long-lens cameras across the
road. One by one, they'd be shot, going in or coming out, their
images imprisoned by a rusted thumbtack against a wall in
some clapped-out office south of downtown.

Hastings exchanged looks with Luchino, who offered him a French cigarette. Yellow paper; black tobacco. Harsh and strong as the mistral. Of all the men in the room, Luchino was the mystery. Hastings had heard he'd started up like him; on the legit in a war, a seventeen-year-old franc-tireur nailing Nazi officers with precision shooting in the maquis, then elbowing his way into the black market as a gofer during the USS Corsica period. Cigarettes gave way to heroin; Bonifacio to Marseille and the French Connection, Luchino always around to deliver a bullet to anyone who got in the way.

Hastings watched Nicoletti and Alderisio sitting in the corner like two classroom dunces. They were not friends, they didn't even like each other, but they were forever linked by the primordial bonds of blood—both family and spilling. Hunched and illiterate, they avoided any communication, even eye contact, barely acknowledging anyone else in the room. Association was complication—what if they had to whack you going out the door? Their heavy presence created a claustrophobic gloom. The only jauntiness came from Roselli, drinking scotch and talking about a visit he'd made the summer before to Agrigento. 'Fucking amazing. Those Greeks. Those Romans. Building goddamn temples you wouldn't believe. History. There ain't nothing like it.'

'Who gives a rat's ass about history?' The dulcet tones of Momo, as he came through the door. 'You're all here to change the future, not fuck around with the past. And you're doing it by putting a bullet in the president.'

There was the rasping irritation of a dry flint, then the silence of flame. 'Why?' Luchino asked.

'Ain't none of your fucking business, *why*?'

Luchino leant forward and exhaled with a brief, sharp thrust and the flame disappeared. 'When I kill a man, I want to know why. It is not a right; it is a requirement.'

'Be careful, my French friend. In this country we don't ask questions.'

'I am Corsican, not French. And in my country even the dead ask questions.'

'Well, in my country the dead shut the fuck up and stay that way.'

Luchino stared at Momo for a long moment. His face had been polished bronze by the sun: more a visage on a coin than something living. 'Any brute can kill . . . ' He half-glanced at Nicoletti and Alderisio, his eyes passing judgment. 'But to end a man's life under carefully controlled circumstances and then to elude capture is another matter. For that, there is a psychological element. And this requires an understanding of the motives behind such acts.'

'His brother is causing—'

'Shut up.' Momo barked at Roselli, then turned back to Luchino. 'We want him dead. That's motive enough.'

Luchino smiled and nodded, stubbing out his yellow cigarette. It was not a gesture of capitulation, it was a moment of resolve. He had just come to the same conclusion as Hastings: kill the others. Steal the money. Run.

Roselli led the way into a windowless room, Hastings pausing before going inside. He could sense death the way a fisherman could sense a change in the weather: through his bones; reactive, not deductive. His eyes swept the surfaces: bloodstains mopped off the floor. Cordite blush on the furniture. Bullets wormed out of walls by prodding fingers. The room was a sponge of evil acts and wicked memories. Carnage, cruelty, suffering.

Luchino felt it too, but the others just sauntered in with the bored indifference of a husband forced along on a house inspection when he has no intention of buying.

There were maps up on the far wall. Little red pins—like schoolboys playing soldier at Soldier Field. The motorcade route. A photo of a gun-crazy chump, posing with an M1 Garand and an angry scowl, his cheeks puffed out in indignation.

'This is your patsy. Thomas Arthur Vallee. A-1 certified nut. Korean vet. Fucked around with some U2 intelligence unit in Japan. Weapons collector. Knows how to handle a rifle.' Roselli tossed a file on a table, then sighted through an imaginary carbine. 'Bang-bang. Happy Deathday, Mr. President.' Momo laughed, but Nicoletti and Alderisio just stared. Luchino's hand hesitated, like a snake handler who had just been bitten the night before, then opened Vallee's file. The word *schizophrenic* stamped on a medical form invaded the room and was mocked by the dual gaze of Nicoletti and Alderisio.

'So what's the plan?' Hastings asked.

Roselli tapped a street on the map. 'Set up a sniper's nest here in the warehouse, where the motorcade slows to take the turn, shooting down as they pass. Four guns in a hotel here, shooting across as they come.'

'Four guns . . . ?' Luchino and Hastings exchanged shadow glances.

'Four.' Momo shouted it as though Luchino were deaf, holding up four stubby fingers. 'Back. Side. Bang-bang and good-bye.' Momo leant over, spat between his feet.

Hastings stared at Luchino. The same thought was going through both their minds. Cross fire. Stray bullets. Confusion. Perfect cover for Nicoletti and Alderisio to fire point-blank into the back of their heads.

Hastings cleared his throat. 'So who takes what?'

'You're the sniper's nest team.'

Meaning . . . 'Just me?'

'Fuck no, the four of you plus the patsy.'

'And who is in the hotel?'

'That don't concern you . . . '

'*Mais* . . . '

'How do you say "Ain't none of your fucking business" in French?' Momo's laugh was more a cough.

Luchino's eyes appealed for solidarity. Hastings turned to Roselli. 'This other team . . . ?'

Nicoletti stepped forward. It was the first time Hastings had ever heard him speak. 'The man said, none of your fucking business.'

Two options. Kill him or walk away. Hastings voted for kill, but before the fatal gesture was released, Luchino had stepped between Hastings and Nicoletti, speaking to Roselli. 'Two teams getting away? In the middle of a firestorm, with hundreds of policemen? I am sorry, my friend, but that's our business.'

Nicoletti got in real close to Luchino. They were all grown men. All killers. So-called professionals. And still they couldn't avoid this—a schoolyard challenge. 'What the fuck's the problem? Just drop the gun and run.'

Alderisio snorted with amusement.

Luchino's voice was low with the effort to control his anger. 'Runners are targets. Runners get chased. Have you not seen what dogs do to passing runners?'

Nicoletti turned to the others. 'What the fuck is he talking about?' Then to Luchino: 'Did you just insult me?'

Hastings couldn't stand it anymore. 'All he's saying is: we don't want to stand on each other's toes . . . '

'What is that, a threat?'

'This is . . . ' Luchino had the blade to Nicoletti's throat. Hastings didn't see it coming. He glanced at Nicoletti, caught the glimpse of nickel in his fist. Nicoletti had gone for his piece and Hastings had missed it too.

Hastings finally got it.

Luchino was better than him.

Full of remorse, Hastings filled both his hands with gunmetal, one pointing at Alderisio, who was liable to get himself and Nicoletti killed, the other at Roselli and Momo—just in case. Luchino nodded, satisfied with his ally. 'Now, *mes amis*, will you let Monsieur Roselli answer the question?'

Roselli slowly raised his hands. 'Settle down, boys, we're all friends.'

'Then you better explain to us who the other team is and how you expect to get all of us out alive.'

Roselli looked at Momo, who nodded. He was famous for hating the sight of blood . . . especially his own, and Momo knew he was just two angry men away from a bloodbath.

'Cubans.'

'Communists?'

Roselli looked at Luchino like he was crazy. 'Fuck no! Anti-Castro.'

The knife under Nicoletti's chin disappeared. It was not taken away; it just vanished as quickly as it appeared. A ghost blade. Luchino either had a gimmick or he was a magician. Hastings kept his guns out though. Everyone was still in that dangerous simmer time, when emotions were so hot, people forgot they were mortal.

'How many?'

'Four.'

Like them. 'Who are they?'

'Put those fucking guns away and I'll tell you . . . '

Hastings watched Nicoletti and Alderisio. 'Everyone nice and calm again . . . ?'

'How the fuck do I know—he pulled the knife.'

'I pulled the knife, my friend, because—'

Nicoletti interrupted. 'I ain't no fucking friend of yours.'

Luchino shrugged with sad acceptance. 'Because—my enemy—you had already gone for your gun. That makes me nervous.'

'Who gives a shit, you fucking frog.'

Hastings made a mental note. Kill Nicoletti before Alderisio. He intervened. 'Castro, anti-Castro. So what? Question is, can they shoot?'

'Ex-military. CIA-trained. They were Bay of Pigs.'

The ones that got away. 'So they're pissed.'

'Awful pissed and pumped and ready to do what it takes to nail the president.'

'Why two teams? You could put two of us in the warehouse, and two in the hotel?'

Roselli looked at Momo uncomfortably, caught out being stupid. Again. Roselli hadn't thought of that question. He was going to have to improvise his lie.

'Backup, that's all. We can't afford to miss.'

Especially if the target had expanded to include Hastings and Luchino. Hastings turned to Momo. 'I don't get it. A Chicago hit. You know everyone will finger you.'

'That's my alibi. I'd have to be nuts to do it on home turf. Besides, what with the Cubans . . . '

He shut up fast. Not fast enough. Luchino tapped the edge of ash from his cigarette. His only outward reaction to the revelation: the Cubans were being set up too. They were patsies. Just like the psycho, Thomas Vallee. And just like Hastings and Luchino. Only Vallee and the Cubans would be blamed, would be hounded down and shot by the police, their bodies displayed like Zapata's alongside posing ghouls. Hastings and Luchino's fate would be very different. They would simply disappear. Luchino's sun-bleached blue eyes stared into his. The secret knowledge was shared. Roselli and Momo had no idea they knew—how could they: they were men without instinct; men without epiphanies. Nicoletti sat there and sulked. Alderisio picked his nose. They were patsies too—only further along in the game. After the bodies and the guns had been taken care of, and the concrete floors hosed down and the drains unclogged of human remains. They were the final act. The dry-cleaning. The polishing of the faucet and the door handle. The endgame in the perfect crime. Nicoletti and Alderisio: a couple of woodlice extinguished with the parting footsteps. Unnoticed. Unmourned. Unmissed.

Never existed . . .

'So,' Momo said, false cheer in his voice, 'I guess that's that.' He clapped his hands together. 'Now we can get on with some trick or treat.'

S chiller has ordered everyone out of the house. Only Old Man Bannister stays inside, resting in his bed with his overpriced society doctor and a suspiciously young nurse. Everyone else is standing on the garden lawn in front of the steps, a regiment of uniformed household staff staring over at the tilled soil in the grove.

Mrs. Bannister stands with Schiller, going through lists and pointing people out. Servants step forward as they are named, like tryouts at a casting call.

'I only count sixteen. Where are the others?' Faces pivot to Morris. He loosens his tie with a finger to the collar, as though already feeling the noose.

'Higgins and Greta have the day off, sir. And Dale is ill.'

Schiller turns to a cop. 'Take them all down to the station and hold them there for questioning. Fingerprint them all. I have two dusting units on their way right now.'

The staff is herded down the driveway towards a bus parked outside the estate. The grease monkey we saw in the garage gives me a queer look as he walks by. He wants to talk. He is alone amongst the others. The rest of the staff is remarkably compliant as they stand around the bus. The Old Man tells them to do something and they do it: mow the lawn; polish the silver; wash the car. Go to jail. Only on this Monopoly board they won't be collecting $200. Old Man Bannister is planning on firing most of them. 'Isn't there anyone you trust amongst them?' Schiller had asked after the phone call.

'Trust? That is not a word one uses with domestic employees, Captain Schiller. I trust in God, Country and myself.'

If Schiller noticed the conspicuous absence of the LAPD in the list, he didn't show it.

'There must be some staff you value over others?'

'Morris. Taylor, the chauffeur. The head chef. That's all.'

'I'll concentrate on them first . . . '

And Schiller had, making sure the three rode separately in patrol cars. I wander over to the bus, tapping a cigarette out of its package. The mechanic already has a match lit. The flame of conspiracy. 'I think I know who did it . . . ' He has a reliable voice, no waver; no plea. He's not selling anything, at least not that I can see.

I suck in fresh smoke, look around. No one seems to be noticing. 'Did what?'

'Made the call. It was . . . ' The doors to the bus spring open with a snapping shudder. A patrolman surges forward, shoving the mechanic, hard, towards the doors. 'Get a move on!'

'Hey, lay off. They're witnesses, not suspects.'

'That's not what I heard . . . '

'Then clean those potatoes out of your ears, 'cause you heard wrong.'

A sergeant comes up in support. 'Butt out, Alston, this is no concern of yours.'

It's that fat fuck, Barnsley. 'I'm Mr. Bannister's personal representative. This all concerns me, Barnsley.'

'Tell it to the judge.'

'I'll tell it to Chief Parker.'

'Fink.'

'Fuck.'

There is the clash of shoulders as we collide, like goddamn mountain rams. Other cops gather round, probably hoping to see Barnsley get his teeth kicked in. They sure as hell don't signal solidarity. The sergeant backs away.

'Your day will come, Alston.'

'It came five years ago, Barnsley, when I left the Force and jackasses like you behind.'

Barnsley adjusts his tunic, hoisting his gun belt. His face ticks with the desire to hurt me. He and the other cop stomp off. I saunter back over to the mechanic. 'Sorry about that. Hope he didn't hurt you . . . '

'I was on Iwo Jima. I don't hurt easy.'

'I was there too. What's your name?'

'Philip Hastings.'

'You been on the job long?'

'A while.'

'And you think you know who made the call?'

'Look, I'm no stool pigeon but . . . ' He glances around. Four or five of the staff are staring at him. Whispers are going out. They know what he's doing. Naming names. It could be theirs. 'There's this kid, Hidalgo. Works as a gardener. I saw him by the phone in the garage.'

A stillness passes between us. It is the transgression. He has given me valuable information. But he has also borne witness against another. I have asked him to do so, and for my troubles I am complicit in his betrayal. In his sin. I offer him a cigarette. He's smart enough not to take it in front of the others. 'Mexican?'

'Cuban.'

'He's here now?'

The very faintest of nods. 'Over by the back there . . . Watching us.'

A gardener . . . 'You ever see him digging around the grove over there?'

Hastings masks his eyes behind his smoke, talking out of the side of his mouth. 'That's all he ever does. Digs holes . . . Then fills them.'

Bingo. 'Thanks. I'll catch up with you at the station.' I drop my cigarette and stomp it out as Hastings joins the others, who all turn their backs on him.

I look at my watch then up at the sky. Then I turn as casually as I can, my eyes making the briefest of contact with the kid, Hidalgo.

He bolts, racing round in front of the bus, heading across the boulevard.

A cop shouts.

There is the screech of brakes.

The hiss of tires locking . . .

And then the empty thud of a body hit hard.

Birds burst from the trees, scattering fragmented shadows for an instant.

Everyone runs onto the road, cars screeching to a halt, the household staff shouting, cops stopping traffic. There is the low sob of disbelief and the stunned mutter of surprise, and the driver shaky on his feet as he protests his innocence.

I stand there, staring at the kid's legs protruding from under the car, sunlight and shadows shifting nervously through the crazy sway of palms.

And then I get it.

I look around.

Too late.

Hastings is gone.

I slap the pocket of my coat. The son of a bitch.

The lighter is missing too.

Schiller steps out of the emergency room, closing the door on the wave of cold air reaching out behind him, trying to tug us both back into the gleaming metal realm of trauma, accident and death. He shivers and pulls out a cigarette. 'Touch and go . . . Doc thinks maybe go.'

I swear. 'Did they at least let you take his prints?' He nods . . . Savouring the silence.

I wait as long as I can. 'And . . . ?'

'Good news and bad news.'

I sigh. Other men play chess. Schiller plays games. 'Okay, start with the good.'

'Hidalgo's prints are all over the phone in the garage.'

'So he made the call?'

'Maybe. Maybe he was just talking to his girl . . . '

'And the bad news?'

Schiller gives his ugly smile and takes one step towards me, cuffs already in his hands. 'You're under arrest.'

'What the . . . ?'

His wheezing laugh echoes off the broken tile walls. 'I can dream, can't I?' He slips the cuffs back into his jacket. 'The look on your face.'

The look on his if I slugged him the way I wanted to. 'Very funny. What's the bad news?'

'Hastings's prints were all over the phone too.'

I swear. He's holding back. There's worse to come, I can

feel it. 'How do you know they're Hastings's prints? Does he have a rap sheet?'

Schiller shakes his head. 'But we've matched them with the tools down there. Who else would they belong to?'

Try the real kidnapper's . . . 'How many other phones are there in the house?'

'Eight. We've got nine matches for all the prints, including Mr. and Mrs. Bannister.'

'Forget them, they were both in the room.'

'That still leaves five others, excluding Hidalgo and Hastings.'

'Was Greta Simmons one of them?'

Schiller shrugs lazily. The sleepless night or the decanter of scotch is getting to him. 'Soon as we pull her in, we'll know.'

Prints on phones, Jesus, we need something more than that. 'How many times do the servants touch the phone, even just to dust it?'

'In my home the dust just minds its own business.'

'Your home is not normal . . . '

'And Old Man Bannister's is?'

'Speaking of which, I've got to get back there. But I wanted to talk to Elaine Bannister first.'

'They're not letting anyone talk to her, at least for the moment.'

I glance at my watch; swear. 'Look at the time, no wonder I'm tired . . . ' And starving. We start heading down the corridor towards the exit.

'Before you go, just one more thing . . . '

This is the real bad news, moving in fast like a storm system off the Pacific. The air is alive with electricity. With the potential for disaster. 'What is it?'

'This Hidalgo kid . . . ?'

The pause is excruciating. Schiller smiles maliciously. This is going to be really bad.

'Well, it turns out he was some kind of a fucking spy.'

'How the hell do you figure that?'

Schiller smiles, picking his teeth with a thumbnail. 'Could be because some FBI agent from Boston just arrested him . . . '

'What the hell has Boston got to do with this?' Schiller shrugs, hands me a card. I read the agent's name: H. Paul Rico. 'What the hell is this about? He can't just march in and arrest an unconscious patient.'

There's a shift in Schiller's eyes. 'I know what you're going to say. I said it, too, straight to the Fed's face. Next thing you know, J. fucking Edgar himself is hollering at me on the phone, telling me to back off.'

I study his eyes for a long moment, then smile. 'You are bullshitting me . . . '

He shakes his head, flicks a piece of retrieved food in the direction of the emergency room's doors. 'Go inside and look for yourself. The kid's handcuffed to his bed. The doctor was awful pissed.'

'But you have jurisdiction.'

'Kidnapping's a federal crime.'

'What state lines have been crossed? Jesus, the FBI can't just . . . ' I see the exasperated look on his face and stop. Of course they can. 'So what does it mean?'

'You're the one getting paid to think, you tell me.'

'Hidalgo was an undercover Fed?'

'He's just a kid.'

A Cuban kid. 'What if he wasn't an operative, but he was on the payroll. An informer, keeping an eye on someone.'

'So why arrest him?'

'To protect him? Or maybe to divert attention.'

Schiller shakes his head. 'You try too hard, you know that?'

'Hastings said the kid was Cuban. Maybe he's a Communist. Maybe the FBI caught him, threatened him with deportation, made him rat someone out.'

'Just like a fucking Red.'

'Or maybe he's anti-communist. Maybe he's against this new guy, what's his name—Castro? Or maybe he was working for the mob in Havana?' Schiller screws up his face. Grey is too complicated for Schiller—he thinks in black and white.

'So where the hell is this Fed?'

'He said he had a car outside.'

'I'm going to ask him some questions . . . '

Schiller grabs my arm. 'Don't mess with Hoover.'

I throw his hand off my arm. 'If it comes down to J. Edgar and Old Man Bannister, I know whose side I'm on.' I push past Schiller, heading towards the ambulance bay.

The sunlight is an assault, leaching the world of vision. I scan the washed-out world, shapes and colours slowly restoring meaning. An empty black '57 Plymouth is parked illegally in the driveway, next to an ambulance. The ambulance driver looks at me in his side mirror. Sunken eyes, black-rimmed and lifeless; contaminated by all the dead and the dying he's been carrying around the city. I sure as hell wouldn't want to be one of this hack's fares. He glares at me as I look through his window. 'Just checking to see the meter's down.' I flash my badge fast, sunlight reflecting off it, hitting him square in the eyes. LAPD, PI, Cereal Box—badges are all the same if they glint. 'Have you seen the agent who belongs to that car?'

'Try the john.' He sneers, withered teeth revealing a deeper, internal decay. 'If you hurry, you might still catch him beating his meat.'

I reach in and snatch the ignition keys from the Plymouth, then follow a dark, half-sunken lane past a stinking platoon of Dempster Dumpmasters, entering a murky kingdom of shadows, leaky pipes and trash cans overflowing with surgical waste. There are gloomy public toilets half-hidden at the end of a sad track of worn linoleum.

Inside are two men in dark suits, both with their pants

around their ankles, one about to sexually assault a handcuffed, half-naked woman; the other about to do the same to a hand-cuffed, half-naked man. I draw my Colt Police Positive .38 Special. 'Stop or I'll shoot!'

The man behind the woman freezes, then turns, his erection pointing straight at me. 'Relax, mister, I don't mind sharing.'

The other would-be rapist quietly adjusts his trousers, going for a Smith & Wesson .38 in a holster attached to his belt.

'Don't . . . '

He raises his hands slowly, his trousers gliding back down around his ankles. 'We're all friends here . . . '

I nod to the couple as I take his revolver, empty the rounds onto the floor, then slip it between my waist and belt. 'Uncuff your *friends* fast, or I'll separate you from your sorry little balls.'

'No need to be nasty, there's plenty to go around.'

The one in front of the girl turns and leers at me. 'Say, I think he likes you . . . '

'Turn around . . . both of you.'

They exchange a look that says they're about to rush me. I have to move fast. I get in first, slugging the big one, then the loudmouth, with the bottom of the gun grip. The big one crumples into unconsciousness at the foot of the girl. The smaller one moans, cradling his head.

'I said, let them go.'

'But we haven't even touched them yet.'

'Shut up. Do as I say.'

'Take your pick. You can have them both.'

I kick him. 'If you don't uncuff them, I'm putting one through your shoulder . . . ' He doesn't move. 'You think I won't do it?' There is a defiant silence in answer, finally broken by me cocking the gun.

'Okay . . . okay, you fucking killjoy.'

Just then the big one moans. The other one tries a grab at

me, but I step back just in time, bringing the Colt's barrel down hard on the back of his knuckles. He curses, clutching his hand in pain. I turn to the big one, sending him back to lullaby land with a kick to the temple.

'Some fucking tough guy.'

'Shut up. Who the hell are you?'

'FBI. Let me go, motherfucker, or I'll have your nuts for breakfast.'

'So you're the one trying to snatch our suspect?'

'I have a warrant.'

'Horseshit.'

'And now you've obstructed a federal agent making an arrest.'

'Don't make me laugh . . . '

'It's true.' He points to the trembling couple. 'Caught them red-handed, lewd and lascivious. Fucking in a public restroom. You're in serious trouble, asshole, obstructing a federal agent in his duty—'

I can't listen to him another minute. I let him have it behind his ear, then find the cuff keys in his jacket pocket. There is the snap of release, then the sigh of liberation. The girl is sobbing. 'Did they hurt you?'

The man looks away. The woman shakes her head, hurriedly pulling up her underwear. 'They didn't have time . . . '

'What happened?'

The woman turns to the man. He avoids her gaze. And mine. 'We're engaged . . .' The couple exchanges a brief look. Something tells me the wedding's just been cancelled. 'We live with our parents . . . '

'We work together.' His voice breaks as he speaks.

'That's how we met. No one ever comes down here. Not normally . . . '

Normally is finished for this couple. Forever.

'No one knows about us . . . ' The man's voice echoes off

the tile walls as he dresses, his back to me. 'And we want to keep it that way.' He turns, his eyes hooded with suspicion. 'No one must ever know about this'

'No one ever will . . . Did they identify themselves as Federal agents?'

'Federal agents? Wait a minute . . . ' The man starts circling me, his fists clenched. Someone jumped him once. He's never going to let it happen again. At least, that's what he thinks. 'They never said a word. And come to think of it, you didn't say who you were . . . '

I snatch the kid by the lapels then send him soaring backwards into the wall. There is the soft crack of his skull hitting tiles. The blow drives the air, and the aggression, out of him. 'Your guardian angel, so show a little respect.' I turn to the girl. 'Tell me exactly what happened . . . '

'We were . . . doing it. And the next thing you know, these two just appear out of nowhere . . . ' She looks away.

'Did they talk about anything? A Cuban called Hidalgo. Or a kidnapping . . . ?'

The girl is trembling. She shakes her head.

I start with the big guy, cuffing his hands to the legs of separate stalls so he's spread-eagle before I frisk him. I find a driver's license inside his wallet. Arthur Leigh Allen, born December 18th, 1933. I pocket the wallet. There's a Zodiac Sea Wolf wristwatch, expensive; probably stolen. I pocket it too, as well as a couple of knives: a USMC KA-BAR and a Frost Moose Hunter. Then I frisk the other assailant, the loudmouth. His wallet's heavy with an FBI shield. The same name as on the card Schiller showed me: H. Paul Rico, from Boston, Massachusetts.

I look up at the couple. 'You two better go . . . ' The one called Allen groans. I let him have another crack across the crown of his head. The girl looks from my pistol to Allen's head to my eyes. 'And I wouldn't come back here for a few days if I were you.'

They're both gone without another word. Outside in the sunshine they'll find relief and anger. Rancour and regret. Why didn't you do anything? How could you have let them jump us like that . . . ? It was your fault, if your mother had gone away like she was supposed to, we wouldn't have had to do it in the john.

Rico's coming round. I grab him by the scruff of his thick neck. 'Okay, you little shit, you have one minute to tell me everything.'

Rico tries to sit up against the wall but slides back down against the tiles, hitting the side of his head against the can. 'Police brutality.'

I grab him by the collar. 'Listen, you fuck, I'll show you some real police brutality unless you talk. Start with your buddy Allen. Is he FBI too?'

Rico gives a disgusted snort. 'That tub of shit? Are you kidding? He's a fucking child molester. I arrested him three days ago in Atascadero.'

'He didn't look like he was under arrest.'

'Yeah well, he was showing me around his network and we decided to have some laughs.' He gives a grunt of merry remembrance, as though recalling a series of harmless schoolyard high jinks.

'You think this is funny?'

'What do you want, tears?'

It takes everything inside me not to bury the pistol barrel deep inside his ear. 'The truth. Who told you to arrest Hidalgo?'

'Hoover. And that's the truth.'

'And where were you planning on taking him?'

Rico clams up. I grab his head and shove it into the toilet bowl, yanking the chain. Water thunders down, nearly drowning out his screams. Something moves behind me. Allen's getting to his feet. I kick him in the shin. He drops to one knee. I

kick him in the windpipe. He falls backwards, gasping. I haul
Rico out of his own private porcelain torture chamber. 'You
got thirty seconds before the cistern refills. Why do you want
him?'

'Miami office wants him.'

'Why?'

'Fucked if I know, I'm just following ord—'

I plunge his head back into the toilet. There is the cascade
of water, and then the sobs of a nearly-drowned man. 'Next
time I'm not letting you up for air, so you better talk: what's
Hidalgo to Hoover?'

'Hidalgo ain't nothing to Hoover, but he's something to
Nixon.'

'Nixon? The vice president?'

'The fucking street sweeper—of course the vice president.'

'What was Hidalgo doing for Nixon?'

'Apart from giving him a blow job . . . ? No!' He screams as
I go to flush his head down the can forever. 'Hidalgo is part of
Operation 40. He's controlled by David Sánchez Morales.
Morales practically runs the entire outfit. Nixon has oversight,
but Morales runs it on the ground. No wonder they keep fucking up: there should be Americans in charge.' He wipes his
stinking wet hair out of his eyes, focusing on me. There's that
snorting laugh again, offensive, derisive; obscene in its total
contempt. 'You don't know what the fuck I'm talking about,
you dumb shit . . . ' Then, 'Let him have it!'

Allen sucker punches me from behind, my ear singing in
agony. Rico charges me, battering into my chest with his sop-
ping bullet head. We career backwards into the sink, my gun
clattering out of my hand. I take the rim hard against my spine.
'When I'm through with you . . . ' Rico is literally frothing at
the mouth. He yanks his gun out of my belt, rams the barrel
under my chin and pulls the trigger. Nothing.

I knock the gun out of his hands and he goes for the throat.

I try to twist him away but his grip is strong. I pivot, searching for a stronghold, my hand finding a faucet behind me. I try to rip it out to use as a weapon but all I do is turn it on. In seconds hot steam is gushing up my back. The tap is so hot I have to let go. My hand flays for something else, and yanks a cake of soap off its metal rod holder. I smash the little bastard in the eye with the soap. He lets out a shriek, and bites my hand. I drop the soap and snatch him by the ears, slowly turning him around, bending him backwards over the sink.

Rico resists every inch. There's an explosion of wood behind me. I glance up at the mist-fogging mirror. Allen has just torn one of the cubicle doors off its hinges and is right behind me, aiming my revolver at my head with his free hand. I'm gone. Then Allen disappears. I catch a glimpse of his feet high in the air, then the mirror clouds over. One last effort, and Rico's head is under the blasting hot water.

He lets out a wild scream, exploding past me in pain, running straight into the door, then rocking backwards, his nose broken from the impact, bits of gristle and blood splattered on the wood. Rico lands hard, out cold. I look down at Allen, taking my gun from his hand. He's slipped on the cake of soap and is out too, a trickle of blood from a crack in his head worming its way across the filthy floor.

I turn back to the sink. The clogged drain is already overflowing. I leave them there. If they're lucky, they'll come to before the boiling water strips the skin off their scalps and hands. If there's any justice, they won't . . .

Schiller and the ambulance driver are lounging against the side of the vehicle, smoking and trading jokes. A real man of the people, Schiller. I wouldn't be caught dead next to that driver—even if I was. Schiller glances up at me, his jaw dropping in astonishment. 'What happened to you?'

'You should see Rico.'

'Are you nuts? You don't touch a Fed.'

I pull Schiller out of earshot of the ambulance driver. 'Fuck Hoover. Hidalgo's not a foreign spy, he's working for Nixon, in some outfit named Operation 40.'

'What the hell is that?'

'No idea, but I intend to find out.' I weigh the set of cuff keys in my hand. 'We uncuff Hidalgo but we hold on to him. He's the only bargaining chip we have. And by the way, there's a fat fuck back inside there who has an outstanding warrant for child molestation.'

I pull out his wallet and hand it to Schiller. 'His name's Arthur Leigh Allen, from Atascadero. From what I found on him, he's a cutter-collector.'

Schiller curses darkly. 'I'll take care of him.' Just then someone bursts out of the exit, making us both start. I spin around, the cop holding his hands up in alarm at the sight of my gun. I holster it quickly as Schiller motions for him to come over. The same asshole who shoved Hastings outside the bus. He's breathless from running. 'Captain? You better come.'

Schiller and I exchange glances. Have they already found Rico? 'Is it the Fed?' I ask.

The cop looks right past me, talking directly to Schiller. 'The kidnappers called Old Man Bannister again.'

Schiller speaks through gasps of breath, struggling in the heat as we trot to a patrol car. 'And did they trace the call?'

The cop hands him a note. Schiller swears. 'How the fuck is that possible?'

'What?'

'The call. Same as before. It came from the goddamn Bannister Estate.'

The siren's still wailing as we pass through the gates. Again I leave Schiller behind as I race up the stairs. Mrs. Bannister's standing at the top. She's wearing black Capri pants and a white blouse tied in a knot at the waist. Gold glimmers around her ears and neckline, and there is the ostentatious glitter of a diamond and emerald chain tracing an orbit about a slender ankle. Her hair is tied in a short ponytail with a red silk scarf. The outfit is more for the beach houses of Rio or the Riviera than for a mansion in the grip of fear. I realize it's the first time I've actually seen her dressed. I'm about to make a crack but she cuts in first. 'He's going to pay them.'

Of course he is. What choice does a father have—especially a very wealthy father. 'How much are they asking?'

'A million . . . '

A good round figure. Substantial enough to cause pain, but not too excessive for an old crook like Bannister. I go to step around her but she gets in the way. For a moment, I feel her breasts against my chest. Their warmth. Their promise. 'Mr. Alston, you're not going to actually let him pay the ransom, are you?'

'You don't really think he's going to miss the money?'

'It's more the principle of the matter . . . '

'When a kid's been snatched, your principles get reduced to basics, Mrs. Bannister. Will he or won't he?'

'Pay?'

'Come back alive . . . '

Inside the room, the lawyer called Granston is standing over Old Man Bannister's wheelchair, arguing with a sour look on his face—you'd think it was his cash that was being put on the line. 'Jesus, Rex, we can't pull that kind of money out of thin air.'

'They said one million and by God they will have it!'

Granston exchanges looks with Betty Bannister as he storms out. Sam's still manning the tape machine, holding one earphone to his head. 'They're sure about the trace?' He looks up with fear in his eyes and nods. Schiller comes in, heaving painfully from his slow trot up the stairs.

'How is that possible?' Schiller roars. 'There's no one else here, the servants are all away.'

'Not only that,' Sam nods to a table. Seven phones are sitting there. 'The one Mr. Bannister is using is the only remaining functioning phone in the place.'

'Jesus, Mary and Joseph.'

'Maybe they're sending your signal back to you, like an echo, masking where they're really calling from?'

Sam stares at me. He doesn't know what the hell I'm talking about. He's not a rocket scientist, he's just a kid in a police uniform put in charge of a goddamn telephone.

'That's not possible,' Schiller says.

I pull him aside. 'It's possible if it's the FBI making the call . . . '

'What are you, nuts?'

'They tried to snatch a suspect, why not a kid?'

He throws my arm off, speaking in a violent whisper. 'Keep your opinions to yourself, will you? The walls have ears.'

He's afraid. Maybe he knows for a fact the place is wired. How would Schiller know? The FBI would never tell him. They hated Schiller almost as much as they hated Parker.

Police Chief Parker . . . Of course. He had never valued his surveillance as evidence but as intelligence. It was the illicit skinny Parker was after, not the legal weight of proof. He just wanted to know who Sinatra was fucking that week. Parker was as bad as J. Edgar: two crippled figures of authority jerking off to the sounds of spinning 7-inch reels. But why bug Old Man Bannister's joint? Parker was a racist who hated gangsters and unions, but who always had a soft spot for the rich.

I can smell Mrs. Bannister's perfume suddenly swelling behind us, like the Sundowner Winds moving across Santa Barbara in April: strong and troubling, spiced with sea, salt and the lemon thrill of magnolia.

'What exactly are the opinions that Mr. Alston should keep to himself, Captain?'

Schiller glares at her, speechless, then pushes past me, staring through the great windows looking down on LA: a city increasingly out of his control. I turn to Mrs. Bannister. 'About who's interested in kidnapping your son.'

She grips my arm. Her fingers are strong. I can feel the heat of her body flowing through them. 'My sister's son.'

The mistake wasn't on purpose. I normally don't slip up on facts like that. But I normally don't talk to women like Mrs. Bannister. 'Son, nephew—what's it matter? He's family, Mrs. Bannister . . . '

Schiller clears his throat, watching Old Man Bannister like a cat watching the neighbour's dog. 'You've decided to agree to the demands, sir?'

The Old Man wheels himself fast towards Schiller, as though intent on running him down. Schiller takes a step back, banging into a table. There is the tinkle of crystal rocking, kissing; nearly falling. 'What choice do I have?' Schiller's big hands nervously calm the sea of glasses. 'If I don't pay, they say they'll kill Ronnie.'

'That's what they always say . . . ' Mrs. Bannister has the falsely reassuring tone of a doctor trying to calm the spouse of a terminally-ill patient. 'It's what they're trading on, fear.'

'What they're trading on is death. I will not sit here and let more innocent blood be spilt.'

Mrs. Bannister freezes. Just for a second, but it's enough. She's the only other person who noticed. She looks up at me. She knows I've heard it too. 'Mr. Bannister needs to rest . . . ' She takes the handles of his wheelchair and starts pushing him out of the library.

'I will not be put to bed like an old man.'

'But, darling, that's exactly what you are . . . ' She turns, a wicked nod to me as she disappears, the wheels of the chair rutting against the floorboards as they go down the hallway. Schiller exchanges looks with Sam. I offer Schiller a cigarette. He ignores it, helping himself to the decanter instead. There is a long pause as he gulps down the brandy, then refills his glass. 'Play that last conversation,' he tells the kid, wiping his mouth with the back of a shirtsleeve.

There's the fast musical hum of voices running backwards. The stolid click of a button, and then spools start to rotate; time begins to miraculously repeat, the same moments happening again and again forever. Eternity inside a plastic box. It is the same voice I overheard before. Thick. Somehow muffled; as though speaking through a handkerchief. I listen but can't catch an accent. 'The arrangements have been settled.' Not fixed, but settled. Oddly formal. Maybe the kidnapper had no education; he was self-taught, and proud of it. Always going after—seeking—the right words.

'I have not agreed to any arrangements.' I can't help smiling at the belligerent pride of the obstinate old man.

'We want one million dollars in unmarked bills.'

The gasp from Old Man Bannister is audible. 'How much?'

'You heard me. Come alone, in a car.'

The instructions don't make sense. There is a pause as Bannister grapples with the order. 'I can't drive.'

'You heard me. Come alone in a car or the kid is dead.' It's as though the caller is reading a carefully written speech that's been checked for grammar.

'But I'm in a wheelchair.'

The tape hisses while the voice considers this unscripted development. Obviously this is news to him. The kidnapper doesn't know Old Man Bannister's crippled.

That means the kidnapper doesn't know Old Man Bannister. Period.

'Then send a driver.'

'My chauffeur?'

A pause as the voice on the telephone grapples with, then understands, the word. 'That's right. Tell him to stand by for instructions. We'll call at three o'clock. Any attempt to follow him, any cops, and the kid is dead, got that?'

'Let me talk to Ronnie.'

' . . . The kid?'

Almost as if he didn't even know the name of the boy.

Almost as if they didn't really have him.

'Please. I need to know he's all right.'

'He won't be, if you don't do what we tell you to do.'

There is the slow heave of the old man's breath, seeking to force his will on the situation, as though the kidnapper were just another banker, or newspaper publisher or judge. 'What is your name?'

The question seems so frankly ludicrous in the context of what is happening—extortion, kidnapping, ransom demand, possible murder—that I laugh. Sam looks up at me, perplexed.

'Call me Jesse . . . '

Not bad. The Old Man has forced a handle on the kidnapper. Although obviously not his real name, somewhere in the labyrinth of personal history and connections, the name Jesse would somehow lead to the kidnapper's identity.

'Jesse fucking James!' Schiller says, excitedly refilling his glass.

'Jesse? You won't get the money until I know Ronnie is safe.'

There is a long pause.

When the kid screams, it's a shock. So loud. So insistent. Sam and I exchange glances. The Old Man's voice breaks in. 'Stop it, stop it,' the Old Man shouts. The screaming ends as suddenly as it began.

I look at Sam. His eyes are welling with tears. He looks away. Hissing emptiness fills the room. Then, after a very long moment: 'Satisfied?' The kidnapper's voice is harsh and determined now. It has crossed a line. I have no doubts about what it implies: fuck with us and the kid's history. 'No more communication with your son. Get the money and wait for instructions. Otherwise we start dropping pieces of the kid all over the city. And the blood will be on your hands, not ours.'

Ours. At least two of them. Does that include the insider?

Old Man Bannister struggles to recover his breathing; his voice broken with horror. And with anger. 'Why in God's name are you doing this?'

Long pause.

You can actually hear the moist satisfaction of the kidnapper licking his lips before he finally answers. 'Because you deserve it.'

Silence stretches between them, waiting to snap. The tapes hiss with suspense. 'One more thing—'

A slender finger with ruby nail polish leans over, and hits the pause button. The tape stretches, almost snaps as it lurches to a sudden stop, tautened tight to breaking on its reel like a victim on the rack. Sam looks up questioningly at Mrs. Bannister. She's staring at me.

'Maybe he doesn't want to hear this part . . . '

I exchange glances with Schiller. 'He . . . meaning me?' I turn to the kid. 'What the hell is she talking about?' His face flushes red and he looks away. 'Play it again, Sam.' He hesitates, then hits the button and the tension of the tape eases, distortion then Jesse's voice filling the room. 'You can tell the private dick I know who killed his brother . . . '

The click of a hang-up cuts off the sound of something almost like a laugh. There's the long white whine of disconnection. And then the smash of a glass as I hurl it across the room.

She hands me a glass. Brandy. All I've wanted to do since I first met her was sweep her into my arms and feel the promise of the dark warmth of her body against mine. I can't take her, but I can take the liquor, can taste the smoke and fire, the dark warmth now inside me. Only burning, not healing.

Schiller wipes his face with a handkerchief. 'How the hell did he know you were here, Alston?'

'It's not like he's Howard Hughes, Captain Schiller.'

'She's right. They've been watching us. From the beginning. For all we know they're watching us right now.' Schiller swears. 'They're professionals, and yet . . . '

'What, Mr. Alston?'

'Jesse sounded so sure of everything; everything except for your husband and the boy. The mark and the victim are normally the only things they are sure of.'

Schiller pours himself a refill. 'What the hell are you getting at?'

'Only a hunch but . . . ' I turn back to Mrs. Bannister. 'Imagine if the boy is not with Jesse.'

'But we all heard Ronnie, Mr. Alston.'

'Did we?'

'What the . . . ' He checks himself, with a glance at Mrs. Bannister. ' . . . Heck are you driving at?'

There is a gleam of self-satisfaction in her eyes. We're on the same wavelength; have been ever since we first met. 'I think what Mr. Alston is suggesting is that it could have been another child . . . '

'Not to put too fine a point on it but . . . One screaming kid sounds just like any other.'

The penny drops, right on Schiller's crown. One of LA's finest cops, and it never occurred to him.

'Where does that leave us, Mr. Alston?'

Us. 'We pay the ransom . . . '

'But what if they don't have Ronnie?'

'What if they do? It's only a hunch.'

'Hunches are what you're paid to have, Mr. Alston . . . So what do you advise?'

'We wait for instructions for the drop.' I look at my new watch. Nearly eleven. 'Almost lunchtime and I still haven't had breakfast.'

'If you're hungry, Mr. Alston, I'll have someone fix you something to . . . ' Her voice trails off. Those days of servants on tap are gone; maybe for good.

'I wouldn't want to put you to the trouble of fixing a meal. In your own home and all.'

'Lay off, Alston.'

She smiles politely at Schiller. 'It's all right, Captain, Mr. Alston's had a shock; like all of us.' She hands him a full balloon of brandy. A vote of confidence. She'd rather have Schiller drunk than in my way. 'I make a wonderful omelette, Mr. Alston. Just as long as I can remember where to find the kitchen . . . '

I turn to Schiller. 'You hungry too?' He's staring at the brandy decanter. Who needs to be hungry when you're as thirsty as Schiller? I follow Mrs. Bannister out of the room; she's very easy to follow. But I suddenly freeze outside the library doors.

Mrs. Bannister has vanished.

Not even the click of heels on the oak floor. I look up and down the hallway. There are trails in the floor varnish from the wheelchair. A wall slides open opposite me. Mrs. Bannister's standing inside an elevator on one leg, rubbing her foot with one hand, holding a shoe in the other. 'The problem with Italian shoes is the better they look, the more they hurt . . . '

'I thought the problem with Italian shoes was that they normally hold Italian women.'

She gives a light whistle. 'Why, Mr. Alston, that sounds like the voice of bitter experience . . . '

'My wife's Italian.' I hear the betrayal in my voice.

She smiles. She's heard it too. The first rule in successful adultery. Mutually denigrate your respective spouses. 'Going down?' I step inside the elevator, squeezing past her. 'I hope you're not afraid of small, tight spaces?'

'I'm not claustrophobic, if that's what you mean . . . ' I lie, feeling the warm flush of her body against mine.

'What I mean is that some men just don't feel relaxed.' She slips her foot back into her shoe. 'In tight spaces, I mean . . . ' She brushes a spot of soil from my shoulder. There is a ring and the elevator doors slide open onto a closed wall.

A crest of panic rises in my chest, then is controlled. 'It was put in when Mr. Bannister had his accident. Although it cost us a fortune . . . ' Us. ' . . . And it's always breaking down. Give me a hand, will you?'

We each take a part of the door frame and pull away from each other, sliding the hidden wall panels open.

We're in the entrance hallway, to the left of the stairway. 'Tell me about the accident?'

'Which one?'

Interesting. I thought we were talking about the Old Man. What other accident could be on her mind? They didn't mean to kidnap the kid? Elaine was supposed to have been dead when they buried her? Elaine was supposed to have escaped unharmed?

I follow her down the corridor. 'Your husband's . . . '

'It was a riding accident.' She crosses the enormous kitchen, passing through bolts of sunshine that pick up the gold in her hair. The diamonds in her anklet sparkle then are lost in the shadow.

'That's why he's in a wheelchair?'

She looks at me. 'Surely you knew that?'

'I thought maybe old age played a part.'

'Don't be coy, Mr. Alston. Men like my husband may get old but they never get feeble. Not unless they're suddenly broken.'

'I heard it was no accident.'

We stare at each other in the long silence. 'My husband was riding his favourite horse. He loved that horse more than . . . ' She didn't have to fill in the missing words: more than his wife. ' . . . Except Ronnie, of course.'

I don't believe her. That's the problem with this kidnapping. Everyone, including the Old Man, insists on how much he loved the kid. But where's the evidence? Where are the photos of father and son crowding the walls and the mantelpieces? Where are the stories of the time they spent together? The trips they took, their outings to the circus, the playground, the movies. Sure the kid was a part of the household, but so was the grand-father clock in the hallway. The alarm the Old Man felt when the kid was snatched? That was definitely genuine. But the love . . . ? It was as if Ronnie were an insurance policy or a bank account, something that had been misplaced or lost. A valuable asset suddenly menaced. There was certainly no sign that Ronnie was a normal, happy child. 'It was a hit and run, wasn't it?'

'The horse was clipped by a truck as it crossed the road.'

'Who do you think wanted to kill your husband?'

'You think it was intentional?'

'If the truck didn't stop, it normally means it was.'

'I think the truck didn't stop because the driver recognised who it was he had hit.'

'Meaning the driver thought Mr. Bannister had it coming to him?'

'Meaning . . . he knew that Mr. Bannister doesn't believe in forgiveness.'

'Something I should note?'

'Something you should avoid ever testing, Mr. Alston.'

'That's a warning?'

'Call it advice.'

M rs. Rex Bannister sat forward in her seat, staring over the shoulder of the chauffeur, watching the lights of the hospital swelling into the night. Her husband's lawyer, Adam Granston, sat nervously in the back beside her, riffling through papers. He handed her one. 'We'll need you to sign this.'

'What is it?'

'Just a document, for the hospital . . . ' The metal of his fountain pen glinted in the lights of the emergency entrance. She didn't like his tone. She never had. And she didn't like his presumption: that she could trust him. As if she didn't know— she couldn't trust anyone in this world, least of all Rex Bannister's people.

'Not now . . . '

'There's no time to discuss . . . '

She pushed the paper away. 'I said, not now.' She was playing her card; and it was an ace. He was the lawyer. But she was the wife. Her husband was seriously—perhaps fatally— injured. The law was on Granston's side, but the drama . . . that was on her side. That was stronger than any legal document.

The car pulled up. Taylor got out and went around and opened her door. She could feel the flush of Granston's anger giving way to nighttime coolness. 'I want to see my husband . . . '

There was the stutter of flashes as they passed the shouted questions of the press, and then she was inside, passing a private waiting room full of aging men. Some averted their faces; others stared at her. With alarm. With hostility. With lust. Some of the faces she recognized from the Star Chamber ceremonies.

A big police captain named Schiller gave her a rundown on what was known. Her husband had been riding a great bay gelding called Goliath. A horse her husband hated. Because the horse had a nobility that the man lacked. Goliath had fought bravely to stay upright after they'd been struck, stumbling all the way down the embankment before its mighty hooves struck the concrete lip of a culvert and its pasterns snapped with the impact, her husband's leg crushed between the unforgiving ground and 1100 pounds of muscle, sinew and suffering tension. His left leg. His left hip. His pelvis. Pulverized.

Shattered.

Irreversible.

The richest man in the country; probably the most powerful, and certainly the most hated was now suddenly a cripple. The very day after his scandalous fifth marriage to the younger sister of his fourth wife. All across America, the same phrase was being repeated with satisfaction: serves the bastard right.

When they came for him after the accident, her husband had insisted they end the horse's life before they did anything for him. Not because he had wanted to put it out of its misery, but because he had wanted it dead. He carried the gelding's blood dusted across his face and clothes when they trolleyed him, delirious, into the operating theatre.

That night a vigil was held at the hospital. The governor and both senators were there. The mayor and the police chief too. So were Howard Hughes and Johnny Roselli. There were Texas oilmen, and even some CIA and banker types from the East Coast. She knew who they were: the shadow men of the True Republic. Wizards without their capes. It gave her the creeps, the way they all just showed up. As if they were malevolent Magi following an evil star. But why were they all there? Were they waiting to see if Rex Bannister would die, so they could haggle and gamble over his assets like Roman soldiers with Christ's robe . . . ? Did they believe he might designate a successor before he died? Or impart some terrible secret that would give them access to the enormous powers he had always enjoyed?

Or were they simply waiting to see if he could survive such a terrible accident; proof that he was, as some half-suspected, the devil incarnate?

She was at her husband's bedside when he came to after the operation. The first thing he asked the chief surgeon, Dr. Lowell Everett, an arrogant man with an appreciative smile for her, was how long it would be before he could ride again. The doctor had laughed; the accident had been so traumatic, the damage so acute that he was sure her husband was joking, so he kidded along: a couple of months; a half-year at the most, but he'd be back up relatively soon, doing all the riding he could ever wish for . . . in a wheelchair.

Her husband had reached down beside his bed, where Morris had left his newly-polished riding boots, one of which contained his riding crop. He drew it fast out of the boot, as though unsheathing a sword, and whipped it forwards and backwards, leaving an enormous X-shaped cut across the front of Everett's face. The doctor stood there, stunned, his cheeks slowly falling open as an eyeball rolled lazily out of its socket and hung like a ripe fruit from a gaping black and red hole.

Betty Bannister managed to wait until the blood began to bubble and suck out of the wound where the doctor's nose had been before she passed out.

He husband had struck Dr. Everett so hard that he had dislocated his shoulder on the return blow; the Old Man's suffering—like the doctor's—would not end as easily as his horse's.

Afterwards, she had learnt that Dr. Everett was in a sanatorium; paid for out of the kindness of Mr. Bannister. The official story was that the surgeon had disgraced both himself and his hospital by driving home drunk later that night and hitting a tree. But Truth in the Bannister Estate was, like her husband's domestic staff, unsentimentally replaceable. Rex Bannister made sure the medical board stripped the surgeon of his license to practice medicine. Not that the former Dr. Everett would have been doing much surgery, after having a scalpel taken to his brain by Professor Boris Landis, the 'Laureate of the Lobotomy.' Her husband would do whatever it took to keep Lowell Everett alive so as to continue his suffering for as long as possible.

The Bannister Way.

The question was, when would her own suffering end?

W as there any truth in that story about your husband
and the doctor?'

Betty Bannister stares at me as though she's just come back from a long way off and hasn't heard the question. She focuses on me; and it's only then that I realize I've been missing those green eyes all morning. 'You don't know my husband, Mr. Alston. He takes personal slights extremely seriously.'

Does that include sleeping with his wife? I tap the bottom of my cigarette packet, three long, slim tubes dancing up to the beat. It's the only thing I have to offer her. She looks at my extended hand, then selects the longest one with the solemnity of someone drawing lots. Fire flares between us; dies with the shock of my breath. I look at the lighter she is holding. Gunmetal with engraved initials. EB. Well, well . . . It looks like Mrs. Bannister might know where we can find Hastings.

She looks away, exhaling smoke into the vast and empty house.

'When was the accident?'

She opens a refrigerator door, light shining on her face, then looks at me. 'It was the day after we were married . . . ' A bloom of cold air rises around her. 'The hospital was the first time I'd seen him since the wedding reception.'

She slams the Kelvinator shut and stares at me for a long moment, then cracks two eggs into a bowl, breaking the shells with short, hard snaps against the ceramic lip. She looks down into the bowl and laughs. I peer over her shoulder. Both eggs have double yolks. 'Good luck, so they say . . . Although I was never one for superstition.' She whisks the yolks into oblivion with dour zeal, the noise echoing off the high walls.

'So that means . . . '

'Well, bravo, Mr. Alston, I believe you've finally figured it out . . . ' There is the hiss of gas and the detonation of combustion.

'Figured what out?'

'My nasty little secret. The marriage was never consummated.' Oil protests on a pan. 'Shocking, isn't it? The young, yearning woman, in her physical prime, wasting away in the bed of an elderly cripple . . .' She sacrifices her mixture to the heat, the eggs puckering in pain. There is the rasp of a spatula and then the omelette is presented to me: golden and burning to the touch. 'The question is, which one of them is the victim?'

'Maybe there doesn't have to be a victim?'

She takes a bottle of beer out of the icebox and pours me a glass. 'Oh, there's always a victim in a loveless marriage. What do you think?'

'About loveless marriages?'

'About the omelette.'

'Very spicy, Mrs. Bannister.'

She takes a long drink from the open bottle, froth clinging to her lips. Our eyes meet. She licks the froth away from her lips and smiles.

Provocation is a dangerous thing. Maybe it's real; teasing reaction like a feather. Or maybe it's just all in your head. There's only ever one way to find out.

I tug her into my arms. We almost kiss but she pulls away at the last instant, opening her eyes with amusement. And something almost like admiration.

She steps close enough to hear my beating heart, her breath fragrant and shallow, her head inclined, hair masking half her face and flowering around her shoulder. 'Kiss me,' she says.

I am embraced by perfume, languorous and yearning, then by her hair and the warmth of her hand on my cheek, her lips full and moist as we kiss, her tongue eager, knowing.

There is a throb of pain and delight as she takes my lower lip between her teeth and quickly, gently bites. She pulls back, studying my reaction. 'I thought so,' she whispers, her eyes full of a knowing confidence as she pulls away, then turns, walking out of the kitchen.

I tug her back into my arms . . . And that's when I see it, over her shoulder. She slowly draws away from me. 'What is it?'

I point to the wall. 'That dark stain there . . . What's missing from the wall?'

'Just a wall telephone. They took it down.'

Where else have I seen a wall phone before? 'The garage.'

'They took that one away too . . . '

Something's eating at me like a fading dream, the struggle to recall it only making it disappear faster. Then I remember. 'Jesus Christ . . . ' She's staring at me in amazement. 'The bomb shelter.'

'I don't understand.'

'Where are the keys?'

She looks at me for a long moment, her green eyes honeyed with panic and I begin to wonder if she might be in on it. Could she be such a good actress?

She unclips a gold chain from around her neck and hands it to me. On the end of the chain are three keys.

'Who else has these?'

'Only Mr. Bannister . . . Why?'

'Don't you get it? There's a phone down there. The call must have come from the shelter.'

She takes a step back, holding onto the doorjamb as though she's about to faint. 'But that means?'

'I know. The kid's been here all along.'

CHAPTER 18
Dallas 2014

JFK loved sex and he loved it most with blondes. Blondes were not Jackie. Blondes were dumb; Jackie spoke French. Blondes were easygoing; Jackie was controlling. Blondes were loud; Jackie was discreet. Blondes looked the other way; Jackie got even. When Jack did Marilyn, Jackie did Bill Holden. Jackie was vengeful, blondes were not.

Or so JFK thought.

But he'd been a politician so long, he had forgotten how to switch off the stereotypes button, and it turned out to be the blondes who gave him the most trouble. In fact it was an intelligent, highly sensitive, extremely vulnerable blonde who may have helped get him killed. A fun night out slowly segued into the Shot Heard Round the World. Marilyn Monroe, the most famous woman in the country and also the most lonely, became JFK's Sarajevo. Marilyn didn't mean to do it. It was all Jack's fault. He was myopic. He never could see past his dick.

Or that, at least is what Mr. Dwayne Wayne, a man with a stutter for a name, is maintaining.

The Marilyn Did It complot was so delightfully frivolous I had to find a place for it in my book on the murders of the Kennedy brothers. It was like a giant champagne soufflé with a chorus girl stuffed inside, ready to pop just as the snooty guests sit down. Say, waiter, what is that blonde doing in my egg whites? The premise was exactly the kind of light relief the book needed. I was so excited, I even called Monica.

'I'm meeting this guy who actually believes Marilyn killed JFK.'

'Is it any more ridiculous than an ass-hat like Lee Harvey Oswald killing the president?'

Only he didn't. Maybe. 'She died a year before Kennedy!'

There is the silence of consideration. 'Maybe JFK killed Marilyn?'

'I doubt that very much.'

'Then someone who was close to Marilyn killed JFK to revenge her.'

'Avenge . . . '

'Avenge her. It's a motive, isn't it?'

'Pretty wild.'

'But possible . . . '

'Anything is possible, angel . . . '

'You're not supposed to call me that.'

Angel. 'Call you what?'

'We're divorced, Lew . . . '

Saying it almost as if it's news to me. Sometimes it feels exactly like it is. Sometimes I wake up and am still surprised to find myself alone. 'You're right, I shouldn't have called.'

'Anyway, it sounds promising . . . '

'Really?'

'Well, more promising than your other leads . . . '

The problem with divorce is that it doesn't stop the knowing barbs. Exactly what made you want to get a divorce in the first place. I can still feel the sting as I look up from the photo of Marilyn singing 'Happy Birthday, Mr. President,' to the man who has promised information linking her to JFK's assassination. 'Some dress . . . '

'Isn't it?' He taps the photo of the crumpled, jug-eared author on the dust jacket. 'Norman Mailer had information proving the connection between the murders of Marilyn and Kennedy but unfortunately it was withheld from publication when his book came out . . . ' Mr. Dwayne Wayne, amateur photographer, would-be bounty hunter and full-time conspiracy buff, shakes his head in regret.

'Why would they leave that out? Claims like that are exactly what sell books.'

'Mailer didn't want to but he had no choice.'

This is the problem with all conspiracy theories. Nobody *ever* has any choice. Things just happen and no one can stop them. Everybody knows that events are covered up, but no one can prove it. No one can produce the smoking gun, although anyone can see it—all you have to do is stare real hard. Evidence is not forensic, it's fantastic. *Blow Up* meets the Rorschach test.

In the Age of Conspiracy, Plausible Deniability has been replaced by Plausible Doubt. Any possible crack in a single detail is enough to bring into question not just an event but an entire political system; the whole course of Modern History. The Conspiracy Theorist is the latter-day boy at the dyke, only instead of putting his finger into the hole, he's threatening to take it out. Catastrophe is better than Cover-up. He is Samson in the Temple. The pillars shall fall, the Son of Sam shall perish, but the truth will out: you don't shave a man's head without his consent. You don't conceal UFOs in Area 51. You don't pretend to land a man on the moon. You don't force Elvis into the Witness Protection Program. And you sure as hell don't blame seven gunshot wounds on a single Magic Bullet. 'You said you'd found a connection between JFK and Marilyn's deaths . . . '

'Murders . . . '

'What was the connection, Mr. Wayne?'

Dwayne Wayne smiles. 'Kennedy was being blackmailed.'

I play along. 'LBJ?' Dwayne Wayne shakes his head. 'J. Edgar?' He wags a finger. Not even close. He's got me. 'I give up. Who?'

'Howard Hughes.'

'What did Hughes have on the president?'

'TFX.'

Tactical Fighter Experimental.

A big-ticket item smack-bang-boom in the middle of the Atomic Age. The largest single government contract ever. Four hundred and sixteen billion dollars in today's currency.

'TFX is an interesting story, but how exactly does it relate to blackmail?'

'Hughes was in bed with General Dynamics. He pushed the F-111 as the winning design.'

'So what? Hughes was a billionaire airman and gambler. He'd be involved in any big aviation contract.'

'This wasn't involvement, this was manipulation. It all adds up. One: Hughes bought his TWA Convair fleet from General Dynamics. Two: Hughes Aircraft bought General Dynamic's Missile Systems Division. Three: both Hughes Aircraft and General Dynamics had access to the same technology—'

'Wait—what technology?'

'TFX technology for starters.'

'The plane was a fiasco.'

'The engineering was a fiasco. But the concept—swing wings, turbofan propulsion, TERCOM navigation—that was perfect, Mr. Alston. Revolutionary. Where did the technology come from?'

'General Dynamics?' He gives me a long, sad stare of amazement, then shakes his head knowingly.

Here it comes, I can feel it: Jerry Fletcher Redux. 'The Russians?'

'Roswell.'

Well, they both start with the letter R. As in ridiculous.

'Not as ridiculous as it sounds . . . ' He intercepts my thought waves. 'Reverse engineering. Hughes financed most of it himself.'

'Mr. Dwayne, I mean Wayne. That is just . . . ' I hesitate, lost for a soft synonym, but he jumps right in.

'Crazy? Is it? Explain how Hughes went from plywood seaplanes to Syncom satellites in less than fifteen years. To soft landings on the moon; to Pioneer and Galileo? Everything that Hughes Research laboratories has done, from inventing lasers and ion propulsion units to reconstructing metallic microlattice comes from the Roswell Saucer.'

Dwayne Wayne stares at me with a bright, intent smile and brown eyes rimmed all the way round by white—if they looked any more startled, they'd burst. Monica's voice comes back to me. 'The problem with you, Lew, is that you're too polite.' I asked her what was wrong with being polite. 'Nothing,' she said, kissing me, 'as long as it's with the right people.' I didn't need my ex-wife to tell me that Dwayne Wayne is not the right people. It is time to pack my bags and leave this madhouse city. 'We're done here . . . ' As soon as I say it, I shudder. I just unconsciously quoted Adam Granston, the horn man. It must be Stockholm syndrome.

Dwayne Wayne blocks my way. 'Kennedy was against the F-111. Hughes had to recuperate the money he'd invested in Area 51, and the only way to do that was via TFX, even if he had to resort to blackmail. Stand back and look at the big picture, Mr. Alston.'

'I'm sorry.' Too polite, again. 'The problem is that no one ever looks at the big picture. Instead, all anyone ever does is peer at the minute details. That's where coincidence exists. And coincidence feeds conspiracy.'

'Coincidence is the first sign of conspiracy.'

'Lincoln was shot in the Ford Theatre, Kennedy was shot in a Lincoln. Does that mean the automobile industry was behind both assassinations? If you want to find connections, you'll always find connections. Like Orion's Belt . . . '

'The constellation?'

'The miniature galaxy in *Men in Black*. Billions of stars inside a tiny globe. The closer you look, the more there is to see.' I gather the little things that are the sum of my existence in this city: iPhone, sunglasses, rental car keys. 'Stop looking so closely at things, Mr. Dwayne.'

'Wayne.'

Whatever . . . 'You need to come up for air.'

'But the devil's in the details.'

'Wrong, Mr. Wayne. The details are the devil.'

'Don't go, Mr. Alston. There's more.'

'I just wish that for once someone actually had physical evidence, rather than wild theories and suspicions.'

Wayne hands me an old manila envelope. On the outside is an address in Chula Vista, California. On the inside are photos. 'How about these . . . ?'

I stare at a face in one of the pictures, her eyes challenging me to look away. I can't. How could I? The eyes belong to Marilyn Monroe.

The night was fragrant with the scent of datura, the bell-shaped flowers hanging heavy amongst lush leaves, like bats enfolded within their wings; nocturnal and still.

Hastings moved through a small orchard of oranges and came out at a kidney-shaped pool. Immediately beyond was a Spanish-style bungalow. This was exactly what LA aspired to be: palms, pool, perfumed. Perfect. But there's one thing a house with a garden can never really provide: security.

Every night across America, trespassers prowled the darkness. Strangers stared through windows, cataloguing secrets, decoding possibilities, identifying valuables. Snapping photos. Windows were tested, locks compromised, interiors cased; animals silenced. Our dreams were patterned by the torch beams of burglars as our wealth was harvested by gloved hands and passed across windowsills. No matter how well-protected, our homes, like our loves, are always vulnerable to the touch of others, to unexpected entries and silent exits; our secrets, like our wallets, slipped into the back pockets of cunning intruders.

The door to the kitchen was unlocked. Hastings paused, feeling the cold flush the kitchen's terra-cotta tiles gave to the summer night. Remembering Bella and the murdered fence. He exhaled but there were no clouds of condensation. The dead weren't walking. Yet.

He listened carefully. Nothing at first, then a moaning. He paused at the entrance into the living room. There was a dull yellow light spilling out from under the door of a bedroom. It wasn't supposed to be like this. The house was supposed to be empty. Maybe a car broke down. Maybe someone got sick and a vacation was cancelled. Maybe the owners had left and the help or a teenage son were taking advantage of the absence. Or maybe Roselli lied.

Hastings had seconds to decide. No one was supposed to get hurt. But no one was supposed to be there either. He was supposed to find the book and get out without being seen.

Without being caught.

He glanced around the living room. A clean fireplace. Shades half drawn. Not much on the walls. It felt like a house that had just been moved into; or just moved out of. It wasn't close to being a real home. He crossed the thick carpet towards the bedroom door, freezing when he heard a man's laugh— light; unauthentic. Through the door he recognized a woman's voice, but couldn't quite place it. Rich with anger. Distended with irritation, and maybe liquor. The man's voice was low with frustration. Hastings couldn't make out what he was saying, just the rhythm of patronizing repetition.

Headlights swept across the room, Hastings pulling back into the shadows beside the fireplace. He could feel his heart beating against the wall as he unholstered a suppressed .45. Two car doors opened, then slammed shut. Visitors. It wasn't supposed to be like this. The whole scene stank of a setup. Of death. Maybe even his.

The doorbell rang.

The door to the bedroom opened and a slight, young man with a long, careless cowlick charged out, heading straight for the front door, never glancing at the shadows where Hastings hid. Hastings looked back at the bedroom and caught the silhouette of a woman projected on the floor, her words slurred with hurt, the hairs on his neck rising in wonder as he was finally able to put a name to the voice. 'Tell him to go to hell!'

The shadow retracted, the voice talking to itself now, distant and sad: 'They can all go to hell . . . '

Hastings crossed quickly, standing in the shelter of the still open door, listening to a flurry of restrained sobs slowly ebbing. He could see through the angle of the living room window that the man was arguing outside on the porch with the two visitors. They looked like government men in dark suits and hats. One held a black medical bag.

The throb rose inside Hastings's head, singing its way across his mind, contracting his thoughts to a single impulse: action.

He listens. It's silent in the bedroom.

He enters the bedroom, closing the door until it's just ajar. Her breathing is laboured but steady. Probably sleeping pills; possibly booze. He feels the dorsum pulse on her right foot. Slow; steady. She's not in any trouble. His eyes travel up her leg to the still-wet trace of lovemaking on the sheet, one of her thighs gleaming with a sticky sheen. It is a private and transgressive moment—the revelation of an intimate act made public; without consent. A classic Movie Star moment . . . if you were *Confidential Magazine*.

Hastings modestly covers the sleeping woman with the top sheet and puts a spare pillow across the bedside lamp. The room drops into twilight, the filtered lampshade still providing enough light for him to see. He sets to work fast, starting with the drawer of the bedside table, stepping back in surprise. Roselli had asked him to find a diary. There are at least twelve books inside the drawer. Hundreds of pages of notes, confessions, pleas, tirades and observations. Names leap out and hit him across the face with their celebrity: DiMaggio, Miller, Sinatra, JFK, Eva Marlowe . . . Rex Bannister.

Hastings swears aloud.

Marilyn stirs, turning onto her back, the sheet getting caught up in her legs. Hastings freezes, staring at her eyes. They stay closed. He approaches the door, and checks outside.

The faces of the three men on the porch are furrowed with conflict. A car is parked across the road, full of darkness. He watches it for a long moment and then sees the telltale red pulse of a cigarette half-concealed inside a closed fist. Someone waiting. Someone watching.

The man in the car across the street raises something to his face. A camera. The men pause on the porch, arguing in hot whispers, unconscious of the dual surveillance.

Marilyn sighs. He looks back at her, a wisp of hair caught across her lips, rising and descending with her breathing, as regular as a metronome. He opens a chest of drawers. More diaries. He hadn't figured on that; he hadn't figured on the naked movie star or the man watching in the car either.

Hastings starts packing the diaries into a vanity case. He checks an antique secretary desk. Nothing but a manila envelope.

Inside are catch-your-breath photos of Marilyn. In all of them her face is creased unconscious from dope or booze. He slips the envelope inside the case and turns back to the sleeping woman. Whatever she's on, she's breathing normally; she's as safe as someone like her can be.

Safer than Susan ever was.

He picks up the bag and goes to the door.

Freezes.

The men have come inside the house, and are gathered around a telephone. Hastings gently eases the bedside phone from the cradle. A piqued voice fills the space between the receiver and his ear. 'She said that . . . ?' Another voice he recognizes but can't quite place: light, nasal, with the unmistakable twang of privilege. 'Do you think she'd actually do it?'

There is a heavy sigh and then someone in the room next door speaks, Hastings hearing the echo coming from the phone. 'Jesus, Jack, you know her; there's no telling what she might do . . . ' Hastings weighs the moment. He could leave now through her bedroom window, while the men are on the phone, or he could stay and try to find out what they are talking about. He has the books. He could get the license plates of all the cars outside. He could put it all together without risking that much more.

He could still get away.

He places the phone on the bed, slips the window latch open silently and starts to climb out when something moves behind him, black and fast. He whirls, his gun drawn. Nothing. He scans the room and finally sees it. Smoke gliding towards him from the pillow on the lamp. It's begun to smoulder. He tugs the pillow onto the floor. The room swells with light.

He drops out the window and backs away, hunched out of view, watching the shadows of the men projected on the wall as they enter the bedroom. He follows the paving stones towards the pool, freezing when he sees the green eyes staring straight at him. Not so much a challenge as an expression of curiosity. A white cat with a grey cap around its ears arches against his legs, its meow alarming in the nighttime silence. Then it scents Bella and disappears with a light, regretful purr.

He's just made it past the pool when it finally hits him—the voice on the phone. And his hand is still shaking when he slips the key into the ignition of his car, almost expecting a boom . . .

CHAPTER 20
Dallas 2014

Dwayne Wayne fans the photographs out on the table like tarot cards. Shots of Marilyn tend to be grouped around several recurring themes. Sexy Marilyn. Playful Marilyn. Wistful Marilyn. Tragic Marilyn. These are unlike any I've ever seen. Real Marilyn. Some are taken beside a pool house in bright sunshine. Impossibly high palm trees sentinel the scenes, slashes of black tapering off in geometric perfection into a background of white-hot sky. In several of the pictures, Marilyn shares a joke with a beautiful young woman in a one-piece bathing suit. In another, both women sit in bath robes, drinking coffee by the pool. Some of the shots are indoors—shadows suggesting a secret intimacy broken by the blurred radiance of lamps or the silhouette of distant hills glimpsed through windows. In one of the photos Marilyn reclines across a sofa, the other woman sitting on the armrest, a hand on Marilyn's shoulder; a gesture of both affection and possession. Both women gaze intently across the room at a man whose back obscures a corner of the frame.

Marilyn seems so powerfully present in the photos that I am overwhelmed by a nostalgia that's closer to personal memory than pop culture history. I may as well be leafing through a long-lost family album, there's such a relaxed candour in these snapshots; as if nobody knew the photos were being taken.

He did say blackmail.

'So what have these got to do with JFK?'

There is the soft shiver of a drawer opening and something

heavy being extracted. For a queasy moment I think it's a gun. But it's an old-fashioned magnifying glass. Dwayne Wayne points to a patch of light in one of the photos. 'See for yourself.' I take the loupe and peer intently at the tiny, microscopic detail—doing exactly what I just said not to: examining the minutiae. Through the lens I can clearly see a face mirrored ghostlike in a window in one of the nighttime shots. I feel my blood pressure drop. The reflected face staring right back at me belongs to Jack Kennedy.

Conspiracy.

For the first time, it almost feels real. Dwayne Wayne slaps me kindly on the back. 'Kind of hard to get your head around, isn't it?'

If they're not fakes. 'How did you get these?'

'These were taken by Walter Stark, a surveillance expert who worked for Howard Hughes. I got them from a lawyer who knew Hughes: Adam Granston.'

Dallas was starting to feel like a very small town. 'Where were these taken?'

'At High Sierra, Old Man Bannister's place in LA.'

I put the magnifying glass down. 'Why would JFK have an affair with Marilyn at the home of one of his father's fiercest enemies?'

His laugh is so explosive it makes me jump. 'JFK didn't know she was going to be there. It was—what do you call it? When there's a strange but happy coincidence?'

'Serendipity?'

'Pretty word.' His laughter is a rumble of thunder, threatening a violent storm. 'JFK had gone there to see the Old Man. He couldn't hold out anymore. He wanted in.'

'On what?'

'The Old Man's cabal, of course'

Of course. 'Mr. Wayne, when you attain the power and influence of someone like Rex Bannister, people often accuse you of belonging to a secret society. But at the end of the day, most monopolies and cartels—'

'Cabals!'

He's very attached to the term. 'Most cabals are merely vested interests seeking to protect their collective advantages, like OPEC or the Big Four. You find them in every society. You even find them in nature. Darwin said that cells of a similar—'

'The cabals of which I speak are outside nature, Mr. Alston.'

'Nothing's outside of nature.'

'My grandfather was a dentist in Tulsa when the Klan burnt down his home in the Race Riots of 1921. You call that kind of hate natural?' His voice tightens, his eyes shining with indignation. 'Jasper, right here in Texas! James Byrd's automobile lynching. You think that was natural?' He's putting words in my mouth. I try to interrupt, but he's on a roll now. 'Smell the coffee, Mr. Alston, all cabals are outside nature and all cabals are evil. The Klan. The Nazis. The banks. Now take a look at the members of the Old Man's cabal. The Mafia. Big Oil. The Intelligence Community. The Military Industrial Complex. Why were they working together?'

'There's no proof they ever were.'

He shakes his head with unsurprised disappointment. 'You need to adjust your vision here, Mr. Alston. You need to start thinking like a Jedi.'

I take a step towards the door. The way things are shaping up, Dwayne Wayne is going to set a new high score on the Dallas Wacko-Meter.

'Howard Hughes and Old Man Bannister used these photos not to destroy Kennedy, but to control him. TFX was the tribune he was forced to pay. Once he agreed, Marilyn was sacrificed. They knew he loved her. It was part of his punishment.'

That wasn't enough? 'And what was the other part?'

'Public execution. Dallas was his scaffold.'

The putter of air-conditioning fills the tense silence, streamers fluttering nervously. It's something I've noticed in the houses of Dallas: the permanently locked windows. Not just to filter the scorching air, but to stop whatever it is that haunts the city from entering. Dallas is the village in the Carpathian Mountains, bolted and breathless; the stain of its guilt running under the very earth. All that crude oil. All that money. All that power. How can truth survive in this air-conditioned nightmare?

The simple answer: it can't. Put 'JFK' and 'Dallas' in any search engine, and you'll get airline schedules, not assassinations.

Wayne starts sliding the snapshots back into their soiled envelope. 'These photos are the smoking gun. Physical evidence that confirms the rumours about Marilyn and Kennedy. They provide the only motive for the assassination that stands up.' He stares at me, his eyes weighing pans, measuring my worth. His smile is not beatific. 'And none of them have ever been published before.'

'You can't even be sure they're real.'

'They're genuine. I want a million.'

'I don't have a million . . . '

'She does . . . ' He jabs a finger at the woman sitting with Marilyn on the sofa.

'Who is she?'

'Her? That's Betty Bannister.'

CHAPTER 21
Los Angeles 1960

C ops crawl over the Bannister joint, two or three to each
room, checking every wall, every panel, every floor-
board. Opening cupboards, wardrobes, trunks. Looking
under beds.

Footsteps vibrate on the ceiling of the top floor as the attic
is searched, bats escaping the strafing intrusion of flashlights.
Dozens more police comb the vast foundations. It's a gold rush
down there. Torches, hurricane lamps. Some are wearing
miners' caps. There is the constant whir of generators.
Spotlights have been set up in the catacomb passageways of
the cellars, dust revolving in the blinding beams.

They haven't found a way into the well yet, but there are
already men tracing the massive old water pipes that striate the
grounds, dating back to the time when the estate's subter-
ranean aquifer provided its own supply of water. The
Bannisters were notoriously independent—social code from
the old days for selfish and avaricious. The elaborate pumping
system not only sucked and channelled High Sierra's ground-
water, but also that of its neighbours. Elaine could have
crawled her way into this ancient water network from another
entrance, maybe on another level or even from another property. But that didn't explain the shoe down in the cellar. Or
what she was fleeing from.

I stumble on an electrical cord as I make my way towards
the dark passage where I found the shoe. There's an old geezer
with survey papers of the grounds. He hears me stumble and

turns quickly, shining his torch into my eyes. 'Found that entrance yet?' I ask, holding my hand up to the light.

The beam goes back to the blueprints. 'There isn't one. Not at this well.'

'There are other wells?'

'Four of 'em. But it's only the north one that has an access door.'

I snatch the paper from his hands. 'Where's the north well?'

He shines the light in my face again, his voice strained with annoyance. 'If you give me back the blueprints, I'll show you . . . Thank you kindly.' There is a crackle as a thin-skinned finger taps even thinner paper. 'Here.'

'And where does it lead to?'

'Straight up.' I grab the torch from him and shine it into his eyes. Two can play at this game. He blinks uncomfortably.

'You know what I mean: does it lead up to where they found her?'

He shakes his head and taps the column behind him. 'They found her above this well. That's for damn sure.'

I shine the light back on the blueprints. 'And we're here, right?'

A harrumph for response. It's a simple compass grid. We're south. The entrance well is north. But something is wrong. On the plans, the north well seems to be freestanding. 'What's all this space here? I don't remember seeing that.'

There is the brief scoffing laugh of a tired and bitter man. Someone who has been forced to suffer fools for bosses; to watch them advance in their careers, marry the pretty secretaries, and leave for Catalina Friday mornings while he had to stay at the office all weekend dealing with a major leak at Silver Lake and ruptured mains in Burbank. His watery eyes drown me in his gaze. 'That's because this survey was done before World War II.'

I stare at him. 'Meaning . . . ?'

'Before. The. Atomic. Bomb.' Spelling it out for an imbecile. Me.

The bomb shelter.

I start running, pushing past cops and workers, going from light to shadow, light to shadow. I run down a second passageway, heading for the shelter. But instead I come to a brick wall.

A dead end.

Then I get it.

Elaine had gone to the wrong well. Like me, she'd got lost. Maybe she panicked. Maybe she took off her shoe and used it to hit the wall, listening for the hollow thud of the cistern. Or maybe she fell in the dark and lost her shoe, but kept on going until she found the right well. The one with the door. Climbing up. Maybe her accomplice promised her he'd clear the entrance. Maybe he got spooked when I called out to him, and saved himself, knowing he was leaving Elaine to suffocate.

Metal glints ahead of me. I rush inside the bomb shelter. Two cops are going through everything, dusting, taking photos. I scan the walls. Steel, steel. Concrete. Steel. What the hell did I expect—it was a goddamn bomb shelter. No sign of a brick wall. But I know I saw a brick chamber somewhere earlier.

The secret room with the altar.

I trot down the side passage leading to the door. It's still locked. I cough my way through the dust up some steps, exiting into daylight pandemonium. Mrs. Bannister and her husband were the only people with the keys. She told me so herself. There's no sign of her in the grounds. Just cops. Everywhere. And firemen. Even military reserves, combing the estate grounds. Bloodhounds strain at leashes, their handlers working grids. Press hounds snap back at them, news crews filming. And huddled around three black cars—the men in suits. FBI. Judgmental and silent. Waiting for the right moment to exert their power. To step in and take over the case. None of them has a broken nose. Boston was leaving this part of the investigation to the Los Angeles office for the moment.

Schiller wades out of the havoc of the household, shaking his head in disgust. 'You could have warned me!'

'I told you already, before we discovered Elaine Bannister's . . . ' I was about to say *body*, but she's still technically alive. 'I checked the bomb shelter, I checked the cellars—there was no one there.'

'The call had to come from there! They must have been hiding—and you missed them.' I try to defend myself, but he talks over me, raising his voice so Bevo Means can overhear as he passes. Subtext for the journalist: His fault, not mine. 'There must be somewhere else in the cellar. Somewhere you missed.'

You.

Means freezes, staying close. He gets the picture. He was the reporter who dubbed Elizabeth Short 'The Black Dahlia'. I wonder what names he'd come up with for Elaine Bannister.

'What if they came back here, just to make the calls?'

'And drag the kid along with them?' Schiller shoves the still eavesdropping Means roughly on his way. Blaming me is one thing, that helps the Force; but this open discord is another thing all together. This is too close to chaos.

'Maybe it was just someone imitating a kid. Remember, the kid never spoke.' He just screamed.

'What are you getting at?'

'Maybe it was a woman. Maybe it was a recording.'

'And maybe it was a fucking parrot. I've got Parker scream-ing in one ear, Old Man Bannister in the other, and the fuck-ing Feds squeezing my balls. Not to mention the press, turning this into a sideshow.' He rips a *Herald Examiner* out of a pass-ing reporter's hands. 'Have you seen this birdcage liner? They're already comparing it to Little-fucking-Lindy. And look here . . . ' He folds the paper back to the front page, thumps the greasy headlines with his stumpy fingers. ' . . . Not a single fucking word about a parrot.'

FBI agents turn and stare. I usher Schiller away from them. 'What if they used some kind of electronic gadget that kept bouncing the origin of the calls back to the receiver—to the Bannister Estate? To confuse us?'

'Well they've done an excellent fucking job, because I've never seen a sorrier, more confused investigation in my life. And as for your Buck Rogers bullshit about radio waves, I don't buy it for a second. They were right here, making the call under your private dick nose.'

'It just doesn't make sense.'

'Fuck sense. They did it. Period.'

'All right, let's skip the how and go for the who . . . ' Schiller nods, looking at me with pleading eyes. There's fear there. And confusion. Save me, he seems to be saying.

'Jesse will be calling in an hour. In the meantime, I want another talk with Mrs. Bannister . . . alone.'

'You're married, Alston—and in case you haven't noticed, Caterina is a good woman.'

What I have noticed is Schiller's eyes all over Cate every time they meet. 'Lay off with the sermons, this is strictly work. What about the nanny?'

'We picked her up at her mother's place . . . ' There is a long pause. 'Jordan Downs.' Well, what do you know? A fierce and famous racist like Old Man Bannister hiring a nanny from Watts. Was he softening in his old age? Or was he simply setting Greta Simmons up for a kidnapping rap? 'She's making a statement at the station.'

'Do me a favour and bring her here when she's done. I want to walk her through her final movements with the kid. In the meantime, we need to talk to Elaine Bannister.'

'Talk all you want, it won't do any good.'

'She's not . . . '

'Dead?' He bites off the lip of a cigar and shakes his head impatiently.

'So she's awake?'

He spits the cob of tobacco triumphantly. 'Even if she was, you'd get more conversation out of an Idaho potato.' His laugh is an internal rumble, as though he were painfully digesting his own joke. He reads from a piece of paper torn from a prescription form, hesitating at each syllable. 'Obtundation . . . That's it.'

'What the hell does that mean?'

'It means, for the moment at least, that Elaine Bannister is a Grade-A, Chef's Specialty vegetable.'

Jesus Christ. 'She's comatose?'

'Total state of shock. The doc said some people suffer from . . . ' Reading from his scrap of paper again: 'Status epilepticus. Words like that, make me glad I'm a cop.'

As if they'd ever let a man with fists like his near a scalpel. I snatch the paper from him. The name on the script is Landis.

'Doc said emotional or toxic shock can bring it on.'

Toxic.

Toxic might be poison. Poison could explain why someone was trying to bury her. Toxic might be drugs. Elaine could be a hophead or powder jockey. That could explain why she was crawling through pipes practically naked in the middle of the night.

Maybe she snapped when she heard about the kidnapping. Or when the divorce became final. What does that do to a mother: to lose her infant child forever? 'Nobody's seen her since the divorce, when Old Man Bannister got full custody. Why was that, do you think?'

'Because he kicked her out of the house.'

'I mean—why did the Old Man get full custody?'

'I don't know, the normal reasons . . . ?'

Only, there's no normal in the world of Old Man Bannister. 'Question is: when did Elaine Bannister go nuts?'

Schiller presses so close, he bumps me with that barrel chest of his. 'You're telling me the Old Man sent her crazy?'

'It figures, doesn't it? He wants full custody. No judge is going to hand over a kid into the care of a mother who's a turnip.'

'We've got no proof.'

'We start by finding people who knew her over the last twelve months. Something's got to turn up . . . And, if we're lucky, the trail will lead back to the Old Man.'

Schiller just stands there, staring at me, trying to tear a flake of tobacco from the corner of his mouth. This is a long shot, but the only one we have. We both know we're in trouble. All we've got are three leads: one near death, one missing, and one who can't speak. Plus a stolen lighter with initials telling me a truth I can see but don't want to acknowledge. That Mrs. Bannister's caught up in all of this. 'Even if Old Man Bannister was involved, why would he or anyone else bury her here, right under our noses? Admit it, Alston, it just doesn't make sense.'

Unless there is a reason none of us have seen yet. 'Unless they wanted her found.'

'Why even risk it?'

Good question. There was only one answer: they didn't care if she lived or died; they knew she'd never talk. They just wanted her found. She was a secret message written in an ancient language that only one person still remembered: Old Man Bannister. 'Blackmail.'

'Blackmail? Why blackmail him when they're already extorting ransom for the kid?'

'What if it's unrelated?'

'A coincidence like that? Are you kidding?'

'Okay, it's a long shot, I admit it, but here's another angle: imagine for a moment that Elaine was in on the snatch.'

'A mother kidnapping her own son . . . ?'

'Wait and listen for a moment, will you? Let's say they need her to snatch the kid but when she sees him, she goes nuts . . . '

'She was already nuts!'

'We don't know when it happened. Maybe just seeing the kid sends her bananas. The kidnappers were just using her to get the kid, but when she does, she snaps . . . '

Schiller's eyes open in stunned illumination. He actually gets it. 'And she doesn't want to give the kid back!'

'She wants to keep him, and to hell with the goddamn ransom . . . '

'Only the others, the ones who are using her, don't give a fuck about the kid. They want the dough.'

'They want the dough, and now Elaine is getting in the way, acting like the mommy she was never allowed to be, complicating everything.'

'So they decide to kill her . . . '

'Not kill. They're in it for the money, but they're not killers.' Can I really be sure of that? What if they're the mob? They wouldn't hesitate to kill a kid for a cool million. Schiller seems to be reassured by what I've said though. 'It's money they're after so now they decide to double down on their bet against the Old Man. Now they have the kid, and they also have proof that Old Man Bannister should never have had custody in the first place.'

'What proof?'

'Elaine Bannister and her sob story. A mother who's ready to die for her kid.'

'But who cares if the kid stays with the Old Man or not?'

Schiller's still a cop even with that liver. I think about it. 'Maybe someone close to Elaine?' Like Betty Bannister for instance. Was that whole line about not talking to Elaine just a lie? Or is there someone else in the family with a special interest in who's looking after Ronnie? 'Or maybe they don't give a damn about Elaine. She's just another racket to them . . . ' In which case it could be professionals like Johnny Roselli. A kid, a zombie broad. It's all the same when money's on the line. You use them, and if you have to lose them, you don't hesitate. Business is business. 'There is one other explanation . . . '

'Give it to me.'

'What if there's a whole group of kidnappers with only one thing in common?'

'Being . . . ?'

'What is it that anyone who has ever had any dealings with the Old Man always says about him?'

'First-class son of a bitch.'

'You got it. They hate him. Every single one of them. His past and present business associates, all his opponents, even his political allies. They fear him. They need him. But most of all, they hate him. Especially his ex-wives.'

'I think it was that fucking crumb, Hastings. A grease monkey working for the Old Man who took a look at all the dough just lying around, and said—why not me?'

Hastings . . . I had almost forgotten about him. Iwo Jima vet. Smart enough to have escaped. Smart enough to have stolen evidence. And who had fingered Hidalgo before anyone knew about the Feds' interest in him. 'Any luck with the all-points?'

'It's still too early.'

'What I can't figure out is how come the kidnappers know so little about the Old Man . . . And so much about me.'

Schiller steps in front of me, anxiety filling his meaty face. 'Don't make this about Tommy . . . '

'What if it already is?' I look around the estate grounds. Tommy bought it in a mansion just like this in Brentwood, walking down a pebble driveway. The burglar must have heard him coming a mile off, and sapped him hard as he turned the corner. They figured he thought Tommy was the old man coming home, or maybe just a servant. But when he saw Tommy lying there in his uniform, his jaw broken, he knew what had to be done and opened Tommy's throat with a long, sharp blade.

Two minutes later, give or take, Tommy was dead. Golden Gloves. Purple Heart. Sergeant in the marines; sergeant on the Force. All that service. For nothing. In one night my brother had been turned into a dead chump.

The burglar had picked up Tommy's piece, walked back to the squad car and blown Tommy's partner's brains out. That had been the first thing I saw when I got there at dawn, brains sticky as egg yolk on the trunk. The blood had pooled calmly round Tommy, dammed by the pebbles, so completely still in the early light that I could see my own reflection in it. The blood of my parents. And of me. Tommy, white and empty, dead from a sucker punch, his own gun turned on his partner.

I knew what had to be done. I had pushed past the others, driven home, and loaded my car with rope, lighter fluid, a hand drill, a hacksaw, a fish fillet knife, ten feet of garden hose, a box of cigars, a bottle of brandy, three vials of ammonia and a pair of bolt cutters. Twenty-four hours later I hadn't found Tommy's killer but I had solved nineteen other cases and was off the force.

Big-time cover-up all round.

And Tommy's killer was still out there, hiding behind the corner at the end of some pebble driveway, waiting for another sucker just like Tommy.

I look at my new Zodiac watch. 'It's time to talk to Jesse.'

Twenty-seven hours till the hit in New York City. Time enough to panic. To feel the twin tidal currents of remorse and ruthlessness. Time enough for Hastings to try to figure a way out.

It was going to be a bedroom whack. JFK would be officially staying at the Carlyle but would be screwing at the Sherry Netherland. The heavy security would be at the wrong hotel. The skeleton Secret Service crew actually with the president would be no threat. Hastings would be in disguise as CIA. He'd arrange broads and booze for the Secret Service boys. The others had been told to assemble in the lobby twenty minutes before midnight. Hastings and Luchino would be jumping the gun by nearly three hours.

He left to stake out the hotel for safe exits, emergency retreats and possible traps. Then he went for a walk in the park. He felt exhausted from the pressurized atmosphere of overheated hotels. He needed the stinging clarity of cold air and traffic.

New York seemed unreal after the shadowless mountain mornings and ocean sunsets of Los Angeles. The trees in the park were all stripped naked, throwing up their bare branches in surrender to the frozen sky. Car horns echoed off the canyons of apartment houses. Manhattan imagined itself to be the centre of civilization, but Hastings felt removed from all human order and companionship. He was alone.

All across the city, museums were closing, offices were

emptying, and storefront grilles were being locked. Trains were departing the city for suburban homes flickering with the fevered contagion of television.

Hastings slipped into a bar. The Cocktail Hour. One is not enough and three too many. But who's counting? The Hour extended itself effortlessly, glass rims blushed with lipstick; heated air soiled with cigarette smoke. Knees touched under tables. Eyes invited. Mouths lied. 'My wife doesn't understand me.' 'My husband takes me for granted.' 'I never thought you felt the same . . . ' Pockets were rifled for change, telephone receivers raised from their cradles, home numbers dialled. 'Held up at work.' 'Better go ahead and eat without me . . . '

The elegant ritual of collective anesthetization. The debate between the olive and the pickled onion. Lemon rind or Maraschino cherry. As for the rest, a dash of bitters is enough for the entire city. Ice is stabbed and fractured like a frozen carcass, comets of sheared cold glittering across clothing to amused applause. Bartenders shake drinks with a musical, metallic chime. No one remembers who ordered them. Nobody cares. A hand touches an arm, an arm brushes a breast; fingers drop to a knee, skate along the sleek path of nylon. Longing mouths are denied union. Perfume is breathed. Jokes are whispered; laughter is light and calculating. Cigarettes are exchanged like promises. Sentences trail away. Gazes are avidly met or studiously avoided. Watches are checked. Timetables don't wait for small talk.

Hastings sipped his scotch on the rocks; looked around. Everyone was leaving, his solitude magnified by the empty tables in the mocking mirrors. Ever since the War, his existence had been dominated by death. Avoiding it, then delivering it on command. Everyone in the city will suffer the same fate. Nobody is spared. Yet they all turn their faces from the inevitability. The Grave or the Flame. Too impossible to imagine. Too gruesome to accept.

Everyone except for Hastings. Not after all that had happened. Not after all he had seen. All he had done; was about to do. One of the telephone booths was free. His fingers found the numbers in the dark, the dial a wheel of fortune. His destiny awaited an answer to his spin of fate. There was the click of response. ' . . . Mrs. Bannister?'

There was a protracted, shocked pause. Then her voice rose with amazement. And recognition. 'You . . . ?'

'We need to talk.'

'Not on the phone . . . ' She had already told him two things. Her phone was bugged. And she'd been waiting for this call. It had been three years but the voice still thrilled him: a delicious surge of pleasure pitted with the promise of pain. Her scent. Her intimate taste. The quicksand of desire and despair. 'Meet me.'

'Where?'

'Our old place . . . '

Why LA? he wondered. Was she planning on skipping town? 'When?'

'Fifteen minutes.'

It took a moment for Hastings to understand she meant the New York Roosevelt. Her surveillance must be total. 'Make it twenty.' She hung up. A long, breathless pause. Then the faint snapping signal of eavesdropping. Hastings cradled the phone and thought about who was behind the tapping. It had to be Hoover. But why Mrs. Bannister? His ex-boss's soon-to-be ex-wife. Like him, a one-time suspect in a kidnapping.

He remembered the rule: the hardest fall is always for the wrong person.

Susan had been the right person. Hastings had married Susan straight off the train coming back from the war. He thought he could put the Pacific behind him by walking down an aisle with his high-school sweetheart. Hastings found out a week after the wedding that Susan was eight weeks pregnant with her uncle's child when a rock smashed through the window.

Through her sobs, Susan managed to tell him the whole story in the course of that night. The abuse had started when she was just a girl. First it was her teacher: Hasting's own stepfather. Then the preacher, long gone. Then the mayor. And then her uncle, who ran the gas station on the interstate. She wasn't the only one. Sons and daughters were traumatized.

Shame and culpability turned the husbands violent. The men were short-tempered and cruel with their wives—who were judged wanting compared to what the husbands had been violating night after night: hurting and damaging children just for a fast shudder of pleasure. The men kept their secret the way men always do: with liquor, brutality and sullen silence; the women struggled with the burden of their knowledge and their hatred of their husbands. Many pretended they didn't know, choosing ignorance over despair. Some beat their daughters. Others ignored them. One or two defended them; tried to even save them. Susan's mother didn't care. Her own ordeal had seen to that: the town was already second generation; socially entrenched, like church on Sundays and the Labor Day picnic.

Susan had been passed around amongst the Elders but now she had a husband who loved her. Even after she told him. A husband who promised to save her. A husband who said it wasn't her fault. The pendulum swing was too far and too fast for Susan. She had been blamed from the very beginning. Because of Eve. Because of the weaker sex: provocative and shameless. The men were blameless. It was always her fault. She, the temptress. A Jezebel.

A woman.

Hastings's four years overseas had introduced him to war and death and despair but had spared him the abusive savagery of his hometown's complicit cruelty; its sanctimonious denial, its vicious easy formula: victim as predator.

Those missing years were about to catch up with him.

He found her in the river. Dead, along with the unborn child he would have raised. He had wanted to take her away from the past and out west to the future, to Dallas, or further, to California. To follow the sun to a place where no one knew them or their past. But her sunset couldn't wait.

There was no funeral. The church would not allow it. Suicide was the public reason. Fornicator was the private one. The men folk had no control over their throbbing pricks and rancid minds. She made them do it. She deserved everything she got. And they gave her plenty. No one came to the burial, not even her mother. Hastings dug the grave himself. Then he went back to the hovel they had rented; that he had been prepared to call a home.

The following night it was a new moon. A perfect Kill Night in the Pacific. When the tormenting mud and underbrush transformed into the hush of silence and cover. A sorrowful rain made the leaves of the sweetgums bow their stars to earth. Hastings went out and stalked the Elders of the town armed with his *navaja sevillana*, won off a deserter from Franco's Guardia Civil in a poker game in Manila in 1945.

Before he killed Susan's tormentors, he forced them all to write suicide notes with the promise of fast dispatch and the physical evidence of noncooperation: the wrinkled member of Susan's uncle. The trembling, self-pitying confessions were testaments less to guilt and shame at the horror their lust had wrought than to disbelief that their arrogant and enduring immunity was coming to a premature end.

The police found the bodies of twelve leading citizens, including the sheriff and the judge, the following morning. The Adelsberg Suicides made the town notorious, and remain to this day America's most startling sequence of spontaneous, simultaneous suicides. The county coroner knew that one man might be able to open his throat with a razor, but twelve on the

146 · TIM BAKER

same night? It was obviously murder, but the motive as outlined in all the confessions was so unsettling that the coroner rubber-stamped them all as self-homicides. The truth was too ghastly. And too close for comfort. The coroner had been missed by Hastings and became Adelsberg's Ishmael.

Case closed.

Hastings watched the families of the twelve men burying their dead one by one in unhallowed ground, in earth that had been made sacred to him by Susan's presence. He waited in their old home, but nobody came. Either they didn't figure it was him, or they knew and were too afraid to go after him, like the Shogun's soldiers with the wounded Ronin.

After three days of silence he disappeared, heading west like he had promised Susan.

Dallas. Phoenix.

Los Angeles.

He found menial jobs. He slept in dives. He was back in the foxholes of the Pacific—not living, just surviving.

More than a decade passed. It seemed to him like an eternity.

Then one night in LA everything changed.

His life.

Betty's.

The entire country's. The Bannister case saw to that.

Hastings stepped out into the Manhattan night, the rain perfect camouflage for his tears.

G reta Simmons, the nanny who was the last known person to have seen Ronnie Bannister before his disappearance, doesn't look too distraught. At least, not on behalf of the kid. She does seem a little concerned about her own professional prospects however.

It was her bad luck that she was on deck when the good ship Babysitting hit a reef. The captain always goes down with the boat. She's already out of a job whether they find the kid or not. It's only natural she's looking more worried for herself than for the kid. After all, she let him out of her sight. Even though the kid was tucked safely in bed; even though she did her rounds when she was supposed to, even though it was a roster that chose her that day, she's to blame. Always will be. This case will follow Greta Simmons for the rest of her life. Her obituary will read: 'the nanny who lost the Bannister kid'.

But none of that is what's really bothering me. The question—and it's a big one—is whether Greta Simmons was in on the kidnapping.

'Let's run through that last hour again . . . '

Greta sighs, like I'm an encyclopaedia salesman who won't take no for an answer. 'Listen, I told the police everything. There's nothing else to add—'

'Let me be the judge of that, will you?'

She gives me the kind of look people would love to give a cop but never dare. But with a private dick—that's another matter. A PI is a man with a tarnished badge, a crooked rep and a pocketful of flashbulbs. Someone you don't have to pretend to respect. 'I want a lawyer.'

Greta's a tough one all right. Violent father. Abusive partner. Neglectful boyfriend. Philandering husband. Selfish son. Greta's tough enough to have had to deal with them all.

'I want an answer. Why did you leave the kid alone all that time . . . ?'

'I didn't.' She straightens in her chair, her lower lip curled in anger. 'I put him to bed, switched off the light and closed the door, like I always do. I checked on him again. Twenty minutes before I went out . . . '

Him. Not Ronnie. Not the poor, dear baby. Him. I've seen more emotion in strangers coming out of Del Mar Racetrack, talking about a horse they hadn't bet on falling as it went into the straight.

'Only twenty minutes, huh?' Greta had originally told Schiller she'd looked in on the kid just ten minutes before she went out. Now she's telling me she checked in on the kid twenty minutes before. Lying is bad, we're taught that it gets us into trouble. But exaggeration is a different matter. Everyone does it. It doesn't make you feel bad about yourself. On the contrary, I can tell from the self-righteous stance Greta adopts, leaning in towards me ready to argue the point, that in her mind she believes it herself. It can't have been more than twenty minutes, forty minutes, an hour. 'Only you didn't check on him twenty minutes before you left, did you, Greta? You took a powder and left him on his own for nearly two hours.'

'That's a lie.' She wraps a silk scarf around her neck, preparing to go. I can't tell if it's wishful thinking or sheer audacity. 'Talk to my lawyer.'

'What are you trying to hide, Miss Simmons?'

'I've done nothing wrong.'

'You lost a child under your care.'

'Ronnie was in bed. My duties were completed for the day.'

I have a hunch there was only one way to ever truly complete your duties in the Bannister Estate, and that would be to hammer in the last nail in the Old Man's coffin. 'But you checked in on him later, you said so yourself. Why?'

'Habit . . . ' She sees the look in my eyes, pulling back with annoyance. 'I'm a reliable person.'

'You may deny it, Greta, but you were still responsible for the boy, even when he was asleep.' She tries to answer but can't, overwhelmed by indignation. 'No one is accusing you of neglect . . . Not yet.'

She masters her emotion, her voice low. 'What are you suggesting?'

'You were the last person to see Ronnie Bannister in this house.'

'I'm not saying anything until I see my lawyer.'

'A lawyer's not going to get you out of this fix, young lady. You put the kid to bed, left the window open, locked the door and made a call.'

'That's a lie!'

'There are witnesses.'

'Who?'

Aha. Always play the hunch. 'Doesn't matter who, what matters is they saw you on the phone.'

'You're lying.' She turns to Schiller. 'Who saw me?'

Now we're getting somewhere. There's a change in her eyes, like the fulcrum on a set of scales. An adjustment; not in her favour. Someone saw her with a phone in her hand. Only no one did; at least not that I'm aware of. I'm running on intuition, on gut instincts; I'm running just like a cop. I feed her a name. 'Morris.' She raises her face in pleased defiance, like a defence attorney crossing towards the witness stand, getting ready for demolition. Morris is not going to hold up under cross-examination. Time to call in a surprise witness. 'And Hastings.'

I score. She takes a step back, her eyes opening. Fear. Lots of it. Right there on her face. 'Level with me, Greta, or you'll be spending tonight behind bars . . . Maybe the first of many.'

Wrong call. Fear gives way to defiance. 'Lay off.' She slaps me. Hard. 'You're no cop.'

'But I am . . . ' Schiller to the rescue, coming in just like he always does, when the action's nearly over. He pulls out his cuffs, grabs one of her wrists. Those cuffs were made for Mickey Cohen's goons, not for a slim nanny who speaks with a lilting voice. No matter how tight Schiller clamps them, Greta's slender hands are going to slide free. But the notion of restraint, arrest, incarceration does the job, reducing her to tears.

Another victory to abusive men.

'Talk to us, Greta, and we'll see you get off. That's right, isn't it, Captain?'

'Sure,' Schiller drawls solicitously, slowly putting the handcuffs away. 'We'll talk to the DA.'

'We'll tell him you were coerced. That you were a cooperative witness. Hell, you might even be in line for a piece of that reward money . . . '

The silence of the room buzzes all around us, throbbing with the insult of having eavesdropped on what was just said. Greta straightens, throwing her shoulders back and lifting her chin. There is a pause as she looks past us. Schiller and I exchange looks. She's taking the bait. She's ours.

And in that instant of smartass male complicity, she rushes between us, her scarf trailing behind her, touching my face with a caress both intimate and defiant.

She jumps.

There is the shock and shattering racket of glass as she goes through the window, then the wind is inside the room, ripping and probing on the tail of the curtains as they billow madly around us.

'Sweet-Jesus-fucking-Christ-all-fucking-Mighty!' Schiller

turns to me, his face awed and uncomprehending: the cop who thought he'd seen everything suddenly transformed and contrite.

I shove past him, rushing across the snap and glitter of broken glass to the gaping insult that was once a window and look down. Greta Simmons's lifeless body lies broken on the ridge of marble steps, the wind flicking the scarf about her like little boys taunting a dead animal, tugging on its tail.

Evelyn Rutledge is not a natural blonde, but she is a natural beauty. Two things she shares with Norma Jean Baker, who stares dolefully over her shoulder. The black and white still is from *The Asphalt Jungle.* In her late thirties, Evelyn bears more than a passing resemblance to Marilyn Monroe. It's the sense of a tender beauty that would bruise if touched the wrong way.

The Spanish-style house in Vickery Place is large and airy and opens onto a shaded garden. Datura flowers hang stricken by the heat, filling the air with the scent of their poisonous promise. It's almost a shock to see such open access to nature, such disregard for the claustrophobic control of air-conditioning. There's even birdsong. Evelyn Rutledge offers me a glass of French rosé and bowls of Brazil nuts, Japanese crackers and Greek olives. Evelyn Rutledge is the United Nations of Dallas and seems proud to be the rest of the world's ambassador, the rest of the world in Dallas being everything outside of Texas. She confirms her own alien status here. 'I'm from South Carolina but grew up in Savannah. I got a job as an intern in the Menil Collection. I just love Rothko. That's where I met my late husband. He was visiting the chapel. We moved to Dallas after the wedding. My family never forgave me for marrying a man older than my own father. But when Mr. Rutledge suddenly passed on, and I inherited his estate, they were more than willing to forgive. Unfortunately . . . ' She shrugs, refilling our glasses. 'After all that had been said, I just didn't feel the same way. The move to Texas wasn't as hard as you'd think . . . ' I have a feeling I've already reached the end of the Mr. Rutledge part of the story. ' . . . Although I do miss being close to the sea. Even when I was in Houston, Galveston was just not the same.'

'I suppose not . . . ' The only thing I know about Galveston is the song. Something about a gun. Neil Diamond. Or was it John Denver?

Evelyn Rutledge's claim to have psychic evidence about the JFK assassination puts her firmly in the same category as her plate of almendras, but she is by far the most civilized and approachable of all the conspiracy theorists I have visited so far. And definitely the most alluring. She places an olive pit companionably next to one of mine, her liquid brown eyes assessing me. There is the hint of a smile. 'I see that you're divorced . . . '

She says it as though I'm stepping out of a large building marked 'Divorce Court' to loud applause with a decree pasted to my forehead. Could this little tête-à-tête be some kind of awful mistake? Has she confused me for someone from an online dating service? 'What . . . ?'

Her smile is no longer camouflaged. 'I see it in your hands, Mr. Alston.'

'But you haven't read my palms . . . '

'I read people, Mr. Alston. Your ring finger still has a circular indentation between the second and third joints. The hairs above the knuckle have been worn away by time. You wore that ring for years.'

'Seven years.'

'And . . . ' She gives a pleasing if wicked smile. 'In the interests of transparency, as they say, I also looked you up on Facebook.'

'But there's nothing about my divorce on my Facebook page.'

'True. But it led me to your wife's—your ex-wife's page. All her friends are obsessed with the divorce. Not to mention

Monica's wedding announcement.' I try not to show any reaction. But what can I do? She just told me she reads people. 'I'm sorry. I didn't know you didn't know . . . ' That wicked smile again. Liar, liar. She's not the only one who can read people.

'I hope that made you feel better.'

There is the teasing tumble of more wine. And then her fingers touch my hand. A thrill passes through me. Another response I can't hide. I want to ask Evelyn who Monica is planning to marry but not only would it be humiliating, it would be wrong. I am here to do my job, to pretend to be interested in initials like ESP, JFK, CIA and LBJ. Then I have to go back home to an empty house in Sydney and make sense of this shifty alphabet soup. Besides, as soon as I leave Evelyn Rutledge, I can find out myself. If Monica hasn't unfriended me.

Evelyn Rutledge puts me out of my misery. 'His name is Kaplan . . . Alan Kaplan.'

My mind runs after faces with names, like a dog chasing a car. Then I have him. Not quite the face, but a handshake. Firm and, in hindsight, oddly satisfied.

Eight years ago, I was handshaked through Monica's previous life and now I had been handshaked into her future one.

When we met, she fell hard. It had never happened to her before. When she proposed, I accepted without hesitation. She was the most exciting person I had ever met. Hard to believe after all that's happened, but she felt exactly the same way about me. She found me handsome; I reminded her of John-John Kennedy. Monica had palled around with Caroline in Martha's Vineyard the summer of '97 and developed a huge crush on the dashing Junior. I never cared for them; they were just another celebrity couple, but I did feel a wave of sadness after the plane crash. Monica believed in the Kennedy Curse. It was at least as convincing as the Curse of Tutankhamun. But why would such curses be reserved just for powerful families? They could equally apply to families no one's ever heard of. Families just like mine.

I had already been married twice before, but with Monica, if felt different. When we finally surfaced after our first three weeks together, very sore but hardly sorry, we were focusing on the future—Us Together Forever. She took me on a tour of the faculty where she worked. This was her mentor, her colleague; this was her former student who was doing his doctorate. Always 'pleased to meet you'. Then the circuit got bigger. This was her old mixed-doubles partner. This was a friend from up at the lake; or down at the gym. The motorcycle club—Monica rode an Indian Chief.

I didn't get these impromptu social calls at first. We'd be on our way to the beach and stop off at some university facility, or go by a gallery or rehearsal space, and Monica would introduce me to another guy. Quite a few were older than me, a couple were younger than her. Occasionally it was a woman.

It was a professor who gave it all away. He didn't want to shake hands. He just wanted to talk to Monica. Alone. I stood outside the frosted-glass door, his muffled voice pleading at first, almost sobbing, then rising in outrage and anger.

Did they know about all the others; did they think it was only a matter of time before they'd lose her? Had they ever even cared about her, or was she just a convenient and easy pleasure on the side—erotic fast food? Were they secretly relieved that they could simply give up the stress that goes with adultery and go back to their families, hiding their reckless episode with Monica in the attic of their memories? Along with all their other clandestine indiscretions, embarrassments and fantasies: the students and the secretaries and receptionists in Friday-afternoon offices.

Then around two years ago, there was Kaplan, a distinguished-looking French teacher who reminded me of myself, only a little more old-school, a little more stylish. More Cary Grant than John-John . . .

I didn't realise till it was too late. The story of my life.

J FK's daiquiri sits untouched by the bed, melting ice draining the high lime tint. Eva Marlowe stretched across the president, her nipple raking the hair on his chest as she helped herself to his drink. Eva liked to screw as well as the next woman, but she wasn't exactly crazy about Jack's 'lay back and give it to me' style. It was all about dick; nothing for Dora.

Eva was a party girl with an artist's mind. When she was up on the screen, audiences only ever saw her beauty. They thought that's what gave her sex appeal. But her crooked smile hid a huge intelligence. Eva knew that nothing got a man up so fast—or deflated him so quickly—as a well-chosen word, and Eva had plenty of those in her repertoire.

She was able to hold her own with most men, whether they liked it or not. Dukes or playboys. Cowboys or bandits. Presidents. She practically collected them. Adolfo López Mateos was the first. She had loved him. Here was a man who wasn't interested in power for its own sake, but as a means of making people's lives better. When Alfredo became president in '58 he wrote down a list of things that would help the ordinary Mexican's life become better: compulsory education; increased minimum wages; farmers' markets that cut out middlemen. Housing. And then he set out in a methodical fashion to try to achieve as many of those goals as possible. It was all a little too radical for a few, very important people and Eva wondered if the terrible migraines Alfredo started suffering weren't caused by some kind of slow-acting poisoning. A hugely popular, internationally respected social reformer was always a threat to those intent on preserving the status quo—the status quo being accumulating the greatest amount of wealth amongst the fewest possible individuals. The Bannister Way.

President Goulart of Brazil was one of the most chivalrous men Eva had ever met. But he could also be surprisingly earthy. He had a real love of music and popular traditions. And was tenacious and effective where it counted. His land reforms terrified the oligarchy.

And then there was Jack. Small beer by comparison, and she wasn't just thinking of his politics.

'What are you thinking about . . . ?'

' . . . Politics.'

'Jesus.'

'What?'

'Politics is the one thing I don't want to think about. Not tonight . . . ' For such a famous voice, it wasn't that attractive. 'Tonight, all I want to think about is . . . ' He leant over and touched her between the legs. 'Sex.'

She had foolishly thought he was going to say 'you'.

Who was she kidding? Sure, he was the president, but he was also a louse. She threw off the sheets and got out of bed. He reached for her waist, but then froze, groaning in pain. Tonight's specialty: naked president with bad back. She must be slipping.

Eva knew she should offer to give him a massage. But she also knew where that would lead. She crossed the room to where her bathrobe hung across a chair, freezing as a man entered, unannounced, through the front door of the suite, holding a camera in his hands. She ripped a sheet off the bed, covering the front of her naked body. 'Who the hell are you?'

JFK rolled off the bed to the heartbeat of the shutter, Hastings shooting as he approached—snap, snap, snap—thinking: head shot, chest shot; kill shot.

Eva started to scream. Hastings had her, her squirming body warm in his arms. 'Shut up or we're all dead,' he whispered into her ear. She spun around, slapping him hard across the face, but keeping quiet. Eva was a trouper. She tossed her robe to JFK, who had taken shelter between the bed and the wall. He was going for the phone. 'Forget it . . . ' Hastings said, 'it's dead.' He lowered the camera and stepped back, the silencer long and lethal in his hand.

Both Eva and the president stared at it, the gun controlling the scenario. 'Do you have any idea—'

'Listen to me!' Hastings said. 'Your life is in danger.'

'And yours isn't? Coming in here and threatening me with a gun.'

Eva stepped towards the door. 'And how about my life, is it in danger too?'

Hastings turned to Eva, recognizing her for the first time. 'Step away from the door, Miss Marlowe. He's the one they want; you're just an incidental target; "the broad in the bed".'

'I resent that.'

'What are you talking about?' JFK thumped the phone, trying to get a dial tone. 'And where the hell is my protection?'

'It was supposed to be Chicago. Soldier Field. You know that.'

'Know what?'

'Shut up.'

Eva turned to Kennedy, outraged. 'How dare you talk to me that way.'

Kennedy looked at her for a long, incredulous moment, then gave a short, scoffing laugh. 'I'm sorry if I offended the lady.' He turned to Hastings, cinching the bathrobe around his body. 'How do you know about Soldier Field? That was top secret.'

'I was the man who was supposed to shoot you there.'

Kennedy stared at him for a long moment. Again the light,

scoffing laugh. Somewhere between disbelief and reluctant admiration. 'I'm glad you had a change of heart.'

'Why are you warning us like this? Why not just call the cops? And why the goddamn camera?' She turned to JFK. 'It doesn't make sense, Jack. He's probably a shakedown artist from *Hollywood Whispers*.'

Hastings looked at his watch. 'I'm here because in precisely three hours, people will force their way into this room to kill you both.'

'That's ridiculous.' JFK said it with a lack of conviction unimaginable in most politicians. He was almost human. 'I have . . . ' His voice faded. Men who know victory also know defeat.

'Security? Not tonight.'

'So what are we going to do now, pose for some more snap-shots?'

'I'm getting you out, Miss Marlowe. But first we have to get the president out.'

'Whatever happened to women and children?'

'Relax, Eva, I'll take care of you. Why the camera? She's right. This is a shakedown, isn't it?'

'Insurance, that's all. You leave me alone and you'll never see these photos.'

'Of course he'll leave you alone if what you say is true.'

'Keep out of this, Eva . . . She's right. How do I know any of this is true?'

'You don't, *Monsieur le Président*. You just need to make a leap of the faith . . . '

Hastings slowly turned. Luchino was standing by a newly-opened window, the curtains rippling around him like a great cape, a gun pointing at the others. He saw the instinctive quiver in Hastings's hand—the one that was holding the gun.

'Calm down, *mon ami*. We are on the same side, remember?'

Eva pointed at Luchino. 'I like him more.'

Luchino bowed gallantly. 'My friend and I, we are in trouble. Explain to them.'

'We were hired to kill you, but we don't want to.' Hastings shrugged. 'It'll be tough enough standing up to them, without having to worry about your people coming after us too. We need to make sure that doesn't happen. That's why we need the photos.'

'If it's amnesty you want, I'll give it to you.'

'Not amnesty, amnesia.'

'That's it?'

'And a million.'

'Who's behind this?'

'Everyone. No one.'

'What about that lunatic Howard Hughes?' JFK caught the trousers Hastings tossed him. 'Or Old Man Bannister? I bet that son of a bitch is in on it too.'

'If we knew for sure, we'd already be dead.'

Hastings nods at Luchino. 'We're going. We'll take care of the girl.'

'I don't like the sound of that.'

'Trust me, you'll be safe.' Hastings handed Eva her dress. 'In the meantime, you better clean yourself up, Mr. President, you look like shit.'

Kennedy froze, staring at them. 'Who are you people?'

Hastings and Luchino exchanged looks. 'The best,' Luchino said.

'Give me one reason why I should trust you.'

'Because we're the ones holding the guns and we haven't used them.'

'You used a camera though, you sanctimonious bastard,' Kennedy said, tying up shoelaces.

'Relax, Jack, if they wanted to hurt us, they would have already done it.'

He started doing up his shirt, dropping a cuff link in his

impatience. Luchino picked it up and handed it to him. Kennedy snatched it from his hand. 'I'll have your hides, I tell you that, if you don't hand over that film now.'

'You give us two million and the photos will go away.'

'He just said one.'

'A million each, *n'est-ce pas*?'

The president gestured to Eva as he did up his tie. 'What about the girl?'

'I'm a lady, show some respect.'

'She's safe with us, and that's a promise. We'll get her out of here, no questions asked. But if anything ever happens to her that we can trace back to you . . . '

'We will certainly not like it.'

Eva nodded towards Luchino. 'The perfect gentleman . . . ' She turned her back to Hastings. 'Zip me, will you . . . ?'

The glide of the zipper filled the silent room.

'So we have a deal?'

'Fuck you, yes . . . '

'A pleasure doing business with the Land of the Brave.'

'Fuck you too. And de Gaulle.'

Luchino offered his arm to Eva, who shook her head. 'I'm walking out of here unescorted. And I'm going home on my own.'

'Such a pity, a beautiful woman like you . . . '

'Drop dead, if you pardon my French.' She looked back at JFK. 'Despite early indications, it turned out to be a memorable night after all . . . '

JFK stared at her, straightening his collar. 'Best if we not see each other for a while . . . '

'Is never long enough for you Jack, 'cause it does me just fine.'

Hastings walked Eva out of the room, her high-heeled shoes dangling from one hand. He slipped something into her bag. If she felt it; she didn't show it. He turned to the president. 'We'll be in touch.'

'How will you get in contact?'

'I have your direct number.'

Kennedy's jaw dropped, exposing gleaming white teeth which made his face look even more tanned by contrast. 'That's impossible. Wait a minute. What are your names?' But they were already walking out the door. Hastings paused, turning back to the president. 'I want you to know, I was there . . . '

'There?'

'Brentwood. The night she died . . . ' The door closed behind him. The president stood there for a long moment, then sat down on the bed and put his head in his hands.

Why in Christ's name did she do that?' Schiller shakes his head, watching the ambulance doors close on what, less than twenty minutes before, had been our only important witness—in custody, that is; and still capable of talking. Press hounds snap away, the pop of their bulbs punctuating Schiller's breathing. Greta Simmons hadn't just killed herself. She had also probably just pulled the plug on the kid.

'Fear . . . ' Only this was no fear for self. This was fear on a grand scale. The kind of fear that cripples just by imagining it. The kind of fear that doesn't just end lives but whole worlds.

Schiller thumps me in the chest with his stabbing fingers, a cigar, like a burning fuse, locked between them. 'This was your fucking fault. I told you to go easy on her!'

It wasn't that Schiller meant to lie. Greta wasn't the only one who was afraid. Schiller knew fear as well. That's what being on the Force too long does to you. First it makes you sick with yourself. Then it makes you sick with all humanity. And then, after years of disillusionment and self-hatred, something unexpected happens—a magical adjustment, like after that fifth shot of whiskey. Suddenly nothing matters anymore. You wake up one morning and realize you just don't care. You start to glide. You learn to live with the condition of being, not caring. The same things happen but you're no longer implicated. You're simply a bystander. Not innocent. Not guilty. Not even aware. You're just there, repeating lines and gestures automatically, pulling out cuffs or badges, weapons or tickets according to minor cues. Knocking on doors or ramming them open, walking away from sobs or curses. Constantly moving away from everyone and everything. Reacting but never feeling. You have finally found your balance in indifference. That's what the Force does to you after all those years. The great self-survival paradox: inhuman but alive.

And then something happens that threatens your blissful emotional numbness. And when it does, you don't react in anger or even in shock. Just in fear; fear that you might start caring again. That you might become human again, and you'll do anything to stop that: lie, cheat, maybe even kill.

Schiller looks up at the busted window, terror in his eyes. 'What makes you so afraid you have to commit suicide?' Asking the question as though he were talking about himself.

Greta wasn't afraid: she was terrified. And this wasn't a suicide, it was a sacrifice. Greta Simmons didn't give a damn about Ronnie Bannister. But she gave her life to protect something. 'The question is: who was she protecting?'

'The kidnappers.'

Faulty cop logic. 'She could have turned them in; could have even walked with some of the reward money.'

'The Old Man would never have allowed it.'

He's right. The Old Man was too vindictive to allow anyone connected to the case to just walk. Including Schiller and me. When this is all over, he will find some way to punish us. Even if we get the boy back safe and sound, we will still incur his wrath. It is the common caprice of the tyrant. Everyone is to blame. 'It's not the kidnappers she's protecting.'

'Who then?'

'Try this: they snatch someone close to Greta, then blackmail her into helping them kidnap the Bannister kid.'

'A hostage . . . ?' Schiller stews on it, turning it over in his mind's digestive tract, warm acidic fluids working hard to break down an unorthodox idea. 'How the fuck would killing herself help the hostage?'

'From the moment she was taken into custody, the hostage was compromised. If Greta squealed, they'd snuff the hostage. She knew they wouldn't hesitate.'

'But how would they know what she said?'

'Let's say she was being tailed.'

'No one was tailing her. I would have known.'

Twenty bucks to the right cop would have made sure he never knew. And normally they would have been doing Schiller a favour: not knowing was not caring. 'Let's say we were being bugged. Let's say they knew she was being questioned. She knows they're listening. Don't you see? She does it for them. It was theatre.'

Schiller's eyes bulge at the notion. 'What's to stop the bastards from killing the hostage anyway?'

'Nothing. But at least Greta did the best she could. At least they know she didn't rat anyone out. If the hostage lives, he'll know Greta sacrificed herself to save him. Maybe she wanted to punish him with the memory. And even if they still snuff the hostage, at least now she'll never know about it.'

He's half-convinced.

'We need to find everything we can about Greta Simmons. Where she was born, where she came from, if she had husbands, lovers . . . '

'Captain.' Sam's face appears through the smashed window. 'It's time.'

'After we're done here, you and me both, we talk to Greta's mother.' Schiller stomps across the shattered glass, heading up the steps. A reporter runs up to him. 'What about the rumour that the nanny died under interrogation?'

Schiller stiffens, staring hard into the as-yet un-rearranged features of the newshound. 'Interrogation? This ain't the fucking SS.'

The reporter doesn't like the tone. He follows us, persisting. 'Bet you gave her the third degree, just like Violet Sharpe.'

Schiller wheels on him, shoving his open palm hard into the reporter's face, the great mass of his hand completely covering it from sight. 'Take a hike, you muckraking piece of shit.' The reporter staggers backwards and falls on his ass in a fountain. His peers applaud and jeer him, some taking photos as Schiller disappears inside. I start to follow, freezing when I get a glimpse of something reflected in a shard of broken glass. A face at the high window. Like a ghost surveying a ruined world. Old Man Bannister peers towards the horizon, a corrupt and brutal pharaoh contemplating the destruction he has wrought.

And as if in response to this painful epiphany, a keening wail fills the air, low and faraway, slowly rising in pitch. At first I think it is the Old Man, lamenting his sins; but it is coming up from the valley, looming towards us. Birds break from the trees in panic, escaping the arrival of troubled spirits. Other sorrowful voices join in the grieving howl, vibrating off the hills as they multiply and approach, the hair rising on the back of my neck. Schiller's heard it too, slowly turning towards the approaching sirens.

The first motorcycles enter the great gates, hovering around an armoured car like wasps.

This is what a cool million gets you: Head of State security.

The convoy pulls up, tires shrieking on gravel, sirens slowly retreating like departing spirits at a séance, cops dismounting, taking up positions. Inside the armoured car, a child's life is hanging in the balance.

Upstairs, the lawyer, Adam Granston, is standing on one side of the Old Man, Mrs. Bannister on the other. All three stare at the ivory-handled telephone as though it were a scorpion, its tail raised, ready to strike. A grandfather clock begins to chime, its musical rumble reverberating in the silence of the empty house. One, two. Three.

Nobody breathes.

Schiller looks at me.

The ring is like a gunshot fired without warning, everyone

reacting with the shock. The Old Man snatches the phone so quickly he drops it; curses . . . 'Hello?' There is an inhuman whine at the other end. 'Hello . . . ?'

Mrs. Bannister pulls the phone from his grasp and returns it to its cradle. He looks up at her, speechless at her temerity. 'They'll call back . . . '

The kidnappers will be either awful angry or awful scared to be hung up on. I'm banking on the second. You don't just blow off a million bucks if someone hangs up. You get back on the phone and give them another chance. You negotiate. The ransom goes up. Or down. You threaten. You reason. You cut them a break, or a body part. You do whatever it takes to get the goddamn loot.

Again everyone jumps when the phone rings again, but the shock has already been replaced by a sense of professional action. This time Schiller cues Sam to start rolling the tape and Mrs. Bannister answers the phone, calmly passing it to the shaking hands of her husband.

'Hello?'

'Listen carefully, I am only going to say this once . . . No police. We see any police and the kid is dead. Got it?'

'Yes.'

The lisping voice continues. 'Load the money into four large suitcases—black, all the same size.'

'The same size.'

'Put them in the back of the car, not the trunk.'

'Not the trunk . . . '

'Just the driver, understand?' He's not going anywhere near a fancy word like chauffeur. 'The driver goes to the corner of Jefferson and Lincoln. Four o'clock.'

'But that's only one hour.'

'The driver's not alone, the kid is dead.'

'He will be alone.'

'He better be. Tell the driver to wait at the gas station.'

'What does he do there?'

'He waits by the phone booth, and when the phone rings, he answers it. Got it?'

'And you will tell him what to do?'

'He will follow instructions or the kid is dead.'

'He will, he will.'

The voice is growing looser, more assured. He's going off script, happy with the fear he has created. Happy to have the power. 'We see any cops, we smell a setup and the kid is dead. Anything suspicious and the kid is dead, got that?'

'Yes.'

'Say it . . . '

The power has taken over. He can't let go. It doesn't make sense. He didn't know the Old Man was in a wheelchair, but one thing's for sure: he hates him. I look up at Sam. He's nodding, almost smiling. He knows what the kidnapper has forgotten—this call's way too long. They're getting their trace. Sam's hand scratches. Not here, please anywhere but here. The pencil stops its journey. I can tell from the way he is concentrating, it is a real address. He's trying to locate it. Opposite us, the call is still going on.

'Any police . . . '

'Any police.'

'And the kid is dead, say it.'

'Ronnie . . . dies.'

Disconnection buzzes through the room. Old Man Bannister gazes at the telephone the way Cleopatra must have gazed at the asp after its bite, then lets it drop with a mixture of disgust and regret, the ivory mouthpiece shattering on the floor. He heaves his chair towards me at a surprising pace, so fast that for a second I think he is trying to run me down. 'You will find these men and bring them to me.'

I exchange looks with Schiller, our minds alive to what would happen if I did.

'Promise me.'

'Mr. Bannister, you know I can't . . . '

The Old Man snatches my necktie and pulls me down towards him, his brute force surprising. 'You find these men and bring them to me and I'll tell you who killed your brother.'

He releases me, riding backwards across the room, like a lifeboat cut away from a sinking vessel. My head thumps with the dual destructive promises of revenge and hatred. Revenge for Tommy and hatred for the Old Man. Mrs. Bannister pushes him out of the room, her eyes seeking to communicate with me, imploring me not to listen to him. Schiller pulls me aside. 'Forget about Tommy,' he whispers. 'He's bluffing.'

I remember the look in the Old Man's eyes when he pulled me down towards him, his sickened breath fouling the air around us. You don't need to bluff when the cards are all marked and you're the only one who knows how to read them. I shove past Schiller and grab the piece of paper with the address. 'Alameda Street?'

'Chinatown.' He snatches the phone, already barking orders into the handset. 'Six squad cars, now!'

'Are you nuts? You heard what he said about cops.'

'That was for the drop-off at Jefferson and Lincoln.'

'You've got just under an hour to pack those suitcases and get the driver to the rendezvous.'

'Where are you going?'

'I'm going to stake out the phone booth, follow the pickup, nail the kidnappers, get the boy, and then find out who killed my brother.'

C amelot was Animal White House, a frat party on a grand scale, with JFK as amphetamine-fuelled house master, McNamara as the needy nerd, McGeorge Bundy as the nasty prick, and Rusk as the loveable Dean. Key Kennedy aides played the salivating frat brats, profiting from the mayhem whenever and wherever they could, especially when it came to the gals. This was the mid-century continental shift in the American political landscape. Tammany Hall was beer and bucks. Camelot was gear and fucks.

King Jack didn't need Viagra, his lifestyle was his own little blue pill. He didn't know that part of his problem came from quack doctors pumping him full of all-American, red-blooded testosterone. He didn't realize that his craving for salted peanuts and his suntanned good looks were connected to Addison's disease. Amphetamines, hydrocortisone, anabolic steroids and call girls. These were the treatments liberally doled out in the Mad Men days to America's youngest president, and paradoxically, one of its sickest. JFK cried out for a rehab clinic, but by the time Betty Ford came around, it was all too late.

The Secret Service was in on the act too. They all knew about JFK's shenanigans. They didn't care as long as King Jack maintained his Round Table policy; as long as they got their fair share of bare derrière.

Sex was JFK's snake oil. It was his pain's H-Bomb. The agents of the Secret Service didn't have the same excuse. The

Secret Service boys didn't suffer from bad backs; they didn't score daily jabs of speed, whizz and throttle; they didn't cramp up with chronic pain; their skin didn't glow orange like a lava lamp. They drove muscle cars, ate apple pie and used racist insults. And, according to Annette Martinez, they killed the president.

'Why did they stop the presidential limousine when fired upon?' she asks, freezing the video and pointing to the evidence: brake lights red as police sirens pulsing at the back of the limo. 'Why did they specifically act against operational procedure? When you're fired on, you flee. They ignored protocol.'

Annette Martinez has a point. I watch the film again on her home cinema setup. Her screen is so large, I have to move my seat backwards.

I had been prepared to lump Annette Martinez in the same basket as Dwayne Wayne and Miriam Marshall, but looking at the footage she's showing me, I have the feeling that I was wrong; very wrong.

The braking limousine is one of the great enigmas of the Kennedy Assassination, and one of the only existing examples of actual physical evidence that there may have been a conspiracy. Red means stop: even the Warren Commission must have known that. Ms. Martinez is right—why did they slam on the brakes instead of putting the pedal to the metal? The first answer that springs to mind is the most alarming: to allow an easier target. It's a lot harder hitting a head that's moving. Why didn't the conduct of the driver, William Greer, come up at the Warren Commission? Another easy answer: nothing came up at the Warren Commission; it was what went down that counted.

Greer is not the only person of interest in the presidential limousine. Sitting next to Greer in the front of the Lincoln, agent Roy Kellerman hunkers down in the passenger seat, showing a disconcerting lack of interest in events right behind him as bullets zing around the limo like crazed pinballs.

172 - TIM BAKER

We have been taught that the Secret Service is there to 'take the bullet' for the president, but Kellerman seems to be taking five, not a slug. It's as though his earpiece was tuned to the Mantovani Strings, not the Dead Kennedys. There is never any sense that he is about to leap out of his seat and sprawl across the president—to realize the Secret Service agent's ultimate fantasy and transmute into a human shield. From the president's limo, there was not even a duck, let alone a cover.

At least Greer managed a look over his shoulder, and it was that distracted glance, like a flustered cabbie turning to watch a sex act in the backseat, that gave birth to one of the most persistent of conspiracy rumours: that Greer himself fired the shot that killed JFK. As Greer turns in the Zapruder footage, he appears to be holding a pistol in his hand, pointing straight at the president. It fooled me when I first saw it. But after several reruns, the 'pistol' turns into the top of Kellerman's head as it catches the fast, metallic glint of Texas sunlight, then, after a couple more viewings, it turns back into a pistol. What is disconcerting about the illusion is that the appearance of a 'pistol' aimed at Kennedy coincides exactly with the lethal head shot. The timing is perfect. It's like the Spinning Dancer silhouette: changing backwards and forwards constantly. Gun, head. Head, gun. Gun, head, head, gun.

But the footage Ms. Martinez shows doesn't appear to be illusionary. Time and time again, in an endless loop of responsibility, Greer and Kellerman appear to do nothing. They sit still as crash-test dummies as they take the 90-degree turn from Main into Houston, and then the 70-degree turn into Dealey Plaza. The Killing Field.

There is the first shot . . .

The limousine's brake lights come on and the car slows almost to a complete standstill. Both Greer and Kellerman as well as Governor and Mrs. Connolly can be seen lurching forwards with the sudden halt. Then there is the kill shot. The explosion on the right side of the president's head, coming from the front of the president and to his right. The limo speeds away, but it's too late.

Forget the hospital, it was already time to visit the morgue. JFK is DOA.

The body was taken to the Dallas coroner's, which had jurisdiction. But the city's forensic examiner, Dr. Rose, was stopped from performing the autopsy. At gunpoint. The only time a weapon was drawn in Dallas, it was not to defend the president but to threaten a doctor trying to uphold the law. Dr. Rose had to make do with the autopsy of Lee Harvey Oswald, while the president's remains were effectively kidnapped and sent to Bethesda Naval Hospital for a nightmarish autopsy straight out of *The X-Files*.

Ms. Martinez shows me amateur film I've never seen before, shot in cheery Technicolor hues, an impossibly optimistic world that never actually existed. It is footage mainly of the crowd waiting with enthusiasm and excitement. A police officer forces a number of bystanders off the edge of the road and back onto the curb. The crowd complies with obvious regret. This was before the Vietnam War, in the days when one cop could still tell ten people what to do. The streets are wide; the motorcycle cops impressive as they herald the president's limo, SS-100-X zooming past the camera, which is on Jackie's side. Jackie looks radiant; Jack looks handsome. They are a young, dynamic couple: confident; easygoing yet dignified. If you saw them, you'd say they were in love.

'There.' Ms. Martinez's voice brings me out of my reverie.

She has frozen the footage. An agent is riding on the back of the president's limo, just moments before the shooting . . . 'Why did he drop back to the follow car just moments before the shooting? Answer me that, Mr. Alston.'

The use of my name cannot strip away the rhetorical nature of the question. No one can answer anything. Dallas is a perfect

174 · TIM BAKER

matrix of give and take, assertion and denial, truth and deception. Affirmation meets Rebuttal in an endless, senseless dance. Head, gun, gun, head. Dallas is the cradle of ambiguity and its homecoming queen is the Spinning Dancer.

I glance back one last time at the silver screen when a notion hits me with the force of a Magic Bullet.

What if the driver, Greer, realized that shots were being fired from in front of the vehicle? From the Grassy Knoll. Wouldn't the normal physical reaction—as opposed to the trained Secret Service response—be to slam on the brakes? Isn't that what we'd all do at night, driving on a rain-slick road in the countryside when a child suddenly appears, staring into the headlights with a ball in his hands? We're supposed to decelerate slowly and gear down. But instead we slam on the brakes, and the tires lock, and the sweet hush of rubber on wet macadam gives way to the screech of lost control as we careen towards the very object we are trying most to avoid.

Greer hit the brakes the way we would all hit the brakes: because his gut told him to. The brain is always left behind in the panic rush of adrenaline. Bullets were coming Greer's way from the Grassy Knoll and he blanked out—he just couldn't remember what else to do except stop and wait for the cops.

Ms. Martinez believes the evidence of the archive films points to a conspiracy. But what if the conspiracy didn't involve the Secret Service? What if the film proves there were other shooters on the Grassy Knoll?

'It's such a crying shame,' Ms. Martinez says.

Shame is right. The Assassination and its aftermath is a well of tears. It is the fatal junction. When citizens stopped believing in their government and gave up on notions of social cohesion. When words like 'Belief' and 'Faith' broke off from the continental shelf of Solemnity and began to drift into the Sea of Irony. When 'I have a dream' turned into 'We have a nightmare.' Vietnam and Watergate, Martin Luther King and RFK.

AIDS. Famine. Global Warming. Globalization and the Not So Free Market. A half-century-long rampage for wealth, and it all went one way. Less *Trickle Down*, more *To Have and Have Not*. The rich got super richer. And the poor got fired and evicted.

Would it have been any different if JFK had not been killed?

Almost certainly, no.

Yet people need to believe in the possibility of Change; of Parallel Universes.

Maybe that's the biggest Conspiracy Theory of them all: that one man can actually change the State of Things.

'A crying shame . . . ' Ms. Martinez repeats, actually wiping away a tear as she guides me to the front door.

I find myself nodding in dutiful sympathy, like an usher at a funeral home. At least Ms. Martinez has closure. She's skipped to the last page of her whodunit and found the killer. Case closed. She is not haunted by car horns like Adam Granston. She's not selling information for a bourbon and Coke like Tex Jeetton, or chasing a million bucks for a photo like Dwayne Wayne. She has been spared Alien Abduction. She has her assassination movies to watch on her home cinema system. She doesn't like their endings, but at least the narrative makes sense.

To her.

But what about the rest of us? The ones who can't make sense of our own times and our own lives, let alone something that happened half a century ago. Everyone carries a Dallas inside them. A milestone event rich with alternative endings. I know what mine is: the Bannister case. The destruction of my father and the belief that he was innocent. But there is something else there that is stronger than regret or remorse; something that puts me in the same category as my witnesses. It is the conviction that one day I will uncover the truth. Not that I will ever solve the mysteries of the murders of Jack and Bobby, but I will discover what really happened to Ronnie Bannister.

BOOK TWO
The Big Deceit

CHAPTER 28
Los Angeles 1960

I pull the curtain back just far enough to see out.

Old Man Bannister's driver, Taylor, parks the car just past the gas station. He looks so vivid and vulnerable through the unforgiving snare of the binoculars that I can hear the slam of the car door in my mind as he gets out, sweat stains shining through the livery of his chauffeur's uniform.

Taylor walks back towards the gas pumps, shaking his head at an attendant who comes out, heading over to the telephone booth standing just beyond the john . . . Leaving a million in cash unattended inside the goddamn car. I can even see the sparkle of the keys he's left in the ignition, dangling beside the wheel.

I replay the call in my head. Was this the plan? Didn't they tell the chauffeur to drive up to the telephone, or was that just something I assumed?

This is the problem with ransoms—too many instructions, too many people looking over their backs, too many tails to lose. With all the second-guessing, the whole damn thing becomes so complicated that people get confused.

Honest mistakes are made.

And innocent children are slain.

Or maybe the driver got it right. Maybe Taylor was doing exactly what he was supposed to. Maybe they were planning a simple snatch and run right there, out in the false open—a terrain that was actually cluttered with obstacles, hiding places and getaways. Maybe the attendant was one of them.

Or were the kidnappers watching anxiously right now, as nervous and surprised as me, cursing the driver, urging him to go back and wait inside the car. Protect the cash from a potential thief who could end up driving away with more than he bargained for.

The fleabag hotel I had found for the stakeout was perfect cover and profiled a clear view of the terrain even without the binoculars. So perfect in fact that I took the time to check the rooms in case the kidnappers were set up here as well. But all I found was an exhausted, middle-aged couple sleeping it off and a young, newly-arrived Okie already on his second pint of rye. There had been no suspicious cars out in the parking lot at the back, but I overfilled the oil in all of them anyway. You just never know.

I survey the streets one last time then go back to the gas station. It's all clear on my side. But my side is only part of the picture and as far as I know, what is going on down there is being shot in VistaVision. I check the time. Ten minutes and counting . . .

The driver looks up suddenly, as though someone is pointing a gun at him and then he grabs the door of the phone booth, yanking instead of pushing, the whole booth shaking with the force of his frustration. With his fear.

An auto mechanic comes out of the service garage, wiping his hands on a rag, and calls out, annoyance on his face. Message received. Taylor shoves the door so hard, he staggers in, and I see him grimace as he hits his ribs against the phone shelf. It would be crassly comic if a child's life wasn't at stake.

Taylor answers the phone. Why are they calling early? I sweep the field of play. Nothing.

An oil tank truck slows to turn into the gas station, obscuring the phone box and the car. I watch it belch black fumes into the air. Smoke signals. Communication from the old days. Did the kidnappers know there was going to be a delivery? The whole truck shudders as it waits for the traffic to pass, the first impatient horns already serenading it with LA's highway melody.

Finally the traffic thins but the tanker just sits there, black clouds of exhaust coughing blindness across the road, choruses of angry horns protesting its stubborn immobility. A green Oldsmobile 98 sedan streaks out, overtaking through the oily fumes, the driver's voice loud and foul, then lost in the screech of brakes as oncoming traffic nearly collides with him.

I pull the cabin of the truck into hard, clear focus. The windshield is camouflaged with grime and dust, and a thousand splattered insects. Almost impossible to see out of. And impossible to see into.

Drivers get out of their cars, exchanging outraged comments as they begin to converge on the truck with all the seething determination of a lynch mob marching towards the county jail.

I focus again on the tank truck's windshield. A passing Dodge pickup shafts reflected sunlight into the cabin. Just for a second, but enough to confirm my suspicions. The cabin's empty. The driver has gone.

I burst out of the room, tripping on the trash cans that have been deliberately stacked there. An almighty crash as I skip and tumble across tin. Asphalt meets the flesh of my palms. Asphalt wins. The realization stings up from my hands to my too-slow brain.

Setup.

They knew I was there.

I kick in the Okie's door, my piece in my bleeding hand. My curse fills the empty room.

Even before I reach my car, I know something's wrong. It sits, queasy and lopsided, like a punch-drunk fighter who can't get off his stool for the last round. It's nursing two flat tires. I rush onto the street and start trying cars. The second one's unlocked. A Chevy Nomad. I tear out the ignition plug, and hot-wire it fast. There's a shout behind me as I pull away from the curb and then I'm speeding towards the gas station, a taxi skidding and swerving as I cut so close in front of it I can smell the fare's perfume. I hit the hand brake, swinging me round the front of the tanker and into the garage. One empty telephone booth. One chauffeur on his back, moaning. Beyond Taylor, on the other side of the station, the limo squats guiltily, its doors still hanging open in total surrender. Empty.

The ransom is gone.

The abandoned tank truck sits in the afternoon sun, like a time bomb about to explode; angry horns still protesting. An attendant climbs into the cabin, then falls back in shock, landing on his heels and turning. 'There's a man in there . . . ' he shouts, pushing past me. 'Tied up!'

I look at my watch. Five minutes before the designated pickup. Has this been a hijack or a diversion? Decision time. See what I can get out of the driver or try to give chase. But to what . . . ? I scan the surrounding landscape. Nothing but cars. Cars everywhere. Speeding, crawling, slowing; overtaking. Snarling. A typical street scene in LA. Inhuman. Mechanized. Brutalized by vehicles.

I don't need Schiller or anyone else to tell me the awful truth: I have fucked up.

Again.

And then I spot it: a beat-up Mercury Eight, puffing smoke like Casey Jones as it burns off the excess oil. It's making a clean break, heading towards the coast. Tires squeal as I pull out into the traffic, someone shouting an insult as I cut in front of him, and accelerate, driving against the flow of cars. Wails of terror. Crisscrossed messages. Hateful klaxons trying to hammer me into unconsciousness.

There is a skid, then the sorrowful double thump of collision. Not me. Hubcaps soar past like flying saucers.

I peel off down a driveway, straight through a wire fence. The car shivers and shudders, crumpling mesh and metal, and then I'm bumping my way across a paddock, towards the road the Mercury has taken. The paddock goes green with lettuce, the wheels sluicing up salad behind them. There is a close detonation, and the side mirror explodes in comets of crystal. Through the rearview mirror I see the old man waving his fist at me, the shotgun in his other hand, angry dogs giving chase. I accelerate, slapping down another wire fence, concrete protesting against the undercarriage with a metallic rasp.

I hump off the curb, the wheel resisting like a tiller against a king tide as I yank and heave it into me, spinning the vehicle onto the street. Although I can no longer actually see the Mercury, I can still follow the chug of its chimney exhaust, leaving a trail of smoke above the crown of trees.

I lurch up onto a curb, sparks turning the muffler into a Roman candle, taking a shortcut back behind a schoolyard, then shuddering back onto the silent hush of bitumen, kids pointing and running after me. I hear their taunt. Bank robber. Bank robber.

I turn at the next corner, slowing right down, scanning the branches beyond for any sign of my lead. I can't have lost the car. It would be unforgiveable. What about the kid? What about the money? And what about Old Man Bannister? I wouldn't last very long.

I check the cross streets.

Empty. Then I see it, abandoned in the driveway of a boarded-up warehouse. I pull up in the shade of a sycamore a block away and watch. Nothing moves on the street except for a wasp tapping a forlorn Morse code on the pane as it tries to B&E the car. Once, when I was still courting Cate, we got invited to a big house out at Rancho Los Feliz—friends of her folks; although you wouldn't have known it. She said it was because their family was from Calabria and hers were from Piedmont: reverse prejudice, made possible courtesy of the American Dream. They had cleaned up in New Jersey thanks to a chain of Buick dealerships and had moved to California for the sunshine and the movie stars. It was a barbecue—one of those affairs where husband and wife keep bickering about the marinade and who had burnt the spare ribs and forgot the ice—and if that wasn't bad enough, all the way through we were plagued by wasps. Tommy showed up late—he'd been on patrol—and saw us all slapping at the bugs. He shook his head, went into the kitchen and came back with two beer growlers half-filled with Coca-Cola. 'What, you're on the wagon now?'

'Are you kidding? This is for the goddamn wasps . . . ' He set them down on a step nearby. Within thirty seconds the wasps were gone.

It was just before sunset when Cate glanced over at the step and screamed. We all got up to see. Even Tommy couldn't believe his eyes. Inside the two jugs were thousands of dead wasps. So many that the coke was lapping out of the lips of the bottles. It was as if there was just a faint smear of liquid on top of two bottles full of drowned and drowning insects, stinging each other as they crawled downwards, further and further away from the only route of escape. Tommy stared at it for a long moment, and then broke into a savage, satisfied laugh. 'Look at those greedy little suckers!' Cate slapped him. Later she said she didn't know why. She started to cry. I had to take her home. I heard Tommy making some crack to the others about how Cate was always like that when she drank. Only she hadn't touched a drop all day. That was the last time she ever saw Tommy alive. I knew she never liked Tommy. But at the funeral she wept. She told me it was because of the wasps.

I lean over and flick the glass on the other side of the wasp and the bug takes off. I glance around at the street's windows, looking for prying eyes. Shifting curtains. For the glint of a gun barrel aimed my way.

Then I catch it, red and white and moving too fast, a Ford '58 Fairlane Skyliner pulling out behind the warehouse, turning onto Hudson. It's already three blocks ahead of me. I hold back, on the cusp of nearly losing it. The car looks too flashy to be theirs but it's the only thing that's moving, and if I was one of the kidnappers, that's what I'd be doing.

I follow gently, just catching them as they take a right onto a back lane. I continue straight on. It's them all right, doing the circuit, making sure they're not being tailed. I pull over and reach into the glove compartment for the street map before remembering: it's a stolen car. And I'm officially a thief. I take my chances and figure I can grid them. North by northwest, that's the only way they can go for now.

I cruise slowly, sticking to the main roads, and when I'm convinced that they've lost me, I nearly hit them as they're coming onto Main. I brake so hard, I hammer my knees against the dash, the steering wheel cracking across my sternum. I swear, making eye contact with the driver. He stares after me with dark, hollow eyes, then flips me the bird. I gaze after the car. He turns to the man in the passenger seat, telling him what he's just done. There is a flash of a smile on the passenger's face. Then they're lost to the blur of distance. I give them four cars between us before I follow.

The face. I knew it. Memories of lowlife hideouts drift sadly by, a down-and-out litany of post-hope environments, like Tommy's growlers, teeming with cruelty, their doomed inhabitants stinging each other to death as they swarm and surge and push ever further down into the drowning darkness. No wonder Cate wept.

I force myself to continue the search as I follow the Skyliner. It was the eyes I remembered. Eyes I should never risk forgetting. The eyes of a killer. The way they stared into me before the driver softened their hatred with a juvenile gesture, seeing me for who he thought I was: just another dumb moving target.

Then it hits me. He was in a uniform when I saw him. I am positive. But which uniform? I nearly have it when they take a left, onto Hawthorn Parade. Now I know I'm in trouble. The traffic would peter out at the Southern Pacific railroad junction and they'd spot a tail. But for the second time I get lucky. The Ford pulls into a driveway, number 669. I cruise past, watching them in the rearview mirror as they walk towards the front door, two men struggling with suitcases, looking nervously around . . .

I pull over, trying to figure it out.

We weren't fifteen miles from the Bannister Estate. Could they have been holding the Bannister kid all this time right under the City's nose?

I get out and look around. A curtain across the road falls back into place. Nosy neighbours? Or accomplices to kidnapping? No time to check now, I have to follow the two men.

I make it across the lawn of 669 without being seen, and duck under some bushes. They are in bloom, the perfume odd and pungent; sweet yet strangely disturbing—almost putrid. There's a window just above my head and people are on the other side, talking. I can't make out the words through the glass, but I can hear the tone. One million bucks has just entered the equation. This morning they were just a couple of petty criminals, and now they're tycoons. No one's going to take that sea change away from them. Not the police, not the mark, not the snatch . . . And certainly not their partner in crime.

This is always the last dance. When the money's on the table, the knives come out. Friends are no longer trusted. Cohorts become traitors. And blood brothers turn out to be shameless strangers. Petty quarrels give way to avarice; anger to murder. Spoils are contested; lives ended quickly. Fast, close and dirty. Point-blank; until there's only one man left standing, with a suitcase in either hand.

I risk a quick look and catch sight of the driver walking into another room. I try the window. It opens like a breeze.

The house is stuffy, as though it hasn't been aired for

months. There's food rotting on the floor alongside the dust, and a strong stench of booze and ammonia. Of death . . . or is it just the scent of those flowers outside?

The voices are strangely clear now. There are three of them, arguing, from the back of the house, probably the kitchen. I case the surroundings quickly. There's a staircase.

I take the stairs, three at a time, the floorboards creaking gently underfoot, and come to a gloomy landing, the windows pasted over with newspapers. That's a bad sign. So is the foul smell as I go down the hallway to the door at the end. I hesitate, pressing my ear against the wood.

Silence. And then a sound emerges, like the faraway, droning hum of a distant freight train slowly approaching.

I gently turn the door handle.

The lock sighs open with a lisped click. I draw my piece, then yank the door open and enter low, ready to shoot.

Something leaps up at me as I hit the room—black, whirring; full of menace, the flies all about me. The air is alive with them. I quickly shut the door behind me, enclosing myself in the stench of that quivering room. It's like the meat markets in Manila just after the war, when you never knew exactly what it was dangling from those butcher hooks, trailing blood away from the pulse of insects.

The smell rears hard at me as I approach the Murphy bed in the centre of the room, flashing me back to Manila, then back further to Iwo Jima itself.

I retch in the corner, then turn back to what is left of the kid, the screams of the war slowly leaving me, the smell of cordite shifting back towards the all-too-familiar horror of rotten flesh.

The body appears then disappears, appears then disappears under the tide of flies.

Through their hovering shadow, I can see the kid has been mutilated the way the bodies of abducted boys always are. I brush at the swarm, peering into their dark, dread territory.

The poor, poor kid; the bastards downstairs had really gone to town on him. I touch his arm, pulling away in shock.

It's impossible.

This was no ordinary kidnapping, if there was such a thing. This was something else entirely. Whoever did this to the kid had gotten what they wanted. At least a week ago. Because that's about when this child died.

The flies drummed their way into my brain. So either Ronnie was kidnapped earlier, and no one even noticed. Or else Ronnie's kidnapping was covered up for days . . . But why?

Maybe it was simply because no one had the guts to tell Old Man Bannister. So they kept him in the dark. Old Man Bannister saw the kid so infrequently, he didn't even notice when he was absent. So much for his love.

I leave the room, the flies throbbing against the door as I close it on a nightmare I had never quite expected. The kid was dead. Maybe, when I was back on the Force, if I had been a little bit smarter, a little bit sharper, I might have caught the people who did it; might have put them behind bars so that five years later they'd have still been locked up; and the kid would still be alive and laughing, and playing with toy trucks.

There is no mercy, but by God, there would be reckoning.

I make it back down the landing, my legs nearly giving out twice. I pause at the top of the stairs, my weapon still in my hand, and when the wave of nausea and regret finally passes, when I have recovered enough to know I'm not going to pass out, I go quietly down the stairs and across the room, the two extra clips and my brass knuckles knocking against my leg. I can only hear two voices coming from the kitchen. That could mean that one of them had already gotten away. Or that one of them had already been snuffed.

None of that mattered anymore.

All restraints were lifted.

The kidnapping of the decade was about to go large.

T he story was on every radio station, every newspaper banner, on every TV. It was Little Lindy all over again. A rich, famous and arrogant father punished for his sins with the loss of his son.

It wasn't just Tabloid. It was Biblical.

It was too bad about Hidalgo, Hastings hadn't meant for him to get hurt. He had figured that the safest place for Hidalgo would have been down at the station. He'd never figured on Hidalgo doing a runner.

Just once, he wanted to help someone without it blowing up in everybody's face. He wanted to get it right, for Betty; to lose the jinx for her. He needed her more than ever.

And the thing was, now she needed him.

Hastings had found out Hidalgo was working for the Feds about three weeks earlier, when he spotted him snooping around Betty's Caddy in the garage. He grabbed Hidalgo by the scruff of the neck, the kid's hand already in her Kelly bag. Hastings had shoved him against the wall, Hidalgo thumping against the tool brace. A screwdriver fell from its cradle, stabbing into the workbench. Hidalgo snatched it and struck out at his face, Hastings pulling back just in time. The lunge surprised him. He never knew Hidalgo had it in him. He was going for his eye. If he had made contact, he would have blinded him, and then Hidalgo would have had no choice but to double down and go for his jugular. Who would have thought?

Hidalgo was just like him—he had the instincts of a killer.

Hastings grabbed him by the wrist, turning and bending it backwards, snaring him with the physics of the human body, the logic of humerus and scapula. Down and around, he continued the sweeping action, rolling him onto his knees, his arm fully rotated and reversed, flexed at an acute angle against the weight of his chest. He grabbed Hidalgo's thumb in one hand, bent the wrist with the other.

'First, I'm going to snap your thumb. Then your wrist. Then I'm going to dislocate your shoulder . . . ' He leant his weight against the arm, driving it forwards, towards his head. Hidalgo groaned in agony. 'Then I'm going to pop your arm from your body. And then I'm going to start on your legs. You got ten seconds to avoid becoming a freak on Nightmare Alley. Talk, kid . . . '

'I don't know nothing . . . ' Hidalgo let out a scream. 'Okay, stop.'

Hastings pulled back, taking the pressure off the arm. 'Who told you to snoop around Mrs. Bannister?'

'A Fed.'

Hastings was so surprised, he let go of the kid. Hidalgo retrieved his arm, cradling it against his chest like a lost puppy that's just been found. 'What does the FBI want with Mrs. Bannister?'

Hidalgo looked up at him, fear and pain in his eyes and something else besides. A lie forming fast. Hastings kicked him in the ribs. 'The truth.'

'This Fed set up my boyfriend. He was going to do us for lewd and lascivious unless we . . . co-operated.'

'What Fed?'

'His name's Rico. From Boston. A real piece of work.'

'What's he doing in LA?'

'Spying. On everyone. Every-fucking-one! Businessmen, teachers, writers, rocket scientists. But most of all movie stars.

They're listening in on everyone. Nobody's safe. Not even the biggest stars. So someone like Sal . . . '

'Sal who?'

'Sal Mineo. The actor.' For the first time, the fear in Hidalgo's eyes was gone, replaced by incredulity as he gazed into Hastings's unregistering face. *'Rebel Without a Cause.* Plato.'

Hastings shook his head.

Hidalgo's lips curled in disdain. 'He's famous . . . '

'So what's the racket?'

'Blackmail. How do you think they got Jerome Robbins and Robert Taylor to testify against the Reds? By appealing to their civic duty? Crap! By threatening to expose them—not for being commies, for being gay.' Hidalgo got up off the floor, still cradling his arm. 'It's an easy choice when it's the only one you've got: lose your job and go to jail—or talk a little.'

'What do they want to find out about Mrs. Bannister?'

'Everything . . . '

Including him? 'What have you told them . . . ?'

Hidalgo looked away.

Everything. 'I don't care who you spy on—leave Mrs. Bannister, and me, out of it.'

'Easy for you to say, I—'

Hastings tapped him on the chin. 'Got it?'

Hidalgo rubbed his jaw, anger in his eyes.

And that was the last thing Hastings saw when he spoke to the private dick outside the bus . . . The anger in Hidalgo's eyes.

Hastings needed to find this actor, Sal Mineo. He needed to find out what the Feds wanted with Mrs. Bannister. Most of all, Hastings needed to know what they had on him.

He got himself a glass of water and checked the back room. All was quiet. The water had a metallic aftertaste, like the pungent flint of oysters. The stench of the hawthorns outside hadn't only permeated the air, it had contaminated the water. The aroma was elemental and alarming, with its bitter traces of formaldehyde, almonds and death. The entire street was in bloom, but instead of festive springtime it felt more like All Hallows. Oppressive and rotten. He was getting cabin fever.

He turned on the radio, keeping the volume low, listening to the news. The hysteria had built to overwhelming proportions. Everyone could sense it: the decade not six months old, and already this was the crime that would define the Sixties. An evil old man; a wicked young wife; an innocent child. A lethal cocktail of guilt and retribution, served up to the smug Everyman. The Big Fall before The Big Sleep.

He changed stations.

Miles Davis. *Elevator to the Gallows*. Hastings sat in the shade in the back of the room and lost himself in the horn. Foolishly, he started dreaming. He and Betty Bannister, walking hand in hand along a boulevard in the Latin Quarter. It was twilight. Hot as hell. They stop under a chestnut tree by the river. The leaves rustle above them; a benediction from the Gods. He leans in to kiss her: his woman, his lover; his lady in Paris . . .

The lady vanishes like the music.

A newsflash. Hastings woke with a start, leaping to his feet. Please stand by, the voice said, they were going live to the Bannister Estate. Captain Schiller's voice rumbled official confirmation that the boy's nanny, Greta Simmons, was dead.

Hastings didn't switch off the radio, he yanked it out of the wall and battered it senseless against the table. He assassinated it.

Even without the details, he knew her death could be traced back to him. This had always been his curse: to be doomed to hurt every single person he had ever tried to help . . .

He froze. There was movement on the street. The room whined with extended silence. A shadow shimmered across the drawn curtains as a car slowed outside . . .

Hastings went to the window and lifted the edge of the curtain before pulling back in shock. That private dick, Alston, had just pulled up in a Chevy Nomad on the other side of the street. Impossible. No one knew about the hideout on Hawthorn Parade.

No one except Mrs. Bannister.

Hastings got his gun, secured the silencer, and went back to the window, again drawing the curtain slowly. Alston was alone. He was crossing the lawn of one of the houses opposite. Hastings remembered what Greta had told him. Half the joints on this block were owned by Roselli. It could be that Alston was after someone else.

He watched Alston as he climbed through the window of the house.

The low buzzing drilled its way through his skull. Balancing him. There was no time to mourn Greta. He had to act now. He unlatched the back door, sunlight slapping him with the promise of pain.

Hastings swung the garage door open. Greta must have known they'd force her to talk in the end. She was protecting someone. Not him. Not Betty Bannister. Certainly not the kid. It had to be Elaine.

Their cover was as good as blown. He and Betty weren't just running out of places to hide. They were running out of time.

CHAPTER 30
Dallas 2014

C onspiracy was back in fashion.
    All it had taken was one whistle-blower from the NSA.
    That's when I had come up with my idea of developing
a list of expert witnesses—personalities who represented all
the major conspiracy theories of the assassinations. Some, like
Adam Granston and Tex Jeetton, were among the usual suspects, already well known to JFK conspiracy buffs. Others, like
Annette Martinez and Dwayne Wayne, had made their presence felt in recent years, pushing their opinions—and their
personalities—via aggressive forum contributions on every site
from *JFK Lancer* and *The JFK Assassination Debate* to *The
National Enquirer*. Evelyn and Miriam Marshall were local personalities I'd discovered by focusing on small Dallas community sites. But the gemstone jewel in the crown of all the witnesses is Leopold Steiner, former Stanford Law Professor and
renowned criminal appellate attorney who had given up both
careers to concentrate on the JFK Assassination.

Leopold Steiner lives in a comfortable loft in West Village,
Uptown Dallas and welcomes me with a wry smile and warily
cocked head. 'The journalist . . . ?'

No, the trapeze artist. Steiner vigorously shakes my hand,
checking behind my back before closing and bolting the door.
His head tilts all the way to the other side of the spectrum.
'Funny . . . '

I can tell it's not 'ha-ha'.

'You're not by any chance related to . . . '

'Nick Alston? He was my father.'

Steiner gestures to a glass conference table heavy with documents and photos stacked with organisational purity. The only non-business touches are a blue dahlia growing in a hand-painted pot, a tray of kumquats, and two glasses of water with crushed ice and slices of lime—all suggestive of an austere flair for healthy, minimalist living. He nods proudly at the display. 'The national plant of Mexico . . . '

'The kumquat?'

'The dahlia. I made the pot myself.'

'Nice . . . ' I suppose. It's definitely not bad.

'It's something I've taken up since moving out here. The adobe tradition . . . ' He offers the kumquats to me as though they were a platter of chocolates. 'Help yourself.'

I take a bite of one, zesting the air with the faint perfume of orange. 'What's so funny about my father?'

Leopold Steiner raises his eyebrows in unsurprised consideration. He has a likeable face; suntanned and remarkably smooth for a man who must be hitting seventy, with a band of closely-cropped silver hair around the sides and a tousled shock of yellow white on top. 'I knew Betty Bannister. Back in the old days. It was right after I came out. Believe it or not, I used to be a regular at Studio 54. That's where we first met. I'll tell you one thing, sport, she was the most beautiful woman I've ever seen. Even more beautiful than Bianca . . . Nice watch.' He reaches over and takes my wrist, helping himself to a good look. He stares up at me. 'As far as I'm concerned, it's still the greatest unsolved case in history . . . '

'JFK?'

'The Zodiac killings. Given the amount of forensic evidence available, it's baffling the case was never solved. Like Elizabeth Short. What does that tell you?' I pause for a second, actually weighing a reply but he's already answering for me. 'Investigative and procedural incompetence is often a sign of conspiracy. A smokescreen for the masses.' He pops a kumquat, speaking through the happy, golden rind. 'Higher Powers.'

'Just like the JFK Assassination?'

'You've got it, sport . . . '

'Speaking of which, I believe you've assembled a list of suspects?'

'It's so much more than that . . . ' He slides a sheaf of papers towards me, our faces reflected on the glass table as we both stare at it. 'I've put together the most comprehensive list of persons of interest ever assembled. People we know were in Dallas, either on the eve or the day of the assassination. I call them the Dallas Fifty.'

He hands me the typewritten document. I glance at the first names: LBJ, Nixon, Bush, then flick through the other pages, catching sight of familiar and not so familiar players and suspects. I'm already having doubts. Just because he's a brilliant lawyer doesn't mean he's right. In fact, the more brilliant you are, the more convinced you become, and that's precisely when you're most likely to be wrong. Certainty always leads to blindness. Look at the hundreds of amateur sleuths on Reddit who went after the Boston Bombers, certain of their conclusions. And yet not one of them got it right.

I glance up at Steiner. He taps the top of the first sheet of paper. 'The first three names. What do they tell you?'

Ever since I was a kid, I hated being put on the spot.

Leopold Steiner sighs at my hesitation. 'It never fails to amaze me . . . '

The spacious loft suddenly feels uncomfortably small. 'What?'

'The inability of people to see things that are staring them right in the face. All in Dallas that day. All vice presidents who became presidents. Inside the White House from 1952 until 1992 almost without interruption. Thirty-four years at the epicentre of power, just the three of them. And when Nixon is actually forced to resign, who replaces him as President? Gerald Ford, a member of the Warren Commission. Don't you get it? Dallas shaped the United States for two generations.' He pops a kumquat fast into his mouth as though it were medication for a cardiac crisis, his shoulders slumping in sadness. 'How many generations do you suppose it'll take to change it back . . . ?'

Interesting take. And poetically prescient. After all, the city of Dallas was named after a vice president. 'So what you're saying is that the Kennedy Assassination was a coup d'état, launched by a triumvirate of vice presidents?'

Leopold Steiner explodes with a roar of frustration. 'Nothing is ever that simple. That's your problem—you seem to think it is. I've read your pieces about Kennedy. Your obsession with his affairs. Look beyond the intercourse, sport.'

'What else was there? His political achievements weren't all that substantial.'

'Of course they weren't—because they shot him. What president could bring about meaningful change in less than three years? Not even FDR. But the intent was there. He was going to drop LBJ, bring the troops back from Vietnam. Break the Mafia. Break the Fed. Break the Military Industrial Complex. End Segregation. End Big Oil's tax concessions. Fire Hoover. That's why those sons of bitches nailed him: they actually thought he could do it.' He taps the list of suspects. 'Like some of the people here. They thought they were so smart, they could get away with murder.'

They must be really smart, because they did. The doorbell rings.

Steiner glances across the room nervously. The bell rings again. He smiles. 'The postman always rings twice. I asked him to. In Dallas you can never be too careful . . . '

On that paranoid note, he grabs a fistful of kumquats and heads to the door, pointing to the papers on the way. 'That list is for you. There may be some suspects even you haven't heard of.'

Steiner has numbered each name. I glance at the last page. At the bottom is suspect number 49: Eugene Hale Brading, aka Jim Braden. An associate of Johnny Roselli and Jack Ruby. It says he was detained attempting to leave the Dal-Tex Building immediately after the assassination. I can't believe what I read next. It says Brading was also detained by LA police the night of the assassination of Bobby Kennedy. If true, it is the first evidence I've come across linking one suspect to both crime scenes. I could lead with this revelation in part two of my book, dealing with Bobby's murder.

I turn the page over. Nothing. 'I'm missing the last page . . . ' No answer. The list is audacious not just because of who he includes but who he leaves out. And the biographical notes are thorough. Two of the witnesses I've already interviewed are included: Tex Jeetton and Adam Granston. One degree of separation between JFK and myself. The closest I've ever been. I search the table for the final page. There is a single last kumquat lying on its tray. He won't miss it.

I look at my watch. Zodiac time should include the sign for each month. Something Evelyn no doubt would appreciate. I had promised to be at her place before sunset. She said she had a surprise for me. Where the hell is Steiner? I pick up the list and walk down the hallway, stopping at the front door. It's wide open. No Steiner, no postman.

'Hello . . . ?' There's another apartment opposite. I ring the bell. Footsteps, and the woof of a little dog. A middle-aged woman answers the door, a Silky Terrier darting out, sniffing my heels suspiciously. 'Is Leopold Steiner there by any chance?' She points to the open door opposite, then slams her own, almost locking the dog out. I call Steiner's number. It goes straight to voicemail.

I take the stairs down to the lobby. There's no sign of a super. There's no sign of anyone. I send Steiner a message saying I couldn't wait.

It's only when I'm leaving that I see them, scattered across the lobby floor. A fistful of bright orange kumquats against the black marble. I pick one up. There are teeth marks around the middle, as though Steiner had just been biting into it when . . .

Schiller stands over the two men, shaking his head. 'No wonder they kicked you off the Force.'

'Can I help it if they resisted arrest?' I look down at the pair, their hands handcuffed behind their backs, their faces lacerated, bones shattered, tendons snapped, muscles displaced. 'The rats had it coming to them.'

'You think I don't know that? But I need them to talk. What good are suspects who can't open their mouths? Hell, from the look of them, they don't even have any mouths left.'

I prod one of them in the ribs with the toe of my shoe. There is the hint of a groan. 'Give them a couple of hours . . . They'll talk.'

Schiller looks around, his voice dropping—an almost impossible feat for a man with forge bellows for lungs. 'The Old Man wants to see you.'

I figured he would. What will he do when I tell him? That the kid is dead, the money is gone and one of the suspects too.

'Police Chief Parker too.'

'Fuck Parker, he's not my boss.'

Schiller pumps my sternum as though he's trying to find the off button. 'He's worse: he's judge, jury and fucking executioner. You better show a little respect, or else Parker's going to learn it to you.'

'Teach.'

'You get the drift. Whatever it takes to understand the lines you don't want to cross.'

'Thanks for your concern.'

'Fuck you. Your career's destroyed, and you've got no one to blame but yourself. So shut the fuck up and do your job. This one that got away. You say you know him?'

'I'd bet my life.'

'Which ain't worth much right now. That means he would have recognized you . . . '

'It doesn't always work that way.' I was trained to retain the atlas trace of cheekbones and hairlines, scars and tics, broken noses and the rainbow glint of gold teeth. To read expressions. Memorize cars. Interpret routine. Understand habitat. Gauge getaway routes. Punish alibis. Lie detect. It was a constant, shifting puzzle of pattern recognition and intuition. It takes time. It's harder than you'd think. People are lazy; particularly criminals. It's just too much effort to be perpetually alert. To sleep with your eyes open. There are two and a half million people in this city and I had recognized one of them. Out of the literally tens of thousands of faces that had passed me by, I recalled this one. The sneer. The sunken eyes, tar-pit black. He got as clear a view of me as I had of him, but he didn't clock me. He saw a victim he could insult with a gesture of his hand and a sidelong sneer. A forgettable encounter. That would be his downfall. He was a water. He gave me too much to work on and didn't take anything back in return. Sooner or later I would remember. Then I would nail the bastard. And I would correct his arrogant indifference.

An ambulance man stumbles coming down the stairs, nearly falling, the wheels of the trolley he's guiding clattering out of control for a nerve-splitting instant. 'Christ, be careful,' roars Schiller, then crosses himself. 'What they did to that poor kid . . . '

'If there's a God up there, it happened after the kid was dead.'

'And if it didn't?'

'Then there's no God up there.'

This case was very dangerous for a man like Schiller. I saw what the discovery of Elaine Bannister did to him; her tear from the grave rattled him as much as Christ's nail holes shook up Thomas. What did Greta Simmons's suicide do to his belief system? Such a traumatic event can only ever do one of two things. Strengthen it. Or shatter it.

And now the body of the boy being carried outside was putting him on the brink. Schiller had paid his dues as a member of the Hat Squad. He was an old-school cop: easy choices, hard fists. But even he wasn't strong enough to endure one onslaught after another. Then again, as we were all going to learn, neither was the nation. Nothing would ever be the same. Not after this.

We watch them wheel the corpse onto the street, see the lurching shadows cast by the flashbulbs outside, the press moving in close, consuming the carcass, so that the ambulance attendants have to jostle their way forward; jackal snarls and hyena growls venting the air, everyone feasting on the crime, tearing at the carrion that was once a little boy, the ambulance attendants trying to force open the doors against the clawing crush for the . . . 'Jesus H. Christ!'

Schiller looks at me as though I were a snake suddenly weaving its way up out of the drain in his kitchen sink. 'What?'

'The driver!' My whole body shivers with the recognition; with the goddamn implications, door after door opening, images coming at me out from the past, every one of them revealing ugliness and truth. 'The fucking driver. I got him, the son of a bitch.'

Schiller tears his cigar out of his mouth and stomps on it, as though it were alive. 'Don't just stand there looking like you're having a heart attack. Talk to me for Christ's sake! What about the driver?'

'The ambulance. Linda Vista . . . '

Schiller looks up at the corpse being loaded into the ambulance, then back at me. 'Linda Vista? But the ambulance is going to City Morgue.'

'He was the ambulance driver at Linda Vista.'

'What ambulance driver?'

'This morning, outside the hospital, when I was with Rico, remember?'

He scratches his head. 'Vaguely . . . '

He doesn't remember a thing. 'Don't you get it? Where do ambulance drivers go?'

'To accidents . . . ?'

And him a captain. 'Where do they take people?'

'To the hospital . . . '

'And where else do they take people?' Schiller's thinking. I point to the ambulance in front of us. We say the words together: 'To the morgue . . . '

'Don't you get it . . . ?' He stares at me, his head tilted, straining hard; willing himself to understand but not quite managing. 'What if they snatched another kid's body from the morgue? Or from some goddamn funeral home?'

Schiller's stumped. 'But why would they do . . . ' His jaw drops. 'Oh, Jesus, Mary . . . ' And fucking Joseph, he gets it at last. He turns, watching the ambulance scream away. 'You're telling me that's not Ronnie Bannister inside there . . . ?' He shakes his head. Too big a leap of faith. He can't just go from case solved—no matter how unsatisfactory for the kid and the Old Man—to case still wide open, and getting more complicated by the second.

'The ambulance driver has access to stiffs. They heard about the kidnapping and snatched the body of a dead boy who's the same age as the Bannister kid. Then they pretended to be the kidnappers and staged the ransom.'

Schiller takes a few moments to stew on it. He grew up with meat-and-potatoes criminals. He's not used to exotic varieties of crime. 'But that means . . . '

'Ronnie Bannister's still out there. And if we're lucky, still alive.'

Schiller swears. 'Chief Parker just called the Old Man and told him they'd found the body of his son.'

'Parker's wrong. That kid's been dead for days. Those cuts were done postmortem, I'd stake my life on it.'

'If you're wrong—'

'Fuck wrong. What if I'm right?' I start hustling Schiller out through a side door. 'You've got to send someone over to the DMV.'

Schiller looks at his watch. 'They're closed.'

'Wake 'em. Have them pull the records of all the ambulance drivers. Match their licenses with their certificates. We can nail him through the records.'

'If you can recognize him . . . '

'You saw him too.' Sullen silence. 'Don't worry, I couldn't forget that face, even if I wanted to.'

I head towards my car. Schiller calls out to me. 'Where the hell do you think you're going?'

'Linda Vista.'

He freezes; ossified by fear. 'Are you out of your mind? We've got to get back to Parker, to the Old Man. They're both expecting us.'

'They can wait. I've going to Linda Vista. That's where this case gets solved. Maybe someone there knows the name of the ambulance driver. He might even have been the guy who dropped Hidalgo there.'

'Could be . . . ' Schiller rubs his chin speculatively with those giant hands of his, adjusting the jaw with great, rolling curves, like a cow chewing its cud. 'But if he wasn't? You'd just be wasting time.'

'Not if Hidalgo's awake. Not if I can talk to him, or maybe even Elaine Bannister.'

'A dying man and a woman with a lima bean for a brain? Neither of them are talking.'

'We've still got the driver.'

Schiller follows me to my car. 'What if nobody knows the driver at Linda Vista?'

'Then I'll try the morgue, and if no one knows him there, I try every funeral home in the city.'

'But . . . ' The question hurts him to ask—but he has to: 'Why?'

'You think it's normal to even think of snatching a kid's body in the first place? Criminals have no imagination. There's only one reason they did it: they snatched the kid's body because it's their MO. I think they've been running a protection racket for stiffs. Snatching and selling corpses; trading body parts . . . '

Schiller's face twists in disgust. 'Who ever heard of such a thing?'

'Just because we live in modern times doesn't mean they've stopped ancient rackets. Grave snatching is as old as the pyramids.' I slap my pockets for my car keys and then I remember. I swear. 'I need a car.'

'What happened to yours?'

'Long story.' I point to the one I arrived in. 'That one is stolen.'

'Evidence. We'll impound it.' He gestures to the mayhem outside the house. 'Pick a driver. Stay in touch . . . '

I nod to a young cop. 'Marching orders. We're going to Linda Vista.'

The cop looks at Schiller. He doesn't like taking orders from a civilian. Schiller shoves him towards the curb. 'Take him wherever he needs to go. He's working for Mr. Bannister.'

The cop looks back at me with different eyes. Servile. Greedy. I smile. 'Help us find the kid and you might even get a piece of that reward money.' That's all it takes: the fat tip at the end. Nobody cares about the going. It's only the pay-off that counts, everyone jostling right at the finishing line, pushing and shoving to get to be the doorman with the open palm and the false smile. Charon in a peaked cap and livery suit.

The cop glances over at the house, puzzled. 'But . . . Haven't they just found the kid?'

'Don't believe everything you read in the papers . . . '

'It's already in the papers?'

Literal guy. I better be extra careful with traffic directions. 'Forget about it, kid, and get a move on. We got a lot of turf to cover.'

He switches on the siren. It starts up as a hesitant, simpering moan, augmenting to a throaty protest with a touch of evil in the lower registers. Then it starts to sing its song, remembering the melody, rising high above the other cars, swelling up to our lonely, empty sky.

I settle back in the seat, watching the traffic ceding to us—not with deference but with resentment and fear; like in the old days when the king's bodyguards marched before him with whips, clearing subjects out of the way. Red pulses on and off, reflecting against the hood and flashing across our faces, masking then unmasking us in the colour of blood. In this world, we're all stained with guilt. It's not about doing right, it's too late for that. It's just about atonement. And a dash of revenge.

I think of Tommy's killer—out there, drinking a beer, the sun on his face. One day I will find him and kill him. It suddenly feels like old times again. Back on the Force. In a squad car with a partner I don't trust, cars scattering out of our way. Owning the street.

Rows of telegraph poles fly by, post after post, their arms stretched out like the crosses of Spartacus and his crucified army, leading all the way back to Rome.

'Where did you say we were going?'

'Linda Vista.'

'What's at Linda Vista?'

Maybe a name for the driver. Maybe a word from Elaine Bannister. Maybe a clue that will save a kid's life.

I turn to the rookie. 'Why don't you mind your own business, shut your fucking mouth, and drive.'

H astings watched Walter Stark get out of his car and slam the door, pausing to look up and down the street before crossing to the porch at the end of a well-kept pathway. It was a mob safe house, on the right side of Griffith Park—if you were a dentist. If you were a mobster, you were a long way from home.

Stark slowly unlatched the screen door, listened against the wooden door, then tried the doorknob. Locked. He sorted through a hoop of keys in his hand, looked around once more, then started comparing keys and lock. He was halfway through the loop when he found what he wanted, opened the door and disappeared inside.

Hastings had been waiting all day for Stark to show. Roselli had put out the hit, right after New York. Maybe Roselli thought Stark had something to do with tipping off Kennedy at the Sherry Netherland. Maybe Roselli thought Stark had found out about the new arrangements in Dallas.

Stark was a full-time burglar and a part-time hit man. Capable of taking out Hastings if he had a little luck on his side. And from what Hastings had heard, luck was something Stark carried with him at all times, alongside his skeleton keys and glass cutter.

Howard Hughes hired Stark as he own yeggman, always over easy. It might have been the Hughes connection that had brought down the contract on Stark. When you're as powerful as Howard Hughes, your enemies become desperate. They'll take any target, no matter how petty. They'll slash your tires, poison your cat, piss in your swimming pool. Killing Stark would be like putting a rock through Hughes's window. An anonymous manifestation of hate and frustration, but a minor inconvenience for Hughes, in the run of things.

Hastings glanced up and down the street. He'd been waiting in the car for hours, watching the purple noon swell into the blinding yellow nothing of a phosphorescent LA afternoon. A white butterfly settled on the windshield, magnified by the sun. Every line of its segmented body was bleached of colour; X-rayed and exposed. It fluttered away, leaving a faint powder behind. Hastings hit the windshield wipers. One single arc. That's all it took to remove all trace of the butterfly ever being there. Whether it's the blade of a windshield wiper or a *navaja sevillana*, the results are always the same: now you're here; now you're not.

Hastings got out of the car, walking quickly across the road, a large brown shopping bag cradled in each arm. He'd cut a hole out for his right hand, which held a suppressed .45 hidden amongst the masquerade of retail. The other bag was full of post-hit cleaning material. He rang the doorbell with his elbow.

An alarmed silence sweated its way through the door. Hastings could feel the fight-or-flight reflex pulsing on the other side. But played out in a suburban landscape, where drama constituted a neighbour's dog shitting on your lawn, it had lost its fatal resonance. It was about avoiding the landlady or hiding the bottle of gin under the bed, not taking a copper-jacketed .45 to the chest. Hastings rang again. Stark decided to speak, his voice dry with apprehension. 'Who is it?'

'Groceries.'

A long pause. Stark wasn't supposed to be there. He was weighing risk and consequence. It couldn't be the cops, because they would have just kicked the door in. The shrink who lived there was with his receptionist at the Hotel Bel-Air. Who could it be but the delivery guy? 'Just leave it outside.'

'Right next to the tip?'

A laugh. Stark's sense of humour was about to get him killed.

The door unclicked.

Stark had a sheepish smile on his face and two coins in his hand as he opened the door, his eyes meeting Hastings's through the screen, the smile gone with the flash of realisation: in a moment all of this would end. The shadows in the house from the drawn blinds; the glimpse of blue sky through the screen, the red Dodge passing on the street outside; the smell of newly-mown lawn and the insistent bark of an unseen dog. The mild headache he had endured those last three days, the throat raw from smoking; the hard-on he woke up with that morning.

Memory was about to end. The sound of his parents fighting through their closed bedroom door; falling on his first bike ride then, only three years later, singing papers through the air and slapping doors like targets; kissing down in the clearing by the river, solving the mysteries of adolescence. Early marriage—unhappy, broken. War. Survival. Women; mostly paid for. Work: always begrudged until he started with the crew. Then work became the thing most lived for. Almost a love. The best part was always the run at the end to the jingle of treasure inside black satin bags.

And it was that elation that Walter Stark took with him as the two holes appeared in the screen, the bloom of fragmented metal powdering the air, inconsequential as the butterfly's dusty trace; the shots swallowed inside the silencer with the soft, soothing plop of a falling pillow, the best burglar in California already dead on the floor. Inconsequential for the neighbours who later thought they might have heard something; for the cops who chalked the outline of the body on the floor;

for the newspaper subs who argued over the layout before it got pushed to page eight anyway; for everyone except the victim. Balloons exploding at a birthday party. A father on his knees finishing the decking out back. It sounded like something normal, not a killing.

Hastings closed the door behind him and pulled out the shower curtain. He combed the man's pockets. Some cash. The usual ID, both real and phony. A hatcheck receipt from The Carousel Club. Dallas. That took Hastings one step closer to understanding why. A book with phone numbers: very reckless for a man in Stark's position. Another possible why. Hastings collected the two shells, bundled the body in the shower curtain, and started the scrub-down of evidence. It was an oddly domestic scene.

Thirty minutes later, all was in order. No prints. No trace. No clues. Every year thousands of people disappeared. Lonely people, crazy people. Those who estrange; and those who are estranged. Stark would be just one more in that sad numbers game.

Hastings sat on the sofa, going through Stark's address book. Chicago names . . . Momo. Alderisio. Nicoletti. Accardo. Dangerous names to speak out loud, let alone write down. No wonder they wanted him dead. Stark was originally from Chicago. But he'd drifted towards Texas and the West Coast. Why put up with shitty weather when there were easy pickings in Hollywood and Vegas. The west was the best.

There were lots of Dallas contacts: Adam Granston; Jack Ruby; Joe Civello. LA names. DeSimone. Roselli. Hastings. New Orleans names. Carlos Marcello was the only one Hastings had heard of. Alek James Hidell kept reappearing, always with Lee Oswald and OH Lee.

Hastings started connecting names to towns. Miami won by a long shot. Maurice Bishop. Orlando Bosch. Bill Harvey. Felipe Vidal Santiago. David Sánchez Morales.

He turned to the last few pages of the book, filled with notes, when a name reached out from the past and slapped him hard across the face. Nick Alston. Stark even had his address, which was impossible. No one knew where Alston was. Hastings went back to the Miami names. Now they were making sense. They weren't connected to the Mob, they were connected to the Company.

Hastings was officially out of his depth. He tore out the page with Alston's address and set it alight. Then he went upstairs to the shrink's study. It was time to get the second part of the job done.

Hastings had already been to the doc's Beverly Hills office the night before. The locks on the filing cabinets had been comical. He had simply levered up the tongues with a knife blade. At home, the shrink had added a combination padlock to the top shelf of his filing cabinet, a red flag that told Hastings everything he needed to know. Access was easily obtained with the help of a simple tin shim. Hastings went through the files, starting at the middle, coming quickly to 'M'. As he was taking the Monroe documents another name caught his eye: Marlowe. That file went too. He closed the cabinet and was about to reapply the lock when an instinct hit him. He went through the files once more, this time starting at the beginning, stopping at 'B' for Bannister.

He reinserted the lock and was doing the final wipe-down for prints, when he noticed the unsealed stamped manila envelope on the desk. Stuffed full of legal documents. He rifled through them. The wife must have found out about the receptionist. He emptied the contents, hiding them behind a row of encyclopaedias on a bookcase, then wrote his pseudonym and his address in Chula Vista on a piece of paper and pasted it over the address on the envelope. He went downstairs and got to work fast, going through all three files, lifting the documents he wanted, including all the notes from Eva Marlow's last session, when she talked about the visit he and Luchino had paid her in New York. He slipped the documents and most of the photos into the empty manila envelope and sealed it. He would drop it off at the first mailbox he saw. There was enough dynamite left in the files to keep Roselli busy.

Hastings looked up from the envelope, his gun already in his hand. But all he could hear was the loud putter of a refrigerator struggling against the heat, and the distant splash of an outdoor swimming pool. He was jumpy. Hastings turned on the radio low, wiping the switch with his handkerchief. *Midnight* by Hal Singer. Sensual. Stirring. A dangerous place to be. He looked at his watch. It'd be dark in an hour. The shrink had booked a table at the Dresden for eight. Plenty of time to get rid of Stark's body. To go through all the details one more time. Fly to Dallas the following morning. Meet up with Luchino. Stop the hit. Escape to Houston by car. Fly back to LA. Pick up Bella from the kennel. Go straight to Big Bear Lake. Wait for her; then run. It was so clear. It was so risky. Hastings closed his eyes and, without seeking it, fell asleep to the lament of Charlie Shavers's trumpet.

* * *

He dreamt of the war; of cleaning his rifle after a tropical storm. He dreamt of mud, of leeches burrowing into his legs. He dreamt of the torment of mosquitoes at dusk and the terrible thirst at midday. They were running uphill under the volcanic sun, chasing retreating enemy forces when they were ambushed. The crack of a bullet through somebody's helmet; the splinter-crumple of skull; the hump of a body falling in sparse undergrowth. No cover. No shade. No shadows. The swoon of machine-gun fire tearing up the terrain; the click of broken rock, flint splinters in the face.

Hastings elbowed his way forward, the air scorch of bullets

tracing the blue sky with the riot of combustion. He kept going, doubling up behind the high ground. On his own. Clear sight lines into the three nests that were holding back both companies. Grenades. Gunfire. The rush of others joining him. The swivel and slit of bayonets. The nests had fallen; the first of many. When they finally came out onto a stream, he sank into its tannic waters, sunburn and blisters thumping from the temperature change, and drank until he heaved. He was nineteen. They had forced this upon him; island upon brutal island. This was war; he was changed forever. He thought back to the deer that morning with his stepfather. The silver silence of dawn. The patina of frost on the leaves. The fog of his breath affirming his decision. He had let that creature live when dozens of men had been denied such grace. That thing of beauty had survived. And then the slap across his ear, the sting in the bitter air. If a stepfather could do that to his own son; what could a stranger do to an enemy's? The war gave him the answer. The tiny river danced to the whistle of bullets. It had already begun again. Hastings hauled himself out of the miraculous water and up into the foliage, ready to kill once more . . .

On the sofa, Hastings moaned and turned. Across the room, the plastic-clad corpse of Walter Stark stared back at him, like a mummy from a lost civilization, immutable and accusing.

Evelyn sits opposite me, the candles blushing her body with a rose-coloured glow. She moves the ruins of our dinner to one side and picks up one of the large candles, cradling it within her fingers. 'Let me show you where I work.' Without waiting for a response, she leads the way down a long corridor, tiles winking at me under the flush of candlelight.

I have to bow to pass through a vaulted passageway into a huge room with a glass cupola. Evelyn places the candle inside a deep crystal globe carved into the shape of a pinecone. Instantly the room leaps into magnified illumination, waves of unsettled light everywhere. Three walls are consumed by high bookshelves. A moveable brass stepladder is attached to horizontal rods, allowing access to the highest volumes. Its highly -polished surface mirrors the flickering flame. The last wall is bare except for some artwork and a king-size bed.

'This is my study.'

I gesture to the bed. 'You do your best work asleep?'

'Much of my work concerns dreams. Where better to sleep?' She climbs one of the brass ladders. 'I have a book that will—' There's the crack of her heel catching between rungs and she slips. Evelyn reaches for support, clasping at books that tumble, the ladder rolling wildly on its tread towards me.

I catch it as it sails past, gathering her in my arms, her body nestled against mine. A long unspoken moment passes then she tugs me up towards her, moving against me, a barely discernible undulation of the hips. I can feel her heart against my chest, beating fast.

She slowly turns and reaches up with both hands, hoisting herself almost out of reach, nearly breaking contact, then lowering herself against me again, one of my hands gliding along her calf, the other finding the zipper down her back, which purrs as I open it.

Evelyn lets go of the bars, trusting me to stop her fall. My lips trace their way up her spine towards her neck, her heat elemental, like a desert wind. She glances at me over her shoulder, her face masked by hair.

I turn her gently and peel the dress from her, the silk straining then freeing itself from her body. Evelyn seizes the rungs and pulls herself up, out of my reach. I see a smile through her hair as she lowers herself upon me, her hand seizing a fist of my hair as her breathing begins to quicken.

I lean out on the ladder then return, one of her legs locked around my waist, the other over my shoulder, Evelyn drawing herself up and lowering herself down: two rhythms, one intent.

I s this the one?'
I stare down at the paper marked Hidalgo and nod. 'What's
your name?'

Defensively, 'Huston.'

'Huston, do you know the guy who brought him in?'

'I wasn't on duty when he arrived. But the driver should
have signed in somewhere . . .' More papers get shuffled desul-
torily, as though an old, drunken cardsharp were going
through his rounds for the last time. Basic moves, but still
beyond the dying hustler's shaking hands. Papers spill, gliding
to the floor. Finally something of significance is retrieved.
'Here we go. No wonder you're looking for him!' He looks up
at me. 'Archer is one strange bird, all right.'

I snatch the paper from him. He works for CHD. We've got
him.

I call the Bannister Estate. Mrs. Bannister answers, her
voice rich, deeply textured; thrilling in its promise. 'It's Nick
Alston, Mrs. Bannister. I need to talk to Schiller.'

There is the pause of power interrupted. 'I'm sorry but the
Captain's speaking to my husband, Mr. Alston.'

'It's an emergency, Mrs. Bannister.'

I wait on the line, listening to distant murmurs. A voice
rises, argumentative, then drops fast—easily defeated. Schiller
startles me, booming into the phone: 'This better be good.'

'We got him. Works for CHD. His name is Nelson Archer.
Lives at 66 Kenton Avenue, El Monte.'

'That's near Legion Stadium.'

'We need him, Schiller.' I hang up and turn to the talking filing cabinet. 'Where are you keeping Hidalgo?'

'I'm not keeping him anywhere . . . ' He points to a sleepy wall clock that seems stunned to be consulted with such urgency. 'In fact, I'm officially off duty. Try reception.'

Hospitals. Churches for the nonbeliever. Penance is out, Penicillin is in. And the corridors of the Emergency Ward have become the Stations of the Cross, universal suffering displayed one lonely bed at a time.

A light flickers like a nervous tic over emergency reception. I flash the badge, gravel down the voice. 'We have a suspect here, Hidalgo.'

She looks up at me with a slow, vindictive smile, like a house detective who has just caught the girl creeping out of the room. 'There's been a lot of comment . . . '

With one single phrase, she has turned my intimidation against me. 'Comment?'

'Police brutality. Handcuffing a seriously injured man to his bed.' I had forgotten all about Rico's cuffs. How the hell did that happen? Forgetting was never like me. 'The next-of-kin is most irate . . . '

'The family is here?'

'His brother's waiting at the bedside.' She glances over my shoulder. 'He's been here for hours. He was kind enough to give me his autograph.' I turn, peering into the room. There is a slim young man with shoulders hunched. 'He was so good in *Giant*, I cried . . . ' Her voice keeps going, like a sports announcer describing the scenes after the match, unable to stop the rush of vocal adrenaline. 'When the train pulls away and his coffin is just standing there . . . '

'What did you say next-of-kin's name was?'

She looks at me with sympathetic amazement. 'You don't recognise Sal Mineo?'

'Sorry, lady, I don't eat popcorn.' The kid looks up at me as I walk into the room, rising not in greeting, but in nervous defence. I walk over to the bed and start trying the keys I'd lifted from Rico. There is the crisp click of liberation.

'You didn't have to do that . . . ' He starts circling, his hands moulding the air, as though searching for something to break. 'It's not like he's going to run away. Not after you ran him down.'

'Shut up, kid. The prick who handcuffed him was a Fed named Rico.' Colour slides from his face, emaciating it. 'That's right, and he knows all about Operation 40, so you better start talking or I'm taking you in.'

Something in his eyes.

If it were fear, I'd recognize it.

If it were hate, I'd deserve it.

It's something a hell of a lot bigger. There's an earthquake going on inside that head of his—a seismic shift. I instinctively take a step back, as though his skull were about to explode.

'You think this has anything to do with Operation 40 . . . ?' His voice is a wheeze of contempt.

Silence needles his question. How the hell would I know? I'm in the dark. I swallow my pride. It humps its way painfully down my ganglion-riven throat. 'What is Operation 40?'

A malicious hiss of satisfaction. 'It's nothing . . . '

'Nothing? That's not what Rico said.'

'It's everything.'

'Look, I'm trying to help you here . . . ' His short, incredulous laugh would kill me if it were a bullet. 'But I need you to help me first. Why does Rico think your brother's tied up with this Operation 40?'

'First, he's not my brother . . . '

'But the nurse said . . . '

He repeats my phrase with a mocking tone. 'But the nurse said . . . !' His face gets in close to mine. 'You fucking idiot, he's my lover.'

I grab him by the shoulders. 'Look, buddy, I'm here to help.'

He pulls away from me with wiry ease. 'Like all the other 'helpers'?'

'What others? What is this racket, Operation 40?'

'Racket's right. It's just a fancy name, a swanky title, that's all; a lousy gimmick. A Hollywood hoax to sell the packet to Washington.' He stares at me, his head tilted, as though the whole planet is about to slide over with it. 'You think senators would vote funding if it was called 'Operation Phony'? Do you think even they would be that stupid?'

'Okay, already, it's a racket. So what are they selling?'

'Shakedowns, blackmail; smut photos. It's the red scare but with sex. It's unaccountable, untraceable money. Lots of it. They say it's to fight communism, but that's bullshit. It's a heist. A scam to get Dick Nixon into the White House.'

'And how's it going to do that?'

His head suddenly springs back up as though a trigger-trap's been sprung inside. 'By shaking down the biggest name there is: Old Man Bannister.'

The Old Man. Again. He didn't just have a finger in every pie: he made them all himself. The Cosmic Baker. 'What's he got to do with it?'

'What hasn't he got to do with anything . . . ?'

'All right, settle down . . . '

'Settle down? You sons of bitches nearly killed Félix.'

'I had nothing to do with it,' I lie. 'Calm down and tell me where Hidalgo—Félix—fits in.'

'Pedro Díaz Lanz tapped him. It's worse than the Black Hand. They needed someone inside Old Man Bannister's household. Fucking Díaz. He said he'd get Félix's family out of Cuba. It was bullshit. He'd burnt all his bridges after the leaflet drop over Havana.'

I don't understand a single word he's saying. I've got to

focus. Fast. On answers I understand. While Mineo's still caught up in his rage of words. 'So Rico works for Nixon?'

'Rico's from Boston.' The fuse of information is guttering. His eyes narrow; judgmental and cruel: why waste words on a moron like me.

'Who then?'

He shakes his head, appalled by my detective powers. 'Joe Kennedy, of course.'

'But Rico also works for Hoover?'

'He's a Fed—of course he works for Hoover.' He gives a disgusted sigh, like a priest giving up on a rummy sinner. What's the use? Three Hail Marys and get the fuck out of my sight.

But he's given me enough. It's the first real lead I've had all day. Hoover is happy to have Rico moonlighting for Kennedy—as long as Rico gives him the skinny on all that he learns. But back doors generally swing both ways. What has Rico been feeding Joe Kennedy about Hoover? And what has Hidalgo been feeding Rico about Old Man Bannister?

'This is connected to the kidnapping?'

He's right up there, in my face again. 'As far as Hoover is concerned, this is connected to Rock Hudson.'

It takes all my control not to slug him. 'Cut the wisecracks. Answer the question.'

He does a slow turn, walking back over to the bed, taking Hidalgo's hand as he sits down in a chair. 'Hoover's got a thing about Roy.'

'Roy?'

'Rock Hudson. Rico was using Félix to get to me, so I could get to Roy. We stalled him, honest. And while we were stalling, we found out about Joe Kennedy.'

I offer Mineo a cigarette. He accepts. There is a whisper of a match between us. 'What about Joe Kennedy?'

'He's obsessed with the Bannister kid. Hoover never figured

it out. So Félix started to watch. To listen. Things are awful wacky in that household. The Old Man's wife—'

'Mrs. Bannister?'

'Mrs. Bannister—wouldn't go near the kid, let alone the Old Man. She's the only one who can stand up to him. If she doesn't like what the Old Man says, she just wheels him away and closes the door. She runs the household.'

Sounds like she runs the Old Man. And if she runs the Old Man . . . She runs the goddamn country.

'What about Philip Hastings?'

'The mechanic?' A knowing leer blooms across his face. 'They spent a lot of time together. Plotting, Félix called it.' I see red: her negligée.

'What about her sister, Ronnie's mother?'

'Elaine? A total nutcase.'

'Felix ever see her at High Sierra?'

'Never. But we used to see her all the time at the Green Door and the Club Laurel. She was into weird drugs, shit like jimsonweed and peyote. She spent a lot of time with the nanny. The one that's missing.'

The one that's dead. Sal Mineo is giving me a lesson in a city I thought I knew. 'Listen carefully. What do you know about the Old Man being blackmailed?'

'You're talking about the kid.'

'What about the kid?'

He starts to laugh, smoke escaping from him like steam from a boiler that's about to explode.

'What's so funny?'

He points his cigarette at me as though it were a smoking gun. 'Figure it out for yourself, Einstein.'

Rico's working for Kennedy and Hoover. Hidalgo was working for Rico. He was also working for Morales and this Díaz, who are both working for Nixon. The arithmetic doesn't add up. Rico, Morales and Díaz are just foot soldiers. That leaves Kennedy, Hoover and Nixon. Scratch Hoover—he's ubiquitous anyway. Kennedy and Nixon. Now that's what you call a conflict of interest. Joe Kennedy's son running against the vice president for the biggest prize in the country: the right to award government contracts; the right to grant amnesty; the right to push the button and blow us all to Hell.

But where did Old Man Bannister fit into the picture? I toss the two-faced coin into the air. It comes up heads.

'Kennedy is blackmailing the Old Man?'

'Nothing like that.' Mineo looks away, tugging a piece of tobacco from his lip. He frowns, and it dawns on me: there'd be no way to tell if he were acting. 'More an edge . . . He wants influence over the Old Man.'

'What kind of influence?'

'He wants the Old Man to throw his support behind his son's candidacy.'

That didn't make sense. 'The Old Man hates Kennedy. And he owns Nixon.'

'You shouldn't be smoking . . . ' I turn. The nurse doesn't see me. She only has eyes for Sal Mineo. She shrugs apologetically. 'There's oxygen in the room . . . '

'We're nearly done.'

She ignores me, smiling one last time at Mineo before disappearing. He frowns as he takes a big suck of smoke, his eyes narrowing from the heat. 'So now what? Are there going to be any charges against Félix?'

The FBI and LAPD could crucify them both just on morals charges. I drop my cigarette to the floor and step on it, grinding it out like the truth, leaving a crescent of smeared ash on the linoleum. 'He hasn't done anything wrong . . . '

There is a moan. Mineo slowly rises to his feet. 'Félix . . . ?' He strokes Hidalgo's brow. 'How are you doing, baby?' Hidalgo opens his eyes. They struggle to focus, but when they do, when they meet Mineo's, something passes between them.

A luminous message. I had nearly forgotten—it's been so long: the way Cate used to look at me. 'See you around . . . ' Mineo doesn't look up. He doesn't even register I'm going. In his universe, I no longer exist.

The nurse at reception looks at me coolly. 'He didn't seem too pleased with your visit.'

'You were eavesdropping.'

Defensively—'You were both speaking very loudly.'

'Pardon me for living, I didn't realize this was a library.'

She looks away. She's made her choice. The movie star, not the flatfoot.

'I need to see Elaine Bannister.'

She opens a large, handwritten ledger, and runs past names with the aid of a ruler. 'Elizabeth Bannister?'

'Elaine . . . '

She looks up at me triumphantly. 'There is no Elaine Bannister.' She snaps the registrar shut with undue force, as though imagining my nose between the covers.

'That's impossible. She was brought in this morning, buried alive.'

The nurse nods. 'That would be Elizabeth Bannister—Room 14.'

Although she's been washed, there's still the aura of the grave about her; a shading of ethereal grey that denies the presence of the sun, that speaks of the lurking menace of the tomb. Her breath is regular but slow, almost silent. She is so completely self-effacing in her state of semi-existence . . .

I pick up the chart hanging from her bed. The name Elaine Bannister is clearly typed. Why then was she registered as Elizabeth in the admissions book? I stare at her calm suffering caused by the indignities of medically-assisted survival, enduring this life in a bed she didn't choose, separated maybe forever from her child.

The hand on my shoulder makes me jump. The doctor

stares at me through thick spectacles which enlarge his eyes. Eyes like his have no right to be magnified. 'No visitors. Mr. Bannister's orders.' The only thing that's missing is the click of the heels at the mention of the Old Man's name. I shove my badge in front of his Coke bottles. His eyes travel the not-too-gleaming badge, worrying the tarnished surface, the mug shot photo, the smear of ink for a signature. 'Get out, *ja*?'

'You work for the Old Man? So do I, and I'm going to report your lack of co-operation.'

'That is ridiculous, no one can accuse me.'

I make a bet with myself: plenty of people could accuse him of plenty. 'What's your name?'

'Landis. Doctor Professor Boris Landis.'

'Don't you types salute?'

He frowns, handing me back my badge. 'I assure you I enjoy the complete confidence of Mr. Bannister.' Translation: I have no hesitation in doing the Old Man's dirty work. And the Old Man knows it.

'In that case, Professor Confidence, tell me why this patient's name has been deliberately falsified.' He glances at the clipboard. 'Falsifying medical records. That's a criminal offence.'

He takes off his gold-rimmed spectacles and polishes them with a silk handkerchief. Stalling for time. 'I was unaware any name was changed. Certainly not with my authority.'

'Who registered this patient?'

'That would be Mr. Bannister.'

'Mr. Bannister was here in person?'

'That, I cannot say.'

I want to kick the equivocating bastard in the balls. 'What the fuck can you say?'

'*Was fällt dir ein*! I am professor emeritus at the George Washington University. I will not tolerate being spoken to in such a manner.'

226 · TIM BAKER

I pull out my cuffs. 'I'm guessing you'll tolerate it more than spending a night in the lockup with a couple of homeless vets of the Battle of the Bulge . . . ' The whine of the cuffs opening shrieks between us. 'So tell me: why the confusion over her name?'

'*Nein, nein, nein.*'

'That makes twenty-seven. And that's how many years you'll get as an accessory to kidnapping if you don't answer the question.'

He stares at the cuffs with such fear that, goddamn it, for an instant a sliver of pity slots through me. 'Twins, don't you see? They are twins.'

Elaine and Elizabeth. *My friends call me Betty* . . . Elizabeth is Betty Bannister. But why did Mrs. Bannister tell me Elaine was her half-sister? Because she didn't want me to know she had a twin . . . ? Or she didn't want me to know who her father was? I stare at the woman in the bed again. All this time I've been looking at her as a victim—the miraculous survivor of a bungled murder attempt or frantic escape—never as a real person; an individual. All this time I was just seeing soil and survival; dirt and despair. Near-death, not life. An apparition, as close to a ghost as you can get—buried alive. All this time I've been looking at her like a cop, not like a detective.

I gently cover one of her eyes with a lock of hair and switch on the bedside lamp. Through the shade of the grave, it's now unmistakable . . . Unmistakable only because now I know what I'm looking for: Betty-goddamn-Bannister to a T.

'Who changed the name of the patient? Tell me.'

'Not me.' Landis backs away, banging into a gleaming metal trolley. There is the racket of falling trays and pans echoing off the hard floor. His shaking hand points to the bed chart. 'The name is there . . . '

I grab the chart. The name is there all right, on the bottom of the third page under authority of next of kin for procedures: *Rex Lionel Bannister*. I grab the little bastard by the cuffs of his white coat. 'What the hell is this?'

He backs away from the chart, as though expecting me to slap him with it. 'What?'

'This procedure the NOK has authorized?'

He takes the chart, adjusting his glasses. '*Ja*, transorbital leucotomy . . . It is nothing, a common procedure performed under local anaesthetic.'

'Can the technical bullshit. What is it in layman's terms?'

'Lobotomy.' Stretching the four syllables as though the 'common' procedure had already been performed on me.

'That woman is a witness to a crime. You touch a hair on her head, and so help me God . . . '

'You don't understand.'

There's plenty I don't understand. 'You better explain it to me then, doc . . . '

He points to Elaine Bannister like a tour guide pointing to a statue in a museum. 'This procedure is not for Elaine . . . '

'Then why is it marked on her sheet?'

'Because she is incapable of giving consent.'

'Consent for what, goddamn it?'

He shakes his head, marvelling at my ignorance. 'For the procedure on her child . . . '

I snatch the chart from him and go back to the last page. Unpronounceable medical terms, hospital stamps and fucking Latin. Then I see it. Ronald James Bannister. The kidnapped kid; snatched before they could poke a knitting needle into his eye. And this is what awaits him if he's brought back alive: Herr Doktor and his procedure.

Jesus Christ, is this a kidnapping . . . or a rescue?

I shove Landis out of the way, my footsteps slapping an angry passage out of the stinking hospital.

The rookie cop is lounging by the squad car, chatting up a

nurse, unable to hide his annoyance at my arrival. He flicks his cigarette between my legs. 'Back to the Bannister joint?'

'We're taking a detour. To Sunset Boulevard.' The moment I'd been dreading ever since I first spoke to the Old Man had finally arrived. It was time to make a house call on Johnny Roselli.

CHAPTER 35
Los Angeles 1960

Johnny Roselli's house lay at the end of a crest of long, open lawn on North Linden Drive. Sparse. Hyper-manicured. No trees to hide behind. No cover; no ambush. No surprises for a man who preferred to spring them. Whatever direction you approached the house, he'd see you coming, silhouetted against the wide, empty space, like a moving target at a rifle range.

Roselli's home was less than two blocks from where Benny Siegel was shot dead. Roselli had learnt from Benny's mistake. After all, rumour had it that he and Johnny Stompanato had been the triggermen.

The rookie cop looks at me like I'm nuts when I tell him to pull up outside Roselli's joint. Rookie cops know where all the gangsters live. They're like Hollywood tourists with stars' homes. 'Mr. Roselli's place?'

I stash my Colt Police Positive .38 Special, Allen's KA-BAR and his Moose Hunter, a couple of spare clips, my cuffs and my knuckle dusters under the front seat of the squad car. 'What's your name, kid?'

'Gillis.'

'Let me give you a word of advice, Gillis. Never say *Mister* Roselli. It only makes you sound like a shit-heel on the take . . . ' I slam the door hard, wishing his dirty little fingers were in its hinges, and march across the lonely lawn.

Before I'm ten paces from the door, two goons come out, their bodies lumped by weapons and the desire to use them. 'Who the fuck are you?'

'Tell your boss I'm a representative of Mr. Rex Bannister. He's expecting me . . . '

Two small heads swivel painfully sideways, cutting through acres of sinew and muscle, just so they can look at each other. As if either of them had the brains to make a decision like this. One of them grabs me. A voice booms from the other side of a screen door. 'For crying out loud, how many times have I told you? Never frisk outside! What will the goddamn neighbours think?'

If they had any brains, the goddamn neighbours would pull up stakes and move to another city—pronto. Living next door to Johnny Roselli is like living next door to the Nevada Atomic Bomb Test Site.

They shove me inside, the screen door slamming on the back of my heels, frisking me with a contained brutality, as though I were to blame for their mistake outside. And in a way I was. I can't imagine that Mr. Roselli receives that many visitors, and my hunch is that most of the ones who enter his home never come out again. At least not in an identifiable state. Word on the street was that Roselli had a basement pizza oven even busier than Big Tuna's in Chicago. I raise my hands to help them with the frisk—co-operation is better than incineration—but these goons are strictly old-school: they don't appreciate assistance. I get my arms yanked and twisted and my back pounded as though I were Tommy Dorsey choking at the dinner table. One of the gorillas paws my wallet out of my inside jacket pocket—along with its lining—and tosses it to Roselli, who's dressed in a silk dressing gown and leather slippers: quite the lord of the manor. All that's missing is the pipe and the pooch with the paper.

'Say, that was a fifty-dollar jacket.'

Roselli handles the wallet as though it's just been retrieved from a piss trough, peering at what's inside. 'A private dick wouldn't spend more than twenty bucks on a suit, even if it was for his own wedding . . . ' Dark eyes, hollowed by all the evil they had witnessed, ride up from the badge, staring into mine. 'Let alone for his fucking funeral.' He tosses the wallet back to one of his Neanderthals, who shoves it into my outside jacket pocket, the shriek of the pocket tearing filling the room. 'Jeez, you're falling to pieces. I think a visit to your tailor is in order.' Roselli laughs at his own joke, always the first sign of a man without class.

Roselli nods towards the centre of the room. I slowly walk towards the fireplace, the goons two steps behind. Escape routes are scarce. Either into the great unknown behind the kitchen door, or up the chimney.

Then it hits me.

The chimney in the star chamber, in the cellars of the Bannister joint.

The old entrance in the north well had been transformed into a chimney for the fireplace there. That's why I hadn't notice it, and when I went back to look, the door to the star chamber was locked. But it wasn't locked when I first went there the night of the kidnapping. That's how Elaine entered the old aqueduct system. Via the chimney. The question was—

'Wake up, scumbag!' Someone slaps me hard across the face. 'I'm talking to you.' I rub my face, coming back to immediate, painful reality. 'I said: how do you like my home . . . ?'

The joint's certainly swanky. 'Must have cost a bundle . . . '

The asshole preens. 'It don't come cheap . . . ' He smiles, the proud homeowner of a five bedroom Spanish Colonial in Beverly fucking Hills, and me, a poor sucker living in a dump in Westlake.

Well, fuck him. 'Sure . . . They're all smart operators out here. They know a pigeon when they see one.'

A right to the solar plexus.

Gasping pain.

Thank God it was Roselli. If it had been one of his goons,

they'd have busted my ribs, burst my spleen. Maybe punctured a lung. I wheeze my way back to an upright position, sucking in enough air to speak. 'Face it. No matter how much you puff out your chest, they see a chump, not a champ.'

Roselli turns, bends down to pick something up from the table. I flinch, expecting a gun. Schiller always said I never knew when to keep my mouth shut.

He always said it would end just like this.

But Schiller is wrong—this time at least. Roselli hasn't gone for a gun, he's gone for a cat. A white cat with a grey cap around its ears. Two green eyes gaze into mine as its whiskers come forward. I feel a soulful communication. How did either of us wind up in the same room with this hoodlum? Roselli cradles the cat in his arms. In the silence, I can hear it purring a message at me: help me escape and I'll do the same for you.

'I don't like dogs,' Roselli says. 'There's something about them. The way they bark. The way they see things us humans can't see . . . Ghosts.' He takes a shot at a smile; almost gets there. 'Can you imagine what it would be like if there was a mutt in this house? Nonstop fucking barking. Barking all the fucking time. Yapping at a crowd of dead fucking men.'

'Worried about the neighbours, huh?'

The way he's staring at me leaves no doubt: as far as he's concerned, I'm already a member of his household's ethereal congregation. I rifle in my trouser pockets for a pack of cigarettes. One of the goons already has my arm, slowly pulling my hand out, his thumb almost breaking my wrist with its pressure. Roselli sees what it is I'm holding and nods. After all, a condemned man is entitled to a last smoke, especially if he has to listen to a speech about cats and dogs.

'But I like cats. Know why I like 'em?'

'Cute and cuddly?'

'Wise guy . . . ' He slowly puts the cat back down on the table. It springs away fast, disappearing under a sofa. 'It's because they're like people. They don't hunt just to eat, they do it for fun. A cat will keep a mouse alive for days. Just for amusement.'

My hand is shaking as I light my cigarette. They all notice. It's always that part of ourselves we trust the most that betrays us. He nods to the goons. There's a brass candlestick on the mantle above the fireplace. And a framed mirror behind it. It's not going to be pretty. They'll get me in the end. But I'm going to separate them from as many pieces of their anatomy as I can before they do . . .

Roselli clicks his fingers and the goons both freeze. He cocks his head, and then I hear it too—a sound slowly seeping into the room, changing the air pressure like a tidal flood, bringing us back to the now of the city outside, not the mayhem and murder about to erupt in this room. The approaching sound begins to build in layer upon layer of keening volume.

For me, it's the cavalry.

For Roselli, it's a killjoy teacher, breaking up a schoolyard brawl.

Sirens.

Roselli looks out across the killing fields of his front lawn, past the trunks of felled trees to the sidewalk curb, the first squad cars already pulling up, strobing the windows with the insistent flutter of red. 'What the . . . ?' He looks back at me.

Improvise a lie before he's tempted to shoot me anyway. 'Mr. Bannister wanted to make sure I'd come back safe and sound.'

Roselli's curse is dark and savage. Even the goons step back in shock. He snatches my tie, pulling me so close, I can smell the acrid tilt of digestive acids stewing on their problem. 'Listen, you smartass fuck. You tell the Old Man he's not welching out of the deal. He keeps the kid, but we keep the money, got it?'

' . . . But the kid's dead.'

There's the pucker of internal detonation, his eyes quivering

234 · TIM BAKER

as though about to shuck themselves out of his skull in phosphorescent amazement. 'Are you fucking nuts? That kid was dug out of a grave—of course he's fucking dead.'

The banging at the front door makes him turn. Maybe he didn't see the look on my face. I knew it: the dead kid was a ringer. One question nailed. But the most important one is still unanswered: what happened to the real Ronnie Bannister?

The racket at the door's getting louder. The goons go over and lean against it, as though expecting battering rams. Roselli shakes his head like a man whose rent money just came in fourth at Hollywood Park. 'What a fucking hullaballoo!' He looks at the police through the window, then back at me. 'Do you have any idea what the neighbours are going to think?'

The cops are coming through the door. I've got maybe five seconds on my own with Roselli. I grab him by the throat, either side of the Adam's apple. 'Tell me where I can find the real Bannister kid or I'm going to pluck me a piece of fruit.' I let go just enough to let him talk. 'You dumb fuck,' he wheezes, 'there never was a Bannister kid.' His last word comes out as a squeak: 'Period.'

Someone grabs me by the shoulders and spins me round. It's my old pal from LAPD, Sergeant Barnsley. He goes up to Roselli. 'Everything all right, Mr. Roselli?' His cap may as well be in his hands.

Roselli has to massage his throat before he can answer. He points to my torn jacket. 'I was just fixing a sandwich for this itinerant type, you know? This here vagrant.' He catches the look Barnsley gives me. 'Well, no big deal, right? Robin Hood shit. Do it all the time. I even help out at the church, ask anyone . . . '

'Thank you, Mr. Roselli . . . ' Barnsley turns to me. 'You're under arrest.'

'Cute.'

There is the hard snap of cuffs on my wrists. 'Grand theft auto.'

'What the . . . ?'

'A 1957 Chevrolet Nomad, stolen earlier today, abandoned on Hawthorn Parade.'

'You have got to be kidding?'

'Well, what do you know? And to think I let this miscreant into my own home.' Roselli turns to me, sucking his lower lip in false regret. 'Look at you . . . I brought you into my house, offered you the hand of friendship, and what do you do? Bite it. You lousy crumb. Do you have any idea how much you let me down?'

'You can never be too careful, Mr. Roselli . . . '

'Ain't that the truth?' He looks away then sucker punches me in the balls. 'See ya, chump.'

'We're very sorry, Mr. Roselli, it won't happen again.' Barnsley pulls me back up to my feet and drags me through the front door, nearly stepping on the cat, which knows an escape route when it sees one. Roselli calls out. I slip my leg back, blocking the screen door from closing behind us. There is a flash of white as the cat leaps to freedom. Roselli shoves pass me, nearly tripping on my leg, racing after it. 'Lily! Lily, come back, goddamn it.' He loses a slipper as he disappears into the neighbour's garden. Perfect. Both of us get away in the end.

Barnsley heaves me across the porch and frog-marches me towards a patrol car. 'You fucked up once too often, Alston.'

'How the hell did you know I was here?'

'Gillis radioed you in.'

Well, what do you know? 'The kid deserves a medal for looking out for me.' I glance over at Gillis and nod my thanks.

Gillis flips me the bird. 'He wasn't looking out for you, you dumb fuck, he was looking out for us. We've got families. Mortgages. How could we get by without Mr. Roselli's help?' Gillis opens the back door of the squad car with a mocking bow. If he weren't in uniform, he would have mooned me. Barnsley slams me against the trunk of the squad car. 'You're stepping on all the wrong toes, Alston. If you don't wise up, we're going to have to order you some custom shoes . . . '

'Is this the part where I'm supposed to cry?' There is the stern wood of a nightstick cracked across my skull. I hear a noise like a branch snapping. Then my face is in the lawn. Ants riot down there in the Forest of the Great Green Blades. Hard hands hoist me up, potato-sack me into the car. My eyes sting with the hot salt of blood.

Robot voices invade my brain, the shriek and stutter of radio transmission wobbling through the shadows. Barnsley protests, spraying spittle in his fury. ' . . . The captain said what?' Barnsley throws something. It slams against the dash then recoils backwards like a Slinky, the radio mic bouncing on its curly cord. Static protests its violent treatment. Gillis glances back at us. 'What is it, Sarge?'

'Fucking Schiller!'

'What'd he say?'

'We have to go to El Monte . . . '

'Why, Sarge?'

'How the fuck do I know, it's an order.'

'Nelson Archer . . .' My voice sounds like a radio signal from Mars. '66 Kenton, El Monte.' Then we must have passed through an asteroid belt, because all further transmission is lost . . .

CHAPTER 36
Dallas 2014

Being in Dealey Plaza is almost like standing on the moon. Wondrous and impossible; foreign yet intimately remembered, as if stepping into a recurring dream. This is the terrain of history, and there is a sense of awe and disbelief. It's like visiting the Coliseum. But Ancient Rome is linked only by imagination. With Dealey Plaza, you have the Movie of the Week version of history.

Despite the change in dress and vehicles, there is something eerily timeless about the location. It is the closest I have ever felt to stepping into the past. It's not the tug of nostalgia or the allure of conservation; it is visceral. It creates a yearning to go back in time and stay there, to start over, to rediscover one's youth; to avoid all your mistakes and to live your life once more; to be young again, to go on living forever, starting here in this most famous of killing fields.

I take out my iPhone and begin the process of lining up my present with these images from yesteryear. I align myself with the trees and retaining wall; with the picket fence. This is the spot where the brake lights came on, just as the presidential limo was approaching the Grassy Knoll.

The Grassy Knoll.

A name that conjures up a children's picture book, not a brutal public killing. A more famous location than the Sea of Tranquillity yet further from our comprehension than any heavenly body.

The characters who have been captured around the mythic

terrain of the Grassy Knoll have passed through conspiratorial analysis and the collective unconscious and entered into folklore.

There, standing on John Neely Bryan North Pergola—a name that teeters between Shakespearean grandeur and parochial pomposity—is the figure of Zapruder, imperious and aloof, watching the assassination like Zeus surveying the fall of Troy; a pagan idol about to receive blood offerings.

By the curbside in front of the Grassy Knoll is the famous Umbrella Man, who pumps an open black umbrella into the air just as the shots rain down, as the president is hit; as he clutches at his throat with that gesture of terrible despair. Locked forever in the bright autumnal sunshine and the brilliant tones of Kodachrome and memory, the very incongruity of the preposterous Umbrella Man signals an intense alarm, like a stranger suddenly taking the father's seat at the family dinner table.

In the Zapruder footage, JFK appears to look directly at the Umbrella Man just prior to being hit. In that fraction of a second did the president see an eccentric or an enemy? Or did he not even notice the black umbrella, that sinister intimation of the storm cloud that was about to envelop the nation?

The suggestion by some conspiracy advocates that the umbrella was an assassin's tool, shooting poison darts or ice flechettes at the president, is frankly ludicrous. And yet it points to an even greater absurdity. At that very moment, in the apply-named Fort Detrick government facility they were attempting to develop exactly those kinds of weapons. When you play with the devil, you get what you deserve: bacteriological aerosols; platinum-tipped darts; ice flechettes; entomological warfare.

Kennedy was not shot by an umbrella gun as he passed in his limo. But for half a century the nation was taken for a ride by the mad-scientist brolly brigade. Unauthorized vulnerability tests on the New York subway. Thousands of troops marched into atomic mushroom clouds or sprayed with Agent Orange. Shellfish toxin. Anthrax. Tularaemia and Sarin. This was the Cold War. A plague—including *the* Plague—on both your houses. Thousands of innocent civilians were cursed with contamination, used as unknowing guinea pigs in a host of experiments involving everything from the secret administration of LSD and nerve gas to medically-induced syphilis, hepatitis and cancer. Criminality and impunity triumphed. Human rights were trampled. Liability was ignored, blame denied, records destroyed.

The real absurdity is not that some people might actually believe an umbrella killed the president but that most people don't even know about the ragged history of US government-condoned human experiments and their consequent cover-ups; or its military labs' development of weapons of mass destruction with eccentric and unstable delivery systems. This knowledge has gone the way of the Slave Trade and the plantations, of the Trail of Broken Treaties. Of the Tulsa Race Riots . . . Buried by public indifference in the face of enduring official silence and lies, it is a denial bred from fear of prosecution, civil liability and class-action lawsuits. Thoroughly understandable—if you were the guilty party.

The leaves of the trees around me that are living witness to these events vibrate in the light breeze: whispering their message. And what they seem to say is: they did it. They got away with it. Like they always do.

CHAPTER 37
Los Angeles 1963

astings checked the street again, then dragged the body out of the garage and into his car, which he'd parked in the driveway. This was always the hardest part: lifting all that dead weight. Getting it in the car fast before the neighbours notice. One time he had actually put his back out from the strain. He'd been barely able to drive. He was so bent over that his face was almost touching the steering wheel. Afterwards he had dropped himself off at a local hick hospital. They put him in traction, which only seemed to make it worse. A nurse gave him a number: a Japanese masseur. She walked on him, toeing pieces of his spine back where they belonged, fisting muscle out of the way, opening up tendons with knowing fingers. She gave him a set of painful exercises which he did every day. It wasn't just for his back, it was for his penance. His back hurt because he was alive when he shouldn't have been; because he killed to make a living. Because he was an evil man. His back hurt because his own body was scrambling to escape, mutinying from the tyrannical captain who forced it to live in stinking galleys; to present on deck each time there was an execution; to mount guard over the corpses and dispose of the bodies overboard without ceremony. Feeding the knowing sharks that followed his wake. Hastings was a killer because he had lost his soul. He was a ghost; butchered on the islands of the Pacific. The spasms of his back's muscles were simply early signs of rigor mortis, held at bay by a lousy layer of ice; a cheap trick by a second-rate mortician.

He dropped Walter Stark's body at Bluff Cove, the sea receiving it with restrained enthusiasm. The drive back was full of dark memories of meeting Betty Bannister at the Roosevelt in New York. Afterwards, she said she'd even run with him. She said they could meet up in Big Bear Lake, at the old ski lodge, three days after Dallas, before heading south. Staying in towns with mythic names. Acapulco. Veracruz. If they needed to head further south, they would. They'd go to Rio or Montevideo. To a place where the nights were warm and you could smell the ocean. A place with enough people not to be noticed; where sins from out of the past would never catch up with them. A place where they would be able to stay lost forever. And maybe even forget all they had done.

He turned on the car radio. Coleman Hawkins. *Midnight Sun*. Even at night, there would be no easy escape into shadows. Maybe this time it would be different. In only five days, they might be together on a dark road heading south. If he wasn't already dead.

He dropped the envelope at the mailbox on Wilshire, circled the block twice to make sure he wasn't being tailed, then headed back, parking three streets away from his place. He couldn't hear his own footsteps because of the nocturnal clamour of crickets and frogs, exultant under a waxing crescent. Their song seemed to surge as he approached the house, as though trying to remind him of the ancient superstitious warning: beware the deadly transit between the Hunter and the Frost Moons.

In the old days he would have listened to them.

But the old days were coming to an end . . .

They grabbed Hastings before the door was fully open, his key still in the lock, hauling him into the dark mass of the interior; fast fingers grabbing his neck, his arms; his hair. His ears were yanked downwards to the floor. Fists found spine and kidneys; knees smashed into his body as his wrists were twisted, captured and locked.

There was the bite and sting of metal traveling across his skin, catching and tearing in his hair.

Sensory dislocation.

And then he was snared, upside down, listening to the whine of grating rope as he rotated on its iron clasp, his hands bound behind his back.

The work was done.

The work-over was about to begin.

Hastings turned his face just in time, the rake of knuckle-dusters sliding along his cheek, somehow missing the holy trinity of jaw, cheekbone, teeth.

But the blow still sliced the inside of his mouth against his incisors, still forced the scatter-spray of blood. He worked on the tear inside his mouth—the only thing that might save him. He swirled and spat out blood and saliva; thick and wet. He forced more up out through his nose. He gagged and choked on it. And then he waited.

The vocabulary of interrogation is known to all. There were only two possible responses to his theatrical display.

Go easy.

Or finish him off.

'Go easy, we need him to talk . . .'

Hastings hung there, slowly rotating, the twin drip of sweat and blood tambouring onto the floor. There was the murmur of consultation, then the stillness of decision. He tensed his stomach muscles just in time for the kick, twisting with the movement, sending the power in the blow away from his body, but grunting as though it had scored maximum impact. The force travelled off the skirting strike, yet still he could feel what was behind it; why it had half-missed. There was real anger there. Hatred. Something irrational yet targeted, dedicated to hurting him. The voice came to Hastings's rescue. 'Go easy, I said . . .'

In the silence, Hastings's body spun its way to a halt, the

rope protesting with a slow, grinding whine. There was a moment's pause—absolute stillness—and then the rope recommenced the journey back to where it had come from, condemned by the physics of torture, turning him anticlockwise, the constant backwards and forwards spinning motion creating a separate nausea, another level of discomfort to add to the clenching pain of the cuffs and the rope, the loose cuts inside his mouth, and the racketing silent ache of bruised body organs and muscle; everything magnified in this upside down world of agony.

Hastings struggled for an answer to a single question. Not why or what, but who.

The angry kicker was a clue: this was personal as well as professional.

A strange, rolling noise approached his hanging body through the darkness. Hastings didn't look towards it. He had witnessed enough interrogations to know what the colossal mistakes were, and acknowledging the presence of something new and strange entering the torture chamber was one of the worst types of errors: it prepped you for pain. For terror.

Fear was the ally of the tormentor, just as anger was the ally of the sufferer. Imagination magnifies agony. Anger terminates it. And that's what the tortured crave from the very beginning of their ordeal: not an end to the questioning but an end to life itself.

The only thing more astonishing than how much pain and suffering a human can endure is how easily human life can be snuffed out. People were impossibly stoic and resilient and at the same time incredibly fragile—that had always been the paradox of human life, of the species that can bestow such loving tenderness one moment and such vicious cruelty the next.

Hastings had been forced to learn this through the prism of war. His dark knowledge forewarned and armed him. Even harnessed and swinging upside down, he felt somehow in control. He was aware. He was watchful and waiting. Through his fluttering eyelashes he could see a reflection in one of the windows, but it didn't make sense at first: a strangely shifting half-figure.

There was the stutter of rolling thunder again, like the heavy mass of a supercell storm building on the horizon, and then Hastings understood.

A wheelchair.

Old Man Bannister was back on his feet—so to speak.

'Good work.'

'Thanks, Mr. Ba . . . '

There is the crack of something unforgiving and then the shriek of hallucinogenic pain. 'Silence!' Hastings caught a glimpse of an exposed ulna bone before blood rushed in to cover it up, like an adulterous wife pulling the sheet up in flimsy protection against the explosion of flashbulbs.

A riding crop from the sound of it. The Old Man's weapon of choice.

A rearing horse. A terrible accident. A face split open like an overripe fig. Nightmare photos held in ink-soiled hands. This is what sold newspapers today. Not simple murder but carnage so gruesome it was beyond all human imagination. Cruelty so extreme, it could never be conjured by mere thought or theory—but only by bloody action. For once an evil deed is enacted, it becomes incarnate; proliferative. It is like splitting the atom. There is never any turning back. January 1947. Elizabeth Short. His welcome to Los Angeles. Jack the Ripper for the Atomic Age.

Hastings woke up to the sound of the taboo tapping of his blood against the hardwood floor. It was a very bad sign to have blacked out that early. Loss of consciousness was the emergency exit for further along in the interrogation; the opt-out clause: deliberate conceptual annihilation.

Something prodded him in the shoulder.

He could smell the leather as the riding crop rose towards his ear. A flick of the wrist and Hastings would lose it.

'I will only ask you once: what did you do with Stark?'

'Dropped him in the ocean.'

'Where's the file?'

'What file?'

For the first time in the interrogation Hastings was caught unawares. The punch seemed to come out of nowhere. He didn't even feel the change in air pressure. It was suddenly inside him, like an internal explosion. Then it was all over. His cry, shaped as much by surprise as pain, echoed back at him from off the floor below his head.

'I am going to ask you once more. I warn you, if you lie, you will never leave this room alive. But it will be days before it's over. Long, hard days . . . ' The Bannister Way. 'Now tell me—where is the file?'

'Which one?'

'I warned you not to play games.'

'There are three files!'

The silence of intrigue. Old Man Bannister was hooked. But how much time had he really bought? 'Go on . . . '

'The files are in my car, under the backseat. There's Marilyn Monroe and Eva Marlowe . . .'

'And the last one?' The riding crop tapped him. He couldn't just give up the name like that. He had to wait until the Old Man asked again. Or he lost an ear. 'Whose file is it?'

He swallowed, not from fear but relief. 'Your wife's, Mr. Bannister . . . '

A breathless hush. Had he overplayed his hand? Hastings closed his eyes, trying to anticipate what was about to come next. The riding crop. A fist. If he were lucky, the swirling twist of a bullet. He closed his eyes and tried to think of Susan but all he could think of was Mrs. Bannister. Imposter, adulterer; maybe even a killer. Just like him. Face it, he told himself, Susan was a lie. Betty Bannister was the one. She always had been. She was also his express train to Hell.

He caught the glint of a well-honed knife. He tightened his stomach muscles, opened his jaw and hunched his shoulders, trying to protect his neck as much as possible.

There was the whistle of velocity as his body careened out of control, speeding through space like a comet, smashing into the sky. Then the world tipped upside down and he was compelled by the arrogance of gravity; crushed by it and sent crashing back to earth. His legs showered down after him, battering against wood. Pain erupted between his ears. The sky had become the earth. And the earth had become his tormentor, stepping on his bones.

He was of no further use to them. It was already the endgame. This was it. The Long Goodbye. Crisscross. Another line drawn through an already deleted name. All that was left were the practical details. He was interested in a detached way in what was going to happen next. What sorrowful grave were they preparing for him? The noble boom of sea surf or the hollow flop of wet cement? Maybe a pig-iron furnace in an off-hours foundry down south. Or the hog farm of some Okie. Or would they simply leave him in the desert to be picked over by the blazing sun? By ravenous wildlife. Too lazy to even shovel out a shallow grave.

Barnsley hauls me out of the car, thrusts me towards a house. Schiller turns, swearing when he sees me. 'Jesus, Mary and fucking Joseph, what happened to Alston?'

'Resisting arrest.'

'What are you talking about?'

'Grand theft auto.'

Schiller palms Barnsley in the chest, almost toppling him. 'Get those cuffs off him, you moron.' He tugs me after him when I'm free. 'Can you still think?'

'Arithmetic is out . . . '

'At least you can talk . . . ' He yanks me to the front door. 'Because you're going to have plenty to say about this.' A young man in his early twenties looks at me with surprise and some shock. He turns to Schiller. 'What happened to him?'

'He fell over your doorstep . . . ' Schiller leads me inside, sits me down at a laminated kitchen table. On a counter opposite, a television shows images of the Bannister Estate, the sound turned down. 'Alston, meet Nelson Archer . . . '

I stare at him. How is it possible? He puts a glass of water down in front of me. 'Let me take a look at that wound . . . ' He looks up at Schiller. 'Captain, I should file a complaint . . . ' He walks over to a counter. 'Police brutality.'

'Give it a rest, he's not even one of you people.'

You people. Archer unsnaps a black case, takes out medical equipment. He puts two tablets down before me, then fills a kidney-shaped metal dish with cotton wool. He squeezes something on my temple. 'Ouch!'

Schiller laughs. 'Tough guy, my ass . . . So what is a doctor doing driving ambulances?'

'I'm a third-year med student at Meharry . . . I've taken a sabbatical.'

Schiller growls, the way he does when he doesn't like what he hears, but knows someone is telling the truth anyway.

'That means a break, Schiller . . . '

'Shut up and take your pills.' He peers into Archer's medical bag. 'So why'd you come all the way to LA, doc?'

'To earn some bread . . . ' He sticks something else on my head that hurts like hell. 'There's not much work in Nashville these days.' He suddenly grabs my hand, turning it over. 'When did this happen?'

'The bite . . . ? This morning.'

'It's already turned septic.'

He douses it with something that burns like the blazes. I let out a cry. Schiller laughs. 'Let him have it, doc.'

Archer runs his fingers along the base of my jaw, then under and behind my ears. 'What's this?'

'How do I know, it's on the back of my head.'

'A contusion . . . ' More wet sting. High bite; low burn. He pushes hard on my temple, the heartbeat throbbing giving way to a slower, less painful tightness. 'That'll do for the moment, but it'll need stitches. You should also get a course of penicillin and a tetanus shot for the hand.'

'Rabies, more like it . . . '

A light shines in my eyes. 'Mild concussion.' He steps back, looking at my torn jacket. 'Mister, you're a mess.'

Schiller thumps me on the back. 'It's official.'

'Thanks for the diagnosis. Listen, Archer, did you or did you not collect a young Latino male from Laverne Terrace this morning?'

Archer shakes his head. 'They don't send me to that part of town. They prefer to keep me over on South Central.'

Schiller nods. 'With your own kind . . . '

Archer gazes up at Schiller not so much with reproach, but worse, with sad confirmation. If the world starts going to hell, I can't imagine Nelson Archer telephoning LAPD for help. 'So why did one of your colleagues finger you as the driver of Felix Hidalgo?'

'Colleagues?' The laugh's a bite. 'I can only imagine that was Huston.'

Archer's bright. 'Why do you say that?'

His eyes glance up at Schiller. 'Let's just say he doesn't like people of "my kind" . . . '

Schiller clears his throat. Guilty as charged.

'Listen, Archer, I'm looking for an ambulance driver. Grey-faced, sweaty. Nasty-temper. With eyes . . . '

' . . . Like you'd find in an ancient skull? That'd be Deckard.'

'Know where he lives?'

'As far away from me as possible . . . ' He is about to say something, then stops.

'What?' He shakes his head. I nod to the TV. 'Listen, this is about that kidnapped kid . . . '

He hesitates. 'Okay. I've heard rumours that he works for people involved in . . . Black magic. Necrophilia. Shit like that. I mentioned it to our supervisor. Next thing you know I'm being accused of taking unauthorized coffee breaks and making excessive overtime claims.' He shrugs. 'I don't need sheet music to know the score.'

'So someone's protecting Deckard.'

He snaps his medical bag shut. 'You said it, not me . . . '

'Wait a minute.' Schiller rushes over to the television, nearly tripping over an electrical cord as he turns the sound up. Archer and I crowd around the screen. A reporter stands outside the gates of High Sierra as a hearse pulls out, followed by a Rolls-Royce. The reporter says that following the positive identification of the remains of Ronald Bannister, the only child of . . .

'What the . . . ? That's impossible.' Unless Old Man Bannister has been in on the kidnapping from the very beginning . . . 'Where's your phone?' Archer points to the hallway.

Schiller crowds behind me as I dial. 'What the hell is going on?'

'Deckard is the key. I'm getting his address.'

'But the Old Man said . . . '

'Fuck what the Old Man said. We can't save the kid, but we can nail his killers. Meet me outside with a car . . . Hello, operator?'

The operator's voice whispers in my ear—distant and séance spooky, my hand obediently scribbling letters as though controlled by a Ouija board planchette. Deckard provided the poor kid's body. He was the flypaper that would stick this rap to Roselli. And with any luck, there'd be enough glue left over to catch the biggest bug of all.

'Mister? Are you alright?'

I come back to reality: standing with a dead phone in my hand in a dump in El Monte. I turn from Archer down to the scrap of paper, my scrawl slowly focusing back into something I can actually read. Deckard lives at the Sea Slums. It figured. A sewer rat like him.

I pull a card out of my wallet and hand it to Archer. He turns it suspiciously, as though expecting it to sting him, then reads the name on the front. 'James L. Tolbert, Attorney-at-Law . . . ?' He looks up at me questioningly.

'I didn't mean to get you involved in any of this, but now you are, there's nothing I can do.'

'But I didn't do anything . . . '

'Sorry, Archer, but in this city that doesn't mean shit. If you need a lawyer, call him. He's a good man.'

Outside a squad car is waiting. Fucking Gillis is driving. Schiller sticks his head out of the passenger-seat window. 'What did you find?'

I stumble to the car, reading the address from the paper. 'Deckard. He lives at Windward Avenue, Venice.'

I get in the back of the squad car. Gillis avoids my eyes in the rearview mirror.

'You figure this Deckard is dangerous?'

'Sick is what he is . . . '

'Maybe we need backup?'

'With a hero like Gillis on board, we'll be able to handle a crumb like Deckard.' I slap Gillis across the crown.

He shakes his head, smooths down the Brylcreem cemetery of his hair. The car surges forward angrily, Gillis taking it up into top, grinding the accelerator into the floor as though it were my face.

The streetlights flicker chaotically as they come on all around us, like an amateur band warming up, tuning the whole city for the big event: sunset. A band of gold arcs across the sky, a red harvest of emotions that will soon swell, gutter and die. Like the love in our lives. Like our lives themselves. Birth. Then Lucky Break or Unlucky Break. Then Death. It's a simple as that: one, two, three. That's all it takes; just three steps up to the scaffold.

The address is a broken-down boardinghouse. Punks like Deckard don't know how to be original. The criminal mind. It's like wildlife migration or summer forest fires. A predictable force of nature. It would be so easy to snuff it out if it weren't for another wholly foreseeable and recurrent event. The Police mind.

Cops and Robbers.

Celestial Harmony.

Like the Drinking Bird's head and tail, the two are dependent on each other, kept apart but moving in concert, sometimes up, sometimes down; but always connected by the common interest of motion, the shared desire to maintain the status quo, and the compelling logic not of morals but of physics.

That's why PIs get results. They're outside this construct. They're free radicals. They fuck up all the cosy arrangements.

I kick the door in with the first attempt, the wood flying off its hinges, Deckard sitting on his bed in his underwear, looking up from the mini maze puzzle he's holding in his hands. He drops the toy, the glass shattering, the tiny balls hitting the floor and scattering for cover, clicking down cracks; Deckard crossing fast to where a .45 lies beside an open pot of glue. I feel the pop of his cheekbone as it cracks, then the flutter in my knuckles I always get before the simmer of bruising sets in, Deckard lying crumpled on the floor.

Schiller hoists him up and ham-hocks him in the face then drags him back up off the floor. 'I ain't asking but one more time.'

Deckard backs away, one eye already closed, blood sheeting out of his broken nose. 'What's the fucking question?'

Schiller looks at me for support. He doesn't know what the question is either. 'The kid that you stole for Roselli . . . '

Deckard throws his body against the wall, hammering the back of his head on the mould-stained wallpaper. 'I didn't kill the kid—he was dead already.' As if that made it okay to steal his body and chop it up. 'You gotta believe me.'

'Was Roselli behind the kidnapping?'

Deckard looks up at me, snot bubbling out of his bleeding nose. 'Please . . . they'll kill me.'

'And you think we won't?' Schiller pistons him in the guts. Deckard drops to his knees. 'Answer the question.'

Deckard's on his hands and knees. Clinging to the floor-boards, as though they were a raft in a heaving sea. He tries to speak but breaks down into sobs, muttering something. Schiller treads on one of his hands. 'Speak up.'

Deckard painfully tugs his hand out of the mousetrap of Schiller's fireman-size shoe. 'Please don't hit me. I forgot what the question was . . . '

'Was Roselli behind the kidnapping?'

He clutches his crushed hand as though it were a magic ticket that would get him out of this fix. Would change his destiny; turn him into someone else. Someone who didn't rob graves for a living. A human being. 'Roselli saw an opportunity and he took it. I mean, who wouldn't? Can the Old Man talk? I don't think so. He wasn't born yesterday, no sir, not with everything lined up like that . . . '

Question: what the fuck is he talking about?

Answer: nod to Schiller and we'll find out.

He throws him across the room. Deckard lands on the bed

and trampolines off it. The shatter of a shitty lamp, shards in Deckard's hair.

'What opportunity? Answer or he throws you through the fucking window.'

'Roselli knew.'

'Knew what, goddamn it?'

'He knew the kid wasn't really kidnapped. Roselli's smart. All he needed was . . . Was . . . '

The putter of a puny voice, silenced by its sins. All Roselli needed was a body. All Roselli needed was to threaten to expose the Old Man as a liar. Roselli was an old-school shake-down artist and his mark was the richest man in the world. But there's still something I don't understand and it's funda-mental: why did the Old Man lie about the body being his son's? I pick up the glue and smash it against the wall. Deckard flinches. 'You better clear that head of yours, because you're not making sense. Was there ever even a kid to kidnap?'

Deckard gazes at me, tears puckering the grime on his face. 'What?'

I can feel the big heat surging beside me as Schiller steps forward to harm. I can barely hold him back, like a jockey at the starting gate. 'Last chance, loser, so you better answer me. Did the Bannister kid ever exist?'

Schiller turns to me, his jaw hanging in surprise at the ques-tion.

'Sure, there's a Bannister kid, only he ain't kidnapped . . . ' Deckard starts to shake, looking at the glue from the broken pot quivering on the floor, knowing he's already said too much. 'Please . . . Leave me alone.'

'Can it with that Garbo stuff. Roselli knew who the real father of the Bannister kid was. So do you . . . '

'I don't, honest . . . '

Schiller picks up the bed, rams it into Deckard. It doesn't

really hurt him. But the way Schiller just picks it up. The simple ease of his strength scares the living daylights out of him.

'Who was he?'

'Please . . .'

Schiller grabs Deckard and runs his head through the wall. Shrieks and shouts from the room next door. Schiller pops Deckard's head out of the hole, like a goddamn wine cork. His ears hum red with blood. He mouths a single word: *Please*.

I snatch the .45 from the table. 'Listen, you sorry piece of shit. You tell us who the father is, or I'm pulling the trigger . . .'

Tears twist through the white plaster on his face, his blood turning him into a garish clown. 'I'm dead if I tell you.'

'What are you now?' Schiller says. There is the glint of a lighter and then the whoosh of a curtain on fire. Schiller yanks it free from the window, flames twisting at arm's length. 'Talk or I'm shoving this down your fucking throat . . .'

'Howard Hughes! Please. It was Howard Hughes.'

Schiller throws the fireball on the floor, stomps the life out of it as though it were a roach.

'The bodies. Where did you get them from?'

'Everywhere. City Morgue, until Curphey got wise. There's a funeral home in San Diego and one in 'Frisco. Mainly for parts, understand? And West Hollywood and Echo Park for the, well . . . Young ladies.' He shrugs helplessly.

Schiller stares into Deckard's dissolving face. The cuffs come out.

There's someone at the door. Correction. At the hole where the door used to be. 'Who's paying for this mess?' Schiller exhibits Deckard like a crow displaying a broken egg. 'Bullshit. He owes six weeks' rent.'

'Well, ain't you the dumb fuck?' Schiller shoves a passage through a crowd of hostile bystanders: junkies, hookers, johns and hustlers: the usual suspects along the polluted canals of Venice. Gillis opens the back door of the car, careful not to touch the plaster-powdered, bloody welt that passes for Deckard.

'He rides up front.' Schiller bellows. 'I don't want to let him out of my sight.'

Car doors close fast, like window shutters in front of an approaching lynch mob. Gillis pulls out recklessly, accelerating with a hot-rod hooligan shriek, almost hitting three rummies swaying across the street. He slams on the brakes, all of us lurching forward. There is the crack of Deckard's head against the dash and the click of metal coming from under the passenger seat. I'd completely forgotten. The knives. The ammo.

My gun.

Too late.

Gillis sees it and swears.

There is an atomic flash: yellow, then white. Heat bursts as the shot erupts inside the contained coffin of the car. The thunder of Zeus.

And then the hollow patter of broken glass. The cordite cloud lifts and Schiller and I sit up slowly, our heads rising through the shimmer and the smoke, our ears ringing.

The passenger door is wide open. Deckard is gone.

Gillis is slumped against the steering wheel. Schiller jerks his body back. 'Are you hit?'

Gillis opens his eyes, his voice at the other end of a long tunnel. 'I don't think so . . . '

'You'd know it if you were.' Schiller follows me out of the car. 'Trust a fucking glue head to miss at point-blank. Where'd he go?'

A woman hanging out of a second-floor window points into the canal. 'He jumped! Right there.'

We stand on the bank of the canal, gazing into the oil-tarnished surface of the water. The last of Deckard's bubbles burst like afterthoughts on the surface. 'And him still cuffed!'

I head back to the car, picking up the revolver that Deckard tossed in his mad dash to escape by drowning, and then I retrieve the rest of my arsenal from under the seat, trying to ignore the sobs of Gillis.

'Why the hell did he run?'

I'd been in Roselli's home earlier that day. I knew exactly what made Deckard do it. The same thing that made the rest of them crawl through ancient pipes, struggle up through soil. Crash through windows; fall through air. Race across highways. Panic. Flee. Do anything to avoid the gods of cruelty: Roselli and his pizza oven; Old Man Bannister and his riding crop; the Frost Moose Hunter of Hoover's renegade agents. The knowing ice pick of Boris Landis.

It was as if Los Angeles were no longer a city but a sepulchre; a mausoleum metropolis where the only signs of movement were the rigor mortis contraction of locking muscle. And the lisp of smoke from the funeral pyre, caught in the Santa Ana winds.

CHAPTER 40
Dallas 2014

T he restaurant is low-ceilinged and dark, the kind of discreet place you'd steal into with your mistress, only to discover your wife in a corner booth with her lover. Evelyn reaches across the table and takes my hand, nursing it palm up, as though trying to get in a fast reading. 'You're hungry,' she says, with clairvoyant-like authority.

It's an easy assumption. We'd spent half the night and most of the morning making love and then walked for two hours through the historic centre. Who wouldn't have an appetite? 'I thought New York was the only city left where people still walked.'

'San Francisco. Savannah, of course . . . But a Virgo like you would prefer European cities. I can imagine you walking for hours in Rome.'

'You're right, only I'm not a Virgo . . . '

Evelyn runs a red fingernail across my palm. 'But that's impossible . . . '

'Want to see my birth certificate?'

She laughs. 'There must have been some kind of exceptional celestial event that occurred at your birth. Were you premature?'

'I know I was precocious.' It's time to come clean with her. 'To tell you the truth, Evelyn, I don't believe in any of that stuff . . . '

'You should open your mind. Your life changes when you have the courage to follow your Zodiac.'

I'm not one of those people who call credulity *courage*. 'The only Zodiac I've ever paid attention to is this one,' I say, pulling my sleeve back to display my watch.

'Very retro . . . '

'It was my father's. He gave it to me just before he died.'

'I'm sorry . . . '

'Don't be, it's a good memory.'

Evelyn unclips her pocketbook, taking out a deck of tarot cards. She sees the look in my eyes and smiles. 'Indulge me,' she says, dealing five tarot cards facedown: anonymous yet somehow accusatory. With the speed of a stinging wasp, she turns them over.

I'm not crazy about my hand.

She taps the Fool. 'You.'

'Thank you very much . . . ' I crane my head to look in detail at the card. The Fool is teetering on the edge of a cliff, a dog barking a warning at his heels. 'Cute dog.'

'In this arrangement, the Fool also signifies the son. The son who's condemned to search for the Truth denied.' Her finger glides across the surface of the card, pointing to the abyss beyond the cliff. 'This then is his Quest.' She nods to the Hierophant. 'Which leads here, to the father.'

'He doesn't look very happy.'

'His authority is being challenged. But it's not only that. The Fool is looking forward, but the father is focused on the past, for he is also the judge.'

'What crime has been committed?'

She points to the next card: Death. 'Murder.'

'Most foul . . . '

Her eyes flash with annoyance. 'This is serious.' Before I can say anything, Evelyn continues, touching The Hanged Man. 'The judgment has already been made.' She looks up at me, her eyes luminous with professional exhilaration—like a medical scientist who has just made a major discovery. The person sitting opposite me is transfigured; I don't know her anymore. It's as though I've been seated at the wrong table. I feel like calling the waiter over and asking him to explain this mistake.

'That's one interpretation. They could mean anything.' They could mean nothing.

'There's no "could" with the Tarot.' She pushes the last card, which shows a tower being struck by lightning, towards the Fool. 'The Tower is your domain in every sense of the word. Where you come from; what made you. Your hardships and successes.'

She goes to draw another card. 'I wish you wouldn't.' But it's too late, she's already turned it. She stares at me.

'I knew it.'

'Knew what?'

Evelyn is trembling as she gazes at me. 'You're the Magus.'

The throb of the cork at my side makes me jump. In the heightened silence between us, the tumble of wine is a cascade. I go through with the ritual, swirling the glass, breathing in the fragrances of the white wine. Notes of almonds with a hint of straw. And something I recognize but can't quite name. Pungent; overripe. A fruit or flower . . . Some childhood memory, emphatic in its importance yet somehow disturbing. The more I try to recall it, the thornier it becomes, pushing me away until it's lost altogether and I am back in a fancy restaurant, nodding approval to a waiter.

'You saw it, just then. You know you did.'

'I was just trying to recall a smell. Wines are so complex these days.' I turn to the waiter for support, but he just stares into the middle distance.

'It wasn't the wine, it was you. Something from your past.' My past feels like it ended several weeks before when my wife divorced me to marry a French teacher. Evelyn stands. 'I'll be right back . . .'

The empty space left by Evelyn's departure is filled by the

restaurant's music. I hadn't even noticed it before. They're playing an orchestral version of *It's A Most Unusual Day*. The fact that I even recognize it is almost as disturbing as the show Evelyn has just put on. Too depressed to continue wondering whether the card reading was a result of her forgetting to take her meds, I check the *Dallas Morning News* on my iPhone. Cowboys. Expressways. Local weather. State weather. National weather. I can remember the time when people had better things to do than spend their life looking at weather reports. There's something about a local murder. I feel my blood slow as my heart slams on the brakes. Even the screen on the iPhone seems to dim with shock. I read it again. A former underworld figure, LeRoy 'Tex' Jeetton, was found shot, execution-style, inside his car. Three to the head. Three to the mouth. The punishment for an informer. Local police figured it was a settling of accounts.

The thought occurs to me before I can block it: was Tex's murder linked in any way with our meeting? As far as I can recall, there was no one else in the bar, except the bartender. I dropped him home, at a ratty little place in Oak Cliff, round eleven. Did someone follow us? Did they take my license plate? I make a mental note to change my rent-a-car that afternoon.

Evelyn comes back and we eat our lunch in silence. It is not the simmering hard silence that punishes a table after a fight; it is a harmonious, respectful silence; peaceful and welcome. She doesn't mention the cards again and I certainly don't mention what happened to Tex.

It's always a shock to leave the artificial twilight and the air-conditioning behind, to step out into the glare of unfiltered afternoon sunlight, the pith of humid air heavy as a summer cold. In that first exit moment, when the senses strain to adjust from the camouflage of fabrication to the authenticity of reality, it feels as if anything can happen.

And it does.

Dwayne Wayne reaches out of the dazzle of sunshine, takes

my arm and pulls me into the back of a large, dark limo. Before I even have a moment to register what's happening, it has happened. I have been abducted.

I look back through the tinted windows at Evelyn, who glances abstractly after the car, then turns and walks back inside the restaurant, as though she just remembered she had left her phone behind.

The car slows and stops for a red light. I lurch away from Wayne, yanking hard on the car door. Locked. I try the window. The same. I thump the glass, the car pulling away. Dwayne Wayne chuckles to himself. 'Evelyn called. Told us what was happening.' There is a disconcerting panting coming from somewhere inside the car. I hope it's not from me. He smiles, shaking his head. 'You didn't have a clue, did you? Damn, we're good . . . '

The panting grows in intensity—like someone losing a fight against a fatal asthma attack. 'Who's *we*?' My throat is so dry, my voice cracks. I start to slowly ease my phone out of my jacket pocket.

Wayne chuckles again, barely able to contain his mirth. His head lolls back towards the window Evelyn had disappeared from. 'Her . . . ' He nods to the driver. 'Him . . . ' The driver turns around. Adam Granston. The Man on the Horn.

'Tex is dead,' Granston says.

I lean forward peering into the front passenger seat. Granston's beagle is on the floor. One mystery solved. I almost have the phone out. Wayne hasn't noticed.

'Did you hear what I just said? Tex Jeetton is dead.'

'I know.' 9 . . .

Granston shakes his head in sorrowful disbelief, talking in a soft, contemptuous rush. 'You know he's dead. But that's not knowing. Knowing is understanding *why* he's dead. And you don't have a clue.'

Silence. Broken only by the gentle hum of the air-conditioner and the heartbeat pant of the dog. *1 . . .1.* The soft lisp of connection. Too late. Wayne spots the phone in my hand; snatches it away with a grin. 'All electronic devices must be switched off.'

'What the hell is going on?'

'We're protecting you.'

'Abducting me, you mean.'

'We're taking you to a safe house.'

'Kidnapping me!'

'Saving your sorry ass. As for the kidnapping . . . ' There is the pop of unlocking doors. 'You are free to go.'

'Right, jump out of a speeding car—what kind of choice is that?'

'A choice.' Granston chimes in, his eyes in the rearview mirror crinkling in a wizen approximation of amusement.

Ever the lawyer. 'Where the hell is this safe house?'

'We're nearly there . . . ' Wayne helpfully shows me his GPS. 'Old Preston Hollow.'

The name rings a bell. I have to keep them talking. The more they say, the less of a surprise I'll have waiting for me when we arrive—I hope. 'Why take me to a safe house?'

'We have information.'

'That's what Tex said too, but he was lying.'

'E. Howard Hunt?' Wayne purrs the name, like a father trying to get his child to eat his peas. I don't respond. I don't like peas. 'He wasn't lying.'

Bullshit. 'So what information do you have that's more original?'

'More original than Original Sin?'

Granston's eyes flicker doubtfully. He looks even more worried by Wayne's bizarre comment than I do.

I nod to the front. 'What's in the box?' Wayne starts to look over to the passenger seat before he stops himself. His eyes flare with anger. Not good for me but good for the situation. Anger leads to mistakes.

'You think you're so smart and you don't know a thing about the Bannister case.'

'That's enough.'

Too late. Granston's ire confirms my suspicions. This has got nothing to do with JFK. This is about my father. Granston and Tex both knew about him. And these two clowns taking me for a ride may be carpooling but they sure as hell don't act like they're real partners. Wayne glares at Granston, then settles his great bulk back into his seat. He speaks in a long, raw mutter. 'Damn, it's more than enough. It's all he'll need.'

'Need for what?'

He turns, his eyes simmering with the sugar hit of insider dope. I feel a sucker punch coming somewhere. 'For comprehension of the situation, Mr. Alston, and believe me, we certainly have a situation here.'

'Kidnapping. Abduction. Unlawful detention. Theft.' That last one scores an amazed, outraged look. I nod to my phone that he's still nursing in his great hand. He reluctantly passes it back to me. 'You used to be a bounty hunter, didn't you?'

'Bounty hunter, my ass. He was a bondsman.'

Wayne shakes his head in wounded disbelief. The car bucks its way over a grille, passing the glare of private armed security, then coasts down a tree-lined driveway into unknown territory.

An enormous mansion comes into view, Gothic and brooding. 'Well, what do you know—Hogwarts!'

A reluctant smile slides its way across Wayne's face as he shakes his head, giving up on further communication. I catch a glimpse of a weather-worn plaque as we pass. The car glides to a stop and Granston kills the ignition.

We sit there, the dog bevelling the silence with its pant. Wayne nods to my door. I get out, look around the luxury estate. The air is humid and pressurized. I feel like I've just stepped into a crowded elevator. Something touches my ankle. I look down at the beagle. Was it a warning; or a territorial challenge? Granston jingles some keys in my face. 'Let's get this over with!' Like an impatient hit man.

I stay by the car, making sure my phone is on. 'Get what over with?' Granston looks at me, shakes his head, and then palms the air away between us, as if getting rid of a noxious smell.

Wayne pats me on the shoulder. 'The Truth . . . ' Capitalized.

The Truth was replaced by the Real years ago, and no one has ever been able to tell the difference. 'And what is the Truth?'

'You're safe now. You're protected by Howard Hughes.'

H astings knew all about interrogation.

He remembered pulling the flap open on the captain's tent and finding the Japanese officer groaning senselessly in a chair, his trousers pulled down to his ankles. It was February 1945 and Susan was still alive. Tommy Alston, Marine sergeant and designated rifle company sadist, had hooked up a field radio to the officer's privates. 'This is useless,' Captain Harper had said in his Ivy League baritone, prodding the half-conscious prisoner, the skin between his waist and knees charred black like overcooked spare ribs. 'He'll never talk . . . '

'Sure he'll talk,' Tommy said. 'Otherwise he gets more of the same.'

'You gave him too much,' the captain said with a mixture of pride and reproach. 'He's too far gone, he can't feel a thing anymore. But the other fellow . . . ' The captain nodded to where the other prisoner sat, staring at him through strangely opened eyes. Captain Harold Harper III—rifle company commander, USILA All-American, scion of the Philadelphia Harpers—had snipped off the prisoner's eyelids with silver toenail scissors engraved with the initials H.H. 'The other fellow's seen everything. Now all we have to do is strap the wires on. We won't even have to juice him. He'll tell us where they're dug in.' Harper suddenly turned, staring at Hastings standing at the entrance to the tent with an SCR-300 strapped to his back, the antenna scrapping the top of the tent. 'Who gave you permission to enter?' Hastings handed the captain a field radio. 'It's the major, sir. He's raising hell.'

Harper snatched the handset from Hastings. 'Yes, sir?'

Hastings looked from the staring Japanese prisoner to the one dying of his third degree burns then back up to the sergeant. Tommy stared defiantly back at him. 'So help me God, Hastings, if you ever breathe a word!' Hastings looked away. The captain handed him the handset, unholstered his service revolver and shot both prisoners right there. Blood lashed the canvas. 'The goddamn major will be here any second.' He turned to Hastings. 'Don't just stand there, help the sergeant with these bodies. Get a burial duty together, pronto.'

That night they went through the last of the lower, southern tunnels, torching them with flamethrowers. Fire licked the night, sending shadows leaping across the rock. Savage screams echoed like lost souls from the lower depths. By the next morning Suribachi had fallen and everyone thought that meant the island was theirs. They were in for a surprise. Another month of fire, thirst and blood. No one understood why the brass wanted the island. All this suffering; all these casualties—for what? A dead volcano without a harbour? It was the airfield. The world's biggest gravestone sitting there in the Pacific, just three hours' flight-time from Hiroshima.

It was someone in 3rd Platoon who found Captain Harper at sunrise the next day. If he noticed Harper's eyelids were missing, he never mentioned it. The captain was posthumously awarded the Bronze Star. A couple of the men griped it should have been silver but the truth was that the major never liked Harper; and neither did the men for that matter. Hastings would have nailed Tommy Alston too on the island, but a sniper hit him in the shoulder on March 1st, and bought Hastings a ticket out of the theatre of war and into the house of horror that was waiting to ensnare him back home in Adelsberg.

In the years after, his dreams were plagued by the penetrating, lidless gaze of the Japanese prisoner. Staring not just in horror, but in helpless agony. Hastings had seen detainees blinded under barbaric interrogation but never the reverse—someone inflicted with unlimited sight: ultravision. Captain Harper and Sergeant Tommy Alston had created a new, terrifying order of existence, denying their victim the last resort: the shelter of not seeing; of being able to turn away when confronted with true evil. And having witnessed this appalling new condition firsthand, Hastings had become infected by it. He too was cursed with unfiltered perception, his eyes always aware, always riveted on that which must never be witnessed.

A decade later, Hastings was walking through Beverly Hills late one night when he heard a woman's scream and then the sudden hush of a hand across a mouth. It was a new moon; a perfect Kill Night. He followed the noise up a long pebble driveway, passing the parked squad car, seeing through the shadows what others would have missed; the drag lines, mute and accusatory. He tracked them into the estate, finding one shoe, his footsteps silent as he walked the soft, betraying lawn that rode the centre of the driveway—nature his accomplice. He silently turned a corner. Two men. Their uniforms almost indistinguishable in the dark. One was wrestling with a woman's wrists, the other with her ankles, both struggling to hold her down. Evil acts. It could have been Susan. It could have been any woman: any woman foolish or audacious enough to dare to cross a slim space of private grass at night on her own. To dare to think she was safe even for a moment from the brutality of men.

The cop who held the legs tore off the woman's underwear and tossed it into the night, where it fell like a wounded bird.

Hastings stepped forward, rage and despair in his heart. 'Stop.'

Both men froze. The one who had the legs let go and slowly

stood and turned, facing Hastings, his badge catching the glint of a shard of light, then falling back into shadow, his hand slowly rising to his hip. 'Take it easy, buddy, we're making an arrest.'

'That's not what it looks like.'

Tommy's head inclined in consideration. He knew that voice. 'Hastings . . . ?' He stepped towards him, his hand dropping. That was when Hastings saw it. The insult of Tommy Alston smiling. And the smile said to both his partner and to Hastings: he's one of us. 'Relax . . . She's just a coloured maid.'

Hastings almost broke his own fist, he hit Tommy so hard. He felt the pucker and snap of Tommy's jaw breaking. Tommy's partner sprang to his feet, drawing his weapon. Hastings hefted the limp body of Tommy towards him, using it as a shield, unholstering Tommy's service revolver at the same time. Mexican standoff. Almost. Hastings had Tommy as his very own bulletproof vest. 'Put the gun down . . . '

'Fuck you.'

'You heard the man, put it down.'

Tommy's partner turned to the girl. A victim only seconds ago, she was now a witness. A threat. Something to be taken care of. After Hastings.

'Drop it, or you're dead.' The cop stared hard at Hastings; recognizing his killer's soul. He dropped the gun. 'Turn around . . . '

The cop started to turn to mush. The girl had held on. She had fought them off; both of them. Tommy's partner had lost his gun and then he had lost his fight. His snivelling filled the rushing quiet of the mastered night. Hastings spoke directly to the woman for the first time. 'Look away, please.' The sobbing of the policeman surged. Hastings unfolded his *navaja sevillana*. It travelled across skin with a silver hiss, unfolding internal mysteries. Hastings dropped the dead bundle to the ground. Sergeant Tommy 'Frankenstein' Alston lay motionless, only his newly-freed blood still moving, slowly snaking out of his opened throat and finding refuge in the damming pebbles of the driveway. Hastings looked up at the other cop. So riveted in his fear, he hadn't even sensed the execution of his partner. He turned back to the woman. She watched until the swarming eddy calmed into mirrored stillness, the very last bubbles puncturing; forlorn. A universe without oxygen. Without hope. She looked up at Hastings, her eyes brilliant, as she mouthed two words: 'Thank you.'

There was a groan of horror—the other cop had finally worked up the courage to turn, perhaps convincing himself of salvation after all. When he saw Tommy's voided body, he bolted; fast feet fleeing back to the universe of the squad car. Back inside the car, everything would revert to normal. He would become a cop again, not a rapist. He would become the Law. The cop reached under the dash for the shotgun. But it was already too late, a bullet had passed effortless through the windshield, spiked a passage through his skull, and hubbed its way out with a significant section of his brains—his memories; his hates. His broken promises and youthful aspirations twisted too easily by greed and the lazy solutions of bribery and corruption. It all showered out behind him; an afterthought, already drying on the trunk of the car.

Hastings turned back to the woman. 'What's your name?'

She hesitated, for a second. Enough to let him know she was smart enough to be careful, and honest enough to be trusting. 'Greta Simmons.'

'Greta, do you have a car?' She nodded. He wiped his prints off Tommy's revolver. 'Can you give me a lift?'

She considered for a long moment, then nodded again, walking ahead of him, stopping to pick up her underwear and her shoe.

They drove in silence through the turbulent darkness. 'Where do you want me to drop you off?'

'Chinatown.' He looked at her, the headlights of the approaching traffic illuminating her injuries. 'You need to see a doctor.'

'You got there just in time.'

He looked at her wrists. 'You need to put something on them.' She looked away. The motor struggled with the silence. 'You live back there?'

'Do I look like I live in that neighbourhood . . . ?'

'So you work there?'

She turned to him, sharply. 'I'm not a domestic.' She muttered something he couldn't quite catch.

A wail rose out of the night. Greta reached over and turned on the radio. Bird with strings. *Laura.* The police car passed them at speed, hitting their faces with the slap-flash of red light. Hastings turned, watching the colour dissolving into the darkness behind them. He turned back to Greta. 'Where you from?'

She was about to answer but then stopped herself with an angry shrug of her shoulders. 'Somewhere else.'

'So what were you doing in Brentwood?'

'What are you, a cop?' Hastings looked away. She waited a moment, then sighed. 'I was . . . seeing someone.'

'Maybe you should start seeing someone else. Why didn't he come to help you?'

There was the simmer of consideration in the car. Of truth-sharing. Greta made her choice. 'It was a she. And those cops have been shaking her down.'

Hastings offered her a cigarette. The interior of the car flared with the nostalgic flicker of a campfire, then dissolved into an intense, heightened darkness. 'Who's their mark . . . ? I mean, who's your—'

'Companion will do nicely. Elaine Bourdonnais.' She glances sideways at him. 'Know her?'

'Should I?'

'Depends what crowd you run with . . . '

He fills the car with the white glaze of smoke. 'I don't run with any crowd.'

'I believe it. Otherwise I'd know you. What's your name anyway?'

'Hastings.'

'That's it—like a city?'

'Philip.'

'What do you do, Phil?'

'Stay out of trouble.'

She smiles. 'Well then, you've rescued the wrong person.'

'There's no such thing as the wrong person when you're rescuing someone.'

'Is that a fact . . . ?' Greta pulled up in front of the pagoda then turned, gazing at him with intense interest, as though suddenly discovering immense possibilities. The stutter of firecrackers made her start. They both glanced over to where some teenagers were gathered on the sidewalk, dancing away from the tiny explosions. She turned back to him, her eyes reflecting the dappled colours of the Chinese lanterns. 'I saw what you did back there . . . '

'And I saw that you hardly blinked.'

'I spent some time with Madame St. Clair in Harlem. I got to see a thing or two with her . . . '

Hastings flicked his cigarette out the window, its golden ash pushing fire through a piece of night, a poor man's comet, already extinguished. 'It's the seeing that does it.'

'Does what?'

'Makes it seem normal.' Hastings got out, walked around the front of the car, than leant in towards the driver's window. 'Thanks for the lift.'

'If I ever need to find you?'

He shrugged. 'On any given night, I could be anywhere.'

'I get it.'

'It's not that. I just set off in one direction and then keep walking.' As if to demonstrate the technique, he took a few paces down the street but then stopped and turned. 'Although . . . there's the Casablanca. It's a jazz club on South Kenmore. Hal Singer and Steve Potts are in residence this month. I plan to spend some time down there.'

She called out to thank him but it was already too late.

* * *

Foam flooded his mind; sucked air out of his lungs. Hastings came to in the surf. He raised his wounded head, the wind moaning into his consciousness as he clawed his way onto dry sand overlooked by the cliffs of Point Dume. He stared up at the rock face, loose sand needling his face with the sting of the wind. He had no memory of what happened from the moment they cut him down until he woke in the seething sea. They might have gotten careless. They might have been disturbed by witnesses. They must have thrown him off the edge and figured he was gone for good.

They figured wrong.

A king tide and luck saw to that.

He got a lift with a Mexican fisherman who loaned him a towel that smelt of calico bass, warmed him with hot coffee and a packet of Faros, and dropped him off outside a gas station on Ventura near Agora with enough change to get back. '*Gracias, amigo.*' The fisherman smiled, his teeth full of gold. '*De nada, camerado.*'

While Hastings waited for the 6 A.M. bus from Salinas he went through the plan once more. He would go on to Dallas and save the president. He'd meet Mrs. Bannister at Big Bear Lake. And then they'd run.

But before they started running, he was adding a new detail. He was going to figure out a way to kill the Old Man.

CHAPTER 42
Los Angeles 1960

I look at myself in the bathroom mirror, the surface fading fast behind the blur of humidity from the shower. Just as well. I didn't like what I was seeing. I finish shaving staring into the blind fog on the glass, the contours of my face familiar to my hands, to the rasp of the well-honed blade, avoiding the more sensitive parts of my jaw. Of my trouble-inviting big mouth.

My body stings from the needles of hot water and the bruising of the last eighteen hours. I dry off and bandage myself up, then walk through to the kitchen wearing just a towel. The cat appears silently at the window, laps its milk, devours the curl of ground beef I share with it then disappears out through the rear window, back into the night. It got what it wanted: it doesn't need company. Unlike the rest of us. I switch on the radio. Billie Holliday. *The End of a Love Affair*. Too close for comfort. The pan spits and protests as meat and eggs sizzle. The last thing I ate was the omelette prepared by Mrs. Bannister. Tonight feels like the flip side of the American Dream: the beginning of *The Lost Weekend*. I uncork a quart of JTS Brown and take a bottle of Golden Velvet out of the Amana. There is a noise behind me. I spin around, knocking my fork to the floor.

'Nick . . . ?' Cate bends down, picks up the fork. I catch a glimpse of her naked body through the neckline of her negligée as she leans forward. There was a time when we couldn't get enough of each other, making love in the shower, at the movies, on the porch at midnight, in the back of taxis, in half-open doorways. Once I pulled her into the Bradbury Building and we fucked in the darkened corner of one of the balconies. It was twilight. Deserted. Silent except for the squeak of a mop and bucket somewhere far above us, echoing in the building's empty corridors. Then the ping of an elevator. We both froze, clinging to each other as though somehow that would make us invisible. An attractive brunette stepped out, stopping when she saw us, Cate's back to her. She opened her mouth as though to scream. I shook my head. The woman was motionless, except for her eyes. They were everywhere. I started again, sinking slowly back against the railing, gently tugging an unsuspecting Cate on top of me, hoisting her dress up high above her hips so the brunette was sure to see everything. Cate rode me as I watched the brunette, spellbound, watching us. When it was over, I kissed Cate like I'd never kissed her before; it was strange, I was so proud of her. There was a fast click of heels behind us. Cate turned but the brunette was already gone. Cate and I had our own home. We were just doing it for the kicks. It was our private fever. I remembered the brunette's eyes that night when I made love again to Cate, but the next day I had forgotten them; even their colour. I only had eyes for Cate. She was the one. It was an obsession. But like all great passions it burnt faster the brighter it was. Now I can't even remember the last time we made love.

'I didn't mean to wake you . . . ' I go to switch off the radio.

She stops me, staring for a long moment, her hands fanning my face in astonishment. 'What happened?'

'Drink?' She shakes her head. The glowing warmth of bourbon; the frosty awakening of the beer chaser. I sigh. 'One too many doors slammed in my face.' There's a frown, of concern. I remember I used to love it. Before I forgot that it was ever there. 'Don't worry, I saw a doctor . . . '

'So did I . . . ' She looks away. 'Nick, I was pregnant.'

'Was?' I slowly stand. She nods, looking up at me.

We had given up on the thing we had wanted so much for so long. It had been the thing that had led us into marriage in the first place. To have a family. And it had been the thing that had killed our marriage when we couldn't. We didn't formally give up on each other. It just happened, the way it always does. We just stopped loving each other, sharing confidences, living together. We drifted apart because it hurt so much when we were together. Unable to have what we wanted. Unable to even talk about it anymore. And now this. It wasn't fair. I didn't even know until it was over. It was all too fucking late.

I sit down opposite her, staring into her eyes. 'Why didn't you tell me?'

She takes the cigarette out of my mouth, inhales deeply. 'Because it wasn't yours, Nicky.'

I hadn't seen that coming.

Silence. Long and hard, broken only by the gush of smoke she exhales and the internal snare drum of my furious heart. I have to clear my throat before I can speak, and even then, my voice breaks. 'Who?'

'It doesn't matter, Nicky . . . '

'The hell it doesn't!'

'Let it go . . . ' she says, grinding out my cigarette. 'I have.'

This had been the news I had waited for all those years, then given up on. Then forgotten about altogether. That's what felt like a cheat. Not Cate, sleeping with another man. After all, how many women had I slept with over the past two years? I wished I had known before Cate had lost it; I wished I'd had that moment of thinking it was mine. Even if it was a lie, it would have been enough.

She looks up at me, tears in her eyes. I grab her wrists, pull her close to me. 'I'm so sorry, baby.'

I feel the tightness in her beginning to crack, the low trembling growing stronger with her sobs. A married couple, at the end of their rope. Holding each other in a crappy little kitchen with a flickering fluorescent light. Good times all forgotten. Future no longer imagined. Present just passing nods through windows as one drives away from the other. Bedside lamps no longer synchronized. The end of the road. 'When did you lose it?'

'Last week . . . '

'Why didn't you tell me?'

'I couldn't. Not without lying.'

'You didn't lie now.'

'Now it's too late to lie. Now it's all over . . . '

She lets go, her tears fierce as a summer storm. I hold her to me. My girl. My fiancée. My bride. My woman. We stand there, the weight of our worn history amplifying her sobs.

The phone rings. 'Don't . . . '

'Baby, I have to . . . ' Cate breaks reluctantly from me. I lean over, snatch the phone off its cradle.

'Mr. Alston? You've got to come over.'

Her voice is strange—tense and distant. 'Sorry, Mrs. Bannister, I'm off duty . . . '

'It's my husband, Mr. Alston. He's missing.' The dial tone purrs in my ear. I hang up. Cate takes my hand. 'Come to bed . . . '

'I can't sleep now, baby, I got work to do.'

'I don't mean that.'

We step into the bedroom together. It feels both strange and familiar, like running into an old friend from school. Cate kisses me gently on my lying lips. I sigh. I can't help myself; it's too strong. I have to ask: 'Do I know him?'

'Let it go, will you, Nicky,' she says, pulling the straps of her negligée over one shoulder, than the other, allowing it to glide down her body. She unwraps my towel, tosses it to the floor and then pulls me into her arms.

Wayne and Granston escort me across a marble entrance. Orchestral music, majestic yet ominous, swells from somewhere beyond a curving staircase: Prokofiev. *Romeo at Juliet's Tomb*. Is someone, right now, preparing my own grave?

Wayne opens a wood-panelled door. I turn before I enter, looking back at him and Granston as though they were going to jump me. I can't imagine why they would, and yet I can't imagine being kidnapped either.

I glance around the enormous living room. Formal, lifeless; resplendent with antiques. Not so much furniture as trophies; stamps of power pressed into innocent teak and oak. I turn to Wayne, who hovers at the door. 'I'm entitled to a phone call and a lawyer.'

He points to a phone, then catches himself, and closes the door behind him. There is the sinister rasp of a bolt turning outside. I try the door handle. Locked.

I look around the great room, but it appears empty. Then I see her, an elderly woman with a large mouth and highly amused eyes, dressed in cashmere and silk, sitting in a Louis XV armchair. Rubies glitter on her ears and around her throat. 'All this talk of kidnapping is really unbecoming.' She gestures to a sofa in front of her. 'If you were brought here, it was for your own safety. Besides, we have all the information you've been looking for.'

'About the Kennedy assassinations?'

'About the Bannister case.' Her dyed auburn hair masks half of her face as she reaches down and plucks a cigarette and lighter from the coffee table. 'Admit it, Mr. Alston, that's why you're really here. Your father's unfortunate association with the case locked you into this obsession. A downward spiral . . . ' She smiles sadly at me. 'You shouldn't have to do this to yourself—you're throwing your life away looking at one thing when you should be looking at another. Besides . . . ' There is the grind of flint finding flame, and the swift inhalation of combustion. 'When it's all said and done, Jack and Bobby were such heels. Don't waste your time on them. Your father was so much more interesting.'

A plume of smoke crosses the room. I can smell its charmed breath of spices and cancer. There is a long silence. She's made her speech, and now I was expected to make mine. We stare at one another, each waiting for the other to crack. She smiles. 'Do you know who I am?'

'Betty Bannister.'

The intake of her breath is so sharp that for a second I think she's having a heart attack. I rise to my feet, but she flags me back down. 'The very thought!' Her laugh is warm and indulgent. Authentically amused. I realize that whoever she is, I think I like her. 'I am . . . I was Eva Marlowe.'

'The movie star?'

'How very kind of you to remember . . . Sometimes I do feel like Norma Desmond.'

'And now you're running with bounty hunters?'

She doesn't understand at first. 'Oh, Dwayne.' Her laugh is like a reed instrument. Musical; resonant without being overwhelming. 'He does have an active imagination. Of course everyone likes to think of themselves as a hero.'

'Heroes don't kidnap people.'

'You were brought here for your own protection.'

'Where's here?'

'Caddo. That's the name of the house. Sonny—Howard Hughes—gave it to me. He knew I couldn't stand Texas. Sonny was always like that, just couldn't take no for an answer. It'd drive him crazy, and let's face it—he was pretty damn crazy to begin with. Poisoned chalices were always his favourite type of gift . . . ' Now I remember where I knew the name: they used to call Howard Hughes "The Headless Horseman of Old Preston Hollow". 'On the other hand, how could any sane person refuse a place like this? Wait till you see the grounds. A drink, Mr. Alston?'

I look at the bottle of single malt she's holding. Older than me. 'Please . . . ' I nod to the shelves of books. 'You're a reader?'

'I love reading, though I'm too impatient to be a great reader. I just finished *The Day of the Jackal*. I actually met de Gaulle. Appalling bore. I was living in France back then. We all were. We were tax exiles, although we pretended it was for the culture . . .' Eva Marlowe looks up at me, coming back from Paris when it sizzled. 'What were we talking about . . . ? Oh yes, the library. Sonny was always fascinated by the esoteric. Freemasons, Ancient Egypt. The Knights Templar. Prophesy and fortune-telling. Even Ouija boards. Anything to do with magic . . . He just hated the notion that someone might know something he didn't.'

'Meaning he was gullible?'

'On the contrary, he was alert—always looking for an angle that other people overlooked. Sonny used to say that superstition was simply knowledge that educated people ignored. He called it his double indemnity. When he found out this house had been built on a Caddo Ghost Dance site, he was hooked. He believed there was some kind of ancient power buried under the earth. That's why he installed his library here. For its magical properties.'

I flash back to Evelyn and me in her library last night . . .

'Evelyn uses it all the time.' Eva Marlowe mind-reads me.

'She says it's unique. Apparently Yale would like to acquire it. There's a lot of material about Skull and Bones; material they'd prefer to keep hidden . . . ' She stands and removes a slim leather volume from a bookshelf. 'But there's one book that shouldn't remain hidden any longer. It was given to me by two men I met in . . . unusual circumstances.'

'What circumstances were those?'

'I'm afraid I can't tell you. There's a third party involved who has already suffered enough.'

'Do you know the names of the men?'

'Even if I did, I wouldn't be able to tell you. They said they were killers. I believe they were actually spies. One of them was French. The other man, the American, gave this to me. It's a diary. You must promise, under no circumstances, to discuss it with anyone, including Dwayne and Adam. Especially Adam.'

'You don't trust Granston?'

'He's trustworthy. Up to a point. But he's too much like Tex Jeetton . . .' She knows—knew—Tex too. 'Haunted by all the glass keys they had to smash after every door they locked. There are things you should never go back to. That's easier for a woman to understand than a man. But then there are things you must go back to, out of respect for the victim. Like that book . . . '

I open the volume. Pages and pages of tight, neat writing. The blue ink has faded to a bronze-hued tint, and the paper has been sun-scorched by time into a burnished, fragile transparency. 'This is Marilyn Monroe's diary?'

'One of them. The one that concerns you. The one that talks about the Bannister case. It explains it all, starting with Sonny.'

'What did Hughes have to do with the kidnapping?'

'It's all there. Sonny blamed Bannister for the election of Kennedy. That was not supposed to happen. Nixon was supposed to have been elected. Especially with everything they had over JFK . . . '

'And what did they have over him?'

'Joe Kennedy was very active in Hollywood, both sides of the War: Gloria Swanson, Marlene Dietrich. Clare Boothe Luce—you know I once turned down the offer of playing Crystal in a remake of *The Women*? It just didn't make sense: why would you want to remake a Cukor classic?'

'Please, Miss Marlowe. What were you saying about Joseph Kennedy?'

'He had an affair with Adèle Bourdonnais—the greatest beauty of her day. Their children married Rex Bannister.'

'Children?'

'Twins. Elaine and Betty.'

'And Rex Bannister knew this.'

'Of course—everyone knew it. Why do you think he married them?'

I look back at the diary in my hands. Turning the pages. A name starts to appear, recurring more and more frequently: Bannister. Adèle, Elaine; Elizabeth . . . Betty. An ancient Photostat slips out of the back of the diary. I unfold the hard, grey shell. It is a Texas State Board of Health Bureau of Vital Statistics Standard Certificate of Birth for a Joey Mack, born October 8th, 1957. I look up at Eva Marlowe. 'Who's this?'

'Remember the body your father found? Everyone said it was Ronnie Bannister? They even buried him in the Bannister tomb. It was all a lie. It was this child, this poor child, Joey Mack . . . '

'How can you be so certain?'

'Who else could it be? Didn't your father ever tell you? Ronnie Bannister was invented to stop Kennedy.'

'Invented?'

'I'm sorry. I thought you knew. The Bannister child never existed . . . '

Cate straightens my tie. Steps back, then adjusts it. 'Come home soon.' I snatch up my car keys. Then I remember. 'Baby, can I take yours?'

She comes out onto the street with me. 'Be careful . . . '

I see her in the rearview mirror, the screen door closing behind her, hiding her like a veil. I go through my calculations. Take the Old Man for as much as I can. Sell the house. Go. Somewhere where there's sunshine and a sea to wash all the grime away. I switch on the radio. Mingus. *Flamingo* from *Tijuana Moods*. Why not another country? I want out of LA. If it doesn't happen soon, it never will. I'll be like everyone else, trapped in Cemetery City.

The gates are open at High Sierra. No cops; no reporters. It's like everyone got embarrassed and ran away. Branches sway with the restless wind, Cate's car swerving up the gravel path. The quiet is unnerving after the carnival scenes with the press hounds. Distant barking tells me the only dogs left are safely stowed in their kennels. There is a plaintive sound to their howls, as if they know the truth: the kid is dead, the only suspect who could give up Roselli is dead, and this whole stinking thing has been a setup from the very beginning.

I look down on the lights of LA. The real LA. Of families and squabbling kids, dirty dishes and blaring televisions. Couples arguing or copulating. Children crying. Cats sleeping or prowling. The mysteries of the mundane; the things that keep us sane. But up here, in High Sierra, other mysteries apply:

wealth, control, dominion; limitless power. Up here, it's Olympus; a whole, separate cosmology. And we poor mortals don't have a clue that it even exists until we accidentally collide with it, through happenstance or catastrophe.

Through visitation from the Gods.

Broken glass crunches underfoot, all that's left of the memory of Greta Simmons. Stars flint their hesitant light into the windy sky above the mansion. Datura flowers bloom in moon glow, honeying the air with their disturbing lemon scent. I shiver. The entire estate seems deserted at first, but then I notice the glow from the pool house and walk round the side, my feet loud on the heavy pebble driveway. This is how Tommy got it, in a lonely place just like this, his footsteps down a mansion's pebble driveway betraying him to his killer.

There is a noise behind me. I whirl, the gun at her face, so close to the final consummation of barrel, bullet, bone. Yet she doesn't start. She just stands there, letting the gun rest against her cheek, as though it were the lips of a lover. 'Kind of edgy tonight, aren't we, Mr. Alston?'

'You could have gotten yourself killed, Mrs. Bannister.'

She shakes her head, hair falling across her face, across my hard barrel. I draw it slowly away and see the white oval impression it's left on her tanned cheekbone. 'I give you more credit than that.'

'What are you doing out here all on your own?'

'I thought I heard a car . . . And what are you doing out here, Mr. Alston? Haven't you read the papers? The case is closed.'

'But you called me?'

Panic spreads across her face. 'Mr. Alston, I assure you, we haven't spoken since Captain Schiller was here.'

One of us is being set up. 'We need to talk . . . '

'Can't this wait?'

'It's about your husband . . . '

'What about him, Mr. Alston?'

'Do you know where he is?'

She hesitates, then shakes her head. I start heading towards the house, but she takes my arm, steers me away. 'Please, Mr. Alston . . . You must go.'

'I want answers. Now.'

She stares into my eyes; a testing look. Challenging. Judgmental. She sighs. Capitulation? Or resignation? 'All right. But not in the house . . . It's not safe.'

'Why's that?'

She doesn't answer, she just walks away . . . I follow the sway of her hips across the gardens, watching her body slowly appearing through her white silk dress as we draw closer to the glow of the pool house. It's lit by dozens of floating candles flickering on the surface of the water, reflected in the skylight.

'Power company cut you off?'

'You know what they say about the rich . . . We're poorer than the poor.' She's looking at me the way she did when we first met, regal and with amused defiance as she crossed that immense hallway, coming to me proudly in her revealing neg-ligée, her silk robe sweeping the marble floor.

If this encounter had happened earlier today, there would have been no hesitation. I would have tugged her into my arms, and kissed her. But something unexpected had gotten in the way . . . Cate.

As soon as we're in the pool house, her attitude changes. 'We must be quick,' she says, glancing over my shoulder. 'There are people everywhere.' Who is she talking about? The estate's deserted. 'Ronnie's life is in danger.'

'Stop the charade, Mrs. Bannister. There never was a Ronnie Bannister, it was all a . . . ' My voice falls down a well when I see it, framed beyond her left shoulder at the other side of the pool house.

The telephone on the table.

She follows my gaze then turns back to me. 'The calls. They didn't come from the bomb shelter, they came from here . . . Didn't they, Mrs. Bannister?'

A look of horror passes across her face, and she takes a step backwards. I start to turn.

Too late.

There's a blow from behind, the blood hot down the back of my shirt then cold with the swimming pool, candles dancing in the water above me, her face disappearing as I sink, flames extinguishing like meteors, till everything closes and goes black.

* * *

I come to in a cellar, the smell of dust and mildew in the air, being dragged backwards down a corridor. It's all too complicated to absorb . . .

* * *

I'm being thrown down on my back, my head meeting the stubbornness of stone. I open my eyes, the golden and purple pentagram coming into focus on the ceiling above the table I'm lying on.

Altar, Mr. Alston.

Above the altar I'm lying on.

That screwy face inside the star stares at me with a decidedly unfriendly expression. I'm not too crazy about him, either.

My head aches the way it only ever does on New Year's Day.

I crane my neck, trying to scope as much of the room as possible. Over my shoulder I can make out ancient cobwebs slowly turning from the heat of a nearby candle. I try to move and feel the burn of rope around my wrists, ankles and throat. The rope around my left wrist is not as tight as it should be.

Maybe I have a chance after all. Maybe someone is looking out for me . . .

A voice I recognize says, 'He's awake . . . ' A light comes on directly above me, showering me in its big, voltage smile. I close my eyes against the glare and the same voice says, 'Where's the kid?'

I can see nothing but the solar flare of the klieg light, its immense heat hammering into my body, my wet clothes already beginning to smoulder under its Fahrenheit dazzle. But that voice? The thick-lipped intonation, laboured and overly precise; the strangely lisped delivery, as though reading from a script he didn't quite understand. Jesse. The man who demanded the ransom.

'What have you done with Mrs. Bannister?'

No response. Guilt? Or satiated exhaustion.

'So help me, God, if you've touched a hair on her—!' There is the wheezing turn of an old wheel and the rope begins to tighten to a sequence of hard clicks. I have just enough time to tauten my throat against its pressure, swelling my Adam's apple into a hard knot against the bite of hemp, sucking breath through my nostrils and expanding my lungs as much as I can, my clothes smoking as though from the pressure. 'Your sweetheart's gone, chump, and she couldn't help you even if she wanted to. This is your last chance. Now where's the kid?'

The rope around my left wrist is giving, but I need more time. I need to go on the offensive. They think I'm helpless because I'm tied up. I need to ambush their smug assumption that they're in control. 'Which kid?' I have their attention, all right. I decide to play a hunch. 'The phony dead one? Or the real living one?'

Stunned fucking silence.

The shocked hush drains the room of all life. Even the arc light above me seems to waver in disbelief.

It tells me something I've never quite stopped believing.

That the Bannister kid is real.

That the Bannister kid is still alive.

And that they know where he is. Or are looking awful hard to find him.

The question is why are they putting on this routine . . . ? The only answer: for the benefit of someone else in the room who's out of the loop. I keep working at the rope around my left wrist. I play the only card I have left, praying it's an ace. 'Jesse led me to the real kid.'

The room simmers with the possibility of betrayal, and right then I knew I figured right, that Jesse had to be there in the room, lurking in the artificial darkness. Time to tease him out with a twist of the big knife. 'He was as sloppy as a dishrag in a chophouse.' I give a false laugh, which comes off as scornful and real. 'You should have heard him trying to talk on the phone! What a riot! Know what we called him? We called him Mumbles.'

'Liar!'

That had to be Jesse. There is a lethal pause and then what feels like a fistful of brass knuckles wallops me hard below the belt. In the convulsive jolt it gives my body, I loosen the rope enough to let me pull my left hand free whenever I need to. I turn my head and the vomit trickles onto the floor. I glance up and spot my assailant retreating into the coward shelter of the arc light's blinding halo. But he isn't fast enough. I get a glimpse of him. His face is mush. Bingo. I've clocked the bastard. Jesse is Goodwin James—Old Man Bannister's nosy reporter turned amateur shakedown artist. 'But seeing you in the flesh what we should have called you was Pruneface.'

I turn to the other side of the room, to where a pair of scuffed black shoes with the soles lifting off the toes half-hides in the shadows. 'And that makes you who? Flattop or Itchy?' I let out a gasping shriek as someone belts me in the guts. I can hardly breathe, but still manage to spit out a curse. I turn my head, dry-retching, my hand free. I just need to stall for the right moment . . . 'Go on. Call the Old Man. Ask him. He knew about the switcheroo. He was the one who told me that Jesse was Goodwin James.'

Boom.

I can feel the panic naming names always causes.

'Why, that dirty . . . '

'Shut up, you fucking prick, can't you see he's lying!' Another voice. Gravelled and coarse. Limned with the drawl of the gutter. Thickened from a heavy cold. Or a broken nose. 'Fuck the old cripple, he's finished!'

'Don't write the Old Man off. He's been one step ahead of you from the start. Call him . . . ' Then I nail the voice. 'Go on—call him yourself, Rico.'

There we go.

Another bombshell in the room. I can almost feel the tremor of its explosion. There's the simmer of exposure. I move in for the kill. 'The Old Man told me everything.'

'And what exactly did my husband tell you?' Her voice is languid; thrilling me with its rich timbre. No matter what, I know I will always be under its spell.

I have to improvise fast. 'He told me why you wanted your nephew dead, Mrs. Bannister.'

Upside down, moving into the aura of the spotlight, comes Mrs. Bannister's face, haloed by radiance. If it's the last thing I'm going to see, I can't complain. An angel would have been proud of a face like that, and pride was the sin that had sent so many of them straight to Hell. 'The arrogance of men . . . ' She grabs me by the hair and taps my head against marble. 'You're always so sure you have all the answers.' I can smell her perfume riding high and imperious above the acrid bile in my throat. I almost had my left foot free. It was one long length of rope and it was beginning to unravel, just like this case. 'You don't even know who Ronnie's father really is . . . '

'Shut up.' Goodwin James's voice explodes behind her. 'The less he knows, the better.'

'What does it matter? He's not going to be around much longer.' The certainty in her voice was devastating. It was the same certainty I heard when she told me she knew I'd find the boy. Could she be lying again? And then I see it: her wink. 'I think Mr. Alston has earned the right to know the truth . . . '

Someone slaps her hard, turning her with the blow, the fist passing close enough for me to seize with my freed hand, swinging Goodwin James over my body as I roll off the altar, tugging him along with me, my right hand still attached, James tumbling onto the floor, his head striking the ground as I fall on top of him, the altar upended, my right hand throbbing and finally free, the unravelled cord tightening about his neck. I look around. Rico has already gone; the only trace of him ever being there is the sole of one of his water-ruined shoes. Mrs. Bannister is on the floor, groggy from the slap. I whisper into Goodwin James's cauliflower ear. 'Where's the boy?'

Defiant silence. I tighten the cord. 'You've got thirty seconds . . . ' A gasp, not of acquiescence but of pain. I wind the rope around my fists, shortening its length to give me added strength, the hemp burning my palms . . . 'Last chance. Where is he?'

Goodwin James makes a rushing noise like a pearl diver coming up for air. 'Hastings. He's with Hastings.'

'Where can I find Hastings . . . ?'

'I don't know—' A choking sound, and something else—a cry: fear of death. He's telling the truth. I let go of the rope, and he sighs into unconsciousness. I struggle to my feet and walk towards Betty Bannister, who slides away from me on the marble floor. I point back to Goodwin James, still crumpled beside the overturned altar. 'You're next, Mrs. Bannister. So help me, God, unless you start talking, you're next . . .'

'I can't . . . '

I grab her wrist and yank her to her feet, half pulling, half throwing her towards the chimney. 'Show me the way out . . . '
She looks at me then points to the chamber door. 'I mean the secret way.'

'What are you going to do?'

'I'm going to find the boy and bring him back alive. Just like I promised.'

'I want him protected.'

'How can I protect him when I don't know where he is?'

'Promise you'll protect him.'

'Take me to him.'

She turns away. I look at the way she's set her jaw. She's strong, this one. Stronger than me. It's hopeless unless I agree. 'All right, I promise. Now get me the hell out of here.'

She steps into the fireplace, triggering a lever under the lintel, then sliding open a panel obscured by soot. I glance back one last time at the still unconscious Goodwin James, then follow Mrs. Bannister into the huge, tubular flue. Iron rungs lead up the ancient well. Halfway up we pass three large circular openings giving on to separate ancient water pipes. I gesture for her to choose one of them. She peers into the darkness, then turns back to me. 'If it's all the same to you, I'd rather not . . . '

Neither would I. 'Where do they lead?'

'Everywhere. To the pool house, the stables, the garage . . . '
The garage—where Hastings worked. 'Some come out into the neighbouring properties. One leads all the way to Greystone Park.'

'Just the thing for a picnic . . . Which one did your sister take?'

She turns, looking down at me. 'The wrong one.'

'Let's hope we don't make the same mistake.'

She doesn't answer; just continues up the rungs. Some are missing. Some feel loose as hell. I look down the shaft and freeze. Perfect. If there's anything stronger than my claustrophobia,

292 · TIM BAKER

it's my vertigo. I look back up at Mrs. Bannister, who's suddenly far above me. Something slides away in front of her and she disappears.

What the hell was I thinking? I've let her escape.

I hurry after her, hoping I can find the trigger to open the secret panel. But then her hand appears, guiding me out of the narrow opening. Shame and relief: maybe I can trust her after all?

Moonlight washes through the great windows, filling the reception hall with a ghostly radiance. She looks around suddenly, putting a finger to her lips. Her eyes are large with trepidation. 'Listen. Can you hear it?'

'What?'

'That strange noise . . . What is it?'

'My teeth, Mrs. Bannister. In case you didn't notice, I took a bath with my clothes on.'

'I'm so sorry, but you see . . . '

I grab her by the elbows and push her back against the wall. 'No, you see! What the hell was that all about? Luring me up here.'

'I assure you, I never called you . . . '

'Just like you never had me sapped and tossed into the pool. I could have drowned!'

'But you didn't. Because I made sure they pulled you out. I had no idea they were going to hit you. After they did, they wanted to finish you off there and then, but I convinced them you had information. Information they needed.'

'Much obliged for arranging my torture. Oh, you're good, Mrs. Bannister, you're awful good . . . ' Something grabs my attention in the centre of the room. A trolley bar. I pour myself a big brandy. 'Let me tell you, it didn't look like you were on my side when they put me on the goddamn rack.' A troubling heat fills me with its sluicing presence. I pour myself another.

'Go easy, Mr. Alston, the night's not over yet.' Hard to say if that's a promise, or a threat. Her face goes blue then yellow with the flame of a cigarette lighter. She hands the cigarette to me. 'I don't know who told you to come out here, but in the run of things, they did me a favour . . . '

'If that's their idea of a favour, next time tell them to just send flowers.'

'We escaped, didn't we?'

'Cute.'

'Who do you think left one of your hands untied?' My face must be looking a little goofy because she's smiling at it. 'Believe what you want, I've been on your side from the very beginning . . . ' She grabs my wrist, her grip fierce. 'They said they would kill me if I didn't hand over Ronnie.'

'What do they want? A million like the others?'

'They don't want money, Mr. Alston, they want control—of my husband.'

'What kind of control?'

'They want him to support Kennedy against Nixon.'

'It doesn't make sense, to kidnap a child just for that.'

'You don't understand, Mr. Alston. My husband decides who becomes president. It's been like that since Dewey lost in '48. Rex gave Truman California, Illinois and Nevada. And Truman gave him Korea in return. There's nothing like a war for making money.'

'But we're a democracy!'

'I'm awfully sorry, Mr. Alston, I really am . . . ' She hurries me across the room. 'Now we have to hurry. Hastings will be getting anxious.' I bang into something in the dark, stubbing my toe hard. The ring of the rocking vase is almost as loud as my curse.

'Please, Mr. Alston, that's Ming Dynasty—it's priceless.'

And my toe isn't. I get the picture.

'Here . . . ' She pulls a long coat off a hall rack. 'That should keep you warm.'

'You take it. You're . . . ' Practically naked in that dress.

'I have this.' She throws on a black satin cape. We wait by

the door, peering outside, searching the shadows for movement, then I yank it open, the shivering wind tormenting us as we run to her car, my hand on her elbow as she almost stumbles. I go to drive but she slips in behind the wheel. I get in on the other side. 'Where to?'

'What time is it?'

'It must be around midnight.'

'There's a pickup on South Street at Broxton Avenue . . . If we hurry, we can make it.'

The squeal of acceleration and the stutter of tires skidding on gravel. She hits the headlights. 'Maybe you should wait until we're out?' There is a shot behind us, agreeing with me. She accelerates towards the gates. I turn back and catch a glimpse of muzzle flash as Rico fires again from a second-story window, the whine of a bullet biting bark close by. The bounce and shrieking protest of chrome against bitumen gives way to the glide of the road as we speed away through the night. I turn to Betty Bannister, her eyes fixed on the road ahead, her hair restless in the wind, the flash of passing headlights peeping inside her cape.

'What's the pickup?'

She turns to me, her eyes emerald in the streetlight. 'Ronnie Bannister of course . . . '

A moment I had stopped believing in: the end of the case. 'Start at the beginning. Who snatched the kid?'

'It was Elaine's idea . . . '

One of my earliest hunches. Not kidnapping for ransom but abduction by a desperate parent. A loon mother battling the most influential man in the nation. That explains Elaine's motive, but what about the others? Their instincts were more predatory than paternal. 'What do Rico and Goodwin James want?'

'They're just foot soldiers.'

'Tell me something I don't know. What's their motive?'

'Manipulation and revenge.'

A car rockets in front of us, Mrs. Bannister almost clipping it, a shouted curse already left behind. I turn back. 'That was a red light.'

'We have to hurry . . . '

'Who's being manipulated?'

She turns, staring at me. 'The manipulators themselves.'

I steady her steering wheel as she strays towards oncoming traffic. 'Can the cryptic stuff. Your husband, is that it?'

'What you have to understand, Mr. Alston, is that Ronnie Bannister is worth hundreds of millions of dollars to my husband. He is the key to the presidential elections.'

'That is the most ridiculous thing I've ever heard.'

'Is it?' A horn sends a wail of alarm our way as she again skates onto the wrong side of the road. I yank us back to safety. She doesn't even react. Nothing seems to rattle her. She is the most unique creature I have ever met. 'Imagine if you had the means of handing the election to Kennedy . . . Or stealing it from him. Wouldn't you use it?'

'This doesn't make sense . . . Hey, watch it!'

Mrs. Bannister brakes fast, a gust of wind filling the convertible, her cape billowing open with its touch. 'Why doesn't it make sense?'

'For starters, your husband made Nixon. Besides, why would he even consider supporting a Democrat like Kennedy?'

'You're talking about political preferences, Mr. Alston. My husband belongs to a small group of pragmatic men who are far beyond mere politics. They operate in a world where the only things that matter are power, money and control.'

'So what is it they want?'

'Depends which one of them you talk to. Sonny wants military contracts.'

'Sonny?'

'Howard Hughes. H.L. Hunt and Clint Murchison want to maintain tax breaks for Big Oil. And Rex wants the Federal Reserve to remain in private hands—his hands—with no possibility of congressional oversight or auditing. Nixon will give them all those things, of course, but Kennedy won't, you see. His father will make sure of that.'

'His father's got nothing to do with it.'

'That's where you're wrong, Mr. Alston . . . ' She leans forward to light her cigarette with the car lighter, exposing the lines of her shoulders. 'The people think they'll be electing Jack but they'll really be electing Joe, and believe me, based upon his past history, Joe Kennedy will block any contracts for Sonny and will certainly oppose any war. He'll punish Big Oil by taking away their tax concessions. And he'll ensure that the Fed's powers are transferred to the Treasury Department.'

'Why would a banker like him do that?'

'As I said, manipulation *and* revenge . . . The Fed wouldn't let Joe join their club. Sometimes, Mr. Alston, when an exclusive club is threatened, the best thing to do is to open your doors just a little wider. But when letting in a man like Joe Kennedy will cost everyone else billions . . . Well, a crack feels kind of like a canyon.'

'Why bother with Kennedy? Why not just support Nixon?'

'Because Rex never permits chance to interfere in any of his business dealings. Besides, Nixon is Sonny's man now. He bought Dick for a lousy $200,000. Rex was very upset, as you can imagine . . . '

As if I can imagine buying a presidential candidate. So this is the Big Steal in our new, modern decade: the presidency. I suddenly feel very old.

The light turns green but she doesn't move. 'To tell you the truth, Mrs. Bannister, I have enough trouble just filling out my income tax. All this talk about banks and the Federal Reserve is way over my head. How exactly does Ronnie Bannister fit in?'

'You disappoint me, Mr. Alston . . . ' She puts her foot down on the accelerator and the car rushes into the night. 'How's this for simple: Ronnie Bannister's father is JFK.'

BOOK THREE
The Long Oblivion

CHAPTER 45
Dallas 1963

Hastings watched the country changing beneath him, the blue promise of the Pacific poorly traded for the equivocal collage of basalt, granite and bruised desert; of lonely roads leading to box canyons and dried riverbeds.

Dead ends.

The click of ice brought him back to the dark, internal reality of the jet plane; of the private claustrophobia of his plans. He reduced them all to a basic, understandable formula: things would work out and everyone would live, or they wouldn't, and everyone would die. Three JTS Browns, a fistful of cashews and a half-pack of Pall Malls later, and Hastings was in Dallas.

He stepped out of the plane, the passenger in front almost tripping down the airstair, the sun angling cunningly into everyone's eyes. Welcomers huddled behind the rope at the other end of a tarmac sticky with afternoon heat and purging jet air, anxious faces peering past him—Hastings, always the invisible man.

Hastings snatched his suitcases from a passing trolley as he walked towards the terminal, Albert Luchino's smile giving way to surprise when he saw his face. He reached for the larger of the suitcases, which held his matériel. Hastings passed him the smaller one instead. 'What happened to you?'

'Someone didn't like my driving . . .'

Luchino tossed him a set of car keys and pointed to a

burgundy Citroën DS19 Cabriolet. 'Maybe you need more practice . . . '

Hastings glanced in the rearview mirror as they left Love Field. A red and white '58 DeSoto Firesweep pulled out after them, riding high through traffic on its blinding chrome. 'Anyone you know?'

Luchino glanced in the side mirror. 'Our friends from Miami . . . '

Miami. Candy-coloured cars and Technicolor shirts. Domino bars with grandpas and gunrunners. CIA listening posts, tapped phones and juiced horses out at Hialeah Park. Always Boom, Bubble, Bust. And now the biggest Bang of all threatening to explode right over the city, a mushroom cloud menace from the sunny south. Castro, Commies and the Kremlin. They did it once, they could do it again. Sub the missiles in, hide them in the jungle and then take the city out with a single OSA torpedo boat.

Miami.

So hot it was atomic. Too big to ignore, too wild to take seriously. CIA were bossing the whole operation, no questions asked. Its agents were going to take down Fidel their way. That meant dirty money and lots of it. Cocaine cash. Gunrunner payoffs. Big Oil dollars by the fifty-five-gallon drum. CIA were loaded. They ran the show. And now Miami CIA had come to Dallas, which meant they knew about the hit and were going to stop it. Or they were going to let it happen. Hell, Hastings thought, they could even be controlling the hit. Anything was possible when you had a room full of exiles, agents and gangsters loaded on Cuba Libres and Gran Coronas playing "who's got the biggest dick".

'I can lose them . . . '

'Don't. It's better for us to know where we can find them, if we need to, *n'est-ce pas*?' French, the language of diplomacy, always served with two bottles of wine. One to get you to talk.

One to silence you, maybe forever. Luchino turned, offering Hastings a Gitanes Maïs as he studied his face. 'They asked me to find some files . . . '

Hastings leant forward, the lighter's flint suddenly loud behind the shelter of glass. He straightened, the wind back in his hair. 'Did you get them?'

Luchino gave a Gallic shrug. 'They sent me to the wrong offices. *Quel bordel!* And you . . . ?'

'I got them . . . But couldn't keep them.' He watched Luchino out of his peripheral vision. A smile. 'Old Man Bannister has them now.'

Luchino shook his head. 'Such a pity . . . ' He pointed to a turnoff heading west. 'Do you know what was in these files?'

'Monroe and Kennedy mainly.'

'*Mais oui . . . Cherchez la femme!*' The DeSoto kept going straight ahead. Even Miami CIA weren't that careless. They were working a team. Hastings's eyes kept flicking back to the mirror. 'It's the Pontiac Bonneville.' Luchino sent the last word quivering with his French accent. Hastings still couldn't spot it. 'Red . . . ' The car was lying far back, concealed behind a Chevy pickup. The driver was very good. 'Don't worry, my friend, it took me the long time with this one too. He is the most talented . . . So, have you told Monsieur Roselli about the files being missing?'

'Not yet.'

'I don't think he will like it.'

'There's nothing to like or dislike. The Old Man's better than him, that's all.' The Old Man was better than all of them. And always would be, until the day someone was able to kill him. Hastings was hoping that day would come soon.

The road was taking them out of town, past used-car lots, scrap metal yards and cemetery rows of nodding derricks futilely fanning the air. The red Pontiac had pulled back half a mile in the thinning traffic. Careful. Astute. The driver was a pro.

An enormous ranch house began to grow on the flat horizon, casting long shadows before it; a fata morgana of the oil lying under the earth, mapping it through the absence of light. Staking it out. Hastings didn't like the look of their destination. His internal Geiger counter was cracking cricket noises. If he didn't know any better, he'd suspect this was a setup, that Luchino was going to do what the others couldn't off Point Dume. 'When did you get into Dallas?'

'Yesterday.'

'And you've already been out here?'

'They brought me straight to this house. Everyone is here, my friend. It's bigger than we ever imagined. Bigger than—' Luchino's voice was lost in the blast of a truck heading east, big wheels spinning dangerously close, smashing Texas distance. A curtain of dust and grit aftershocked them, the whisper of sand peppering the windshield.

'What's that you said?'

'I said, it's bigger than us . . . Here, you turn in.'

Hastings spun the wheel, skidding the back tires, raising a flag of dust to the red Pontiac: here we are, come and get us.

They were stopped by a large contingent of armed sheriffs, Texas Rangers and Dallas police. A man in white short sleeves stepped out from behind them, his face falling apart when he saw Hastings. The man's left arm was bandaged below the elbow. Blood oozed through the dressing, attracting the humming appreciation of flies.

One of the sheriffs turned to the man. 'They clean?' Hastings watched the man struggling with the answer. He half-nodded, looking away.

'Ça alors!' Luchino stared back as Hastings drove on towards the house, passing a slim stand of cottonwoods where a dozen government cars stood in the shade of branches pelleted with the black tremor of crows. 'What did you do, fuck his girl?'

'The Old Man did that to him.'

'Fucked his girl . . . ?'

'Cut his arm . . . '

'So why does he give that look to you?'

'He thought I was dead.'

'Why would he think this?'

'Because he threw me off a cliff last night.'

'*Putain de merde!*' Luchino shook his head in disbelief. 'What chance. In Corsica if we threw you off the cliff, you would not come back.'

'I believe it.'

'You want me to kill him?'

'I'll take care of him later, but tell me his name, if you know it.'

'*Mais oui*, he is Fiorini, a troublemaker, but down here, they are calling him Frank Sturgis.' He laughed. 'Americans and their names . . . '

The red Pontiac squealed as it turned off the road, not even slowing, the police jumping back, allowing it to power past. It hot-rodded after them, pulling up outside the homestead just ahead of Hastings and Luchino. A man jumped out without opening the door, stocky and dynamic; more like a circus acrobat than a mercenary, in white T-shirt, denim and blue suede shoes. 'Hemming. Operation 40.' He said it with false modesty, as though he expected them to be awed by the news; as though he didn't give a fuck who they were. He was the star, they were the extras. Hemming strode into the house, past the envious gaze of a posse of agents, sweat stains tarnishing their suits. Their ties were all unloosened, their jackets all buttoned up. That meant J. Edgar was very close.

'What's Operation 40?'

Hastings got out of the car. 'Just another name . . . ' Like all the other names thugs and killers gave themselves to feel superior to the people they killed. To justify what they had become. Hastings and Luchino didn't have that luxury. They were individuals without names. They were professionals; stone-cold assassins about to break the number one rule: never let it become personal.

Agents stood in front of the door, blocking the way. Roselli stepped out of the house, wiping the sweat away from his brow with a monogrammed handkerchief. He pointed to Hastings and Luchino. 'Let 'em through.' Hastings stepped into the damp, shadowy house. 'The shooters are out the back, behind the stables.' Hastings went first, barking his shin on a little green card table hiding in the darkness. 'Jesus Christ, watch where you're going. You don't want to look like a meathead in front of our guests.'

They passed through a large kitchen, the smell of sourdough bread and cinnamon apples following them outside. The sunlight was even more intense after the gloom of the interior. The air was thick with flies and the keening country perfume of hay and manure. Horses whinnied inside the stables, cuffing the wood impatiently with powerful hooves. More cars were parked out back, sitting hot and forsaken in the sun. A table was set up under a big dogwood, crowded with jugs of beer pearled with evaporating frost, a servant setting down bowls of potato salad and barbecued Elgin sausages. A group of men watched them approaching, whispering to each other. Luchino nodded to them, pouring beers for himself and Hastings. Hastings burnt his fingers picking up a sausage and dipping it in chili. 'You actually going to eat that shit, Daddy-O?' the one called Hemming said. Hastings's mouth went hot with the sausage, then spicy with the bite of sauce, then ice-cold with the beer. It was the first time he had felt truly alive since the Mexican's coffee on the beach at Point Dume. He was suddenly ravenous. 'Like, don't it bug you, chowing down on chopped-up guts?'

'*Andouillette*?' Luchino asked, nibbling the tip of a sausage, then pulling a face. '*Rien à voir.*'

Silence as the men exchanged looks. Hemming narrowed his eyes. 'So who's the French cat?'

'Corsican . . . ' Hastings said, filling a plate with potato salad and sausage. He felt as if he hadn't eaten in a week.

A snort of contempt, posing as humour. A man with a heavy goatee and wearing green military fatigues stepped forward. 'There's a difference?'

'Have we met?' Luchino asked, his voice tight with control as he refilled Hastings's glass.

Hemming nodded to the bearded man. 'He's Loran Hall. You've heard of him. Deputy commander.' He nodded towards a very large man speaking in Spanish to a group of Cubans by the stables. 'And that's El Jefe himself: David Sánchez Morales. One very dangerous mother. He started Operation 40.' Hastings stared at the powerfully built man with his grey hair and dyed moustache. Vanity always meant trouble in their line of work. It required prudence, not preening. Nuance, not narcissism. 'Ex-82nd Airborne.'

Hall laughed, speaking to Luchino. '82nd whipped your sorry French asses during the war.'

'I am Corsican, not French. And I fought alongside your countrymen, not against them.'

Hall muttered something under his breath to Hemming, then turned back to Luchino with a sneer. 'Shit . . . Corsica. Cuba. The same goddamn thing. Tiny fucking islands causing way too much trouble.'

It never failed to amaze Hastings how blind people could be to the imminent threat of death. It was as though Hall had just deliberately glued his head to a railroad track in front of a rapidly approaching locomotive. Luchino stepped around Hastings, sliding a steak knife under his hand, ready to deliver a fatal lesson in manners to the red-eyed young man with a rash under his beard. 'Wait till this is over . . . ' Hastings whispered. Luchino froze. Intelligence guided his instincts. He believed in honour, not pride. But what had just passed between Hastings and Luchino—call and response; restraint and control—had gone unheeded by Hemming and Hall, who were too busy strutting their own importance to realize they were dancing on snakes.

'The three of us control the fucking Cubans.' Hemming pointed to the stables, where a dozen Cubans rested on their haunches, watching out of the corner of their eyes as Morales addressed them. 'Nobody talks to them without going through us, understand?' Like all young hotshots, what Hemming really needed was a swift hard kick in the ass. 'And that goes for those fucks-in-suits over there . . . ' Hastings glanced over at five men, two heavy and three thin, who were talking to Roselli on the back porch of the homestead. CIA. Who else? he thought. Two of them were even smoking pipes.

Hastings served himself more sausages and salad, the raking of the spoon against china chiming musically. Hall shook his head. 'Shit, man, are you here to work, or just for the free lunch?'

Hastings looked up at Hall. 'That mouth of yours is so big, I bet I could shove this plate right down your throat . . . '

In the silence that followed they all could hear the sound of cooking coming from the kitchen's open windows: the spatter of hot fat stinging griddles.

'Whoa . . . Slow down, Daddy-O. No need to blow the jets. We're all friends here.'

'I thought we were all just killers . . . '

Hall took a step towards Hastings, a sheathed bowie knife strapped below his right knee. Ostentatious and threatening. Always cover for unreliable and scared. Hastings could disarm him, chop his beard off and shove it up his ass before he'd even know what had happened. 'What the fuck is your problem, man . . . ?'

'Steady, Loran . . . ' Morales came up to Hastings, standing right beside him, looking him up and down, measuring the flush of heat from Hastings's body. 'Let the man eat in peace. He's travelled far, like we all have.'

Hall hesitated, then stormed off, humiliated by the subtext that even a beatnik dropout like him could understand: walk away now or this man will kill you. Luchino sipped his beer, enjoying the moment. He turned to Hemming. 'You are from Miami, yes?'

'No one's from Miami. I'm from El Monte.'

LA Loser. Nothing more to know. Hastings dipped his last sausage into the sauce, not looking as he spoke to Morales. 'How about you?'

'Arizona . . .' He was Mexican, not Cuban. That meant Morales had been working for CIA long before Fidel grew his beard and flipped his lid.

'And now you both work with the Cubans out of Miami?' There was something that could have been a nod. 'So you were with them in Chicago on Halloween?'

Hemming and Morales exchanged alarmed looks. 'Who wants to know?' Hemming asked, running a comb through his ducktail. Hemming was the Jimmy Dean of Boys Town.

'Two men who were also there,' Luchino said.

'If you have questions about Chicago, ask him . . .' Morales said, nodding over Hastings's shoulder. Hastings turned. Roselli was walking towards them, his head bowed, as though ashamed to be associated with such a crew of felons. 'He's the asshole who screwed it all up.' Tagging behind Roselli, like a couple of empty cans tied to a honeymooner's car, were Nicoletti and Alderisio.

'Okay, everyone, listen up. The last shooters have arrived . . .' Hastings and Luchino glanced at each other. How many shooters could there possibly be? Was this assassination or insurrection? 'I want you all inside for the briefing.' He looked at Morales. 'The Cubans too.'

Roselli turned to go, banging into Alderisio, who was shadowing him too closely, both of them staggering backwards from the collision. Larry and Moe. Roselli shoved Alderisio out of the way, marching inside with as much dignity as he could muster, wearing Alderisio's shoeprints on the toes of his polished wing tips. Morales waved for the Cubans to follow. Hastings watched them getting up, brushing desert dust off their trousers, extinguishing cigarettes. Weary, battle-hardened men, wary of their commander, but following orders anyway. Foot soldiers, all.

'I knew a Cuban kid called Hidalgo . . . ' Hastings said to Morales as they walked back to the house. 'Used to work at Old Man Bannister's joint.' There was a single tremor in Morales's jawline. Good control. 'It was around the time of the kidnapping . . . '

Morales stopped in his tracks and looked all around, making sure no one was lingering. 'The information you have is still valuable. Very valuable . . . '

'What about Hidalgo? He said he was working for you, for Operation 40.'

Morales started walking towards the house. 'I cut him loose. Joe Kennedy got to Hidalgo, worked him against Nixon till Hoover found out. Forget what they say about the Outfit, about the Five Families. It's the Boston mafia that pulls the strings these days, especially that little shit, Bobby, breaking our balls. He's worse than goddamn Castro!' Morales held open the screen door for Hastings. 'Remember what I said about the Bannister kid. Some people would pay big money . . . '

'Some people like who?'

'Are you kidding? Howard Hughes, for one.'

Morales disappeared through the steam. Hastings followed him inside, kitchen clamour greeting him; the opera of pots and pans. Hemming helped himself to a piece of pie as the stragglers traipsed through the kitchen, a pretty young female cook slapping theatrically at him, Hemming dancing out of her way with a winning grin, licking his fingers. He could have been the kid next door in his final year at college, but he was a baby-faced killer in charge of mercenaries damaged by betrayal and defeat. Judge the plan by the planners. It didn't take a giant crystal ball to predict the outcome, Hastings thought—this was all going to be one colossal, fucking mess . . .

They entered a library, the drapes drawn, filling the mistrustful room with the nitro cocktail of contained heat, unstirred air, and impatient testosterone. Chandeliers hung incongruously between the lethal horns and antlers that stabbed out of the walls, lighting the room with a funereal amber glow.

The spooks sat grouped in an adjoining music room, watching them all march in with the appraising eyes of casting directors. For Hastings they were just like the top brass in the Pacific, the old men who stared through binoculars from the bridge as the young men died, whispering orders then impatiently complaining about the wait, as though war were a drawn-out dinner in an overbooked officers' mess.

Hastings scanned the library. New faces. Strange faces. One without any eyebrows or eyelashes, the resulting naked gaze alarming under an orange wig. There were Outfit faces. Small-time hoodlum faces. Three-grand-a-pop killers. There were Dallas police and sheriff uniforms. Hobo hopheads. The picture was getting even clearer. Hastings, Luchino and one or two other professionals would execute the hit, as originally planned. And then the rest of the men in this room would converge and kill the killers. It was going to be the way Hastings always imagined it. The only thing that had changed was the scale. It was overwhelming. It would be mayhem writ large.

Roselli clapped his hands in a futile effort for silence, then barked through the cigarette smoke. 'Everybody, keep it down.' He turned to Hemming and his group. 'For Christ's sake, for once in your life can't you shut the fuck up?' Hemming pulled a face but fell silent fast, feeling the faces staring at him. Roselli beamed at the hesitant quiet in the room. 'That's way better. We got special guests here, so show some respect.' He nodded to the music room. 'Now Frank here is gonna take us through the plans for the Big Event once and once only . . . ' A song started up, tinny music coming from the kitchen. *It's My Party.* Roselli looked up with annoyance, speaking over the music. 'If you got any questions, I don't want to hear 'em. Frank don't want to hear 'em. You go back to your section boss and ask him, understand?'

Sturgis stepped forward, yanking a chart down that was hanging from the top of a projection stand. He tugged so hard that the stand toppled over. Guffaws all around. Vegas vaudeville. A ripple of appreciative anticipation. After the clowns, there's always the girls. Sturgis picked up the stand, briefly making eye contact with Hastings before looking away. Hastings had read him right. He was scared shitless that Hastings knew who he was and what he had done. What he had tried to do. And Sturgis had very good reason to feel scared, starting with the most obvious question: how the hell did Hastings survive the old heave-ho into the sea?

Sturgis wasn't the only one with questions. Why the hate during the interrogation? For Sturgis it had been personal, powering down on every single punch. Somewhere along the line, Hastings had made an enemy but he didn't know why. He needed to find out before he killed Sturgis.

Sturgis prodded the map with a pool cue. 'This is the map of the motorcade, Jackie Ruby got it off the Secret Service, thank you, Jack . . . ' A short, stocky man with a fedora saluted acknowledgment. 'A Team goes here . . . ' Sturgis tapped a building marked Texas School Book Depository. 'Rendezvous with patsy, then up to the sixth floor, last two windows, B Team goes here.' He tapped the building opposite. 'Dal-Tex Building. Second and third floors. Windows and fire escape.'

Hastings exchanged looks with Luchino. Shooting from a fire escape on a main street, in daylight? 'C Team and D Team . . .' Luchino turned to Hastings, mouthed, 'What team are we?' Hastings shrugged. All the shit about team leaders and alphabet armies didn't make sense. It had to be a distraction: cover for the real hit teams. ' . . . At the Trade Mart. E Team on the motorcade going back, right here . . .' Sturgis hit the overpass so hard with the cue, he left a blue chalk mark on the map. 'And Love Field Team back at the airport.' He turned and looked at a young man with a preppy air standing at the front of the music room, who frowned and whispered to a beefy man with glasses next to him. Sturgis looked worried. 'Final backup only, sir. We're talking emergencies here, highly unlikely.' The young man coloured, whether from anger or embarrassment, Hastings couldn't say. 'How come the rich prick gets a name and we only get an initial?' a gangster next to Hastings asked. Henchmen muttered indignantly. 'One more thing: see a camera, nab it. Steal it, break it, buy it. If you can't, put a name to its owner.'

A voice spoke up. 'How do we do that, Frank?'

'How the fuck do I know, use your brains.'

Ruby stuck his hand up. 'What about press? The place will be crawling with them.'

'Forget the newshounds, that'll be handled by our guests.' Faces turned towards the music room. 'One more thing, and this is for all you people dressed up as cops. Anyone detained is to be taken to the sheriff's. Not to the police station, to the sheriff's. You must prevent fingerprinting and mug shots. The idea is to release all detainees within two hours. Got that? Two hours max.'

A tall man with tousled blond hair dressed like a tramp raised his hand. 'How will the cops know it's us?'

'Good question. Anyone detained will be us.'

'What about the patsy, Frank?'

For the first time there was ringing silence in the room. Sturgis turned to Ruby. 'The patsy will not be detained. I repeat, the patsy will not be detained. That's all. Good luck, gentlemen.'

Hastings pushed his way through the crowd towards Sturgis, who was being mobbed with questions. He reached through the others, and grabbed Sturgis around the bandage below his elbow. Then squeezed.

Hastings had to give Sturgis credit. Other men would have buckled under the pain. Sturgis remained standing, steeling his features as he turned slowly to his tormentor. 'What is that, a riding accident?' Hastings asked.

Jack Ruby laughed, his voice nasal and self-important. 'What happened, Frank, got bucked by a filly?'

Some of the men laughed as Sturgis pushed past them, trying to escape Hastings's grip. Hastings pressed harder, Sturgis going white, finally on the verge of collapse. 'Tell the Old Man we need to talk . . . '

'Fuck you, tell him yourse—' There was the shrill, whistled gasp of internal agony, of acute combusting pain, perspiration swelling like blisters on his forehead. Then Hastings let go, Sturgis staggering, then straightening, his forearm slick with blood.

Hastings leant in close. 'What have you got against me?'

'I was on Iwo Jima with Tommy Alston, that's what.' He shouldered past Hastings, cradling his arm as he lurched out of the room, blood pitter-patting after him. Hastings hurried after Sturgis, but Roselli blocked his path, Nicoletti and Alderisio huddling protectively around their boss. 'So? How do you think that went?'

Hastings felt like slapping him. 'What do you think this is, a fucking game show?'

'Now look . . . '

'You look. I'm walking unless you come up with a real plan. And that includes escape routes I trust.'

'Escape routes? What are you, chicken?' Alderisio's sneer slid off his face when he saw the anger in Hastings's eyes. Even he was smart enough to know he'd gone too far.

Hastings wiped his bloodied fingers on Alderisio's jacket. 'Free sample. Next time, it'll be yours . . . '

Alderisio went for his gun. Roselli stopped him. 'Are you fucking nuts?' He turned back to Hastings. 'Jesus, relax for Christ's sake. That speech, it was just for the chump change boys.'

'You're trying to tell me this rent-an-army's here just for diversion . . . ?'

Roselli shrugged his shoulders into a big, fucking question mark. 'What can I say?' he lied. 'Everyone's got a role to play, it's all part of the plan. Here . . . ' He steered Hastings towards the music room, Hastings staring back at a still-seething Alderisio. 'I want you to meet some important people . . . Wal? This is the guy I told you about.'

The heavy man with spectacles turned to them, instinctively pulling his hands in to his sides as though protecting his wallet, his eyes glued to Hastings's forehead as he spoke. 'Sure, sure, Johnny told us all about you.'

Roselli patted Hastings on the shoulder. The hand of Judas. 'The best is what you asked for and the best is what you get . . . ' Other heads turned, eyes locked. Hastings brushed Roselli's hand away, but the mark remained. Roselli may as well have hung a sign around his neck. Hastings: dead man walking. 'Nothing but the best for our pals in Miami . . . '

Wal smiled with a bashful self-effacement. 'Sure, sure, we appreciate it. We always knew we'd be in safe hands with Johnny Handsome . . . ' He rubbed his bulbous nose speculatively, as though it were a tuber that might just snap off, and turned back to the other suits.

'What did I tell you . . . ?' Roselli said, leading Hastings away. 'Salt of the earth . . . '

'Can the bullshit. Where do Luchino and I go?'

Roselli frowned. Very convincingly. 'You and Frenchie? You ain't a team . . . ' Hastings studied his face. Roselli was a good liar about little things and a bad one about big things. This was a huge fucking thing. 'You and Nicoletti in the Book Depository and Frenchie and Alderisio in the Dal-Tex building.'

Meaning Hastings and Luchino would kill the president, and Nicoletti and Alderisio would then kill them. They were back to the exact same setup as Chicago, with the Cubans thrown in somewhere along the line to run false trails and distract any authorities not in on the conspiracy. 'Where are the details?'

'Relax, we all rendezvous with the patsy in Dealey Plaza at eleven sharp . . . Kennedy don't fly in till just before noon . . . '

'What about Morales? Where will he be?'

Roselli wagged a finger. 'Now you know I ain't allowed to divulge privileged information.' He looked up suddenly, his face crinkled in displeasure. Someone had started playing *Rock Around The Clock*—the original version by Hal Singer. Loud. 'It's that juvenile fucking delinquent, Hemming, I'd stake my life on it.' He turned back to Hastings. 'Haven't any of the younger generation heard of Sinatra? What the fuck will our guests think?' He stormed off towards the kitchen. Hastings pushed his way through the library, trying to focus on how Sturgis knew he had killed Tommy Alston. The song drifted through the walls, the lyrics taunting him, as though they knew the answer.

One for the money
Two for the show
Three make ready
Four let's go

It started to come back to him. Hastings was in a bar, cigarette smoke gliding across a spotlight. Onstage, Hal Singer was crying out the song with his raucous voice, raw and rowdy, inciting sedition and excitement, his tenor sax hanging like a gleaming weapon from his shoulders.

Let's rock
We're gonna rock
Rock around the clock

The old Casablanca! On South Kenmore. That's where he'd heard Singer performing the number. And that was where he had met Greta Simmons for the second time . . . It was Greta. She must have talked; that was the only explanation for why the Bannister kidnappers had known about him; why they had dangled Tommy's killer as bait to Nick Alston. And if Sturgis knew, that meant he had been in on the kidnapping too.

Luchino was standing outside the room, half-singing in a broken monotone: 'We're gonna rock, rock around the clock . . .' He smiled when he saw Hastings. 'I have not heard that song since the old days, at the Welcome Hotel in Villa. Ah, my friend, the 6th Fleet . . . What nights. What parties. When people still danced to jazz.' He shook his head sadly. 'We thought we were wild back then . . . We wanted to be bad, very bad . . . But we were just children. Innocent really. We had no idea what bad really was . . . '

'I have to kill a man tonight . . . '

'See what I mean? That, my friend, is bad.'

'For him. Maybe for me . . . '

'Do you need help?'

Hastings patted him on the shoulder. 'I can handle this one. But I'm going to need all of your help tomorrow.'

'Ah yes, tomorrow. *Quelle catastrophe!*'

They walked together through the shadow of the house, out to the front, the shouts from an angry confrontation between Roselli and Hemming fading as they stepped off the ornate veranda into the gardens. An agent stopped them. 'No one's allowed out here . . . '

316 - TIM BAKER

'We're with Wal . . . ' Hastings said. The Fed hesitated, then walked away, shaking his head. He didn't really know what was going on anyway. This meet made Vito Genovese's Appalachian Summit look like a discreet assignation at the Cosmos Club.

'FBI. CIA. Dallas police and sheriffs . . . Texas Rangers. They're expecting someone big.'

'But who, *mon ami*?'

'White House big. Think about it. Who has the most to gain if Kennedy dies?'

'Johnson.'

'And this is his home turf . . . ' The wail of approaching police sirens forced the crows in the cottonwoods to break cover, the rattle of their protesting comb calls and cries mocking them as they scattered overhead, cawing: rock, rock.

A limo escorted by motorcycle cops was coming in. The Fed waved Hastings and Luchino back towards the lawn, away from the house. The limo pulled up, slurring on the pebble driveway, and former Vice President Richard Nixon got out, surrounded by plainclothes bodyguards. He disappeared inside.

The final details. Who got what and when. President Johnson now; President Nixon later. And President Bobby Kennedy? Try never. JFK was already dead. Hastings and Luchino too. Unless they thought of something quick.

Hastings stared up into the empty Texas sky, clouds going to cover, hugging the flat horizon in fear. 'We can still stop it.'

'It is too late, my friend.'

'We can do it. But only if we shoot.'

It took Luchino a moment to understand. 'Shooting and missing . . . ?'

'I have the Book Depository, you have Dal-Tex. If we shoot to miss, they'll abort everything, including the Trade Mart speech. Kennedy will fly out of Texas and if he's wise, never come back.' Just like Hastings.

'There is Love Field Team waiting at the airport but . . . '
There was the reflective pause of a cigarette being lit, then the
exhalation of certainty. 'The young man in charge has the face
of a bureaucrat, not a killer. He will not risk it.' Luchino took
off his coat and laid it down on the sun-bleached grass. 'It could
work. In the meantime I am going to get some rest. I advise you
to do the same. Tomorrow will be the longest day . . . ' He lay
down on the lawn, smoking meditatively, his eyes closed.

Hastings started walking around the side of the estate, glancing in one of the windows. He froze. Jimmy Hoffa sat alone at a
table, playing solitaire in front of a quart of rye. Howard Hughes
was pacing up and down on his own behind him, holding a
white handkerchief over his mouth. But it wasn't the notoriety
of the pair that had riveted his attention. It was something that
stood mostly outside the frame of the window; something intimately familiar and deeply hated—just the front rims of a wheelchair showing.

Hastings made his choice immediately. Forget Sturgis. He
was going after the puppet master.

Hastings kept on circling round the house, nodding to a
group of cops who were playing cards on the back porch. One
of them looked up at him. 'What do you want?'

'Just going into the kitchen, for a beer . . . '

'There's plenty to drink past the stables.'

'Wal told me to bring him a cold one from the icebox.'

The cop put his cards on the table, facedown. 'Wal?'

'From Miami . . . ' Local yokels. They didn't know what he
was talking about. He had to spell it out for them. 'CIA . . . '

The cop straightened in his seat. 'Well, why didn't you say
so?' He went back to the game, glancing at his hand, then toss-
ing in two more chips.

Hastings had the password now . . . CIA. Authority plus mystery always breeds fear. And fear was the skeleton key to everything. He entered the kitchen, scanning the steam and gleam,

318 · TIM BAKER

looking for the pretty young cook who had been flirting with
Hemming. She was over by a portable record player. He
watched her carefully lower the needle. A strange, mournful
atmosphere was born with the music. *Blue Velvet . . .* She turned,
blind and lost, already hypnotized by the chorus, almost walking
into Hastings. Suddenly awakened, she looked up at him, flustered and flirtatious, focusing on his face—liking what she saw.
She smiled. 'You gonna ask me to dance too . . . ?'

'Like Hemming?'

'You know him?' Hastings nodded. 'He runs Operation 40.'

The kid was pimping his outfit for a dance with a cook.
'You know what Operation 40 is?'

She shrugged. 'Oil, right?' He laughed. She looked away, a
little hurt, her smile fading into something mysterious, something potent and possible. This girl had a special glow. His
hand enclosed the small of her back, brought her body into
contact with his. She looked up at him, moving with the music.
She was a good dancer.

'What's your name?'

'Carmen.'

'Pretty name. Tell me, Carmen, what's going on here?'

'Can't you tell? We're having a party.'

'Who are the guests?'

'Just about everyone from the size of dinner.'

'I saw a man, an old man in a wheelchair?'

'I don't rightly know who's here and who's not. I just
cook . . . '

'And dance.'

She smiled. 'I could get into trouble . . . Penny wouldn't
like it.'

Something caught his eye on the counter, glittering cruelly
in the angled afternoon sunlight. 'Who's Penny?'

'Head cook . . . Oh, shoot.'

Carmen let go, and Hastings missed her instantly, watching

her rushing to the stove, lifting lids and pulling away instinctively from the assault of steam, spoons stirring frantically at first, then slowing to a confident, muscular twirl. There was the rap of wood against iron edges, the click of lids being replaced. 'No harm done.' Carmen turned to him, smiling, but Hastings had his back to her as he slipped the stainless steel skewer inside his jacket. The music ended. Carmen sighed into the sudden silence, wiping her hands on her apron. 'That song was my alarm clock. I got to get back to dessert now . . . '

'Maybe I can come by after dinner?'

Her smile reminded him of Susan's: innocent and eager. 'You can help with the washing up.'

He smiled at her. 'Thanks for the dance, Carmen . . . '

She dropped her head to one side, beaming at him. 'My pleasure.'

Hastings headed towards the back porch, turning as he opened the screen door, his face going dark with the force of the western sun behind him. 'Carmen, where are the guest rooms here?'

She threw her head back towards the stoves. 'Other side of the house. The damp side.'

There was the simmer of protest behind her, as boiling water squeezed through a lid and started guttering the fire beneath it. 'Shoot.' She turned the gas down, dabbing at the froth. 'Say, what did you say your name was, anyway . . . ?'

CHAPTER 46
Dallas 2014

The JFK Assassination is my first memory, at least the first one I can put an exact date on: November 23rd, 1963. We were a day ahead of the news when the shots were fired. On the other side of the world in Sydney, it was already the Morning After. The beginning of a long hot summer. Dad had moved to Sydney a couple of years earlier, looking for a place that was quiet and safe, a place where he was sure no one would ever know about his past, his connection with the Bannister case.

The move was supposed to be about letting go of the past. About forgetting. But that's nearly impossible. You can change the bed but the dreamer's always the same. And even in the hot amber sunlight of a Sydney that no longer exists, can a dreamer ever really forget the shadows of a nightmare?

We were sitting in the front living room. A eucalyptus stood outside, its leaves still, protesting another scorching day, the birds that had woken me already going quiet from the assault of the sun.

I had heard the TV from my bedroom upstairs. That's what had alerted me to the magnitude of the occasion. The only thing on television early in the morning was the whining geometric challenge of the test pattern. But this was something extraordinary. A handsome young leader cut down under the gaze of newsreel. This was when the infant medium finally came of age. It was the brave new world of television with real-life murder served up in front of the largest audience on earth.

This was the beginning of news as convenience food. Smooth as a filter tip, and just as addictive.

My father sat in his chair, his ashtray already full. There were two beer bottles—the big ones that came with cork caps—empty by his side. My mother was standing behind him, crying. This is my memory of her; my only real memory. She was weeping at the death of a man I didn't know. The television said that President Kennedy was a man of peace, who would not let the world destroy itself with atomic bombs. A man of change, who spoke of enormous challenges but believed in the possibility of success. A man of justice who fought Segregation. Back then Kennedy was known for his youthful and contagious optimism and the exciting promise of a better world. Today he's mainly known for fucking. It's only human nature, I suppose. Just ask Bill Clinton. It's easier to imagine a middle-aged man screwing a young intern because she'd just shown him her thong than it is to imagine him trying to introduce universal health care or bring lasting peace to Palestine. But back then, in the black-and-white days of television and politics, we didn't know about the bedrooms. We only knew what we saw: a young man killed in public because he was ahead of his time, because he promised civil rights and education and freedom for all, regardless of race or creed or colour. That's why people cried and why people remembered. Because they knew that if they could get the president of the United States, they could get anyone, including us and our families. Our homes and dreams were inconsequential compared to JFK's but they were just as vulnerable. No one was safe. Anyone big or small could be snuffed out with the flap of a dark umbrella on a sunny day.

Dad was trying to explain to me what had happened, his eyes going backwards and forwards, from mine to the television, and it was while he was staring at the screen that he suddenly stopped speaking, his mouth opening in a well of disbelief as he rose from his chair and slowly pointed at the TV. 'Jesus Christ, it can't be . . . '

322 - TIM BAKER

'Dad . . . ?'

'Oh my God, Jesus Christ, it's him.'

I was frightened. 'Dad?'

'There.' He stabbed the screen with a finger. I stared at the impossibly small faces moving in the black-and-white world. 'Did you see him, plain as day in goddamn Dallas?'

I don't know why, but I started crying. I tried to speak but couldn't. He turned to me, tears in his own eyes. And it was that sight, the first time I ever saw my father cry, after everything that had happened; before everything that was going to happen—the heartbreak and disappointments, the illness and betrayals, the foreclosures and the firings—the only time, now that I come to think of it, that I ever saw my father cry. And it was that astonishment that gave me the courage to clear my voice and speak. 'Who, Dad?'

He took a step away from the television, as though it were a loaded weapon pointing straight at him. 'That son of a bitch . . . Hastings.'

* * *

I awake to a hand touching my shoulder. 'Lewis . . . ?'

I leap to my feet, confused and a little embarrassed to have fallen asleep in the armchair. Evelyn stares at me with concern. 'Are you all right?'

I look around the room. 'I was with Eva, when . . . ' When I fell asleep. The problem is, I have no recollection of having been tired, let alone drowsy. I glance out the window. Almost dusk. Jesus, my last day in Dallas and I still haven't been to the Book Depository Museum. I had been planning to visit it after lunch. I hadn't counted on being kidnapped.

'Eva didn't want to wake you, but when they told her the news, she said it would be best for everyone to leave . . . '

'What news?'

'Annette Martinez . . . She was found early this afternoon. She was murdered. A karate chop to the neck.'

I had been shocked when I'd read about Tex's murder earlier in the day, but it wasn't entirely unexpected. Not for someone like Tex, who had belonged to the murky milieu of mercenaries, paramilitary rebels and death squads. But Annette Martinez? She was a gentle yet determined investigator searching for the truth from the supposed safety of her home cinema, armed with nothing but a remote control. This type of sudden and horrific ending was never supposed to happen to someone as normal as her. Besides, I liked her. She was just about the sanest of all my witnesses, Evelyn included.

The door opens, unable to frame all of Dwayne Wayne's enormous body, even if he didn't have a suitcase in either hand. 'It's time.' He disappears.

'Hurry . . . ' Evelyn takes my hand and tugs me into the reception area. Granston's beagle lies in a corner, panting with asthmatic patience.

'Wait a minute, what the hell is going on?'

'You have to leave, we all have to go.'

'Go where?'

'As far from Dallas as we can.'

'But . . . ' I stare into her luminous brown eyes. They've changed somehow. And then I realise, it's not her eyes that have changed, it's the way I'm looking at them. The pleasure of last night has been replaced by doubt. 'You can't think Annette's death involves us?'

'It involves you.' Granston says, coming out of a door, an attaché case in one hand, a walking stick in the other. 'Goddamn it. Nothing good ever comes from digging up the past. Sonny used to say all it did was turn up corpses. And in a city like Dallas, there are more of those than oil.' He points the cane at me. If it had a trigger, he'd pull it. 'This is all your fault, Alston. Prying into things that don't concern you. Just like your goddamn father.'

'You know, that's not entirely correct . . . '

'Shut up.' Granston barks at Dwayne. 'You're as bad as him.'

I've had enough. 'I'm getting out of this madhouse.'

Granston shouts after me. 'Good. Go, and never come back, hear me? Never come back to Dallas.'

Evelyn takes my arm but I shake her hand off. 'Don't be angry, he's just . . . '

'Don't be angry? After being kidnapped and menaced. And you haven't even told me why you did it?' Evelyn tries to answer, but I talk over her. I'm in no mood for civilized conversation. 'All you had to do was ask me, and I would have come here gladly. You didn't have to get them to abduct me.'

'Lewis, believe me. I called them because I was worried . . . '

'Why?'

'Because of the cards . . . Don't look at me like that.' How the hell am I supposed to look at her after what she's just said? 'Then, when they told me about Tex Jeetton, I panicked.' She holds my face between her hands. 'Death is all around us.' The incongruity of her soft touch and her harsh words would make me laugh if it didn't alarm me so much. 'It was for your own protection, Lewis, you know that.'

'Why didn't you just tell me?' A whooshing noise startles me and I spin around, something arcing fast behind me. But it's just an automatic sprinkler system coming on. I turn back to her, embarrassed by the shock it gave me. ' . . . And why didn't you come with me?'

'I couldn't.'

'Why couldn't you? What are you hiding?'

'Oh, Lewis, what I mean is . . . I can't.' She takes a step away from me. 'Be with you. Ever again.'

'You're just like the others. You think I'm the cause of all this.'

'I know you're not. But I also know our destinies are not aligned.'

'Aligned? We're not bookshelves.'

'We're planets . . . '

She opens the door of the limo in the driveway. Eva Marlowe is sitting in the back. She offers me something she's holding in her hand. 'Lewis, it was such a pleasure to meet you. This is for you.'

I stare at her for a long moment, then slowly take the folded onionskin writing paper and open it. Above a drawing of the mansion with the name *Caddo* in copperplate, Eva Marlowe has written another address: 966 avenue Jean Cocteau, St-Jean-Cap-Ferrat 06230 . . . The sprinklers hum all around me, emphasising the silence. 'This is your address in France?'

'This is the address of Betty Bannister. She's expecting you . . . '

Dwayne closes the door, separating us with smoked glass. 'Get in the front. I'll drop you off at your hotel. There's a flight at 9:20 tonight, change at Heathrow for Nice. There are still seats available.'

He slams the door behind him as he gets in. I shout through the window. 'Thanks for the itinerary but I'm flying back to Sydney tomorrow.' The window glides down to half-mast. He gives a sad shrug. 'Don't say we didn't warn you.' The engine starts up, making me jump, the limo reversing too fast down the driveway, gravel snapping out of the way.

'I'll drive you into town.'

I turn back to Evelyn. 'What in God's name makes them think I'd actually go to France? Because they told me to? I'd have to be as crazy as . . . '

'Lewis, you were never going back to Sydney. Not before going to France. You have no choice. You've never had a choice. Don't you understand? Your cards were marked even before you were born.'

S outh Street. Betty Bannister glides to a halt. 'Wait here, please . . . ' She gets out of the car, walking towards the Fox Theatre, its spectral spire a lonely lighthouse in a sky without stars. A smothering ocean fog has come in fast with the midnight tide, salting the city with the metallic embrace of the Pacific. The sea is everywhere, the clash of waves murmuring on the wind; the air heavy with moisture and mist, my own clothes still saturated from the unplanned dip in the Bannisters' pool. A clammy shiver passes through me. Someone's walking over my grave. I get out of the car, watching Mrs. Bannister striding away. I have an intuition—that someone might just be Betty Bannister. Am I being set up? Why did she tell me to wait here? I feel like a dopey hack whose fare is about to do a bunk with the meter still running. Instinct kicks in. I start to follow, sticking close to the shadows along the walls, the click of her heels echoing in the lonely street as she runs across Weyburn Avenue. Goddamn it, what is she up to now? My battered brain, loosened from its moorings by the bruised accumulation of a day of hard blows and sharp cracks, lurches backwards and forwards as I trot after her, playing painful pat-a-cake as it sloshes around the interior of my skull.

She disappears near the movie house . . .

The exterior box office is closed but one of the doors to the cinema is still ajar, a faint light washing out. Lucky break or sucker punch?

The lobby is lit only with the pattern of tiny spotlights shining on framed movie posters: *They Drive by Night, Clash by Night, The Night of the Hunter* . . . It was enough to give me a terminal case of insomnia. The cheery parade continues down the other side of the lobby with a serenade to homicidal romance: *Killer's Kiss, Kiss Me Deadly, Murder, My Sweet* . . . I pause in front of a poster of *The Lady in the Lake* and think of Deckard, drowning in a sheen of oil-slicked water, and then my own lucky escape in the pool. The cinematic Calvary is nearly over. The last poster seems to be talking straight to me: *On Dangerous Ground*.

A soft humming leads me across the lobby. A generator, from the projection room. I try the door. Locked. Where could she have disappeared to? One of the auditorium doors is wedged open by a door pump. A red velour curtain blocks the entrance. Like the curtain in Old Man Bannister's pentagram chamber. Instinctively I reach for my gun before I remember—it's still at the bottom of the swimming pool. If there's somebody waiting for me, they better be unarmed, or else a lousy shot.

I pull back the curtain and enter.

Wooden panelled balconies stare down at me in the acute silence. There's nothing lonelier than an empty cinema. Without the amplified voices proclaiming love and threatening death as giant faces flicker across the weave of silk and silver, the movie palace becomes a public burial chamber, each seat a leather-padded tombstone waiting in vain for a ghostly audience, like a tragic dog sitting patiently beside the grave of its master.

Dead end.

No one.

False lead.

I'm heading back up the aisle when I hear it—so faint it's almost out of reach.

A child, crying.

Instinctively I look up at the screen, that locus of false miracles and deceit. But it hangs blank and unanimated. It's no illusion. The sound is coming from a door leading off the orchestra pit. I take the stairs down, careful not to trip.

Under the stage, it's another world entirely. Luxury cedes to utility, plush carpet to cracked tiles. Barely visible in the nervous flicker of a dying fluorescent lamp, the room is a terrain of obstacles designed to entangle the trespasser. Levers and pulleys, chains and ropes—I try to watch my step. The sound of the child grows stronger before giving way to something else: a murmur and then laughter. It's coming from a spiral staircase that leads to a crummy flop for a super or night watchman. We're a long way from High Sierra. There is a squeal of delight coming from the room next door.

I freeze. It is a moment I had stopped believing in. The boy is alive and I am about to become the man who found the Bannister kid. But finding is not keeping. I look around for a weapon.

'Freeze . . . '

I recognize the voice instantly. Raising my hands slowly, I turn. 'Well, what do you know?' It's him all right. 'I've been looking everywhere for you and now you just turn up, uninvited.'

Hastings tosses me a pack of Luckies with his free hand, holding a nickel-plated Smith & Wesson Chief's Special in the other. 'Funny, you don't look like a guy who's just hit the jackpot.'

I grab a smoke, toss the pack back, deliberately throwing them low and short. He stretches instinctively for the catch. Mistake. The aim of the .38 snub-nosed shifts away from me for a second, and in that moment, I nail the son of a bitch with a short, sharp kick to the chin, snatching the gun from his hand, pointing it at him as he sits up, rubbing his jaw and staring at me with a grin.

'What's so funny?'

'You're better than I gave you credit for.'

'Much obliged. Now get up nice and slow.'

There is the metallic whisper of a gun being cocked behind me. Then her voice, husked with the proximity of death held in slender hands. 'Please, Mr. Alston, I don't want you to get hurt.'

'Ever since we first met, all I've done is get hurt.' I inch away from her until I can see them both, my back against the wall. 'And to tell you the truth, Mrs. Bannister, it's becoming a very annoying habit.' I keep the gun on Hastings, watching her out of the corner of my eyes. I don't like the look of that Colt Single Action Army shaking in her hands. 'I'm here for the boy.'

'The trouble is, Mr. Alston—'

'The trouble is, Mrs. Bannister, that trouble is my business, especially when you're involved . . . Don't!' Hastings slowly raises his hands back up above his head again. 'I'm taking the boy.'

They exchange looks. 'You have no idea what will happen to Ronnie if you return him to my husband.'

'You mean Landis?' She lets out a cry of surprise and in that moment of disorientation, I snatch the gun from her hands. 'Easy!' Hastings almost beat me to it. He takes a step sideways, towards Betty Bannister. I gently ease the hammer back. I've never trusted the Colt .45. Heavy and highly temperamental. Liable to go off when you least expect it, which is nearly always. 'I give you my word: I won't let that Nazi son of a bitch touch the kid. Or his mother for that matter.'

She stares at me. Not so much surprised as stunned. 'But didn't you know, Mr. Alston? My sister was lobotomized right after she gave birth to Ronnie.'

So the Old Man knew from the very beginning who the father was. Knowing the Old Man, he could even have set JFK up. A honey trap with his teenage bride as bait and presidential influence as payoff. But that didn't explain the medical chart I saw at Linda Vista. It said *procedures*. More than one . . .

The echo of Sal Mineo's voice mimicking and mocking me: 'But the nurse said . . . '

The nurse had looked in the admissions book. She had said Elizabeth not Elaine. But if Elaine had already suffered Herr Doktor's operation, that meant the Old Man was lining up her twin sister for a repeat performance. Enforced discretion delivered eagerly by the Laureate of the Lobotomy. After all, the kid wasn't the Old Man's son, he was just a huge chunk of equity in an ambitious shakedown; an across-the-board bet in the Biggest Derby of them all: the White House Stakes. All this time, I'd been wrong; I had been looking at Ronnie with the sentimental eyes of a father. But the Old Man never saw the kid as anything but a human bargaining chip, to be played when the spoils of election victory came up for grabs in November. And the Old Man needed to keep his ace in the hole hush-hush. What use is blackmail if everyone knows the secret? Silence must rule. First the mother, then the boy and finally the only other relative who knew the whole story. One by one, their brains had to be muted by ice picks.

The Bannister Way.

So where did that leave me?

I didn't need a compass needle to see the direction I was heading in: following the footsteps of Hidalgo and Deckard. Of Elaine Bannister and . . . 'Greta Simmons. She was in on it, wasn't she?'

They gaze at me, saying nothing . . . Which says it all.

'Greta used to be a friend . . . ' Hastings says. 'She got me the job at High Sierra.'

'That's where we met.' She says it as though we were a couple of guests getting acquainted at a mutual friend's wedding banquet.

'But then, after Elaine fell pregnant . . . ' His voice drops away. He appears overcome with emotion. It's genuine, but I don't get it. Where exactly does Greta Simmons fit in? 'It was Hidalgo who warned me.'

'About Greta?'

He looks at me like I'm a moron. 'About the Fed.'

'You mean Rico?'

He's amazed I know the name. 'Rico was in charge of the snatch . . . '

Of course. A heist controlled by Boston. Joe Kennedy needed to get rid of the evidence as much as the Old Man needed to hold onto it. And with Rico on board, no wonder they blew the snatch. I didn't have all the details yet, but it was looking more and more as though Betty Bannister and Hastings had pulled a fast one over two of the richest men in the country. 'What were you planning to do with the kid?'

'There's an adoption agency, in Vancouver. I know the woman who runs it. We went to school together.'

'Vassar or Mount Holyoke?'

'Very funny. Barnard as a matter of fact. Now look, Mr Alston, can't you put those guns down? We're civilized people, aren't we?'

That's a loaded question when you're holding a loaded gun. I spin the chamber of the Chief's Special and toss it back to Hastings, filling my pocket with the slugs. 'I swear to God, if you try anything . . . '

He stares at me for a long, hard moment. It makes me want to look away, but I know if I do I might not be seeing anything else for a very long time. 'Relax . . . ' There is the silver shimmer of a blade being folded away. Jesus Christ. Two things. He had the knife out, and I never saw it. He had the knife out, and he didn't use it.

'I should take the kid . . . '

'Why would we allow you to do that, Mr. Alston?'

'Because you've got to run and you won't get far with the kid at your side.' I take her shoulders in my hands, staring into her green eyes. From the room next door comes the sound of the child stirring. She glances at the room then turns back to me. 'We play this right, Mrs. Bannister, and the impossible happens. Everyone gets out alive.'

astings watched from behind the dogwoods as LBJ climbed into the back of the limo with his mistress, the car's headlights long and lonely as they tugged the couple off into the murderous night.

Nixon waved good-bye to the couple, the smile on his face vanishing as he turned back to the ranch house. Hastings watched through the great windows as the oilmen, dons and bankers left for their respective rooms. Old Man Bannister and Howard Hughes exchanged words, both nodding as they left via different doors, the Old Man turning in his chair, berating Morris as he was wheeled out of sight.

Hastings waited in the silence as the rising crescent moon began to scythe a path through a thin bank of clouds shrouding the eastern horizon. The night sky was his watch; its moments of motion counting down not to an act of justice but revenge. It was on another night with a low crescent moon over three years ago that he had decided to tell Betty Bannister about Greta's plan. She had looked up, watching him through the windshield as he approached her car, the radio still on. They listened to *Lament* together in silence, the engine block ticking in the cool air after the song was over. And then he had told her, watching her face in the faint moonlight; enduring her sobs.

It had been the right thing to do, and neither of them owed anything to Greta, especially after what she had done to Elaine, but still it hurt the way betrayals always do. The life of an infant was at stake and Hastings thought that if he could save this child, it would make up for the baby that had been inside Susan when he had lost her.

He had thought wrong.

Inside, the house simmered with the stillness of sleep, the collective breathing agitating the floorboards; furniture contracting under the suppressed tension. From the stables he heard the loud whinny of a horse, prescient with the knowledge of bloodshed. The bone-handle doorknob cracked open, and Hastings entered the bedroom, the scent of medication sluicing through him. He took a small blue bottle of chloroform out of his coat pocket, wet his handkerchief and placed it beside the Old Man's face. He waited through the nervous chiming of a grandfather clock in the hallway, then saturated the handkerchief and pressed it against the Old Man's mouth and nose. His eyes opened in surprise, and Hastings leant over, whispering into his ear just two words: 'It's over.'

The Old Man tried to sit up, his grip fierce and surprisingly strong around Hastings's wrists as he struggled to push the assault away, but then he lilted backwards into unconsciousness.

Hastings removed the handkerchief, revealing the burns around the Old Man's mouth. Even his own hands were stinging from the solvent. He went into the adjoining bathroom and washed his hands and rinsed out the handkerchief, pulling away from the departing fumes. He unwrapped a clean white napkin that held the stainless steel skewer and ran the hot water as he passed the skewer through the flame of his cigarette lighter. It sang when he put it under the water, a brief hiss of pain. He placed it carefully back on the napkin, unfolded his *navaja sevillana*, sterilized it in the same way, then took both weapons back into the Old Man's bedroom.

It was time for the surgery.

Kneeling over the Old Man's body, he edged the tip of his

blade between the upper right eyelid and the eyeball, then slotted the skewer through the space in the orbit. He was surprised how easily the skewer slipped down through the socket until he struck bone. Carefully extracting the knife, he looked around for something to use as a hammer, sliding open the top drawer of the bedside table.

He took the heavy hardcover book out of the drawer and, holding the skewer as though it were a nail, rapped the top with the book.

Nothing.

He did it again, harder this time. Still nothing. The Old Man sighed, like someone who had just remembered he'd forgotten his wallet and had to turn around and go home.

Hastings changed hands, holding the skewer with his left, this time angling it up more towards the top of the head. Holding the book in his fist, he raised it high, then slammed it down with all his force, driving his shoulder into the blow, the skewer disappearing. Hastings worked quickly, arcing it in a semicircular sweep backwards and forwards one way, then changing to the opposite direction, performing the same sheathing movement, so that the two arches would intersect in the centre, forming an elongated oval.

He yanked the skewer out too quickly, the eyeball halfpopping as it crested over the rim of the orbit. Hastings stopped, easing the eyeball back into its socket before carefully extracting the skewer with a gentle twist, its steel misted by membrane and blood.

Hastings washed and dried both his *navaja sevillana* and the skewer, wiped down the taps and basin, then went back to the bedroom and did the same to the bedside table and the bedhead. He cleaned the book of prints, placing it back in the drawer with his handkerchief, noticing its title embossed in gold for the first time.

He listened at the door, then slowly opened it. No sounds

outside. And inside just the laboured breathing of a man trans-formed; a single bloody tear pearling his right eye. Not enough to mourn all those he had harmed in his long and greedy life. But a start nonetheless.

Cate looks out the window, to where Betty Bannister's Cadillac convertible is parked, eating up our shitty little street with its glossy pink expanse. She turns back to me. 'Big Bear Lake . . . ?'

'A ski lodge, you know the type—a real log cabin. In the woods. No one will ever find you.'

'I don't know, Nicky, it just doesn't seem . . . ' Her voice trails away. Too many adjectives to slip into that one small space: right; safe; sane. 'Why can't you come with us?'

'I've got to stay behind and fix a few things first; make it safe for us . . . ' To run, and maybe not get caught.

She glances towards the kitchen. 'I don't even know them.'

'It's a big ask, I know, but it'll only be for a few days, I swear . . . ' She goes over to the closet, hesitates for a long moment, then takes out a suitcase.

The two locks snap like handcuffs as she opens it. 'How about the police?'

'I'm taking care of everything, baby. Look . . . ' I pull out a wad of hundred-dollar bills. 'They gave it to me.' I take her in my arms. The last thing I want is to leave Cate like this. But there's no other way. 'You can trust them. They'll do everything they can to help us.'

I break away from her but she pulls me back, staring into my face. 'Why, Nick? Why are they helping us?'

Because they're two people torn apart by the accumulated history of all their suffering and violence and sin. Just like me.

'Because they're good people,' I lie. 'And because they want the same things we do.' Reprieve. Forgiveness. Escape. Above all that most elusive of dreams: the unheard-of Second Chance.

I take Cate in my arms, her lips generous, her tongue seeking, both of us falling into the kiss the way we used to. When we still believed in a future together.

'Mr. Alston?'

I ease out of the embrace, turn to Mrs. Bannister. 'Don't bother to knock.'

'I'm sorry, but we really should get going if we're to reach the lodge by dawn.'

I turn back to Cate. There are tears in her eyes. 'You know this is what we want.'

'But like this, Nick?'

'Sometimes when you have no choices, you have to accept the ones that are made for you . . . ' I look at my new watch. Carnivore time. 'Mrs. Bannister's right, you've got to go.'

Cate's about to say something when the telephone rings, making all three of us jump. I snatch it from the cradle.

'Alston? Where the fuck are you?'

Like most cops, Schiller's not one to lose sleep over asking an obvious question. 'I'm standing at the end of the number you just dialled . . . Where are you?'

His voice drops to a low burr, almost a pharyngeal impossibility for a man like Schiller. 'With the Old Man . . . We're heading out. To La Jolla.'

La Jolla? 'What's there?'

'The Hotel del Charro . . . '

'There's also a racetrack and a goddamn barber's. I mean why are you going there?'

The voice drops even lower. It must actually hurt Schiller to force himself to speak so softly. 'For a meet at the hotel with J. Edgar. He wants you along.'

'Fuck Hoover, he's not my boss.'

'But the Old Man still is.' I can hear the relief in the way he roars it through the phone.

'Tell the Old Man I'm following up a lead from Linda Vista. I'll call him in the morning.'

'Jesus, Alston,' he lowers his voice again, to the barely audible register of muttered prayers. 'You just don't get it, do you?'

'Enlighten me.'

'It's Hoover. He says they've found the kid.'

A mbulances congregated outside the ranch house like a pack of feasting hyenas, their engines all running, surprising the morning air with the grime of exhaust. Doctors, lawyers and accountants milled with CIA, FBI and Secret Service: a convention of grey flannel suits talking in the covert shorthand of hurried whispers and meaningful nods, self-important with their proximity to History. Momentous decisions were being negotiated inside the ranch house. Power was being divided. Resources allocated. Nations reassigned. The Old Man's empire was being dismantled, one golden brick at a time.

Hemming was the one who blabbed the news at the breakfast table out back: Old Man Bannister had suffered a massive stroke—a nine on the Richter scale. Looked like he was out for the count. Hemming figured the Old Man must have blown a gasket with some broad. 'Maybe that cute little cook in the kitchen? Hell, she'd just about do it to me.'

Hastings let him have it, Hemming dropping his plate of waffles, the horses cracking their hooves against the stable's walls in appreciation of the sight of the young hotshot slowly getting to his feet, still clutching his stomach, the knees of his Dallas police officer's uniform coloured yellow with Texas dust.

Roselli grabbed Hastings. 'What are you, nuts?' Then in a whisper, 'We need that juvenile delinquent, at least for today.'

Hastings threw Roselli's hand off his arm. Message received. Hemming was disposable too. They all were. Who could argue with the logic? Why waste time washing all the dishes when you can just toss everything into the trash? Welcome to the Age of Plastic. Hastings caught Sturgis staring at him through a window and pointed thumb and forefinger at him—you're next.

Luchino watched him with concern as they crunched their way down the gravel driveway to the cars. 'Just something I had to get off my chest,' Hastings said, climbing into the Citroën.

Luchino put a tan leather overnight bag in the trunk, then lit one of his yellow cigarettes, scenting the air with a strong alkaline haze. 'This old man, was he not the one with the kidnapped son?'

'Ronnie Bannister.'

'*Précisément . . .* ' He turned the key in the ignition, as though he were snapping a small animal's neck, then turned to Hastings, the car worrying the birds with its throaty growl. 'Be careful, my friend. The people we work for do not believe in coincidence.'

'Neither do I.'

'*Très bien . . .* ' Luchino drove fast out of the ranch, chickens feather-dancing out of the way. They flew past the checkpoint, Stetsons turning in surprise, Luchino accelerating dangerously onto the highway, tires screeching warning as he glided with confident indifference through the early-morning traffic: milk trucks, oil tankers; pickups stacked with hay bales honeying the air with golden chaff. They sped past a roadhouse, two men in suits and hats standing outside, watching the traffic, one with a walkie-talkie in his hand, the other with a camera. Luchino gave them a *bras d'honneur*, clenching his cigarette in his teeth as he laughed, the car swerving for an instant, Hastings steadying the wheel.

Dallas began to appear, mirage-mirrored on the bitumen's heat haze. It was unseasonably hot for November, as though the whole city were gripped in a fever dream. Hastings could feel the sweat slowly inching down his sides like a trail of scouting insects waiting for the swarm to follow. Heat. Nerves. The old war itch. There was a buzzing inside his head, an internal coring. Not going in, not going out. Just being there.

So many lives were at stake. Starting with the president's. Ending with those of the two killers inside the speeding car. To get it right would be almost impossible. But they had to try.

'I'll take the first shot,' Luchino said. 'Fire right after me.'

That sounded fine to Hastings. 'Just make sure you miss.'

'It will be difficult but . . . ' Luchino gave a sorrowful shrug. Professional pride. Hastings felt it too. Not in the work itself, but in their innate and unique ability. Once a marksman, always a marksman. It was like carrying a tune or riding a horse. Some skills never leave you. Until the vocal cords are severed with a blade, or the horse run down by a truck.

It was nearly half-past nine by the time they reached Dealey Plaza, Luchino parking up beside the railway yards in front of the overpass. The ground was still moist from dawn dew drying slowly in the shadows. Hastings would normally have worried about footprints but the parking was already filling up for the motorcade. That morning's evidence would soon go the way of the traditional Comanche hunting grounds of Texas: overrun and obliterated. Luchino ground out his cigarette against a car tire, then pocketed the butt. Instinctive; intelligent. A Chesterfield or a Camel would be invisible. But with one of Luchino's Gitanes Maïs, he might as well leave his birth certificate.

The pair grabbed coffee in a diner off Elm. 'There are some things you never forget: the first time you made love, the first cigarette you ever smoked, and the first coffee you couldn't drink . . . ' Luchino pushed his cup away. 'New York, September 8th, 1954. My first day in your country. I used to wonder why I was always tired when I came to America. And then one morning at breakfast, I realized: it was because I was deprived of caffeine. Even in prison in France, the coffee is better.'

Hastings filled up his own cup. 'Here's hoping I never get the chance to compare.'

Luchino laughed. 'Ah yes, the devil you know. But you might think about going to Europe. There's plenty of work in Marseille and Palermo for a man with your talents . . . '

Talents. Kill and not be killed. Hastings lit a cigarette, looked at the Corsican. Luchino was already thinking about the pleasures of going back home. But Hastings had no home; not after what he'd done in Adelsberg.

'*Ça alors . . . !*'

Hastings turned fast, staring through the windows after the man that Luchino had just seen. 'You know him?'

'Pietro Cesari, I swear it was him!'

The man with the crew cut turned the corner, disappearing from sight. If he thought he had been recognized, he didn't show it. 'Who is he?'

'An interrogator. The best . . . He started on the Nazis for the OSS. Then on the Collaborators for the Unione Corse. And when they saw how good he was, the SDECE sent him to Indochine. He's still based in Saigon, but now he works for CIA.'

'Are you sure it was him?' Luchino nodded sadly, like a veterinarian confirming there was no alternative to putting the dog down. 'Did he see you?'

Luchino stubbed out his cigarette, tossed coins onto the table. 'There is nothing he doesn't see.'

Hastings stared at the Corsican. There was something about him that he didn't recognize. Something he had never seen before. And when Hastings realised what it was, the hairs on the back of his neck rose in alarm.

Luchino was afraid.

'Let's go,' Hastings said.

Outside, the streets were animated with bunting and flags, cops and sheriffs lounging against squad cars or motorcycles, smoking and squinting into the morning sun. It felt familiar enough to offer cover for the fear they knew was there. For the death that was lurking everywhere. For the secret knowledge that was inside them. There was no sign of Cesari. 'What does it mean?'

'It means, my friend, that if he is targeting your president, there is nothing we can do.'

'If?'

He stared at Hastings, his ancient eyes blinking in the sunlight; guarding their shadows. 'He could be targeting us.'

A tall, military-looking man in a dark suit and a short-brimmed cowboy hat slipped Hastings a hand bill as they passed him. Hastings glanced at both sides of the bill to make sure there was no secret message written on it, then showed it to Luchino. Above the title *Wanted for Treason* were photos of Kennedy mocked up as police mug shots.

'The OAS did the same with de Gaulle. It is the spell of the Griot.' Hastings shook his head. 'A shaman. He has a special power.' He leant in close to Hastings, whispering. 'He tells a story and then it comes true . . . '

Hastings looked back at the man on the street corner, wondering where the tall cowboy would be in a few hours' time if his story came true. Celebrating in a bar, or under arrest for sedition? If Hastings could stop the assassination, then the cowboy would simply trudge back to the printers and order another story with a fistful of dollars and a heart full of hate. But it wasn't just the Griot's story; all the stories of the nation were in the balance. If Hastings failed, then in a year or two, a telegram would arrive at a house in Louisville, Kentucky, and shortly after a star would appear at a window. Black ties would be borrowed. And a church would fill with the scent of flowers and the sobs of family. Maybe a mushroom cloud would fill the horizon south of Florida . . . Or west of Berlin. Maybe flames would tongue the night sky in Watts or Harlem or Memphis. Maybe factories would close in Detroit, schools in Rapid City, hospitals in Pittsburgh. Maybe a few would grow richer while the rest would grow poorer. Maybe guns and drugs would invade the country's towns and schools; radiation poison its air and water. Maybe napalm would blossom over distant green jungles. All of history was balanced, knife-edged and dangerous, on a sunny autumn day in a bustling Texas city. Hastings felt the honed danger of the razor underfoot. One slip and the nation's arteries would split open with shocking speed, venting blood and gore.

They returned to the car, removed their bags from the trunk and walked down to the plaza in silence. If Luchino was worried about Cesari, he wasn't saying. Maybe he was guarding his own fears and doubts inside his silence. Or perhaps he was like Hastings, skimming the near future, jumping to that afternoon when they'd metamorphose from killers to saviours.

When they'd both start running.

Roselli was waiting for them, wearing Hollywood shades, his face turned upwards; a burnt offering to the sun.

'Jesus Christ, when I think of all those years I spent freezing my nuts off in Chicago. To hell with the Windy City, I'll take sunshine any fucking day . . . So, you bring everything you need?' Hastings and Luchino raised their suitcases. 'Fucking A! Let's do this.'

Roselli started to stride towards the Texas School Book Depository but Hastings stood in his way. 'What about the rest of it?'

Roselli feigned ignorance. 'Rest of what?'

'The payment,' Luchino said.

Roselli made a gesture like a bird just shat on his hat. 'What is this, a concert hall shakedown? I told you boys already. You'll get paid after the gig.'

'Problem is, after the gig Alderisio and Nicoletti are planning a little extra work . . . We'd like to spare you the overtime.'

'Wise guy, huh?'

'More "alive guy" . . . Show him.'

Luchino looked all around, then opened his overnight bag. He held it towards Roselli, who refused to look inside. 'Whatever the fuck you're selling, I don't want it.'

'You need to take the look.'

Roselli took a deep breath, like a gambler about to stake his life savings on a pair of jacks. He glanced inside the bag, and saw three squares of ivory-coloured C3 wrapped in transparent plastic and wired to a clock and detonator. Roselli ripped off his sunglasses. 'That looks just like a fucking bomb.'

'That's because it is the "fucking bomb", my friend.'

He turned to Luchino. 'I ain't talking to you.'

'That's his bomb, so maybe you'd better start.'

'It's called *la strounga*. I learned how to make it in Oran.'

Roselli sucked in his lower lip, his chin creasing in phony defiance. 'Your fucking plastic explosives don't scare me.'

'They should . . . '

Roselli grabbed Hastings by the shirt lapels, his eyes bloodshot and murderous. 'What are you going to do, blow me up in the middle of downtown fucking Dallas?'

'Better. We're going to blow up all your guests from last night.' Roselli let go of Hastings, defeated.

'You see, I hid *la strounga* in their bags and . . . how do you say 'chassis'?'

'Never fucking mind, I get the drift . . . ' Roselli went over to a park bench and plunked his weight down. 'It's enough to make you cry . . . ' Luchino offered him a cigarette. Roselli stared at them for a long moment, then knocked them away. 'Who the fuck ever heard of yellow cigarettes? Like smoking old teeth.' He leapt to his feet, reinvigorated by his anger. 'Do you clowns have any idea what you've done?'

'Naturally, *mon ami* . . . And I object to being called the clown.'

Roselli cursed so savagely both men took a step away from

him, avoiding contamination. 'So whose fucking car did you booby-trap?'

'We picked five of them.'

'Oh, Christ! Who?'

'*Mais non, mon ami*, it's not fair, you must guess.'

'He's right. It could have been Hughes or Hoffa. Maybe it was Nixon? Or one of your Big Oil buddies. Or maybe that little banker, what's his name?'

Roselli sobbed twice, the second ending in a snarl. He slumped back down on the bench, a man defeated, staring into the big sky. His voice sounded far away. 'So what do you crumbs want?'

'Alderisio and Nicoletti off our backs.'

'Done.'

'And full payment, now.'

'Give me a break, you know I can't . . . '

'Why?'

'You know why. We never brought the money.'

'Then you have a very big problem, *mon ami* . . . '

'Tell me something I don't know.'

'You need to get the money. Now.'

'No fucking kidding . . . ?' Roselli thought for a moment. 'So what's to stop me just telling everyone to look under their cars?'

'You can do that, if you want. Tell me, who was in charge of security last night?'

A passing klaxon filled the silence. 'Monsieur Roselli, of course.'

'Or you can find out where the bombs are and have your own people remove them nice and quiet. No one needs to know.'

'*Oui*, save face. And your skin too . . . '

Roselli stared at Luchino. 'Fucking French fancy pants.'

'This way at least you know where to look. Who knows, you

might even decide to leave the bombs there when you find out who we picked.'

'Very funny. Wait a minute . . . ' Roselli leapt off the bench, illuminated and wrathful. 'You fucking hustler. You didn't mention the Old Man. That doesn't make sense. He'd be the prime target. Why wouldn't you put a bomb in Old Man Bannister's car too?'

'Because I've already put one in his head.'

This time it was Roselli who stepped backwards. He was like Saul on the Road to Damascus . . . Blinded by revelation. And fear. He crossed himself, touched his corno. 'Mother of God . . . '

Hastings looked at his watch. 'You better talk to your oil-men. Two cases. Three hundred grand each in five-hundred and one-thousand notes.'

'Six hundred grand at short notice?' He actually stopped to think. 'Let me see, Gene Brading's in town.' Hastings knew him. Shakedown artist. 'I could send him and Jackie Ruby to pass the hat around the Oil assholes, but I don't know if we can pull this one off in tim—' Roselli's voice faded away. Hastings looked in the same direction as Roselli. A slim young man with a large head and thinning hair was marching mean-ingfully towards them.

'Hi, Mr. Roselli,' He said with a light, strangely flat voice and an open smile just the wrong side of vacant.

'What the fuck are you doing here?'

'I saw you talking and . . . ' He turned, nodding to first Luchino and then Hastings, 'I figured these gentlemen must be the shooters.'

Roselli grabbed the kid by the shoulders. 'Not so loud, for Christ's sake. We don't want it broadcast.'

The kid frowned, pulling himself free. 'No need to be hos-tile,' he said, unable to hide the hurt in his voice. 'We're all on the same side, right?'

Hastings felt a twinge of pity for this kid. Try as hard as you like, no one can ever be on the same side as the Outfit or CIA. But they were both masters of optical illusion. If you looked in the mirror, you'd swear they were standing right there beside you, arm around your shoulder, smiling . . . When they were really standing right behind you, with a gun pointed at your head.

Roselli seemed taken aback by the kid's naivety. 'Huh? Sure, kid . . . ' He introduced him to Hastings and Luchino. 'This here is the pats—' Stopping himself just in time. 'I mean this here is Lee O—'

'Hidell.' The kid shouted, pulling a face at Roselli. 'We said code names.' He shook hands with Hastings then Luchino. 'Alek James Hidell but you can call me Leon.'

'I'm Elvis and he's Napoleon.'

Leon beamed, nodding at them for the sake of Roselli. 'Code names . . . Good.'

'Leon, or whatever the fuck his name is today, is going to take you to your positions. He's got a job at the Book Depository.'

'That's right, and I can get you into the Dal-Tex Building too.'

Roselli frowned at him. 'How the hell did you know about the Dal-Tex?'

'I saw Wal and Hemming pointing it out to the Cubans.' Hastings could imagine what they'd told the Cubans. Follow him and Luchino out of the buildings and kill them the first chance you get. 'Given the range and field of fire I assumed . . . '

'You're one nosy fucking kid.'

'I'm a spy, Mr. Roselli, what do you expect me to be?'

A passing woman looked up at them. Roselli hushed Leon down with a look of pain. 'For crying out loud, keep it down.'

'Listen . . . Leon? We need a phone, we have some urgent calls to make.'

Leon tapped his cheek with his finger, thinking; actually snapped his fingers. 'There's a phone in the Dal-Tex building. Third floor.'

'What the fuck is wrong with the Book Depository, it's closer.'

'In case you've forgotten, I work there . . . People know me. They might get suspicious . . . '

This kid, Leon, was amazing. Lecturing Roselli, as though Roselli could be taught anything. As though he were Roselli's equal. It made Hastings wonder whether it was possible the kid was with CIA; that he was actually smarter and more senior than he seemed. Or was he just another rope-a-dope, playing cops and robbers like Hemming?

They followed him across the lawn and into the Dal-Tex building, their footsteps echoing loud against the stone floors up into the high ceilings of the sun-hardened shell of red brick. They rode the freight elevator up to the third floor.

Hastings took in the view of Dealey Plaza: one huge killing field. Leon's face appeared reflected in the window. 'So, what's your story?'

Silence hummed like the traffic outside: muted, strained and threatening. 'In Japan, gangsters share fingers, not stories . . . '

'Excuse me?'

'You cut off your finger and give it to your boss, as a mark of respect . . . ' Hastings turned to the kid. 'I mean, who needs a man's story when you've got his fucking finger?'

Leon gave a low whistle. 'Jeez, I didn't know that . . . I've been to Japan too. With the Marine Corps.' Looked like Leon was too attached to his fingers to sacrifice them for a story. 'I signed up right after Civil Air Patrol. They sent me to a spy station in Japan. Kanagawa? Taught myself Russian and volunteered to go undercover as a defector.'

'You defected?'

'You better believe it.'

'So how come they let you back into the country?'

'Let's just say they were expecting me . . . ' He gave a small smile that hide a large pride. 'Afterwards, I infiltrated the Pro-Castro movement.' Hastings didn't get it. How could a kid like this infiltrate the closed, duplicitous world of Castro and Anti-Castro? The only honest answer: he couldn't. 'They think I'm a Commie!' His laugh was unnerving, divorced from any notion of humour; more the jumpy stutter of a fuse burning too fast. 'Pulled one over their eyes . . . '

Hastings had an irresistible urge to grab the kid by the shoulders, to shake some sense into those slightly glazed eyes of his and tell the poor chump the truth.

'Okay, no promises but it's looking good. Those Oil fuckers keep hundreds of grand in their office safes for emergencies just like this . . . ' Roselli paused, mulling possibilities: Oilmen with greedy appetites and more money than they knew what to do with. Too much ready cash lying around. Easy access to office safes. Overall, the big combo was irresistible. Roselli was already moving on to his next operation. 'I should talk it over with Walter Stark. Now about them bombs . . . '

'Bombs?'

'Shut up, Leon, this don't concern you . . . '

'I disagree, Mr. Roselli, this most certainly concerns—'

Roselli grabbed him by his skinny arms and tossed him across the room, into the wire cage gate of the elevator. The hinges squealed and squeaked, and Leon bounced back into Roselli. 'Wise up and shut up.'

'But all I . . . '

Roselli raised a warning finger right in front of his nose. The kid took a deep breath and closed his mouth, tight. Roselli nodded approval. 'What about them bombs?'

'You get the info when we get the money.'

'Money . . . ?'

Roselli flicked Leon hard across the nose. 'What did I tell you?' Then back to Hastings: 'You'll pay for this . . . '

'Tell me one single thing any of us has ever done in our miserable lives that we won't pay for?'

Roselli stared at him for a long moment, then slid his sunglasses back on. 'Ain't that the god-awful truth . . . '

Luchino turned to Leon. 'I was told the second floor.'

'That's right, there's a vacant office, in front of the fire escape.'

'Let's see it,' Hastings said. Leon went to call the elevator. 'Use the stairs. Less chance of people seeing us.'

Leon nodded. As they walked past the telephone booth, Roselli stuck his finger in the return coin slot, checking for missed dimes. The Godfather of loose change. It gave Hastings an idea. He leant in and ripped the receiver cord out of the box. Roselli nodded approvingly. 'Good thinking . . . Elvis.'

'Say, that's the property of Ma Bell.'

'Who gives a rat's ass? You should take a look at your phone bills, Leon. Those crooks are worse than us.'

Roselli and Leon walked down to the second floor, holding on to the staircase handrail all the way. Hastings and Luchino exchanged looks. Maybe no one would sweep for prints. Recklessness wasn't dangerous in itself, it was the hallmark of an amateur. And that's what was dangerous.

'There you go . . . ' He unlocked a door and handed the key to Luchino. Luchino walked in, his eyes calibrating the terrain. 'Perfect.' He snapped open a small carry bag and began to assemble a Kongsberg Våpenfabrikk Mauser M59 sniper rifle with a precision Zeiss scope.

'Nice piece.' Leon went to touch it but Luchino stopped him just in time. 'It's like a Stradivarius, *mon ami*. You can look, you can listen . . . but never, ever, touch . . . '

Leon stood frozen with embarrassment and maybe fear. Hastings decided to rescue him. 'Let's get to the Book Depository.' Leon and Roselli left the room without a word. Hastings paused, then turned back to Luchino. They looked into each other's eyes, then shook hands. It was meant more for complicity and luck, but if need be, it would also serve as farewell. Then Hastings closed the door behind him, his fist protected by his handkerchief.

Outside the sun was brighter, the air clammy with expectation. Hastings could hear music that sounded like it was coming from a carousel. They crossed the street, the asphalt tender underfoot. The music grew louder: unnerving in its inappropriateness; in its insistence on dominating the mood. It was coming from an organ grinder, sitting on the bottom step of the Book Depository. Roselli strode up to him. 'Are you out of your mind? What the hell are you doing here?'

The organ grinder stopped his cranking, the thin music running on into silence. He said something Hastings didn't catch. 'As God is my witness . . . ' Roselli grabbed the grinder by the lapels and yanked him off the steps. 'You tell Marcello go fuck himself.'

A tall passerby stopped and stared. 'Say, leave the poor fellow alone . . . ' He had a strange way of speaking. Mid-Atlantic. Roselli glared at him for a moment, his face breaking out into a leer of recognition. 'Ned?' He removed his shades, the diamond on his pinkie finger flashing. 'It *is* you.'

The man turned back to the organ grinder. 'Good lord, don't tell me he's with you too?'

Roselli shook his head. 'This asshole's with Marcello . . . ' Carlos Marcello was allied with Santo Trafficante. Trafficante was palled up with Meyer Lansky and the Eastern Establishment. Two different worlds, east coast and west coast, colliding in Dallas. You didn't need a weatherman to know a storm was due. 'What is that, Ned, you putting shit in your hair now?'

Ned dabbed his forehead nervously, as though expecting the dye to run. 'I'm incognito.' He glanced at Hastings and Leon. 'So I'd be most obliged if you didn't address me by name.'

Hands on hips, shaking his head in disgust, Roselli watched

Ned hurrying away. 'Goddamn spooks . . . ' He shoved the organ grinder along after Ned. 'It's always about them.' Roselli turned to Leon. 'Move it, we're running out of time.'

'I can handle it from here.'

'Maybe you can and maybe you can't, but I'm not going to find out.'

Leon actually put his hand out to stop him. 'I work here. You cannot compromise my position.'

Impressed, Hastings turned to Roselli, nodding. 'The kid's got a point . . . '

Roselli knew enough to give up. 'Fuck you all, I'm out of here.'

'What about my payment?'

Roselli paused for a moment, but not long enough to construct a lie. 'Jackie will come by with your bag, Gene with Frenchie's.'

'Napoleon's,' Leon corrected.

'What are you, a history teacher?'

'How will we know the other one hasn't been double-crossed?' Hastings asked.

'When you get your bags, you can wave at each other through the windows.' Roselli sulked away, then stopped and took a step back towards Hastings. 'Do you have any idea . . . any fucking appreciation of how hard this has been to put together?'

'Don't. You'll break my heart . . . '

'Wise guy.'

They watched Roselli turn the corner and disappear. 'Unpleasant, isn't he . . . ? You'll find my colleagues much nicer.'

'CIA nice?'

'The workers at the Book Depository.' The air inside was cooler but musty with damp and the strident stench of varnish. 'They're replacing the floorboards . . . ' Leon led Hastings into a changing room and handed him a grey coverall. 'It'll make you damn near invisible.'

Leon was right. No one even looked at Hastings as he was led past the soda pop machine, into the elevator and up to the top of the building. Leon showed him the windows at the end. The trajectory was far more acute than Luchino's in the Dal-Tex building. Did that mean they thought he was the better shot? Or did they just toss a coin. There was a rifle lying parallel to the window on the floor, half-hidden by newspapers—a Mannlicher-Carcano. 'What the hell is that?'

Leon leaned over his shoulder, craning to see. 'A rifle . . . '

'I can see that.' It was a model 91. 'What I want to know is, what's it doing here?'

'I've never seen it before in my life.'

Hastings looked around suddenly. 'What floor are we on?'

'Seventh.'

'We're supposed to be on the sixth floor.' Hastings slipped the bolt out of the rifle, then wiped the weapon down for prints.

'Why did you do that?'

'Call it anticipation . . . '

Hastings pushed past Leon, taking the stairs, Leon hurrying behind him, catching the door onto the sixth floor before it slammed shut in his face. Hastings went over to the far windows. Boxes had been stacked around them, forming a sniper's nest. Leon gestured to it. 'I built it myself . . . ' Hastings ignored him as he started to assemble his weapon, a Springfield Model 1903-A4 carbine. 'Nice,' Leon said. 'What are they?'

'Custom rounds . . . Remember what Napoleon said. No touching.' He started loading the magazine, then glanced back up at Leon and froze. The kid had just drawn a Smith & Wesson .38 Special revolver. It looked like he might have completely underestimated Leon. 'What are you going to do with that?'

'Huh? Oh, this . . . ?' Leon hurriedly tucked the revolver

behind his trousers' waistband, embarrassed. 'I was just—you know: you show me yours . . . '

Hastings finished assembling his rifle, not looking up as he spoke. 'So what's the .38 Special for, cat burglars or target practice . . . ?'

'Heck . . . It's for a job.'

'Really? And what have you got planned?'

'Have you heard of this hotshot called Gerry Hemming?'

Hastings stopped what he was doing, looked up at Leon. '. . . Sure. He's the one that acts like an escapee from juvy hall.'

'That's the one.' Leon said, beaming with pride. 'Well, after we kill Kennedy, we're going to kill Gerry Hemming . . . '

T he Hotel was lit up like an ocean liner beached against the shadowy sea of the Del Mar Racetrack. Black sedans gathered at the entrance gates, their headlights fisting trembling barriers of light. 'You better watch your batteries . . . '

'You better watch your mouth.'

If it isn't my old pal, Sergeant Barnsley. 'Isn't it past your bedtime, Barnsley? Must be a full moon.'

Barnsley's huge hands are at my throat. The heat of his anger roars out through his fingers; they tremble from the barely controlled desire to maim and scar. I reach down fast and snap his balls. Barnsley crumples to the turf. Flashlights circle, then trap me. 'What the hell . . . ?'

I shoulder through them. 'I'm Mr. Hoover's personal guest. He's expecting me.' I point back to the sergeant, sobbing in his sick. 'That man needs medical attention . . . '

'What's wrong with him?'

I make a drinking motion into the torchlight. Someone swears, and they haul Barnsley away, his heels dragging in the dirt. I stride towards the hotel, Feds forming an honour guard all the way into the lobby, most of them cradling tommy guns. I'm frisked next to the porter's desk in plain sight of an old man in a Stetson peering at me through cigar smoke.

'What's the matter, you never seen police brutality before?' One of the Fed's pulls the .38 Chief's Special carefully out of my jacket pocket, as though someone's told him it just might go boom.

The old cowboy draws his cigar slowly out of his mouth and shakes his head sadly. 'The problem with you, stranger,' he says, speaking with a pleasant Texas drawl, 'is you don't recognize your friends from your enemies.'

To hell with sermons, it's too late even for midnight mass. 'Who needs either when you've got clients and criminals?'

He nods and two gorillas grab me from behind, frogmarching me towards the servants' quarters. I turn back to the old man. 'So which one are you?'

'Why, stranger, I'm just a poor bystander hoping he's not going to witness an unfortunate accident . . . '

I'm shoved along a narrow corridor, staff looking away quickly as we pass. 'Who the hell was that, Sam Houston?'

'He owns this hotel . . . ' A hard thump in the back. 'So show some respect, dumbass.'

We cross a large kitchen, the smell of charred steak and coffee reminding me how long it's been since I last ate. Two green swing doors stand at the end, their portholes glittering with treasure beyond. I'm pushed through them, into a ballroom lit with crystal chandeliers, gold-leaf ceilings and statues of ancient soldiers balancing candles on their spears. The doors slowly flap shut behind me, my escort staying on the other side. In the middle of the room is a small, circular table, where J. Edgar Hoover and Johnny Roselli are staring at me. Old Man Bannister sits with his back to me. Schiller nervously waves me over. I start to cross the dance floor, slipping and almost falling on the polished wood.

J. Edgar Hoover glares at me. 'Have you been drinking?'

'Never on the job . . . '

There is the crooked squeak of a wheelchair as Old Man Bannister rotates himself towards me. 'No need to worry then, Mr. Atlas . . . '

'Alston . . . '

'Mr. Alston, because you're no longer on the job. You're fired.'

'Best news I've heard all day.' I nod to the bottle of Dimple Haig sitting in the centre of the table, then go to pour myself a drink. Roselli snatches the bottle away. I tut-tut sadly. 'That's not like the famous Robin Hood of Beverly Hills . . . '

It gets awful quiet awful fast. The legs of Roselli's chair screech as he pushes away from the table.

I go to block his punch to my stomach but at the last second Roselli pulls back and kicks me hard in the shin. My knee crumples fast. I try to straighten. Too late. The toe of his shoe catches me under the chin. I stagger backwards into a service table and knock it over, slapping the floor with an unholy whack, the echo reverberating through my head.

'That was for Lily, you crumb.'

'Lay off.' Schiller shouts, stepping between me and Roselli.

I rub my aching chin, cheap boot polish coming off on my hand. I get to my feet. 'Who the hell is Lily?'

Roselli pulls out a 4-inch Colt Python. Schiller grabs his wrist in one of his baseball-mitt hands and squeezes. 'You know the rules. No weapons inside the hotel.'

Roselli lets out a whine like a steel girder struggling through a wood chipper and drops the gun, the revolver pointing right at him when it clatters to the floor. He dances away in fright. 'Fuck me—that could have gone off.'

'What do you think we'll make of that ten years hence . . . ' the Old Man says. 'The hand of Providence . . . ' He rolls right up to Roselli, leaning out of his chair. 'Or a tragic missed opportunity?'

'Now look, you dirty old man . . . '

'This is no time for squabbles.' Hoover says, slapping the table. 'It's late and I have breakfast with Bing Crosby at the Diamond Club.' He turns to me. 'You're the one who found the body of the boy?'

'The body of *a* boy.'

Schiller grimaces and shakes his head at me. Hoover looks from him back to me. 'You're a forensic pathologist?'

'You know the answer to that.'

'Then leave it to the medical examiners to determine whose remains they are. In the meantime, I want you to know that the DA has spoken to me about bringing charges against you . . . ' He smiles. 'That's right, Alston. Fraud. Extortion. Grand Theft Auto. Obstruction of Justice.'

It's not the certainty in his voice that makes me go weak in the legs. It's the vanity. He is the Oracle. He sees the future and he knows it. 'None of those charges will stick . . . '

'What about Reckless Endangerment with regards to a minor? McKesson came out of Juvenile Court. You know he'll go after you.'

'That is, unless . . . '

I turn to the Old Man. Shakedown time. The Bannister Way. 'Unless what . . . ?'

'You swear an affidavit testifying that the remains are those of my son, Ronald Bannister.'

'And if I don't . . . ?'

'That question is cockeyed, Atlas. If you do, I'll use whatever influence I have to help you avoid prosecution.'

'We won't be able to save your license to practice as a private investigator in the State of California, but we should be able to stop you becoming an inmate in one of this state's penitentiaries.'

'Some choice . . . '

'Our choice. We're being kind here, Alston, we don't need you.'

I turn from Hoover back to the Old Man. 'Why are you going along with this crap? You know that's not Ronnie lying in City Morgue.'

'Because, Mr. Atlas, I always require an edge . . . '

'So that's all the boy ever was to you, an ace in the hole?'

'Business is business. If Kennedy's camp believes that the child entombed in the Bannister mausoleum is Ronnie, they will still require my cooperative silence. After all, a corpse is evidence. And evidence can talk, even from the grave. And if Nixon's people believe that dead child is Ronnie, they too will continue to seek my assistance . . . '

'But if either of them suspect that the remains aren't Ronnie's, your influence is gone.'

'Not gone, but . . . diminished.'

'You've got your politicians figured out, but what about him?' I say, pointing at Roselli. 'He was the one blackmailing you. He was the one who switched bodies.'

'Wait a minute.' Roselli rises, wrathful; and hurt. 'A shake-down is fair game—but body snatching? That's not my style.'

Schiller to the rescue, pushing Roselli back into his chair. 'Take it easy . . . '

'So who planted the body?'

Roselli roars the answer. 'Operation 40, you dumb fuck.'

'We had Operation 40 under surveillance for months and had even successfully infiltrated Hidalgo into the organization, and then you came along and ruined everything.' Hoover sighs sadly. 'I had expected more from a man like you . . . ' He reaches into his jacket, pulls out a document and slides it across the table towards me. Everyone stares at it.

'What's that?'

'The affidavit.'

'But it has to be sworn, and notarized and—'

'We'll tend to that later . . . '

I stare down at the paper. It's like a magic mirror. You see whatever you want in it. I saw a lifeboat. 'What about Ronnie? Don't any of you wonder what really happened to him? Don't any of you even care . . . ?'

A shiver goes through the room. Schiller crosses himself. Even Roselli fingers something around his throat.

Hoover clears his throat, breaking the spell of Guilt. 'The Bureau will look into all matters pertaining to the kidnapping. Including your own personal conduct, Alston.' The pen he hands me is moist and warm from his hand. I look up at Schiller. He turns away.

I sign.

Silence.

When I finally look up from my signature, all three of them are staring at me. I toss the pen down on the table. 'Look at you, sitting all together, smug and happy. Just who the hell do you think you are?'

'I'll tell you who we are. We're the people always in the middle, the people who put their petty grievances aside and learn how to work together. Who are we, Mr. Atlas? We're America . . . '

Hoover nods to Schiller. 'Take him back home. Make sure he stays there.' He looks at his watch, turns to Roselli. 'Where the devil is Hastings, I have Crosby at eight . . . '

'Hastings . . . ?'

Roselli stares at me for a long moment. 'What's he to you?'

I've almost blown it. I talk fast. 'I need to question him, about when he saw the nanny. Him and Morris.'

'Forget it, Alston. You're not talking to anyone anymore. You're through as a private investigator. Take him away, Sergeant.'

'Yes, sir.' Schiller grabs my elbow and escorts me across the dance floor and out of the ballroom, walking so close it's like we're in a three-legged race. There's no force in the big man's grip: it's as though I'm supporting him. He whispers curses as we march through the lobby and down the steps, past the machine-gun-toting Feds. 'You nearly got us killed back there.'

'Quit your bellyaching. They wanted something, I gave it to them.'

'I'll tell you one thing, you were right about them switching the bodies . . . ' Schiller looks back at the hotel with nervous uncertainty. 'And did you see their faces when you opened your mouth about Hastings?'

'What do they care about Hastings?'

'He was Roselli's inside man at the Bannister Estate . . . ' I freeze so fast I nearly pull Schiller over. 'He was in on the scam from the start.'

'Who told you that?'

'Roselli.'

'And you believe him?'

'Who do you believe? Hastings?'

The rasp of the hotel's gravel underfoot fills the long silence between us as we walk back to the cars. This is the last sound Tommy ever heard. The stutter and crunch of an unsteady surface about to give way. 'I just hope . . . ' Schiller's voice wavers. He stops and looks at me. Even at night, I can feel the colossal weight of his huge body's shadow obliterating everything in its path. 'I just hope they don't think, you know? That they have to get rid of us . . . '

'Are you nuts?'

'Well, we are witnesses . . . '

'Accomplices, more like it. Why, the way those bastards made me—'

It comes without warning, the way it always did in the Pacific, when you'd be following a jungle trail, mistaking it at first for the sound of water on stone, the darting repetition almost birdlike, until it wakes you out of your trance of suffering, and you focus back to why you're there—to kill or be killed; the hollow pop defining itself for what it was: the fast, indiscriminate sting of death, Schiller bending his great mass towards the earth, the muzzle flash folding itself back into the camouflage of night.

I cradle Schiller in my arms, the soft murmur of his blood pulsing through my fingers. 'Jesus, Mary and fucking Joseph, I'm hit, Nick.'

There are sounds of running across the paddock, the lightning blaze and stutter response of the Fed's tommy guns and the distant squeal of brakes. I hear the twist of bullets hitting wood; the lisping twang of ricochet. Then it's over. They shot at us. And they got away. Again. 'Hold on, Gus, help is on the way.'

'Jesus, Nick,' he says, 'it's like my mother always said . . . '

Blood eddies from him, haemorrhaging now in hard, accelerating spasms. 'What did she say, Gus?'

'She said . . . She said—'

Already the torrent is slowing. 'Hold on, for Christ's sake, the doctors are coming . . . Gus?'

'Nick? It's like Ma always said . . . '

We are in a pool of life; a great man's force abandoning him—leaving him slick and wet like he was at birth, the natural warmth of his blood already running cool in the night air. 'Gus? Talk to me. What did your ma say, Gus . . . ?'

'Life . . . ' He wheezes the word, his voice transformed, thin and squeezed from quickly-diminishing lungs. 'It's . . . '

There is the tremor of his legs, as though struggling to rise against gravity one last time, and then Schiller goes limp in my arms.

I hope you don't mind,' Ruby says, handing the suitcase to Hastings, 'I helped myself to a tip.' He pulls his hat down low over his eyes to escape Hastings's stare. 'Lighten up, buddy, I'm just kidding.' He hands something to Hastings. 'Compliments of the house.' Hastings ignores the ticket and it flutters to the floor. Leon picks it up, reading aloud, painfully enunciating every syllable of the final word: 'Girls, girls, girls . . . Come ride the . . . carousel?' He looks up at Ruby. 'Sounds very imperialistic.'

Ruby frowns at him. 'What the hell are you, a commie?'

'I'm a Marxist but not a Leninist-Marxist.'

Ruby bumps into boxes as he backs away, yanking open the elevator cage door. 'Screwy!' The door springs shut, nearly trapping his hand. 'The both of you . . . ' he shouts, his head disappearing past the floor. 'Crazier than a pair of snakes on fire.'

Leon gives a long, hollow laugh. 'That's the problem with being a spy,' he says, to no one in particular. 'You end up believing half the things you only pretend to believe.'

Hastings stares at him. 'That's not just a problem with spies . . . ' He places the case on top of an overturned box, snaps it open and is greeted by multiple portraits of McKinley and Cleveland.

'Say, how much is in there?'

The case clicks shut. 'Enough . . . '

Leon scratches his thin hair. 'I don't know about you but I'm not doing this for money.'

'What are you doing it for?'

'Following orders . . . '

'Kid? Take it from me: that's just about the worst reason to do anything.'

Leon wags a finger at him. 'You need to trust your superiors.'

'Even when it means killing a president?'

Leon stares at him, that goofy smile slowly vanishing. 'Even when it means dropping the Bomb. That's the thing about us. We don't ask questions. We just do. And that's why we always prevail.'

'That's some kind of certainty.'

'Haven't you ever felt it . . . ?'

Hastings thinks for a long moment. 'Once, when I was deer hunting . . . But that was long ago.'

'Well, I pity you . . . '

'Save your pity for yourself, kid, you might need it sooner than you think.'

'What's that supposed to mean?'

But Hastings isn't listening to the kid anymore. He's listening to the approaching sirens.

He hurries to his window and assumes firing position. Leon is talking to him, but Hastings cannot hear. He is no longer on the sixth floor of a book depository, he is on the other end of his telescopic sight. His crosshairs panned across the crowds, freezing on a familiar face: a young man in white shirt and dark jacket. 'What the hell is he doing there?'

'Who?' Leon asks, excitedly scanning the crowd with an old pair of Fuji binoculars.

'Down there, along the curb . . . It's the leader of Love Field Team, holding an open umbrella.'

That unnerving laugh again. 'He's nutty, it's not even raining.'

'Don't you get it, you moron? It's a goddamn signal. It's not just us. He's spotting gunfire on-target.'

'What target?'

'The president, goddamn it. He's going to call in fire.'

There is the contained, metallic rasp of a bolt sliding open as Hastings cycles the carbine, the glint of the extracted cartridge rising, and then the fatal forward slamming, tunnelling gold as the cartridge is chambered, the weapon cocked and ready to kill.

The motorcade comes into his field of vision. The sirens retreat, the crowd of bystanders retracting, becoming part of the landscape.

Hastings waits: still, alone; outside of time.

Luchino fires. Hastings sees the twist of freed sunlight bursting from a bullet hole in a freeway sign.

Hastings immediately fires into the curb on Elm Street, ahead of the president's car.

He reloads the rifle, resuming firing position, but this time his mind is not as empty as before. It is filling with a question. Why? Why no response from the Secret Service or police; why no evasive action? Two shots and still the cavalcade ploughs forward.

Luchino must be thinking the same thing, for he fires again, just over the limo, the bullet hitting at the back of Main Street. Hastings sees a bystander near the rail overpass react, struck in the face by debris.

Three shots. Still no response from police or security.

Hastings changes plan radically, shooting at the top left side of the presidential limo's windshield, metal and glass fragments spritzing the air. He was taking the threat to the limo itself.

Luchino fires instantly, following Hastings's lead, clipping the rearview mirror and furrowing out the tip of the windshield.

Still no reaction.

Five shots.

Nothing.

Then he sees it: the glint of metal coming from a storm water drain. 'Jesus, what is that?' he cries.

'What?'

Hastings aims at the rifle barrel and fires, his shot hitting the grill of the drain. A bullet fragment purrs across the lawn on the sidewalk, scarring the grass.

'Fuck, I missed.'

'What is it?'

Hastings watches as the president's body rocks backwards; as he clenches his fists and brings them up to his throat in a reflexive response.

'He's been hit!' The gun from the storm drain disappears.

Leon leans over Hastings's shoulder, shouting with excitement. 'Where? Where?'

'In the throat.' Connally jerks in pain. It's Luchino, forcing the issue. No one's reacting on the ground; no one's reacting inside the car. Someone's got to do something dramatic. Luchino's wounding passengers. Hastings follows suit, firing into the governor's thigh.

Finally a response.

But not the one he ever expected.

The brake lights of the limo come on.

There's a kill shot from the direction of the Grassy Knoll, the body of the president rocking backwards and to the left, an organic comet bursting from his cranium.

Hastings leaps to his feet, disassembling his weapon.

'Did you see that . . . ? Did you see that?' Leon is hollering. 'Those boys are good, I tell you, those boys are real good!'

Hastings braces Leon against a wall, his elbow at his throat. 'You know who did it?'

Leon can hardly speak. 'Sure . . . ' Hastings eases his arm off Leon's windpipe. 'The best outfit there ever was . . . ' There is a sneer of triumph on his face. 'Operation 40.'

A Navy Hospital orderly walks down the empty corridor towards me, his eyes careful to avoid mine. He's carrying something in his hands. A swollen brown manila envelope, stained at the bottom. 'These are Captain Schiller's personal effects . . . ' The paper sticks to his hand when he pulls it away. There is the patter of blood from the rip. The mortal belongings of Captain Augustus Schiller Jr. His badge. His blood.

'Do I need to sign anything?' He gives me a look that tells me I do; that tells me he thinks I'm a troublemaker for even asking: a colossal pain in the ass at five o'clock in the morning. 'Tell you what, I'll come back tomorrow and sign the forms then . . . ' The orderly nods at the lie, and turns without another word. I stand there watching him limp away. Then there's nothing. No staff. No movement. Nothing. Just a buzz from a flickering light. If I had the strength, I'd bust it and shut it up for good.

This is the way I should have felt when I quit the Force. Bereft not just of answers but of possibilities. But I was too full of hatred and revenge back then. And I was certain I would taste it; certain that I'd find Tommy's killer.

This is the way I should have felt when I first betrayed Cate barely three years into our marriage. At least the first time. And maybe even the second . . .

This is the way I should have felt when I came back from the Pacific, my pockets bulging with dog tags and bibles and letters for parents and sisters and girlfriends from comrades and buddies and smart-ass hotshots. From the ones that didn't make it.

And now, when I finally feel the way I should, it's all too late. For Schiller. For Tommy. For Cate. And especially for me.

There's light in the sky outside; it glows white and ghastly. I think of the old Chinese man in Manila, waking in his bed and screaming at the sight of all those bandages, all those white bandages, how he tore them off in a frenzy, and how he died, livid-skinned but naked and at peace later that day. Afterwards a local nurse explained it: white is the symbol of death for the Chinese. And like that old man, I can feel its power now: this white dawn sky is bringing nothing but trouble.

I fish around in my pockets, and then I remember that Cate's car is back at La Jolla. A fifteen-mile walk. I start to thumb it.

I feel the car before I hear it, nosing the air ahead, pushing everything out of its way. Instinctively I step off the road. A blue and white Buick Roadmaster pulls up, driven by a young man in a black suit. In the back, staring at me with a handkerchief half obscuring his face, is Howard Hughes.

The chauffeur gets out, and opens the back door. He's wearing buckskin gloves.

'Nicholas, I'd like to speak with you . . . ' I start to get in the back, but the chauffeur stops me. 'What is that thing you're holding?' Hughes asks.

'The personal effects of a friend of mine . . . '

'The police captain who was shot?'

I don't answer. He seems to know enough without my help. He nods to the chauffeur. 'Your hands, please . . . ' the driver says. 'Without the bag, sir.'

'What the hell do you want with my hands?'

The chauffeur leans in close to me. 'You need to wash them, sir. For Mr. Hughes . . . '

I put Schiller's envelope down on the road. The driver indicates that I should hold my hands out, and he pours something over them. I pull my hands away in pain.

'I'm sorry, sir. Pure grain alcohol . . . ' He hands me a box of Kleenex. I take a fistful and dry my hands. There is an embarrassed pause. 'I'm sorry, sir, it's to hold over your mouth . . . To halt transmission of germs, sir.'

'You know what, I think I'll walk . . . '

'I know about Big Bear Lake, Nicholas.'

I get inside the car and go to close the door, but the chauffeur shakes his head and closes it for me. I turn to Hughes: two men sitting side by side, not touching, covering half our faces. 'How do you know?'

'The FBI is not the only organization that can tap a wire. I've been following you from the beginning, Nicholas.'

'The beginning?'

'Since the call came in about the Bannister kidnapping.'

'And what about Big Bear Lake? You're not planning . . . ?'

'Believe me, Nicholas, if I were planning anything, it would have already happened by now.'

'So what do you want?'

'What do you want?'

'Don't play games with me.'

'Don't you understand, Nicholas? I'm the Supersonic Santa Claus. You can have anything you want. Think about it. Anything. If I were you, I'd know what I'd want. I'd want out. Out of this town. Out of this country. Safe passage for me and my loved ones. As far away as possible.'

'And if I were you, what would I want?'

He smiles behind his handkerchief. 'Oh, that's too easy. Knowledge, of course.'

'What kind of knowledge?'

'The only knowledge that counts, Nicholas: the one that grants peace of mind . . . ' He nods at the chauffeur's eyes watching us in the rearview mirror and the car starts to pull away. I look back at Schiller's envelope, sitting by the side of the road. 'Wait a minute, I need that. It's Schiller's.'

'Captain Schiller has no more need of that than you. Besides, we should get a move on. It's a long drive to Big Bear Lake . . . '

Outside in Dealey Plaza it's pandemonium. Hastings shoves his way through the panicking crowds towards the Dal-Tex Building. '*Putain!*' Luchino says, running towards him, a case in either hand. 'What in the name of the God happened?'

'They killed the president is what happened. It's a setup. You. Me. JFK. Every person in this plaza. Every voter in this goddamn country. It's all just one big con . . . ' They walk fast through the turmoil, heading back to their car. 'They set us up, and they set us up good. We fell for it. We thought Leon was the patsy, when all along it was us.' Luchino suddenly veers back towards the plaza. Hastings follows. 'What is it?'

'Cesari and his men.'

'Where?'

'Up near our car . . . ' He looks at Hastings. 'They know about us.'

They try to cross the plaza, but Dallas Police push them back onto the sidewalk. 'What is it, officer?'

'They're making arrests . . . '

Luchino slaps Hastings's arm, raising his chin towards a man who is being led out of the Dal-Tex Building. He holds up one of his cases. 'It's the one who brought me this.'

'Gene Brading?'

Luchino nods. Ahead of them a jeering crowd has formed. Police are escorting Ned towards the sheriff's office.

'They're rounding everyone up. We've got to get out of here . . .'

They both walk fast, heading east up Main Street, against the flow of people still running towards Dealey Plaza. A cop standing next to his motorcycle stops them. 'Where are you birds coming from?'

'Dealey Plaza . . .'

'What's in the bags?'

'We're travelling salesmen.'

'Got some ID?'

'Sure . . .'

There is the squawk of static from his motorcycle radio. He goes over and listens for a moment, then shakes his head. 'Goddamn dispatch!' He turns back but Hastings and Luchino have disappeared.

Two blocks east they stop running. 'Close, *mon ami* . . .'

'More than close. They've put us on the list of suspects. We need to split up.'

'You will be all right?'

'Don't worry about me.'

'Until we meet again, *mon ami*.'

'So long, pal.'

They shake and then Luchino disappears. The crowds are thinning now, people hovering in doorways, gathered around radios. The flags along the motorcade route hang limp and defeated. A taxi slows beside him. Hastings glances at it. The back window rolls down, Leon waving him inside. Hastings hesitates, then gets in.

'Where's Napoleon?'

'He's gone back to Paris.'

'That's a quick getaway.'

'What about you?'

Leon makes sure the cabbie isn't eavesdropping. 'Mexico. I got a plane waiting.'

374 - TIM BAKER

Hastings nods. 'Smart.'

'That's me. If you want, I could ask if there's a spare seat.'

Hastings looks at Leon's helpful smile. If he were a gambling man, he'd put everything he had on Leon not even making it to the airport. 'Thanks, but I have my own plans . . . '

'South America?'

'Alaska.'

That stuttering laugh again. 'Hope you've packed your winter socks. This will be fine, thank you, driver . . . ' They get out, the hack looking at his tip as though debating whether to toss it back at Leon or not. 'One thing they taught me in Minsk. Tipping is antisocial. Here we are.'

Hastings looks all around. There was a movie house opposite. 'What's *here*?'

'Rendezvous with Gerry Hemming. This is where I come in . . . '

Hastings studies the terrain. Ambush territory. He feels as if they'd just been herded into a box canyon. He wants out. 'Good luck, Leon . . . '

The goofy smile slides off his face. 'You're not leaving?'

'That's exactly what I'm doing . . . ' Hastings starts heading west. He's going to find a car, hot-wire it, and get the hell out of Dallas as fast as he can. He was booked on the 6:15 flight from Houston to LA and he wasn't going to miss it.

Leon follows him. 'It's because you don't think I have it in me, isn't it?'

'I don't know what you're talking about . . . '

Leon grabs his sleeve. 'It's because you don't think I can do it, right?'

Hastings stops. 'You're making a scene.'

'Answer me!'

A couple comes out to watch the ruckus. 'Keep it down, for Christ's sake! Do what?'

Leon pulls out his .38 Special. 'Kill Gerry Hemming.'

There is a shout behind them. Someone's seen the gun. Hastings pushes past him. 'Do whatever you want, I'm getting out of here.'

Leon points the gun at him. 'I stood by you back in Dealey Plaza, now it's your turn to stick by me.'

'You're going to get us both killed, do you know that . . . ?'

'Once a Marine, always a Marine . . . Here he comes!' Hastings glances out of the corner of his eye. A Dallas Police patrol car pulls up next to them. A single, uniformed driver with a slick-backed duckbill. And no partner. It didn't make sense. 'Hey, Gerry, look what I've got for you.' The driver gets out, his face just clearing the car's cherry light when Leon pulls the trigger. Three shots. All point-blank. The officer staggers, then falls. 'I got him, did you see me? I got him!'

Hastings pushes past Leon, staring at the fallen officer. 'You idiot, that isn't Hemming!'

Leon slowly circles round the squad car, staring at the bleeding man. 'But it looked like Hemming. They told me Hemming would be here . . . ' He stares at Hastings, his face a map of confusion.

Hastings doesn't wait. He starts running. 'Hey, come back! Please? Elvis? Come back!'

Hastings runs down Patton Avenue, looking back one last time. Leon is going into the movie theatre. He looks at his watch. Five hours to steal a car, drive 250 miles and catch a plane—without getting caught. And then, if he made it back to LA, the hard part would begin.

A rriving in France had been like a fever dream, the afternoon heat at Nice crushing with humidity. I hadn't slept since the night before last with Evelyn, and even then, we had spent most of our time not sleeping. It took over an hour to get to my hotel in St-Jean, and when I finally arrived I was exhausted but resisted the cool temptation of white sheets striped by the shadows of Italian shutters, and walked down to the nearest beach, Paloma Plage.

The water was cooling and green as jade from the sea grass, the whole scene contained by limestone cliffs enfolding the bay like a huge amphitheatre. A plane flew by, its single prop engine whining high above the shouts of children on the beach as it trailed an aerial banner for a nightclub in Cannes. I swam far out, past swimmers with snorkels and masks and couples kissing on floats; past kayaks and anchored yachts to a great yellow buoy, and watched a three-master sailing by under motor, "The Maltese Falcon". I Googled her when I got back to the hotel. Three hundred feet. Half a million bucks to charter for a week. A sum so far beyond comprehension I needed to get some more air.

I felt better back outside, especially when I saw a one-man fishing boat returning for the day, keying the still waters with its low, persistent wake. At the end of a curving road was an ancient chapel on a hill, and just below it a cemetery, filled with the sickly scent of datura, the pale closed bells digesting their secrets in silence, their poison hidden deep within thorny kernels.

I ate on a terrace in the main square, watching swallows riot around the church tower. I'd never been to the Riviera before. Everything felt beautiful and unreal. We can board a plane at night, get off halfway around the world. But we can't expect to feel the same. It's not just the difference in season and landscape. Movement changes us. Move too fast and we change in ways we don't expect. Ways we never knew were possible. I came to France because I was told to; because—let's face it— I was afraid. Now that I was here, it felt as though I had chosen it myself.

* * *

I wake with a start. For a second I could have sworn someone was in my room. I look out the window. The moon has just come up, simmering crimson and defiant above the waves. How many times do you get to see a moonrise? A sunrise? Like everyone else, I'm locked inside a city, canyoned behind walls and smog and the camouflage of streetlights. When was the last time I bothered to look up at the sky? It was in Mexico, in Ciudad Juárez. But that was a city without stars.

The horror of what happened there still fills my soul with night grief. I have it bad; I can barely breathe from the weight of remorse, especially in the heat of the night. It is more than just fatigue and jet lag. It is as if something has always been wrong with me; as though my timing were off. It is something organic, not environmental. Something deep inside me. Integrated and internal. Not so much a feeling of loss as a sense of displacement. Misplacement. Something is amiss—I've always known it. And here, staring at this foreign moon, I think I've finally figured it out. It's easy, really.

I'm just not me.

Never was.

Never will be.

I stare out into the sea. There's something out there, far out on the horizon, past the blaze of anchored yachts and the drift of green starboard lights. A set of pillars rising from the sea, and just beyond, the mountainous peaks of an enchanted island. I keep losing it, then seeing it again; a fata morgana, the kind of bewitchment that once befell Ulysses. I keep staring until a mist rises, and the apparition disappears.

I drink a half bottle of water, take a piss, wash my face, check that the door is locked and then lie down again. Sleep's out of the question, but if I'm lucky, I'll stop thinking . . .

And it's not until nearly dawn, when the seagulls start their crying, that I not only get lucky, but finally drift away.

* * *

Betty Bannister's house sits on a hill sheltered by a grove of pines restless in the morning breeze, cicadas already frantic with the heat.

The gate is not even locked.

Music comes from a shaded terrace. Lilting; mournful. Compelling. I walk slowly towards it, passing a stone-clad swimming pool, following a trail of wet footprints evaporating on terra-cotta tiles. There's a record player sitting on a large terrace shaded by vines, an LP cover lying on the glass top. I pick it up. *Tijuana Moods*.

'Charlie Mingus. You must know him?' Whereas Eva Marlowe's voice had been liquid and musical, Betty Bannister's was sculptured and grand. And while Eva had hidden her age behind make-up, jewellery and carefully styled hair, Betty Bannister was natural and strong, standing there clad in a one-piece bathing suit and a hairbrush she was running through her hair. It wasn't simply that time had been kind to Betty Bannister; compared to her it had been unkind to everyone else. 'That's my favourite number, *Flamingo*.' She slowly lowers the brush, staring at me. 'My God, you are so much like your father . . . '

'You knew my father?'

'I didn't like him, but I knew him.'

I wasn't expecting that. 'He was a good man. He tried very hard. He had problems . . . ' I don't know whether to keep defending him or not. She just stands there, staring at me. Embarrassed, I put the LP cover down. 'My father listened to this stuff all the time . . . '

'Not you?'

I shrug. 'It has its moments . . . '

'It most certainly does. I'm sorry, can I get you something to drink . . . ?'

I follow her into the house. If there's anyone else in there, they're being awfully quiet. 'It's a lot cooler inside . . . '

'Isn't it? Italians know how to build for the summer. This all used to be Italy, not that long ago . . . ' She opens a fridge. 'Do you like blood oranges?' Without waiting for an answer, she half-fills two double old-fashioned glasses with freshly-squeezed orange juice, then drops in ice and wedges of scarlet orange. Then she fills the glasses to the brim with Campari, stirring them with a glass swivel stick. She hands one to me. 'It's called a Garibaldi.'

'Really? I nearly wrote a book about Garibaldi once. The grandson.'

'I know. When you were in Mexico . . . '

How does she know about Mexico? I sip my drink, waiting for more, but there's nothing. The drink's better than good. It's dangerous. 'I don't normally drink in the morning . . . '

'Drinking's like sex. You don't have to wait until dark to do it.' She looks at me, her eyes flickering with amusement.

I clink glasses.

She gestures to a leather sofa, taking a silk scarf from the back of a chair and wrapping it around her waist. Opposite is a bay window with a view onto the sea and the cliffs beyond. 'That's Italy over there,' she says. 'Bordighera. You should visit it.'

'I thought I saw an island out there last night.'

'The Island in the Clouds . . . ' She stares at me, then smiles. 'You're lucky,' she says. 'You normally only see Corsica in the winter, and even then not everyone can see it. The Corsicans say the island only reveals itself to certain people.'

'What people are they?'

'Very good people. Very bad people. And those who are about to die . . . '

There is a pause as I try to figure out which category I belong to. I change the subject fast. 'How far is it?'

'Ten hours under sail in a stiff breeze. I had a friend from there once; not a close friend, but . . . He did his best to help us.'

'Some people believe a Corsican killed the Kennedys.'

'You can get into trouble listening to "some people". Especially when talking about Corsica . . . '

I wonder what the Corsican word for 'omertà' is? Probably omertà. I point to the *Maltese Falcon* anchored at the other end of the bay. 'It went right past me yesterday. An amazing ship.'

'Registered in Malta. Its owner is from Greece . . . ' That smile again, both mocking and mischievous. 'Two countries that have had their share of troubles recently . . . And yet you wouldn't know it, looking at that ship. It seems to be riding out the financial storms quite nicely, doesn't it? My late husband would have appreciated the irony.'

I gesture to the view. 'You don't seem to be doing too badly yourself . . . '

She puts her glass down on a coffee table. 'I live here because it's beautiful. I live here because I love it. And I live here because I can.'

'All I'm saying is—'

'You're just like your father. Trying to humiliate me. There's something about an independent woman that drives men crazy. I had hoped it would stop when I grew older but . . . ' She gets up and goes over to a drawer, rifling through papers. She slams the drawer shut. 'As for my late husband's fortune, I've given most of it away to charity, and the rest will go there too, after my death.' She hands me a folded piece of paper. 'Which hopefully won't be for some time yet. I promised I'd give this to you one day.'

I take the paper. 'Who did you promise?'

'A man you don't know. Philip Hastings.'

'The killer . . . ?'

She takes a long sip of her drink, watching me. 'If you had ever known him, you'd never have called him that . . . '

I open the paper. It's a State of California Certification of Vital Records birth certificate for Ronald James Bannister. I glance down at the details of the father's full name. 'John Fitzgerald Kennedy?' I scan further. Under Occupation of Father someone has written United States Senator. 'This can't be real?'

'Of course it's real.'

'But . . . We would have known.'

'It depends who *we* is . . . Of course some people knew. You can't keep a thing like that hidden for long.'

I read the name of the mother: 'Elaine Bannister?'

'My dear, tormented sister had one unforgiveable fault. She just couldn't tell a lie. Of course when they found out, they had the birth certificate amended. But you're holding the original in your hands.'

'Is this why Eva Marlowe sent me here?'

She sits down next to me. 'I sent for you. When Eva told me you were in Dallas, I knew I couldn't put it off anymore . . . '

'Put what off, Mrs. Bannister?'

'I hate that name. Call me Betty. I can't put off telling you the truth anymore . . . ' There is a ringing in my ears. She places her hand on my arm. 'Are you all right?'

I feel faint. 'It's about my father, about the Bannister case, isn't it?'

'That's right . . . '

'The rumours were true, is that what you're going to tell me? That he was in on the kidnapping?'

She slaps my face. 'How dare you say that about Nick Alston. He's the man who saved your life.'

My voice is husked with a rising anger. 'What then?'

'It's about you. Don't you understand? Nick Alston was not your real father . . . '

Hastings only slowed down when he entered the lobby of the Roosevelt. Up until then, everything had been a fusion of fast-paced anxiety and anticipation; the streets and the people on them existing outside of the fevered trajectory of memory. There was only his yearning and his remorse. The one thing that had ever tempered the intensity of his mourning for Susan had been Betty Bannister. It wasn't alleviated; it was annihilated. Gone the instant her pink Cadillac convertible coasted into the garage, moving from blinding sun to throbbing shade, her green eyes camouflaging the trip wire he was about to stumble against. The look she gave him had been like a cunning knife, slotting its way quickly and effortlessly through the brittle defence of his rib cage, coring straight up into his heart—desire pumping from him like black blood . . .

And Susan's memory?

Gone, baby, gone.

Mrs. Bannister hadn't been a love affair, she had been a madness. A contagion. A pandemic of lust. Nothing existed except the next moment with her. Certainly not the ghost of Susan. If she had been watching, what would she have thought? Would Susan have been glad that he had finally been able to find an escape from the suffocation of his guilt? Or would she have been appalled at the ease with which he was able to toss her memory away, like a broken umbrella, as he knowingly walked into the face of the approaching storm?

The grandeur of the lobby—the marble, the ceiling, the

glint of bronze and gold; the tick of clocks and tock of high heels and the sight of himself multiplying in unexpected mirrors took him by surprise; brought him back to the reality of New York, not Los Angeles; of autumn, not spring; of 1963, not 1959. Of all the deaths that almanaced the moments in between. Doubt whispered in his ear. What was he doing there? He was like a junkie who had gone cold turkey only to find himself staring yet again at the syringe. Did he really have to do this to himself?

He froze.

Ever since he had hung up the telephone in the bar, he had thought he had come to New York to see her. He had forgotten his mission. He wasn't there to kill a president; but to save a life—and maybe his own while he was at it.

Like most epiphanies, the realization comes too late, for no sooner does it hit him than he sees Betty Bannister waving from a balcony overlooking the lobby.

Uncertainty ends.

Compulsion begins.

The logic of addiction.

He hurries up the steps, her lips a warm promise of an evening of unfolding delight. The key flashes as they pass a lamp. A lock clicks. A door opens. His cold killer hands move across her body. She sighs, raising her chin the way she always used to, offering her throat to his mouth. Their lips meet. He looks at her eyes. She's crying. He slowly draws away.

'What is it?'

'Sonny called . . . ' There is a long, deadly pause. 'He wants Nick Alston's son back.'

'Did he say why?'

'Jack's dropping LBJ from the ticket and when he's re-elected, he's firing Hoover. They're all afraid this time he's going to do it. Only the boy can stop him. Maybe not even that. But they want to try.'

'Alston will never do it.'

'Of course Nick won't. Sonny knows that too . . . But he says he has no choice. If he can't get the boy back, he's got to join with the rest of them. They're all going to kill Jack.'

Hastings goes over to the window, gazing out at the thrusting silhouettes of electrified buildings simmering in the night. He makes his decision, turning back to her.

'Everything's going to work out fine. Just wait and see . . . We'll keep the boy safe and save the president. We can do it. Trust me.'

About the Author

Born in Sydney, Tim Baker moved to Italy in his early twenties and lived in Spain before moving to Paris as director of consular operations at the Australian embassy in France. His short fiction has appeared in books published by Random House and William Collins, his non-fiction in books published by Penguin, *Time Out*, and Facts on File. He currently lives with his wife and son in the south of France.

EUROPA EDITIONS BACKLIST
(alphabetical by author)

Fiction

Carmine Abate
Between Two Seas • 978-1-933372-40-2 • Territories: World
The Homecoming Party • 978-1-933372-83-9 • Territories: World

Milena Agus
From the Land of the Moon • 978-1-60945-001-4 • Ebook • Territories: World (excl. ANZ)

Salwa Al Neimi
The Proof of the Honey • 978-1-933372-68-6 • Ebook • Territories: World (excl UK)

Simonetta Agnello Hornby
The Nun • 978-1-60945-062-5 • Territories: World

Daniel Arsand
Lovers • 978-1-60945-071-7 • Ebook • Territories: World

Jenn Ashworth
A Kind of Intimacy • 978-1-933372-86-0 • Territories: US & Can

Beryl Bainbridge
The Girl in the Polka Dot Dress • 978-1-60945-056-4 • Ebook • Territories: US

Muriel Barbery
The Elegance of the Hedgehog • 978-1-933372-60-0 • Ebook • Territories: World (excl. UK & EU)
Gourmet Rhapsody • 978-1-933372-95-2 • Ebook • Territories: World (excl. UK & EU)

Stefano Benni
Margherita Dolce Vita • 978-1-933372-20-4 • Territories: World
Timeskipper • 978-1-933372-44-0 • Territories: World

Romano Bilenchi
The Chill • 978-1-933372-90-7 • Territories: World

Kazimierz Brandys
Rondo • 978-1-60945-004-5 • Territories: World

Alina Bronsky
Broken Glass Park • 978-1-933372-96-9 • Ebook • Territories: World
The Hottest Dishes of the Tartar Cuisine • 978-1-60945-006-9 • Ebook •
Territories: World

Jesse Browner
Everything Happens Today • 978-1-60945-051-9 • Ebook • Territories:
World (excl. UK & EU)

Francisco Coloane
Tierra del Fuego • 978-1-933372-63-1 • Ebook • Territories: World

Rebecca Connell
The Art of Losing • 978-1-933372-78-5 • Territories: US

Laurence Cossé
A Novel Bookstore • 978-1-933372-82-2 • Ebook • Territories: World
An Accident in August • 978-1-60945-049-6 • Territories: World (excl. UK)

Diego De Silva
I Hadn't Understood • 978-1-60945-065-6 • Territories: World

Shashi Deshpande
The Dark Holds No Terrors • 978-1-933372-67-9 • Territories: US

Steve Erickson
Zeroville • 978-1-933372-39-6 • Territories: US & Can
These Dreams of You • 978-1-60945-063-2 • Territories: US & Can

Elena Ferrante
The Days of Abandonment • 978-1-933372-00-6 • Ebook • Territories: World
Troubling Love • 978-1-933372-16-7 • Territories: World
The Lost Daughter • 978-1-933372-42-6 • Territories: World

Linda Ferri
Cecilia • 978-1-933372-87-7 • Territories: World

Damon Galgut
In a Strange Room • 978-1-60945-011-3 • Ebook • Territories: USA

Santiago Gamboa
Necropolis • 978-1-60945-073-1 • Ebook • Territories: World

Jane Gardam
Old Filth • 978-1-933372-13-6 • Ebook • Territories: US
The Queen of the Tambourine • 978-1-933372-36-5 • Ebook • Territories: US
The People on Privilege Hill • 978-1-933372-56-3 • Ebook • Territories: US
The Man in the Wooden Hat • 978-1-933372-89-1 • Ebook • Territories: US
God on the Rocks • 978-1-933372-76-1 • Ebook • Territories: US
Crusoe's Daughter • 978-1-60945-069-4 • Ebook • Territories: US

Anna Gavalda
French Leave • 978-1-60945-005-2 • Ebook • Territories: US & Can

Seth Greenland
The Angry Buddhist • 978-1-60945-068-7 • Ebook • Territories: World

Katharina Hacker
The Have-Nots • 978-1-933372-41-9 • Territories: World (excl. India)

Patrick Hamilton
Hangover Square • 978-1-933372-06-8 • Territories: US & Can

James Hamilton-Paterson
Cooking with Fernet Branca • 978-1-933372-01-3 • Territories: US
Amazing Disgrace • 978-1-933372-19-8 • Territories: US
Rancid Pansies • 978-1-933372-62-4 • Territories: USA

Alfred Hayes
The Girl on the Via Flaminia • 978-1-933372-24-2 • Ebook •
Territories: World

Jean-Claude Izzo
The Lost Sailors • 978-1-933372-35-8 • Territories: World
A Sun for the Dying • 978-1-933372-59-4 • Territories: World

Gail Jones
Sorry • 978-1-933372-55-6 • Territories: US & Can

Ioanna Karystiani
The Jasmine Isle • 978-1-933372-10-5 • Territories: World
Swell • 978-1-933372-98-3 • Territories: World

Peter Kocan
Fresh Fields • 978-1-933372-29-7 • Territories: US, EU & Can
The Treatment and the Cure • 978-1-933372-45-7 • Territories: US, EU & Can

Helmut Krausser
Eros • 978-1-933372-58-7 • Territories: World

Amara Lakhous
Clash of Civilizations Over an Elevator in Piazza Vittorio •
978-1-933372-61-7 • Ebook • Territories: World
Divorce Islamic Style • 978-1-60945-066-3 • Ebook • Territories: World

Lia Levi
The Jewish Husband • 978-1-933372-93-8 • Territories: World

Valerio Massimo Manfredi
The Ides of March • 978-1-933372-99-0 • Territories: US

Leïla Marouane
The Sexual Life of an Islamist in Paris • 978-1-933372-85-3 •
Territories: World

Lorenzo Mediano
The Frost on His Shoulders • 978-1-60945-072-4 • Ebook •
Territories: World

Sélim Nassib
I Loved You for Your Voice • 978-1-933372-07-5 • Territories: World
The Palestinian Lover • 978-1-933372-23-5 • Territories: World

Amélie Nothomb
Tokyo Fiancée • 978-1-933372-64-8 • Territories: US & Can
Hygiene and the Assassin • 978-1-933372-77-8 • Ebook • Territories: US & Can

Valeria Parrella
For Grace Received • 978-1-933372-94-5 • Territories: World

Alessandro Piperno
The Worst Intentions • 978-1-933372-33-4 • Territories: World
Persecution • 978-1-60945-074-8 • Ebook • Territories: World

Lorcan Roche
The Companion • 978-1-933372-84-6 • Territories: World

Boualem Sansal
The German Mujahid • 978-1-933372-92-1 • Ebook • Territories: US & Can

Eric-Emmanuel Schmitt
The Most Beautiful Book in the World • 978-1-933372-74-7 • Ebook •
Territories: World
The Woman with the Bouquet • 978-1-933372-81-5 • Ebook • Territories:
US & Can

Angelika Schrobsdorff
You Are Not Like Other Mothers • 978-1-60945-075-5 • Ebook •
Territories: World

Audrey Schulman
Three Weeks in December • 978-1-60945-064-9 • Ebook • Territories: US
& Can

James Scudamore
Heliopolis • 978-1-933372-73-0 • Ebook • Territories: US

Luis Sepúlveda
The Shadow of What We Were • 978-1-60945-002-1 • Ebook • Territories:
World

Paolo Sorrentino
Everybody's Right • 978-1-60945-052-6 • Ebook • Territories: US & Can

Domenico Starnone
First Execution • 978-1-933372-66-2 • Territories: World

Henry Sutton
Get Me out of Here • 978-1-60945-007-6 • Ebook • Territories: US & Can

Chad Taylor
Departure Lounge • 978-1-933372-09-9 • Territories: US, EU & Can

Roma Tearne
Mosquito • 978-1-933372-57-0 • Territories: US & Can
Bone China • 978-1-933372-75-4 • Territories: US

André Carl van der Merwe
Moffie • 978-1-60945-050-2 • Ebook • Territories: World
(excl. S. Africa)

Fay Weldon
Chalcot Crescent • 978-1-933372-79-2 • Territories: US

Anne Wiazemsky
My Berlin Child • 978-1-60945-003-8 • Territories: US & Can

Jonathan Yardley
Second Reading • 978-1-60945-008-3 • Ebook • Territories: US & Can

Edwin M. Yoder Jr.
Lions at Lamb House • 978-1-933372-34-1 • Territories: World

Michele Zackheim
Broken Colors • 978-1-933372-37-2 • Territories: World

Alice Zeniter
Take This Man • 978-1-60945-053-3 • Territories: World

Tonga Books

Ian Holding
Of Beasts and Beings • 978-1-60945-054-0 • Ebook • Territories: US & Can

Sara Levine
Treasure Island!!! • 978-0-14043-768-3 • Ebook • Territories: World

Alexander Maksik
You Deserve Nothing • 978-1-60945-048-9 • Ebook • Territories: US, Can & EU (excl. UK)

Thad Ziolkowski
Wichita • 978-1-60945-070-0 • Ebook • Territories: World

Crime/Noir

Massimo Carlotto
The Goodbye Kiss • 978-1-933372-05-1 • Ebook • Territories: World
Death's Dark Abyss • 978-1-933372-18-1 • Ebook • Territories: World
The Fugitive • 978-1-933372-25-9 • Ebook • Territories: World
Bandit Love • 978-1-933372-80-8 • Ebook • Territories: World
Poisonville • 978-1-933372-91-4 • Ebook • Territories: World

Giancarlo De Cataldo
The Father and the Foreigner • 978-1-933372-72-3 • Territories: World

Caryl Férey
Zulu • 978-1-933372-88-4 • Ebook • Territories: World (excl. UK & EU)
Utu • 978-1-60945-055-7 • Ebook • Territories: World (excl. UK & EU)

Alicia Giménez-Bartlett
Dog Day • 978-1-933372-14-3 • Territories: US & Can
Prime Time Suspect • 978-1-933372-31-0 • Territories: US & Can
Death Rites • 978-1-933372-54-9 • Territories: US & Can

Jean-Claude Izzo
Total Chaos • 978-1-933372-04-4 • Territories: US & Can
Chourmo • 978-1-933372-17-4 • Territories: US & Can
Solea • 978-1-933372-30-3 • Territories: US & Can

Matthew F. Jones
Boot Tracks • 978-1-933372-11-2 • Territories: US & Can

Gene Kerrigan
The Midnight Choir • 978-1-933372-26-6 • Territories: US & Can
Little Criminals • 978-1-933372-43-3 • Territories: US & Can

Carlo Lucarelli
Carte Blanche • 978-1-933372-15-0 • Territories: World
The Damned Season • 978-1-933372-27-3 • Territories: World
Via delle Oche • 978-1-933372-53-2 • Territories: World

Edna Mazya
Love Burns • 978-1-933372-08-2 • Territories: World (excl. ANZ)

Yishai Sarid
Limassol • 978-1-60945-000-7 • Ebook • Territories: World (excl. UK, AUS & India)

Joel Stone
The Jerusalem File • 978-1-933372-65-5 • Ebook • Territories: World

Benjamin Tammuz
Minotaur • 978-1-933372-02-0 • Ebook • Territories: World

Non-fiction

Alberto Angela
A Day in the Life of Ancient Rome • 978-1-933372-71-6 • Territories: World • History

Helmut Dubiel
Deep In the Brain: Living with Parkinson's Disease • 978-1-933372-70-9 •
Ebook • Territories: World • Medicine/Memoir

James Hamilton-Paterson
Seven-Tenths: The Sea and Its Thresholds • 978-1-933372-69-3 • Territories:
USA • Nature/Essays

Daniele Mastrogiacomo
Days of Fear • 978-1-933372-97-6 • Ebook • Territories: World • Current
affairs/Memoir/Afghanistan/Journalism

Valery Panyushkin
Twelve Who Don't Agree • 978-1-60945-010-6 • Ebook • Territories:
World • Current affairs/Memoir/Russia/Journalism

Christa Wolf
One Day a Year: 1960-2000 • 978-1-933372-22-8 • Territories: World •
Memoir/History/20th Century

Children's Illustrated Fiction

Altan
Here Comes Timpa • 978-1-933372-28-0 • Territories: World (excl. Italy)
Timpa Goes to the Sea • 978-1-933372-32-7 • Territories: World (excl. Italy)
Fairy Tale Timpa • 978-1-933372-38-9 • Territories: World (excl. Italy)

Wolf Erlbruch
The Big Question • 978-1-933372-03-7 • Territories: US & Can
The Miracle of the Bears • 978-1-933372-21-1 • Territories: US & Can
(with **Gioconda Belli**) *The Butterfly Workshop* • 978-1-933372-12-9 •
Territories: US & Can